Yamashita's Gold

Tate
Holt

Berkeley Hills Books

[signature]

Yamashita's Gold

A Novel

Berkeley, California

Berkeley Hills Books
P.O. Box 9877
Berkeley, California 94709
www.berkeleyhills.com

This is a work of fiction. The events, settings and characters described are imaginary. Any resemblance to specific actions, places, or people — living or dead — is coincidental.

Cover design by Elysium Design/San Francisco
Maps and illustrations by Lisa Schulz

Manufactured in the United States of America

10 9 8 7 6 5 4 3 2 1

Library of Congress Cataloging-In-Publication Data

Holt, Tate
    Yamashita's gold : a novel / Tate Holt,
        p.   cm.
    ISBN 0-9653774-6-6
    1. World War, 1939-1945--Confiscations and contributions--Asia--
    Fiction. 2. World War, 1939-1945--Destruction and pillage--Asia--
    Fiction. 3. Yamashita, Tomoyuki, 1885-1946--Fiction. I. Title.
    PS3558.0423Y35   1998
    813'.54--dc21
                                                              98-36363
                                                                 CIP

CONTENTS

MAPS

Acknowledgments

The author wishes to thank the many people who helped to bring this book to its final form, particularly Donn Tice, Brandon and Debby Nordin, and Heather Graham. And, for their support and inspiration, Tatum, Robert, Nathan and Bob.

Most of all, to John Strohmeier. From our initial meeting through the acquisition process, from your patient reading of the first draft through the final stages of editing, your professionalism has been greatly appreciated. By doing this book, you've made another great adventure possible.

To Laurie,
   because even an island isn't enough

This story contains both fact and fiction.

fact (fakt) n. 1.a. Something put forth as objectively real. b. Something objectively verified. 2. Something with real, demonstrable existence : actuality.

fiction (fik'shun) n. 1. A creation of the imagination

"How often have I said to you that when you have eliminated the impossible, whatever remains, *however improbable,* must be the truth?"
Sherlock Holmes to Dr. Watson
The Sign of Four

The nation of Japan launched its attacks. Their primary target, at least from an American's perspective, was Pearl Harbor. The stealth and audacity of that assault were so shocking that most of the people of the western world overlooked Japan's other initiative, their simultaneous invasion of Southeast Asia.

At face value, it appeared that the secondary strike was also a military exercise. Japan had spent the first part of the century stretching its empire well into mainland China, and this offensive would extend their control all the way down to the Andaman and South China Seas. If successful, the invasion would create defensive strongholds along the entire southwestern perimeter of their new empire. In fact, these military maneuvers masked their true objective. Their real motivation was economic.

After more than a decade of severe financial depression, the rulers of Japan were desperate. Not only were they broke, but their nation was critically overcrowded as well, their people having long outgrown their native islands. Intensely driven by an expansionist vision, they embarked on a fatalistic gamble; they would take the adjacent land masses by force. They chose to finance their military efforts through an equally outrageous method; they would simply steal it. All too well, the Japanese knew that the riches of the neighboring countries included unimaginable amounts of gold and precious gems.

The people of Southeast Asia had never used paper currency. Centuries and centuries of trading and commerce had been conducted with valuable stones and metals, most of which eventually found its way into the incredible collections of their country's royal treasuries. Diamonds and emeralds from Burma and Borneo. Sapphires, rubies, and pearls from Siam and Singapore. And gold. Everywhere there was gold. Nuggets of gold, coins of gold, and statues of gold. More than enough gold to build a new empire.

PART ONE

THE TIGER OF MALAYA

N

SIBERIA

MONGOLIA

MANCHURIA

KOREA

JAPAN

CHINA

MIDWAY
ISLAND

BURMA

IWO JIMA

HAWAIIAN
ISLANDS

THAILAND

PHILIPPINE
ISLANDS

GUAM

MALAYA

BORNEO

GILBERT
ISLANDS

NEW GUINEA

JAVA

SOLOMON
ISLANDS

PACIFIC
OCEAN

AUSTRALIA

AREA UNDER
JAPANESE CONTROL

AS OF DEC. 7, 1941

AS OF MAY 1942

Lieutenant General Tomoyuki Yamashita changed into his dress uniform as he prepared to join his men for their victory celebration in the large hotel that served as their temporary command post. It had not been easy, he considered, but they were well ahead of schedule. Just seventy days ago, he and his 25th Army had descended upon Thailand and taken control of three small fishing villages on the eastern shore of the Kra Peninsula. Sending half his 60,000 troops across the narrow isthmus to the western shore, they had quickly entered Malaya and swept south along each coast before rejoining at the country's southern tip outside the city of Jobor Baharu.

While Yamashita's troops had been badly outnumbered by defending forces, they didn't meet their first real resistance until they encountered the combined British, Indian and Australian forces in Jobor Baharu, directly across the narrow channel from Singapore. Even that battle had only taken two weeks. He had then directed his artillery to begin pounding the tiny island of Singapore with a constant and overwhelming barrage. Yamashita had completed his conquest of the three countries with such speed and ferocity that his adversaries had given him the nickname, "The Tiger of Malaya."

He was flattered by the comparison, since he clearly didn't look like one. At the age of fifty-eight, he was still powerfully built, but at five-foot-six and 185 pounds, he could hardly be considered catlike. As he fastened the buttons on his tunic and his personal valet buffed his boots, he reflected upon the recent successes achieved by his fellow officers elsewhere. They had taken the lightly defended Guam and Wake Island within days of bombing Pearl Harbor. By Christmas, the Japanese had stormed Burma and captured its capital of Rangoon, a major port city on the Indian Ocean. Although fighting still continued there, the Japanese had occupied Manila before the first of the new year and would no doubt soon control the Philippines. And now the latest news: in addition to Yamashita's own conquest of Singapore, Japanese forces had also captured the vast oil reserves in Palembang, Sumatra earlier in the day.

No, he thought as he strode into the dining room to join his men, the victories had not been easy. In just over two months, his Army alone had killed over 138,000 enemy troops and lost nearly 10,000 of their own. Neither figure, however, particularly bothered him. He had successfully executed the first part of his orders and could concentrate on his primary mission. Now that his troops had achieved physical control of the region, it was time to transfer the contents of their countries' treasury vaults to the holds of Yamashita's waiting ships.

His chefs had prepared the traditional banquet of chestnuts and dried cuttlefish, and as he raised his cup of sake in silence to toast their victory, his men bowed in the direction of their home country. Draining the fiery hot liquid in a single swallow, he bowed stiffly in return. Yamashita's top aide handed him another cup and then stepped back to salute him, saying, "Tora, tora, tora."

The General permitted himself a slight smile of satisfaction. The same words that had been used as the code to indicate a successful attack at Pearl Harbor now referred to him as well. "Tiger, tiger, tiger."

Colonel Teiichi Hara was the officer in charge of Yamashita's bounty brigade. Isolated from the General's fighting forces for reasons of internal security, the two hundred men under the Colonel's command were specialists of a different sort. Although most of them carried rifles, their skills could be likened to those of the U.S. Army's Corps of Engineers. They were expert in demolition, logistics and construction, and their orders were simple: take any and all valuables they could find and put them on transport ships.

Breaking the simmering silence of the early morning sun, Colonel Hara's convoy of heavy trucks slowly rolled along the ancient dirt road that led to the Buddhist temple, which was located in an isolated field on a hilltop several kilometers to the northwest of the city. The only local residents they had seen since sunrise had been rice farmers who were tending their submerged fields. The convoy's lead vehicle parked directly in front of the twin stone pillars that marked the entrance to the sacred site as the other twenty trucks came to a halt some distance behind. Four soldiers emerged from the back of the lead vehicle and took positions behind the pillars, readying their rifles in case it became necessary for them to provide covering fire. A fifth solder exited the truck carrying a rucksack and, running in a zigzag pattern towards the temple, soon crouched by the structure's enormous front door.

Colonel Hara sat in his command vehicle and watched as the man set an explosive charge against the massive wooden door and then moved to a position around the corner of the temple. In a few seconds, with a muffled *whoomp* and a cloud of gray smoke, the centuries-old mahogany door disintegrated into millions of splinters. An instant later, the four soldiers ran through the smoke with their weapons ready and raced inside. In less than a minute, their most senior member came out and gave the all-clear signal to the waiting convoy. Not a shot had been fired.

Certain that there would be no resistance, Colonel Hara allowed his Lieutenant to direct four trucks into positions close to the temple's now-gaping entrance. The first truck was empty. It approached the entrance directly before turning in a tight circle, briefly stopped, and then reversed so that its loading area would be close to the still-smoking opening. The second and third trucks were troop transports and each contained twenty uniformed men. These soldiers carried no weapons; the extent of their battle today would be confined to lifting heavy objects. The transport drivers parked their vehicles on the far side of the empty truck and unloaded their passengers. The fourth truck carried supplies: wooden boards of differing lengths, plenty of nails, and assorted hand tools. The driver of this truck positioned it next to the empty one.

Colonel Hara entered the temple and took a quick look around. Like all the others he had seen in the past few weeks, the layout of the interior was simple. The entry-way opened onto a single, expansive hall. The high ceiling was supported by a handful of ornately carved wooden columns that fed into an elaborate system of beams and rafters above. The stone floor was clean and even slightly polished by centuries of contact with prayer rugs and bare feet. Despite the fact that none of the windows held any glass, the walls were clean, and bare of any decoration. There was nothing that might visually distract the temple's occupants away from the altar at the front of the room—nothing, that is, but the awe-inspiring grandeur resting upon its surface.

The Colonel walked towards the stone altar and assessed the handful of artifacts it displayed. Virtually identical to the dozen other temples he had seen since landing in the country, its centerpiece was an intricately-carved statue of a meditating Buddha. He considered this one to be of average size, standing just under half a meter in height. On either side perched two much taller candle holders, embellished with delicate filigree patterns. He could only guess that they were older than the temple itself; the elegance of the craftsmanship was unmistakable.

If the Colonel had examined them more closely, he would have seen that the candle holders had not been formed by a molding process, but that their apparently smooth surfaces and meticulous details had been wrought by hand. Over the course of nearly a decade, and using only a small wooden mallet and a crude bronze chisel, an artisan had lovingly and painstakingly shaped the precious metal through thousands upon thousands of gentle taps. The pair of precisely-matched candle holders represented the culmination of the artist's life's work, and his masterpieces had rested on the mantle of this particular temple for more than twelve hundred years.

On either side of the twin candle holders were several large bowls, so shallow Colonel Hara thought they might be serving platters of some sort. It occurred to him that he didn't know exactly what they were used for and that perhaps he should find out. But then again, he thought, it really didn't matter. All he needed to know was that each of the objects on the altar were made of the same material. Every single piece shone with the shimmering glitter of solid gold.

Signaling to his Lieutenant to begin, he stepped back and casually observed his men in action. The smaller pieces were dumped into a large wooden box. Each of the candle holders—nearly two meters tall—were so heavy that it took several men to lower them from their positions on the altar. One at a time, the candle holders were placed across two heavy timbers which lay parallel to each other on the stone floor. Once properly situated, it was smashed by two men with sledgehammers, who would occasionally stop, rotate the piece, and continue their labors. After ten or fifteen minutes, the sweating men had achieved their goal—the twisted hunk of metal was small enough to fit into the wooden storage bin.

The same process was repeated with every other object that proved to be too large to fit into the box, while the rest of the work crew tackled the statue. That group quickly erected a crude ramp that led from the base of the statue to an industrial-grade dolly. Looping one end of a thick rope around the thickest part of the icon, several men grabbed the other end of the line and unceremoniously dragged it onto the sturdy wheeled platform. Along with the other boxes, it was soon maneuvered outside to the waiting trucks.

There, a team of workmen transferred each piece into one of a dozen shipping crates. Each of the crates were weighed, and when it reached the designated limit, a lid was placed on the crate and nailed shut. A few carpenters quickly built a separate, much larger, container for the statue. Not bothering with fancy dovetail joints, they simply hammered together a series of thick planks to create an enclosure for the dolly. Experience had taught them to leave the wheels in place. To further secure each crate for transport, several thin bands of iron were wrapped around its perimeter and crimped together with a cast-iron levering device. The final step was accomplished by a soldier with a clipboard who made notes on a pad of paper and gave instructions about how the crate should be labeled for shipment. Once the strange black ink markings were swabbed onto the wood, the crate was carefully stacked with the others in the truck.

Colonel Hara glanced at his timepiece as he and his men climbed back into their respective vehicles. General Yamashita would be pleased. All had proceeded according to plan, and the entire process had taken just under two hours. As the convoy slowly pulled away from the ravaged site, the silence of the morning returned.

The selection of the staging site had been easy, since Banjarmasin was the only port within the region that could accommodate the needs of Yamashita's fleet. Designed for the loading of oil tankers, the dock stretched out nearly a kilometer, where it intersected the deepest part of the natural channel of Malatajur Bay. It was easily large enough to accommodate the largest vessels in the Japanese navy.

Colonel Hara stood at the base of the pier and watched the action on the afterdeck of the aircraft carrier *Ryujo*. High above, the ship's crane pivoted its tower out over the dock and lowered its steel cable to the men waiting below. The men took only a few minutes to connect the hook on the end of the cable to the heavy chains that were secured to the corners of a crate measuring two meters square. The crane's operator pulled a lever to take the slack out of the cable, and heard the engine whine in protest as the winch strained to lift the cargo high enough to clear the vessel's side. Once clear, the crane pivoted back and gently lowered the crate into the storage hold below. This same process was repeated with three dozen other solitary boxes before the more traditional cargo nets could be used for transferring the hundreds of stacks of smaller wooden crates into the ship's hold.

The Colonel had conferred with the *Ryujo's* load master about limitations on the weight of the cargo the ship could carry. Although he wished that the enormous vessel could accommodate an even greater load, it presented him with a relatively minor inconvenience. The truth was that he was relieved to be rid of the sheer number of boxes the carrier's hold had swallowed. Moreover, General Yamashita had informed him that two of the other ships of the *Ryujo* fleet, the destroyers *Muzuki* and *Asagiri*, had extra space in their cargo holds and would be available for loading later that day. With any luck at all, he thought, the destroyers would be able to take on all of his remaining chests of stolen loot.

Flipping through the sheaf of papers held by his clipboard, Colonel Hara once again reviewed the inventory being transferred aboard and mentally did the math. The *Ryujo* would accept eight thousand nine hundred and twelve of the smaller cases. At an average of one hundred kilograms per crate, and adding in the total weight of the forty eight larger enclosures, he figured the aircraft carrier alone would transport a little over a thousand metric tons of gold. That should make the Emperor happy. The destroyers would split the remaining seven hundred and sixty crates of gold, along with—almost as an afterthought, considering their relatively negligible weight—the three hundred and seventy two cases of jewelry and precious gems.

On balance, his mission was proceeding very well. Since only the end of December, he had already made hefty cargo deposits into the holds of over twenty ships, and he anticipated repeating the process with an equal number within the next few months. Although he received reports of the casualties suffered by invading and defending forces, because his unit only worked in areas that were occupied and tightly controlled, it had been spared from the mayhem of combat. In fact, he reflected, the only killing he had witnessed at all had been three months earlier when they had entered the Grand Palace in Bangkok. What an ugly scene that had been.

Colonel Hara was assured that the palace had been thoroughly secured by the invading troops. The defending soldiers and their
small cache of armaments had been eliminated, he was told, and
he could expect to find only a handful of royal residents remaining in the vast compound. As Hara's platoons entered the high
white walls through the main gate on Na Phra Lan Road, he noted
the compete lack of activity on the various streets within and assumed that the vaults would be unguarded. He was mistaken.

As soon as his men crossed the threshold of the Phra Maha
Mondop, the Royal Pantheon, they encountered their first attack.
Emerging from the shadows of a corner with a murderous battle
cry, a lone figure dressed in flowing, yellow silk robes ran directly
at them, equipped with nothing more than a glittering curved
scimitar. Not a grenade. Not a pistol. Not even a rifle with a bayo-
net. The man literally ran straight into two dozen combat-ready
assault troops with only a sword. In response, before he'd traveled
ten meters, he was cut almost completely in half by simultaneous
blasts from several semiautomatic rifles.

The first hall was empty, but as the platoon continued deeper
into the royal enclave, similar attacks were repeated. Sometimes
the yellow-robed defenders came in small groups or in pairs, but
always with the same piercing yell and holding only the curving
blades of hand-crafted swords high over their heads. And always
with the same result—with blood from the palace guards splatter-
ing everywhere as the devastating bullets brutally tore into their
flesh. In a vain defense of their heritage, they fell dying onto the
thick, royal carpets without inflicting as much as a single scratch

on the steadily advancing Japanese soldiers.

Finally, as the troops descended the stairway that spiraled down into the royal vault, Colonel Hara witnessed the most definitive display of courage he could imagine. In the smoky light created by dozens of steadily burning oil lamps, his lead troops could see the magnificent chests that lined the perimeter of a huge subterranean room that lay only a few paces ahead. Only two things impeded their progress. The first was a heavy iron gate that barred easy access to the treasures locked within. The second was the body of the final palace guard, who, already felled by a barrage of bullets, lay inertly on the floor just outside the gate. The fatally wounded guard, whose flowing golden robe was completely crimson with blood, also had a thick ebony sash that bound his midsection. Hanging from this belt was a single key.

A soldier bent down to retrieve the key and allow Colonel Hara's workmen to take the royal treasures. Sensing the soldier's hands upon him, the fallen guard opened his eyes, reached into the folds of his robe, and, grabbing a concealed dagger, slashed out at the invader in a final act of defiance. Crying out, more in surprise than from the pain of the gash in his leg, the soldier leapt back and watched as several members of the platoon emptied their guns into the guard. As the sounds of the thunderous volley echoed into silence, the Colonel himself approached the corpse. Colonel Hara bowed deeply to the fallen adversary and then knelt to retrieve the key. Out of his intuitive respect for this opponent, he reached inside the man's blood-drenched robe and took the knife's sheath, and then the dagger itself, as a reminder of his own warrior's code of *bushido*. Fight to the death and never be taken alive.

Handing the key to his Lieutenant, Hara examined the dagger. Probably thirty centimeters in length, its wavy blade was razor-sharp. The handle was made of ivory, decorated with a light brown pattern engraved along either side. The butt of the handle, as well as the hilt and tip of the scabbard, were fashioned from silver, intricately etched with another repeating pattern. The Colonel returned the dagger to its sheath and tucked it onto the belt of his uniform.

In comparison to the value of this trophy, Colonel Hara was unimpressed with the riches contained in the caged royal vault. As usual, he inspected the contents of the dozens of chests that lay waiting inside, and checked with his aide to ensure the accuracy of their written inventory. A case of uncut sapphires weighed nearly eighty kilos, and an even larger chest contained emeralds. Another case, constructed of ebony and teak, held a pair of matching tiaras. Delicately fashioned from solid gold, the headdresses featured rows of rubies surrounded by huge diamonds. The Colonel could not have known that the crowns had been worn only once—at the coronation ceremony of the beloved King Chulalongkorn one hundred years before—and were among the country's most valued cultural artifacts.

But in Colonel Hara's eyes, these treasures were mere trinkets, worthless baubles, compared to the dagger, and the spirit of the fallen guard it represented.

It took the crew of laborers only two and a half hours to empty the vault, which the royal families of Bangkok had filled over the course of twenty centuries. Box after box was carried from the lower level, up the spiraling stairway to the convoy of trucks waiting outside. Every soldier tracked bloody boot prints from the life that oozed from the bodies of the overmatched palace guards. The Colonel examined a handful of objects that were not made of gold and otherwise simply too large to easily transport, and decided to leave them behind. He gave a final set of orders to his Lieutenant, and then climbed into his command vehicle and drove away.

Colonel Hara stood under the enormous canvas canopy that had been erected like a circus tent. Looking around him with satisfaction, he saw row after row of wooden crates, carefully stacked under the protective awning so that his staff could more easily perform their bureaucratic obligations.

He shook his head, somewhat sadly. It wasn't enough that he had faithfully executed his orders and amassed the largest collection of precious metals, gemstones, and historical artifacts the world had ever seen. The boxes would soon be loaded aboard ships bound for his homeland and it was now necessary to ensure that the number of chests he was sending matched the number eventually received in Tokyo.

While a platoon of junior staff members inspected the markings on the boxes and made corresponding notations on their papers, the Colonel paced up and down the aisles. Stopping at one exceptionally large crate, he inspected the black ink markings on its side, *Cirebon, Kraton Kasepuhan*. Without consulting his paperwork, Colonel Hara could recall what was contained inside. Several weeks earlier, as their army had swept through the Dutch East Indies, he had directed the removal of the riches from the town of Cirebon, which lay on the island's northern coast. An ancient trading center, where ships bringing gold and silver from Europe, or silk from China, had once exchanged their cargoes for the exotic local spices, Cirebon was home to several palaces, or *Kratons*, and each of them had provided the Colonel with an incredible bounty. Inside this particular crate, he knew, was the golden statue of nesting birds.

Although Colonel Hara had seen enough priceless sculptures to become jaded, even he was aware that the object had a value that was far higher than its considerable weight in gold. He recognized it as an icon of Islamic faith, and his inquiries had confirmed that the relic had been commissioned by Sultan Syamsudin during the fifteenth century. Over a meter and a half in height and encrusted with thousands of rubies and diamonds, it had taken several of the Colonel's workmen and their heaviest mechanical equipment to prepare it for transport.

The piece was too special to be melted down, he thought. Even though it would probably pay for a number of Zero aircraft from Mitsubishi, the Emperor would probably choose to add it to his private collection once it arrived back in Japan.

The statute was, Colonel Hara considered, along with the fabulous pearl necklace from Brunei, his favorite acquisition. According to the local legend, the Chavet Pearls had been named after their original owner, the beautiful first Sultana of Brunei, and they had been worn by every Sultana since, for more than a millennium. Each of the perfectly-matched black pearls on the strand were larger than a quail's egg, and each was almost mystical in its iridescence. He made a mental note to check on which of the crates contained the necklace. He would keep special track of it and make sure that the Emperor received it personally.

Glancing at the clerks studiously working around him, he continued pacing down the aisle.

Hunched over a tall stack of charts that lay on the table of their temporary command center, Colonel Hara pointed at one of the pages. "Here, General," indicating an area not too far from where they stood on the southeastern coast of the island of Mindanao. "This is the place I have selected to store our shipments until we can find a more permanent location. In addition to our temporary accommodations, there are a number of large buildings that should work, and there's plenty of space for the trucks."

"Fine," responded Yamashita, "Let me know whatever you need. The Admirals have told me to expect their ships here for refueling within the next few days. Evidently the fleet is headed to the north, and they are anxious to get rid of the extra weight of our cargo."

"As you wish, Sir. We will expedite the unloading of our shipments and get them on their way. Only four of the vessels carrying our cargo are not scheduled for a rendezvous with us here soon."

"Excellent, Colonel. Which ships will remain at sea?"

"The *Ryujo*, Sir, of course," replied Colonel Hara immediately as he then consulted his notes, "as well as the *Muzuki, Asagiri*, and a submarine."

"Very well. And what is the total of our current holdings?"

"Well, Sir, please forgive me if I give you more than one answer. We have collected, packed and catalogued more than one hundred and ten thousand crates. As of today, more than half of them are here on Mindanao, and most of the rest are due here within the next few days.

"I cannot give you a reliable estimate yet on the value of the gems, jewelry, or artifacts, and am afraid that it will take some time before our curators can give us that information. I can, however, tell you about the gold. Things have gone according to plan, and we've done very well. All told, we are in possession of more than one hundred thousand tons of gold."

The tone of the conversation between Yamashita and Hara was decidedly different from that of their meeting only thirty days before. For the nation of Japan, the tides of war were beginning to shift against them. What only last month had seemed an undeniable victory had become, quite suddenly, uncertain. They had been dealt some critical setbacks. First in the Coral Sea, then in the critical battle at Midway Island, and now they had lost control of Guadalcanal.

In less than six months, Japan had seized more than a million square miles of land in Southeast Asia. They had driven the Americans from Guam, Wake Island, and the Philippines, the Dutch from the East Indies, and the British from Hong Kong, Burma, Malaya, and Singapore. They had taken New Guinea and the Solomon Islands, and even penetrated Australia as they stretched their dominance over the western half of the Pacific Ocean.

So rapid and complete was their success that they had overwhelmed their own ability to manage it. Communication and supply lines were either nonexistent, or stretched as thin as piano wire. Without a sufficient infrastructure for support, General Hideki Tojo, Japan's Prime Minister and Minister of War, provided the only logical direction to his Generals; he gave them absolute authority to deal with every issue they encountered.

General Tomoyuki Yamashita considered the facts before him. Admiral Isoroku Yamamoto, the Commander of the Combined Imperial Fleet, had confided in him the truth about Midway. Yamashita was alarmed by the strategic implications of the oceanic defeats, and angry with himself for not doing a better job of carrying out his own set of orders. Because he had failed to consolidate the treasures soon enough, some of them were lost forever.

The General reviewed the new report handed to him by Colonel Hara. The battle of the Eastern Solomons had taken thousands of his fellow countrymen to their death. Not only had the fighting been expensive in loss of life, it had been financially costly as well. The aircraft carrier *Ryujo* and destroyers *Muzuki* and *Asagiri*, had been sunk by American aircraft. Their cargoes were now irretrievable, lying somewhere deep within the Mindanao Trench.

It was at that moment that Yamashita decided to embark on a different strategy. The sea lanes were obviously unreliable, and if he couldn't deliver the gold to his native soil, at least he could make sure that it didn't fall into enemy hands. He would hide it here in the Philippines.

"Colonel," he began, "it is time for your team of engineers to begin a new task."

An image of slaves building the pyramids of Egypt formed in Colonel Hara's mind as he looked down from his hillcrest vantage point at the scores of men toiling below him under the midday sun. Working only with primitive tools and their bare hands, most of the men picked and shoveled dirt while others carried it away in buckets. And all these men, Hara knew, were only a small fraction of his laboring resources. A hundred times as many were out of sight, doing exactly the same work deep underground, creating by hand a sophisticated network of tunnels.

Ensuring the progress of the workers were a handful of nearby Imperial soldiers, armed with rifles and whips. The soldiers tended to remain seated in their folding chairs, so the overhanging umbrellas could protect them from the heat of the sun. Barking orders at the laborers was usually enough, but occasionally they would have to lash out with their whips. Rifles were never needed, because the workers from the concentration camps were too exhausted to try to escape. Although Colonel Hara knew that the Hague Pact of 1907 prohibited using prisoners of war for this kind of work, he didn't care. He had an assignment to carry out, and POWs were the obvious answer.

Once every hour, the senior engineering members of Colonel Hara's command would walk through each of the excavation sites and update their notes. Each inspection, they would take a series of measurements and compass headings, and inscribe the results in their logbooks. The Colonel had made them well aware of exactly how important their role was in the overall process, even though he had kept them ignorant of the complete plan. General

Yamashita had been emphatic on this particular point. Aside from just the two of them no one else could know where the treasure was actually hidden.

According to Yamashita's strategy, it was essential for Colonel Hara to make sure that his men operated only on a "need to know" basis. The men who scouted and identified possible hiding sites never knew which ones were actually selected for use. As soon as their part of the process was complete, the General had them transferred to active combat areas from which he knew they would never return. He had teams create elaborate documents to show the precise location and access approach to sites that were simply fake. In several instances, the Colonel's efforts to mislead and frustrate any enemy recovery operation went far beyond the creation of false paper trails; he created decoy sites. He had the POWs dig tunnels to depths approaching one hundred meters and then buried only empty boxes before sealing the excavation's entrance.

The Colonel had several ways to make sure the workers couldn't talk about what they were doing. First of all, the field teams of POWs and guards were never told what they were building or why they were digging. Secondly, each team of laborers only worked on a single site. When a work crew was finished with an assignment, they were not transferred to another site, where they would come in contact with other men and undoubtedly talk amongst themselves. Colonel Hara chose an expedient means of ensuring their eternal silence. He killed them.

When a site was completed, whether or not any gold was buried, the workers would be marched into the tunnels one last time and entombed as the entrance was sealed with dynamite. Sometimes the men noticed the explosives, wired at the mouth of the underground shaft, and anticipated their fate, but not very often. Crowded into the narrow passages at gun point, they realized the futility of resistance, and numbly proceeded inside.

Thus assured that the locations of General Yamashita's inventory would not be revealed, the Colonel devised methods to make sure that all evidence of construction disappeared as well. One of his favorite techniques was to explode a two hundred and fifty kilo bomb on top of the already-sealed excavation site. This was, after all, a war zone. Who would ever know, much less care, about another crater caused by a falling bomb? Besides, between the heavy monsoon rains and the rapid growth of the jungle vegetation, any signs of human labor would fade from sight completely in a matter of months. Concealing the sites was easy, but Colonel Hara was faced with two larger problems. The first was creating the documents that would lead him back to the actual burial sites; the second was to ensure that only the right people could successfully retrieve the treasures.

Three components combined to resolve his site documentation dilemmas. Like the inscriptions on the outsides of the crates, the maps that described the burial sites were written in an ancient hand of *Kungi*. Long ago, this form of notation had been practiced by Japanese religious scholars, but now, unused for nearly two hundred years, it was known only by a handful of academics. Having recruited a pair of such men expressly for this purpose, Colonel Hara further directed them to make their notations exclusively on a special type of paper. The material, a brittle blend of finely processed rice and hemp, burned almost explosively. Should the maps ever fall into enemy hands, the mere touch of the end of a burning cigarette would cause the papers to ignite. If that safeguard was, for some reason, impossible to execute, the papers themselves would crumble into dust if not handled with appropriate care. The final aspect of documentation was the system of markers that he used to identify the specific entry to each site. The markers were critical for a couple of reasons.

In these remote jungle settings, accurate maps were nonexistent. Even someone with the rest of the necessary information could be literally on top of a burial location and, without a reliable marker, still not know the exact point of entry. Precision, the Colonel knew, would be essential for success, because any careless or random digging that did not strictly follow the intended approach would activate booby traps. The Colonel smiled to himself at the notion. Calling his devices booby traps was like equating an ant with an elephant. Booby traps were hand grenades and small mines. Colonel Hara had built his defenses with bombs that weighed up to a ton.

At General Yamashita's insistence, the Colonel and his lead engineers had developed their defensive designs so that the only way to gain access to the gold was through a uniquely prescribed approach. The system of markers identifying the starting point of each site, therefore, assumed immense significance. The markers became the location's lock and the *Kungi* notations the correlating key. The Colonel decided to use large blocks of stone for the markers. He realized that trees could die or be harvested for lumber, and the dense vegetation could obscure the line of sight for any triangulation based on other natural landmarks. The stones were selected from sources close to each site, moved to the excavation, and then carved.

Among the troops under Colonel Hara's command were two extraordinarily gifted sculptors. Whatever displeasure the men may have initially felt about being forced into military service at the start of the war had been completely erased when they learned that they would not spend their war time in combat, but rather in using their artistic skills. They had no idea that the Colonel would have them killed as soon as their contribution was completed.

Under Hara's direction, the craftsmen used an assortment of implements that would have made Michelangelo envious to chisel stones into the likeness of animals. Colonel Hara himself selected the specific animal to be created for each particular site, apparently choosing them at random. Sometimes they were fierce and intimidating images, such as large predatory cats or dragons; other times the carvings were of more commonplace creatures like simple beasts of burden. Hara enjoyed the irony that it was his own craftsmen's art that now marked the burial sites of the cultural artifacts he had stripped from the neighboring countries.

Once the stone carving was completed, a dozen workers used block and tackle to wrestle the heavy figures into place. None of the laborers involved in this task understood why the Colonel was so demanding about the exact positioning of the object.

Observing the swarm of sweating humanity toiling around him, Colonel Hara consulted his notes and concluded that this site required a statue of a panther. While the Colonel rarely paid any attention to the area surrounding a burial site, there was something unique about this particular island location that appealed to him. Sandwiched between the South China and Sulu Seas, the water on the eastern side was a deep, deep blue, but the water to the west was a translucent aqua. The island itself was of reasonable size, perhaps two million square meters, and although it was close to other islands, the topography rendered it nearly inaccessible. Eons of erosion from the action of the ocean had created vertical cliffs on all sides of the island. Rising to a height of between thirty and a hundred meters, cliffs plunged straight down far into the waters below. The only way to approach the island was from its southern tip; the only place with water shallow enough to anchor, and the only part of the island with a beach. Rising up from the tiny patch of sand was a steep, although passable, natural grade that led to the gently rolling hills where Colonel Hara stood, high up on the mesa above.

This location was special, he thought. His first excavation site, in a deep glen nestled between the mountains of central Mindanao, had been chosen by simple expedience. That site was close to their temporary staging area and a readily available forced labor pool. While it had by no means been an ugly spot, the terrain there was nothing in comparison to this spectacular vista. No, he thought, as he examined the oceans surrounding him, this place deserves more than a single marker. There should be two of them. The natural beauty of this location deserved the best.

April 23, 1944
The Philippines

General Yamashita had made it clear to Colonel Hara for some time now—Japan was going to lose the war. While others around him adopted an attitude of resignation, the Colonel rededicated himself to completing his mission, and increased the pace and intensity of his efforts. He and his team of conscripted laborers had accomplished an engineering feat of impressive proportions. They had deposited loot into two hundred and twenty nine locations spread throughout the thousands of Philippine Islands, each one dug deep beneath the surface, and every site undetectable. Should a wandering passerby become curious when they stumbled across a large stone carving of an animal, there was no cause for concern; the markers were simply too large to be moved by the primitive means available to the locals.

Colonel Hara had bigger things to worry about. It was only a matter of months before the Americans and their Allies would retake the Philippines. In discussions with General Yamashita, they had concluded that the Allied attacks would come from the East, so Hara had relatively little time to complete the burial efforts currently underway on the islands of Samar and Leyte. He had already moved the rest of the General's inventory into a storage facility on the main island of Luzon, to the northwest. If he could not quickly complete the remaining excavation projects that were underway in the southern islands, his efforts would not be entirely wasted. He could ship the loot north and convert the sites to decoys.

Under General Yamashita's newest mandate, Colonel Hara would also have to develop new ways to hide his treasures. Without the time necessary to dig deep tunnels, he would have to make use of the natural subterranean passages that were widespread in the country. There were several volcanoes within the Philippines, for example, and each one of them was riddled with caves. There were a handful of abandoned mines that could be used. And finally, there was the ocean. That, he knew, was the ultimate hiding ground.

August 30, 1944
The Philippines

Without having to deal with the time or logistical problems associated with digging tunnels by hand, Colonel Hara quickly made a great deal of progress. His engineers had created a terrific location within a network of caverns that lay at the base of one of the Philippines' most famous volcanoes. Although the passages were well known by the local people, the engineers had found an obscure section within the underground maze and excavated a sizable extension. Once the treasure-laden chests were placed inside the new space, a minor explosion was enough to cause a controlled cave-in that closed off the area, a small stone carving of a tiger's face the only indication of their work.

With General Yamashita's permission, Colonel Hara concealed more than a dozen separate caches in this single location. Because the volcano was situated on the country's eastern side, they both knew there was an imminent risk of an encounter with the advancing Allied forces. Time was scarce, however, and the men had no other choice. As an additional precaution, since they agreed that these particular sites were more likely to be discovered than any of the others, the Colonel installed a new twist on their booby trap designs. Their inventory of large bombs was now painfully low, due to the never-ending battles on the nearby fronts. Without the means to create an overwhelming explosion, they rigged canisters of a recently developed poisonous gas to the site's tripwires instead. Colonel Hara had never witnessed the effects of the new weapon, Sarin gas, but had been told that it attacked the human nervous system with an instantaneously lethal effect.

As soon as the volcanic site was complete, Colonel Hara directed his men to load the remaining crates onto a few ships. Once aboard, the Colonel ordered the vessel's skipper to head for a specific set of coordinates in the sea to the west. Upon their arrival at that spot a few hours later, three small inflatable boats were lowered into the water. With one of his team's engineers aboard each of the tiny water craft, the clarity of the relatively shallow water allowed them to find the intended destination in no time at all. Signaling the larger vessel towards the site, an anchor was soon lowered and the unloading process begun. A team of divers was dispatched into the water. Next, lines from the ship's davits were used to lower the wooden crates to the floor of the ocean where the divers steered the boxes through the final few feet of their quick descent. Once the chests were positioned properly, the divers and inflatable boats rejoined their mother ships and the flotilla headed off to its next location.

In less than a week, the Colonel would supervise and document burials at thirty-nine underwater sites. Aware of the probability of accidental discovery, each of the submerged sites contained only a small number of crates. Given the mild temperature of the water, the Colonel figured that the crates themselves would remain intact for less than a year before the wood began to rot, and then, between the action of the tides and the growth of the ever-present seaweed, the gold would lie undetectable.

With the completion of his war-long mission in sight, the Colonel stood on the deck of his borrowed vessel and once again found himself captivated by the physical beauty of his surroundings. It was, he thought, reminiscent of his favorite land-based hiding spot, which he knew was not far away. For that matter, he thought, he was also close to the burial site of his favorite treasure, the incredible statue of the golden birds from Java. Smiling, he recalled marking the location of that most majestic work of art with the most mundane figure he could envision, that of an ox at rest in a pasture.

Looking at the profile of a small island nearby, he listened to the sound of the surf crashing on the elliptical reef that encircled it. The water was alive with color; the pastel turquoise tint of the shallows in front of him glowed over the bleached white sandy bottom while the deeper sea behind him shone a dark sapphire blue. Yes, he reflected, natural beauty like this deserved a golden offering. Directing his men to take their inflatables to the center of the reef, the last remaining cases of treasure were dropped onto the sandy bottom that lay two fathoms beneath.

General Yamashita and Colonel Hara sat on folding bamboo chairs just outside their camouflaged command tent. The situation they faced was grim, indeed. The expansionist vision of their Emperor had been crushed, and all the gains achieved during the early part of the war were being reversed. To the west, Japanese forces had retreated all the way from India to central Burma. The Americans had driven them from New Guinea, retaken Guam, and decimated a huge portion of the Imperial Navy as they landed their troops on the Philippines and prepared to regain control.

The General had been forced into retreat, and he now deployed his remaining soldiers to harass and delay the invading American troops from three strategic locations. Yamashita himself would direct some of his once-invincible army, now less than 150,000 in number, from this defensive site here, deep within the rugged mountains of Northern Luzon. He ordered another senior officer to take 30,000 men and assume positions in the hills overlooking the aircraft facilities at Clark Field, northeast of Manila. He turned to Colonel Hara and announced his plans for the remaining 80,000 soldiers.

"My friend, it is time to say our good-byes. Our glorious efforts have failed, and we must now prepare for the end. The Americans will soon recapture Manila, and when they do, we have lost the war. No, Teiichi," he said as he raised his hand to stop the Colonel's protest, "we have discussed this before. The only thing we can do is delay the inevitable. I have been told to remain here and await further orders. Those orders, I suspect, will arrive when we surrender."

"But, General! Surrender?"

Yamashita ignored the interruption. "We will certainly lose this war, but Japan will still win in the end. Sooner or later, those precious maps of yours will allow our countrymen to recover the gold. Through your efforts, we have amassed a great fortune, a fortune that will change the economic direction of our nation. Those who follow us will not simply rebuild our country, they will have the financial resources to achieve dominance of the world within the next few decades."

The General stood and Colonel Hara did, as well. "You have faithfully executed every order I have ever given to you, and are a credit to our country. Even though your contribution to our cause has been far more important than those of my other senior officers, I know that you would have preferred to spend the past few years leading men in combat. As a result, I am giving you a final mission, and also giving you a promotion. Lieutenant General Teiichi Hara, you now command 80,000 men. Take them to Manila. Set up your defensive position there, within the walls of Intramuros, and hold off the Americans as long as possible."

"*Hai!*" barked Hara as he bowed deeply to Yamashita. "I am honored, Sir."

Yamashita bowed for several seconds longer than normal in return. "It is I, Teiichi, who am honored."

Lieutenant General Hara stood proudly erect and saluted. "Sir," he began, "if I may, there is something I wish you to have." Hara reached to his belt, removed the ancient dagger he had carried with him throughout the war, and, bowing again, held it out in offer to Yamashita. "Please accept this. It once belonged to a truly magnificent warrior, and should be worn again by another."

Yamashita accepted the silver and ivory weapon. He attached the scabbard at once to his own belt and bowed deeply. "Thank you, General Hara. Farewell, and thank you."

February 22, 1946
Manila, The Philippines

General Yamashita considered the events of the previous year. As he had predicted, they had unfolded swiftly and decisively. Americans had landed at the Lingayen Gulf on the western side of Luzon and driven south, entering Manila on the third of February. There they were joined by another Allied force that had sealed off the Bataan Peninsula and established a line of control that stretched as far as Subic Bay. Though the General's countrymen contested it ferociously, American forces had regained Corregidor, and with it, control of Manila by early March.

General Teiichi Hara had brilliantly led his men in some of the most ferocious fighting of the entire war. Holed up in the ancient walled city of Intramuros, the badly outnumbered Japanese troops had held out for weeks until the American soldiers, using hand grenades, bayonets, and flame throwers, killed every single one of them and reduced the place nearly to rubble. Deeply pained by the loss of his countrymen, Yamashita took comfort in the knowledge that all of the men who had helped hide the treasure had been silenced forever.

By June, the Americans had liberated Luzon, and forced the scattered Japanese troops who remained on the Philippines into hiding. Elsewhere, the Japanese had been driven from Mandalay and Burma before being hit by the atomic blasts on their homeland in August. After Japan's surrender, the War Crimes Trials began. The General, who had allowed himself to be captured in September, was found guilty in December, and sentenced to death.

Alone in his cell, he was at peace with himself. The humiliations of defeat, captivity and interrogation were at an end, all made bearable by the knowledge that he had not only hidden the gold, but had safely stashed the encoded maps. With his silence, his treasure, worth hundreds of billions of dollars, would one day be passed to the right hands. He awaited his date with the hangman at dawn with no regrets.

PART TWO

THE OLD MAN

The two men sat in comfortable chairs by the old man's bed. The figure beneath the sheets drifted in and out of a fitful sleep, kept alive only by the fluids pumped into his failing body by high-tech machines. On the other side of the bed, drab beige drapes covered the windows that ran along the entire wall of the room, masking the million-dollar view of Waikiki Beach and the Diamondhead crater just outside.

The old man was dying, but this was not a hospital. Far from it. The large room was actually part of the penthouse of a high-rise condominium at the most exclusive address in the city. The top three floors of the building had been converted into a luxurious, self-sufficient fortress, complete with the latest life-support equipment. The renovation had cost nearly two million dollars, but the old man could afford it; he lived as if he had all the money in the world.

The two men—one of them forty-five years old, the other in his early sixties—sat quietly, almost formally. Wearing dark business suits, they sat with their hands in their laps, looking at the reclining figure of their friend, their mentor, the former President of their country, Ferdinand Marcos. Waiting for him to open his eyes again and speak, waiting for another precious few moments of lucidity. Summoned by the old man earlier that morning, they had been waiting for more than three hours to hear what he had to tell them. They would wait as long as it took, without complaint. And while they waited, they talked, reminiscing.

The younger man spoke first, "My friend, I have known you for more than twenty years, but you never told me. When did you

49

first meet 'The Old Man'?"

"In the spring of 1966."

"You didn't know him before he was elected?" he asked, mildly surprised.

The older man shook his head, "No, when I met him, he had already been President for a year. I was running a small shipping company and I was contacted by one of his people. He wanted me to perform a service for him."

The two men looked at each other and shared a brief smile. "Performing a service" had become a code name for the key building block of the Marcos empire. Whenever a business would apply for a permit or a license of any kind, Marcos would send an emissary to perform the service of negotiating with the head of that company. Supposedly on behalf of the Philippine Government, the negotiator would agree to grant approval of the company's request on the condition that the business pay an additional service fee. The amount of the fee was the responsibility of the negotiator to establish, but it was typically a relatively nominal amount.

The fee they would pay was not deposited in the Philippine's Central Bank, however, but in the account of another company. A company that had no products, no services, and no employees. A company that was only a shell, existed only on paper, and had but a single stockholder—Ferdinand Marcos.

It was an elegantly simple concept, one that was noteworthy only because of the enormity of its scale. Applied not just to companies that were within certain industries, or to companies that were of a certain size, Marcos applied it to every company that required a permit or a license. Eventually, of course, it encompassed virtually every corporate entity throughout the Philippines.

As Marcos structured it, the simplicity of his plan ensured that very little could go wrong. As long as the company received what it required, he reasoned, they would not complain. When the deposits assigned to a shell company Marcos owned grew large enough to attract unnecessary attention, a new shell company would be created and deposits directed to it instead. Under Marcos' personal direction, the system operated efficiently and encountered only two problems.

The first problem, although predictable, lasted for nearly two years before Marcos was able to find the right solution. The second problem was far more subtle and proved to be much more difficult to resolve. The tougher dilemma, in fact, didn't even present itself until nearly 1970, and it wasn't deciphered at all until well into the next decade. The two men who now sat chatting quietly by his deathbed were instrumental in resolving both of these issues.

The first problem, of course, was how to select negotiators. Negotiators he could trust.

The older man continued, gesturing with a nod of his head at the sleeping figure. "One of his cronies from Ilocos de Norte came to see me and said that 'The Old Man' needed someone who understood the shipping business to settle a minor bureaucratic dispute.

"That was the first time that I met him face to face. He asked me to perform the service of negotiating on his behalf. What he asked me to do was easy enough: look at the accounting books of the other man's business and settle on a payment figure. It was a shipping company like mine, so it didn't take me very long to understand the numbers. In less than an hour, I had a signed arrangement for a payment of two percent of the company's fuel costs to be deposited into the special account. That was all. I went back about my own business and didn't hear anything else from him again for a few months."

There was a loud knock at the door and a nurse marched inside. The older man quit talking while the uniformed woman inspected first the equipment, then the tubes that were connected to her patient's body, and then, finally, the reclining figure himself. Apparently satisfied that everything was in order and that his vital signs were acceptable, she made some notations on a sheet of paper attached to the clipboard at the foot of the bed and marched out of the room.

"What happened then?" asked the younger man.

"He called me personally, and asked me to come to the Palace. I went immediately, of course. I'll never forget it. It was the first time that I had ever been inside the Malacan`ang grounds. The guards waved me right through the gates and were afraid to look me in the eyes. They knew that 'The Old Man' was expecting me, and I was ushered in to see him as soon as I arrived.

"He sat behind that enormous desk of his, staring at me— studying me—while I walked into the room. There were only three pieces of paper on his desk. He pointed at them and said 'Explain these to me'."

"What were they?" asked the younger man.

"He had the agreement with the shipping company that I had negotiated for him and some of the company's accounting papers. One of them showed the total amount of fuel the company had purchased. I explained to him why I had structured the arrangement that way and then calculated the amount of the payment for him. It matched the amount of the deposit the company had made to his special account."

"He didn't expect that, did he?" said the younger man, a slight smile on his handsome face.

The older man shrugged. "I had no way of knowing at the time, of course, that all of the other negotiators had taken some of the money for themselves."

The younger man smiled, more broadly now. "You were the only one who didn't know, my friend. Everyone else knew, or at least had heard stories. The negotiator would agree to a fee of fifty thousand pesos, tell 'The Old Man' that the fee was only forty thousand, and pocket the rest."

The older man smiled. "When I was finished with my explanation, he came around from behind the huge desk and poured each of us a cup of coffee from the serving tray. Himself! He must have taken ten spoonfuls of sugar for his own cup. He had me sit down in a chair, and then paced around behind me, firing questions at the back of my head, finally asking, 'What did you take for yourself?'

"When I told him that I hadn't taken anything, he said 'Why not?' I just told him that the money was not mine. He laughed."

"And he asked you to do him another service?"

The older man nodded. "Yes. The next one was also a shipping company, but it was a much more difficult assignment to complete. It took me three different meetings to get the owner to agree to an amount, and even then I knew that he was going to try to cheat 'The Old Man.'

"Sure enough, a few months later, I was asked to return to the Palace and explain the amount of the company's deposit. They had only paid a small amount, having assumed that they either wouldn't get caught, or that I would be blamed for the shortfall, which is what I explained to him."

He looked over at the younger man. "He obviously believed me, because he asked me to quit my other job and work only for him. He handed me an envelope and said that if I ever needed anything else, to tell him." He looked back at the figure on the bed in front of him. "Inside was the deed to my house. He paid off my mortgage," snapping his fingers, "just like that. I told him that if I was going to work for him, I would need a more reliable automobile. He smiled and said, 'Good idea. No problem.' That afternoon, when I got home from our meeting, there was a brand-new Mercedes parked in my driveway."

The younger man shook his head. "Yes, I heard about that. But what ever happened to the man who cheated on his payment?"

"The same thing that happened to the other negotiators. They just disappeared," he said, lapsing into silence.

About a year after he found a solution for his first problem, Marcos encountered his second dilemma—how to explain the existence of his newly-created wealth. His system was working so well that he was amassing unbelievable amounts of money. Month after month, company after company made their pledged deposits. Millions quickly grew into tens of millions. Soon, Marcos realized, it would grow into billions, and he had no way of tapping into it and spending any of it without drawing undesirable attention to his system.

Marcos again called for his trusted negotiator, and the two men sat alone in the cavernous Presidential office in Malacan'ang Palace. Marcos told him that it would not be appropriate for the leader of a free-world nation to admit to corrupt practices. He needed to publicize an explanation that would greatly enhance his reputation and mystique, not detract from it.

What Marcos decided that he would tell the public was that he had found some of Yamashita's gold. Like his other system, this plan was elegant in its simplicity, and, like the other, equally grand in its scale. The brilliance of the plan, the negotiator saw immediately, was that Marcos never had to actually find any of the treasure, he only had to claim that he had found some of it. It was, he believed, common knowledge that there was no one alive who could possibly dispute the claim. In addition, because the legendary treasure was supposed to be priceless, there was no limit to the amount that Marcos could claim to have discovered.

Marcos then instructed the negotiator to lead a team to implement his latest plan, a team that consisted of only two other men. One of them was a well-known senior member of the Marcos government, the other was the younger man sitting next to him now. They would need to do research about Yamashita and find out everything possible about the treasure—where it came from, what it included, and where it might be hidden. Although they would be a covert team, Marcos had told them, they would enjoy the full resources of the government. They would have an unlimited budget, and would have access to any information they required. They were to let it be known that Marcos was actively searching for the treasure and, whenever they considered it appropriate, allow word to leak out that he had actually discovered one of the burial sites.

Marcos, meanwhile, recognizing that his team might indeed unearth some of the legendary treasure, commissioned the design and construction of a special new facility to handle the smelting of the gold. The facility was being built in a location that was close enough to Manila to allow him frequent visitation and inspection, but far enough from the central governmental offices to keep other, inquisitive or antagonistic members of his regime away.

It wasn't until much later that the negotiator learned that Marcos had not told him the entire story; he had created other teams to carry out additional aspects of his plan.

There was another brief knock on the door and the nurse returned, this time accompanied by two men wearing long, white laboratory-style coats. The nurse carried a metal tray of instruments and hypodermic syringes, and one of the men pushed a small cart containing other medical implements and supplies.

The two seated men watched as the medical crew attended to Marcos. In the span of just a few minutes, they took his vital signs, rechecked all of the equipment and intravenous connections, and hooked up new plastic bags containing clear liquids on the tall stands at the head of the bed. From the other side of the bed, the nurse unobtrusively removed a large plastic bag of pale-yellow fluid, and replaced it with a new, empty one. Once again, she picked up the clipboard attached to the bed and made notations.

Turning to the seated men, she said curtly, "He should be waking up soon. Don't say anything to disturb him," and then, turning on the heel of her white shoe, she marched out of the room, the doctors trailing behind her.

As soon as he heard the door click shut, the older man, returning from his reverie, spoke again. "Yes, he led us through some interesting times, didn't he?" He turned to the younger man. "Will you ever forget our first gold deposit?"

"No, nor will I forget the expression on his face when we told him what we had accomplished."

The older man smiled. "Yes, yes. How long did it take you to plan that shipment?"

"Once Emmanuel told me how much the gold would weigh, calculating the maximum number of cases an aircraft could carry was easy enough. It didn't take long to charter the airplanes, either," he said, considering. "No, most of the time was spent coming to terms with the banks in Switzerland, and negotiating the international flight plan. Credit Suisse and Swiss Bancorp were the only banks big enough to handle billion-dollar deposits of gold bullion, and reasonable enough to not require that every single bar be assayed again."

"Ha! 'Reasonable!' That's a good one. We paid them a commission of ten percent on each shipment just to accept the deposit."

"Just so," said the younger man with a smile. "Still, the discussions took months to complete. It wasn't until we agreed to send them all of our holdings that they were willing to accept a commission that low.

"It was fortunate that I was able to work on the flight plan issues at the same time," he continued. "Finding a city halfway between Manila and Geneva that would allow planes to land, refuel, and not pass through a detailed customs inspection was almost as difficult as dealing with Credit Suisse. But as is often the case, once the problem was solved, the solution appeared to be obvious.

"Once we realized that a charter company received favorable treatment at its home airport, the rest was easy. Renting the aircraft in Vancouver allowed us to fly there nonstop, refuel, and continue on to Geneva without any difficulties."

He thought for another moment and then looked over at his friend. "And the way you kept the shipment out of the hands of the CIA was brilliant. By tricking the mining engineer from Nevada into arranging decoy flights for us through Las Vegas, you not only protected our deposits, but also destroyed whatever credibility he might have had with American authorities.

"After that, the biggest problem we had was that 'The Old Man' didn't like the names we used on their accounts."

The older man laughed again. "It wasn't him," he replied with a grin. "It was Imelda. She thought it was an insult to be called Jane Ryan. She wanted something more glamorous, more 'Hollywood'."

Just as the younger man was about to comment, a single, hoarse cough came from the figure laying beneath the sheets. In a voice that was so soft the two men had to strain to hear, Marcos began to speak. "Mine. It was mine—he stole it from me."

The older man stood up and placed his hand gently on Marcos' shoulder, shaking it slightly. "Nando, Nando! It's me. Wake up."

Marcos opened his eyes. Clouded and rheumy, they struggled to focus. Finally, recognizing the face in front of him, he spoke. In a weary, laboring voice, he breathed, "Ah, you're here." Looking over to his right, he saw the other seated man. "Both of you. Good. I was afraid it was that bastard Roxas."

The older man reseated himself and glanced at the younger man. The appearance of Roxas, a Filipino locksmith, some eighteen years earlier, was the event that exposed another of Marcos' efforts to find Yamashita's gold. Although the exact turn of events would never be known, Roxas evidently discovered some of the treasure within a maze of underground tunnels outside Baguio City in Northern Luzon.

In addition to more than one thousand crates of gold bullion, Roxas reputedly unearthed a Buddha made of eleven-karat gold that stood over three feet in height and weighed over a ton. When the head of the statue had been unscrewed, thousands and thousands of cut and uncut diamonds were revealed inside. Roxas somehow managed to transport the Buddha and its precious gemstones to his home and then resealed the tunnels with blasts of explosives. Incredibly, Roxas then reported the discovery to his local Magistrate, Mr. Pio Marcos, who just happened to be "The Old Man's" uncle.

Not surprisingly, a short time later, Marcos' other secret team intervened. They entered Roxas' home, took the golden Buddha, and then jailed and tortured Roxas. Because Marcos had declared martial law, it was a simple matter to later reopen the tunnels and take the crates of gold bullion to Marcos' newly built facility, where their identifying marks could be removed.

Marcos turned to face the seated men and spoke again. "Did you get it here safely?"

The younger man answered. "Yes. We brought over three hundred cases with us. Some of the gold we shipped on to Geneva, but the rest of it—most of the gems and jewelry—are in the vaults we installed downstairs."

"Good."

The older man leaned forward. "Don't worry. We have done everything you asked us to do."

Marcos shook his head, weakly. "No. There is more," he croaked.

The two seated men shot each other surprised glances.

"Yes. More work to do."

"What is it you need?" asked the younger man.

"Three things," came the strained, almost inaudible reply.

They sat forward.

In a soft, but clear voice, Marcos said, "Find Pérez. Juan Benito Pérez."

He moved his head and stared up at the ceiling. "He worked at the prison at the end of the war." He closed his eyes for a moment, resting. When he spoke again, his voice was still clear. "He guarded the last Japanese Lieutenant captured. Intramuros. Corregidor."

The younger man reached into the jacket of his suit and, withdrawing a pen and a small spiral notepad, began to write.

Marcos continued. "He's waiting. Waiting for you to contact him."

"Where can we find him?"

"Ilocos de Norte. Has papers—" Marcos replied, his voice becoming noticeably weaker and his breathing less rhythmic. He rested silently for another moment before again attempting to speak. Clearly struggling now to make himself heard, he gasped, "Locations—markers. Has a knife."

"No problem," said the younger man gently. "We will find him. What else do you want us to do?"

Marcos tried to turn and lift his head. "Bong Bong—" He said something next that was unintelligible, the words only a sound that were caught in his throat. He tried again. "Keep—Bong Bong,"

The two men looked at each other for a moment, and then the older man spoke. "Yes. Consider it done. We'll look after your son."

Marcos' eyes flew open, "No!" he said distinctly, and then, exhausted, his eyes closed again, his entire body relaxed and he drifted off. The older man leapt to his feet and pressed the button next to the bed. Seemingly in the same instant, the door burst open and the nurse raced towards Marcos. As she neared the bed, she barked at them, "What is it? What happened?"

"He was talking to us about something very important. You must do something to wake him up," the older man said, adding harshly, "Now!"

The nurse glared back at him for only the blink of an eye. Taking a few steps towards one of the countertop life-support machines, she inspected it briefly and then bent down and opened a drawer beneath it. Withdrawing a syringe and a small bottle of medicine, she quickly prepared the needle and injected it into one of the tubes connected to her patient.

She turned to face the visitors. "He will be awake in a moment, but then he must have his rest. I will return in three minutes," she said, looking at them sternly. "That is all the time you will have today." She spun on her heel and marched quickly out of the room.

True to her word, a moment later the movement in Marcos' chest seemed to become more pronounced and his eyes opened. With no apparent effort, he moved his head to his right and looked at his visitors.

The younger man put his notepad down and stood by the side of the bed. "What about Bong Bong?" he said, What about your son?"

Marcos' eyes, blurred and watery, both pleaded and commanded. He opened his mouth and his tongue flicked at his lips. "Keep it—away," he sighed. "Keep my money—," another breath, "away from my family."

"And your third request?"

"You must build—a maze—," Marcos sighed, taking a breath, "—around my money." Another breath. A moment later, "Boxes inside boxes." Another very labored breath, and then, in a barely audible voice, he closed his eyes and whispered his final words. "Businesses within businesses."

PART THREE

BUSINESSES WITHIN BUSINESSES

Dormant for the last seven hours, Nick Gardner's brain erupted with an explosion of ideas, questions, and solutions. In response, his eyelids snapped open with an almost audible sound. Yep, he thought as he glanced at the clock. 4:57 A.M., time to get moving. He rolled slowly out from under the comforter and looked back at his wife, Laurie, to make sure she was still asleep. Even in the pre-dawn moonlight, he thought, she looked as beautiful as ever.

Walking across the room, he entered their bathroom suite and grabbed his electric razor from the recharger as well as a pair of old sweat pants that hung from a nearby hook. He quietly crossed back through the bedroom and took a moment to check out the view. From this vantage point, high up on a hillside in southern Marin County, he could see the sparkling lights of the San Francisco skyline in the distance. The skies were clear, he noted, and he could still see a few stars. He stepped into his sweats and headed down the stairs to the main floor of their home.

Nick proceeded with his usual morning routine, making the coffee and walking down the hall into his office. Before their massive remodeling effort, it used to be the home's master suite; now, instead of a bed, there was formal office furniture, and wainscoting they had painted, as Laurie called it, the color of money. There, he flipped on the switch to his computer and headed for the adjoining bathroom to shave. He emerged a few minutes later, plopped his six-foot, five-inch, 190-lb. frame down on the carpeted floor, and, without undue effort, proceeded to do a brisk hundred stomach crunches. He hated doing the sit-ups, but had found that it was the best way to keep his lower back relatively free from the pain caused by his old sailing injury. Finished, he went back to the kitchen, poured the creamer into his coffee, and then went back to his office.

Nick scooped up the small stack of files and papers that he'd stashed out of sight the night before and sat down at his desk to start work for the day. He took sips of his coffee as he consulted his calendar and made a list of the people he needed to telephone. He flipped open the top folder and glanced at the clock. 5:20 A.M.. He just might get a solid hour to work on it, he thought, before the first call would come. He enjoyed the solitude of his morning routine because it was the only time of his day that he could completely control. Once the phone rang, his day no longer belonged to him, it belonged to his clients.

Nick had founded his company, The Gardner Group, only three years earlier. TGG had grown steadily as Nick had solved some seemingly impossible problems for a handful of initial clients. Over time, Nick had developed a diverse set of clients and had created an extensive network of resources he could call upon when necessary.

The first folder he opened this morning contained some summary financial information he had just received from a new client. The company had just introduced a new product, and the initial sales results were far below their original expectations. Nick began to read through the pages, quickly gaining a sense of the problem.

The telephone rang and he picked it up on the first ring. "This is Nick."

"Mornin', Nicholas, it's Tom. Am I catching you at a bad time?"

"Not a chance. I was just going over some new stuff and getting ready to hop into the shower."

"Anything interesting?"

"I'm not sure yet. This startup software company just launched a new product and it isn't doing very well. I'm not sure if it's a product problem, a bad plan, or just bad salesmanship. I have a meeting with them later today. Things will be a lot clearer to me then. What's new on your end?"

"I'm on my way over to Dorr Industries. You know, when you had me take over as their interim CFO a few weeks ago, it bothered me that I wasn't able to talk to the guy I replaced. Well, now I know why. I've uncovered something that needs your involvement. Is there any chance we can we get together sometime today?"

Nick checked his calendar briefly before responding. Tom was a TGG Associate with considerable financial expertise, and wouldn't have called him at the last minute unless the situation was critical. "How much time do we need?"

"Probably an hour. There's a lot of money missing. I know how and when it disappeared, but I don't know who did it. It's either the owner himself, or the CFO who just left. If it's Jack Dorr, I wouldn't be surprised if he wants me to help him cover his tracks. If it's the former CFO, Jack is not only gonna be pissed, but he'll need help to get some cash and stay in business. Either way, I need you to help us lay out our options."

"I can be there around 11:00. Is that OK?"

"Yeah, that'll be fine. See you then. Thanks, Nicholas."

"No problem. See you later."

Nick hung up the phone and went upstairs to shower. He stood under the scalding stream of water a little longer than usual as he thought about the situation Tom had summarized. In this kind of business, you never knew what might happen next.

After his shower, he ran a comb through his still-damp brown hair and parted it, wishing once again that more of it was grey. At thirty-four years of age, his unlined face was dominated by expressive blue eyes, and he worried sometimes that he looked too young to be taken seriously in business. He dressed in his normal attire for client meetings: pressed and pleated slacks, black socks and loafers, and a custom-tailored long sleeve dress shirt. Heading back downstairs to his office, he seated himself comfortably and began his telemarketing routine.

For the past thirty-six months, Nick used the first hours of nearly every working day in the same way—building his business by looking for his next client. Every professional business adviser knew that solving a client's problems was the easy part of their job. The tricky part was finding the clients in the first place. Much of Nick's success in getting clients was based upon his ability and willingness to do the rejection-filled work of cold-calling—methodically using the telephone to identify prospective clients, qualify them, and try to set up meetings so that he could better understand their problems. And, of course, convince them that he would be able to help them.

Dialing for dollars.

More than just finding prospects, he was expanding his network of people who would be able to steer him towards good leads, or—better still—refer businesses to him. He always started the day with a list of twenty new people, and he rarely stopped until he'd contacted every one of them.

He punched in the first telephone number on his list. No answer. He made a note on the list and called the second number. An answering machine. He left a brief message, hung up the phone, made another note, and continued down the list. He successfully reached his target on the seventh call and made an appointment to meet for coffee later in the week. While he was updating his list, the phone rang.

"This is Nick."

"Nick, it's Rebecca Parker, over at San Francisco National Bank. How are you?"

"Hey, Becky, just fine. How about you?"

"Things are as hectic as ever. Look, I know it's early, but I thought that's when I'd have the best chance to get a hold of you."

"You've got my attention. What's up?"

"One of our biggest customers just introduced us to an old friend of his, a man visiting from the Philippines looking for startup capital for a new business. We don't make that kind of loan, but, as a favor to our customer, Victor spent a couple of hours with him, and came away from that meeting impressed with the possibilities. Evidently the plan looks good, but Victor suggested that we get a consultant to take a look at it. He's already set up a meeting with someone from one of the big accounting firms, but I'd like to get you involved. Mr. Villanueva is leaving town in a couple of days, so if I can set up a meeting for the four of us, can you be here later this afternoon?"

"Sure, happy to." As he listened to her speak, Nick mentally juggled his schedule. Becky was SF National's second in command, and if she could arrange a meeting with a prospect and Victor Crenshaw, the bank's president, it could only mean good things for TGG. "Yeah, I can be there around four."

"That's fine with me. I'll let you know if it doesn't work for the others. See you later."

"You bet. Thanks for thinking of me."

Nick hung up the phone, stood up from his desk, and collected the handful of files he would need for the day. He was in the process of placing them and his cell phone in his briefcase when Laurie entered the room. He turned, and she walked into his arms for a morning embrace. "Good morning, sweets," he said softly.

"Mmm," came the reply. Holding each other for several seconds, they kissed briefly before she sat back into the most comfortable chair in his office. Nick watched as she rubbed the sleep from her light green eyes and swept the stray strands of shoulder-length blonde hair out of her face. "What are you looking at?" she said with a sly smile.

"Nothing. Just you." She had the kind of face that didn't need makeup. Incredible skin, a light dusting of freckles, and beautiful teeth. A graceful athletic body that despite childbirth, still looked great in a bikini. In her early thirties, she kept herself fit by riding her horse and running a household for four. Nick bent down to give her a quick kiss on the cheek and started for the door. "I should be home at a decent hour. I'll call if anything changes."

Nick strode onto the Italian marble tiles that decorated the lobby of SF National Bank at four o'clock on the nose. He smiled at one of the receptionists, and the attractive young woman interrupted him just as he started to introduce himself. "Good afternoon, Mr. Gardner. Go right in; they're expecting you." Her eyes followed Nick closely as he entered Victor's office. She turned to the other receptionist and murmured, "The best ones are always married, aren't they?"

Because Nick had been there several times before, he ignored the lavish furnishings of the office and focused instead on its three occupants. He crossed the large space in a few strides, shook hands with Victor and Becky, and then turned to face the newcomer. As Victor performed the introductions, Nick gripped the man's hand in a firm but not crushing grip, and instantly studied him. Romy Villanueva was around five-foot-six. Two hundred pounds. Dark baggy suit, white shirt, and a narrow, colorless tie. Black hair, and a round, brown face with very intelligent eyes. A big smile with large, even teeth. How old was he, wondered Nick. Mid-fifties? At first impression, his dominant reaction was that the man was—gentle. The man started to speak. "Mr. Gardner—"

"Please, call me Nick. I do much better with first names."

Romy smiled broadly. Very broadly, in fact, exposing a small gap in the right side of his upper teeth, between his incisors and molars. "Yes. Well. I'm very pleased that you were able to join us on such short notice. Mr. Crenshaw, er, Victor, has been telling me about you."

"Don't worry, Nick," interjected Victor. "I was just starting to tell him about the way you helped DKF Productions." He turned back to Romy. "By any standard, it was an impressive piece of work. The good news is that Nick got the company turned around on a dime and it started making money. The great news is that the company did well enough to pay us back all the money I'd lent them."

Banker's humor, thought Nick, as he took control of the conversation. "That was a fun engagement. In any case, Romy, I understand you have an idea for a new business, but other than that I'm completely in the dark. What do you have in mind?"

Romy sat forward in his chair and began to speak in a soft but animated voice. "Have you ever been to the Philippines?" Nick shook his head negatively, so Romy continued. "It is a beautiful country, with much to offer. Despite what you may have heard about last month's volcanic activity, life continues. The disruptions caused by Mount Pinatubo were confined to a relatively small area on Luzon, and everywhere else it is business as usual." Nick smiled encouragement and made himself comfortable in his chair. This was going to take a while. "As you know, all Pacific Rim countries export goods to the United States, but the Philippines doesn't get their fair share of the market. We want to set up a new company to export goods exclusively to the United States."

Terrific, Nick groaned inwardly. The man wants to export a bunch of junky baskets and strings of beads. Just what America needs. "Oh," he replied neutrally, "what exactly would you like to export?" he said.

Romy continued, picking up the pace of his delivery and now beginning to gesture more emphatically. "Things that are unique to our country. Things that no other country can bring to the U.S. Our people, for example. We have an enormous labor pool—millions of educated, well-qualified, English-speaking men and women who would be happy to work abroad for a decent wage. We can provide thousands and thousands of temporary employees on a contract basis on very quick notice." He paused and watched Nick's impassive reaction before continuing. "Other Asian countries cannot do that. And we have many natural resources that are also in demand here, such as tiger shrimp and carrageenan."

"Cara— what?" asked Nick. Victor and Becky glanced at each other, obviously having asked the same question not long before.

"Carrageenan," Romy replied, slightly rolling the double "R's" and placing the emphasis on the second syllable, "is a seaweed. It has a wide number of uses, and is an ingredient that is often found in paint, dog food and cosmetic lotions."

"Interesting," commented Nick. "Well, I don't know very much about either the contract labor business or seaweed, so let's put those ideas aside for the moment. The Gardner Group has had a few clients in the restaurant business, so I am familiar with the profit potential of specialty and imported foods like tiger shrimp. Why don't you tell me a little more about your plans in that area?" Romy went on with his presentation for another thirty minutes, completely captivating his small audience. Nick occasionally scribbled something in his notebook, while Victor and Becky appeared to hang on Romy's every word.

It was, Nick realized, an excellent performance. Romy's delivery was smooth and effortless, an indication that the man had either done a great deal of homework or was a superior salesman. Maybe both. The man possessed a presence that was both commanding and understated, thought Nick, but what impressed Nick the most was the breadth of topics the stout Filipino covered in his outline. Without consulting his notes, he began with an executive summary and then dove into the details.

He spouted statistics on the size of the tiger shrimp market and named a handful of companies that would be competitors. He knew what these companies did well and did poorly, and where significant improvements could be made. He described the profile of a typical U.S. restaurant that would buy from his startup, and listed a number of marketing strategies to first get, and then keep, the targeted customers. He outlined sales expectations which, although apparently logical, were aggressive. This line of business alone, Romy was saying, would have sales of several million dollars and high double-digit profits, all within the space of a year and a half.

Nick's initial assessment of the idea was that it did, in fact, have potential, but almost certainly not as great as the man suggested.

His experience had taught him that results always differed from the owner's expectations. Sales were always more difficult to achieve, the costs of running the business were always higher, and even the most trivial projects always took longer to accomplish. Still, in this case, there was a market for tiger shrimp. Just how big the demand was they would have to find out, but it was something that could be quantified. Nick probed further, testing the degree of Romy's preparation. "It sounds as though you've given this a lot of thought. Do you have any of this in writing?"

Romy grinned hugely, again exposing the gap in his teeth. He reached into his briefcase and pulled out a sheaf of off-white, legal-sized paper that was so thick it barely fit in its dog-eared manila folder. "Yes. Of course, Nick. Here."

Nick accepted the neatly printed plan, scanned the headings on the first few pages, and then briefly studied the summary spreadsheet on the last page. Yep, he thought to himself with a touch of disappointment, it looks like every plan ever written by a first year student in an MBA program. Sales that ramped up from zero to millions without a hitch. Profits that were so high it was like the company was simply going to be printing hundred dollar bills. Looking at the expense section, however, Nick immediately noticed something different. In the financial summary of a rookies' business plan, costs were minimized. In this case, though, there were all the normal expenses, and then plenty of others. The profits were still way too high to be believable, but that was undoubtedly due to the inflated revenue figures.

Nick looked directly at Romy, "So, what this means is that it's a huge market and you'll make a lot of money. Do you have written plans for the other two ideas as well?" Romy had anticipated this request and was already handing him two other thick manila folders. "I'd like to take a little time to look through these so I can give you some intelligent feedback, and then maybe we can get together and continue our discussion. Are you free for breakfast tomorrow? Great. We don't need to take any more of our host's time;

I'm sure they've got other things to do. One last thing before I go, though. Romy, I'd appreciate it if you would tell me a little bit about your background."

"Certainly. I have always been active in a variety of businesses, and have served in the economic offices of our government. For a long time I was a consultant, such as yourself, but for the past ten years, I have been President of the University of Quezon City."

"Really?" responded Nick. "I'm hardly surprised that you've had a wide range of experience, but I never would have pictured you in an academic setting. I'll look forward to hearing about some of the specific projects you've worked on. For now, it looks like I need to do some homework."

Nick suggested a suitable place for the next day's breakfast, then stood and shook hands all around, saying his good-byes. Just as he was turning to leave, Romy inquired, "Please, Nick. Before you leave. I'm sure our hosts won't mind taking another minute or two. It's important for me to understand your initial reaction. What do you think?"

Nick gathered his thoughts before responding. "For starters, I'm not optimistic about your contract labor idea. Forget, for the moment, about the sales, marketing, or logistical issues of running the operation. You've got the INS—the Department of Immigration and Naturalization Services—to worry about. I don't know any of the particulars of the industry, only that there are plenty of countries that allow large-scale temporary work forces to cross their borders. I just don't see it being an easy sell here in the U.S."

"Exporting the other items, though, is an entirely different matter. While your top line, your sales figure, looks almost too good to be true, I haven't asked you what assumptions you used to develop your projections. Maybe they're not as big a stretch as they seem; maybe the sales figure is attainable. But even that issue isn't really important at this stage. What we really need to do is focus less on the size of the opportunity and more on the risks. Let's not worry about how big the potential may be and concentrate, instead, on looking at what can go wrong. First, we need to examine all the potential exposures. If we can solve them, then we're off to the races."

Nick saw the questioning expression on Romy's face, so he continued. "Let me say it a different way. We can assume your production risk is pretty low. I mean, shrimp and seaweed grow in the ocean already, and the Philippines have plenty of that, right? So we need to take a closer look at the market risks, but since restaurants and food processing companies in the U.S. are already buying and paying for the shrimp, that's probably no big deal. Similarly, you don't have a technology risk, or at least not a tough one, for the same reason. People already know how to harvest and freeze-dry tiger shrimp—if that's what they do—and then get it here, so that's not a problem. No, it seems to me that the biggest concern is the competitive risk. Someone else is already doing this. What are they gonna do when we show up and crash their party? Just fold up and go away? I doubt it. And another thing—are your shrimp and seaweed special? Wouldn't it be cheaper for a buyer here to get them from Mexico or South America?"

"I don't know the answers, but those are the kind of questions we need to ask. If you've already got good answers, or we can create them, then everything else sort of falls into place naturally." Nick shook Romy's hand again and spoke first to him, and then to the bank's President. "It's too early to tell. Let me do some homework and we'll talk again in the morning. Victor, would you mind walking me out? There's another issue we need to discuss. Bye, Becky, and thanks again."

The two men left the office and stood in the deserted lobby. "Sorry we had to take up so much of your time. Any comments?"

Victor smiled. "Don't worry about the time. As you know, we do a lot of business with the Filipino community here, and Romy was personally introduced to me by my biggest customer. With the amount of deposits under his control, I can afford to spend a little time helping out one of his friends. Besides, I enjoyed your comments. They were right on the money."

A typical banker's metaphor, thought Nick. "Thanks. I don't like to shoot from the hip, but you know how it works. If you've been going to target practice for a dozen years, when the time comes for you to shoot quickly, there's a pretty good chance you'll hit what you're aiming at.

"Anyway, there's something else I wanted to tell you. I understand that Dorr Industries—," Nick slowed his speech so Victor would know that he was picking his words carefully, "is having a sudden cash crisis. I wouldn't be surprised if Jack called you up for a sizable loan. Although I'm sure your credit department would give the request it's usual sharp assessment, maybe I can help you shortcut it a little. I can't give you any specifics, but I can say that TGG resigned from our engagement there today."

"Really?"

"Yep. Jack's a very charismatic and creative guy, and I like him, but I've got TGG's reputation to worry about. I don't mind pushing the limits of generally-accepted accounting principles, but I can't stretch them so far that they break. Anyway, I'm sure he'll find some hustler who won't have a problem with the way he does business, and I'm sure we'll find another client. Who knows? Maybe it'll be Romy. Thanks again."

"Don't mention it, Nick. Always good to see you. And thanks for the heads-up on Dorr. Becky will give you a call to talk about it. Good luck tomorrow and let me know how things go with Romy."

Nick went to his car and headed for home. He drove through the city streets in silence, further digesting Romy's comments. As he entered Doyle Drive to cross the Golden Gate Bridge, he picked up his cell phone and punched one of the preprogrammed numbers. "Keith," spoke Nick to the answering machine on the other end of the line, "this is Nick. I need some information. Please call me on my cell phone around 6:30 tomorrow morning. I'm having breakfast with a prospect who wants to start an export business, and I need to find out whatever you can get me on the market and math of tiger shrimp and carrageenan. Talk to you later."

Twenty minutes later Nick pulled into the driveway of their home. He loved it here. It was quiet. Nestled in among a stand of oak trees, they enjoyed a private and apparently isolated setting, yet were still close enough to the city to take advantage of its attractions. It was, Nick noted after a moment, even more quiet than usual, and, entering the house, soon discovered why.

Laurie greeted him at the door with a mischievous grin on her face and wrapped her arms around him. It had taken some doing, she explained, but she had managed to park their boys at some friends' homes for the night.

She kissed his mouth and then asked, "How about an omelet for dinner?"

"Sounds good to me."

"Great. Fix one for me, too."

She kissed him again, slowly. Gently pulling away, she disappeared down the hallway. Nick dropped his briefcase in his office, ignoring the blinking light on the answering machine. He had other priorities.

August 1, 1991
San Francisco, California

Nick read through Romy's materials over his morning coffee and marked sections that needed immediate clarification. He left the house at 6:15, and was driving along the Marina Green on his way to meet Romy when his cell phone rang.

"This is Nick."

"It's Keith. Good morning. I got your message last night. What have you gotten into now? What's this about tiger shrimp and carrageenan?"

Nick laughed, an image of his lead Associate flashing through his mind. Blond-haired and blue-eyed, Keith had a boyish face that, as Nick had seen on many occasions, women found attractive. Keith's athletic good looks, however, belied the power of his brain—a virtually encyclopedic memory that teamed well with Nick's more imaginative and creative skills.

"I thought you'd like that," responded Nick. "After working on all those clients without knowing anything beforehand about their business, I thought you'd enjoy a situation in which you actually know what you're talking about. Anyway, thanks for calling me back early."

"Sure, what's up?"

Nick launched into a summary. "Vic Crenshaw asked me to join him yesterday to meet with a prospective client, a guy with a startup plan named Romy Villanueva. I'm on my way to see him again now, and I need you to tell me what you know about shrimp and seaweed."

"I can't tell you that much right now about tiger shrimp. There's plenty of margin potential, but it's a niche market that's pretty small. Carrageenan, however, is a different story. I've had a lot of experience with it; first, when I worked in product marketing for P&G, and then later, when I ran the Research and Development group at the ice cream company. How much detail do you need?"

"I've only got about twenty minutes, so why don't you assume that I don't know a thing and give me your perspective from an altitude of 30,000 feet? If things go well and I end up having another meeting, you can fly down to treetop level and fill in the details."

"No problem. Carrageenan is made from dried eucheuma seaweed. It's been a while since I've looked at any market figures, but the number has got to be big, well over a hundred million dollars a year, and it's growing. There are three different types of the stuff which have slightly different properties. All of them are used as binding, thickening and gelling agents in a wide variety of products, from paint and pet food to shampoos, toothpaste, salad dressing and ice cream."

Keith paused for a moment before continuing. "It was introduced in Europe in the early 1970s, took a while to get through the FDA, and didn't get widespread acceptance until the mid 'eighties. That's the view from a high altitude fly over, at least until the last few months. I don't want to be too technical, but this next part is important. It turns out that carrageenan also has strong water-protein bonding characteristics that make it a superior fat replacement. It's the active ingredient in McDonald's McLean Deluxe. Remember the new burger they just introduced and have been talking about all summer? The one they're spending over a million dollars a day to promote? Carrageenan is the fat substitute they've chosen, and it creates the basis for their 'reduced fat and calorie' advertising claims."

"Whoa, Keith, slow down. McDonald's is using this stuff?"

"You bet. There are plenty of other bulking agents they could have used instead, but the key part is this: carrageenan, like fat, is a carrier of flavor. If you remove fat, you take away the ingredient that transmits most of the taste. People have been reducing the volume of fat in food for years, it's just that McDonalds couldn't make low-fat burgers tasty without using carrageenan.

"Nick? Are you still there? It gets even better. In addition to replacing the fat that's normally added to ground beef, it's starting to be widely used in poultry as well. It's what makes microwaved chicken stay moist. I read somewhere not too long ago that the Food and Drug Administration was raving about its properties, but I can't recall the details. So what's going on, Nick? How did you get involved in this?"

"It's a referral from SF National. This guy is visiting from the Philippines and wants to start an export business. I'm not sure yet whether he wants help finding capital, or if he needs us to revise his business plan."

"It's interesting that he's from the Philippines, Nick, because they already produce three-fourths of the world's carrageenan. I don't know if that's good news or bad news. The good part, of course, is that the right kind of seaweed grows there. The bad news is that there is at least one company who's already established in the business, and who has a long head start."

"Yep, I wondered about that myself. All right, Keith, thanks for your help. I had no idea this stuff was so big. You've given me plenty of ammo for this meeting, but do me a favor and check your files for anything you've got on the competitive production side. If you find anything interesting, fax it to me. I'll let you know what happens next. Take care."

Nick parked in the lot of the Marriott Hotel south of the San Francisco airport and strode into the lobby. He had arranged to meet Romy in one of hotel's restaurants. It was a relatively casual place, in a corner of the lobby, beneath an expansive atrium that opened up to the dozen or so floors above. As he approached, he found Romy already seated at a small table, waiting for him. Judging from the stack of dirty plates, the portly Filipino had been there a while.

"I'm glad to see you make yourself at home," he said as Romy rose, smiling, to greet him. He shook Romy's hand, sat down, and poured himself a cup of coffee from the white plastic carafe that perched like a sentry on the middle of the table.

Nick got straight to the point. "I enjoyed our session yesterday afternoon, Romy, but I have to tell you, I always prefer to meet potential clients for the first time one-on-one. Why don't we start over, now that it's just the two of us? Tell me what you think you need."

Romy relaxed visibly. "I like that, Nick. A no-nonsense approach. As you probably know, the bank also introduced me to a partner from a major consulting firm. He made me uncomfortable because all he wanted to do was perform a study of some kind. But here you are, already getting to the bottom line." He then proceeded to give a five-minute summary of his idea to begin exporting carrageenan that was even more concise and compelling than the one he had given yesterday. He concluded, "Two companies, then. A production company in Manila and a parent marketing company in the United States. We don't need any help with the Philippine part; we already have most of that figured out. Our real need is here. We don't have anyone who knows how to market to the big U.S. food companies. I was told that you could help us there. Can you?"

"The short answer is 'yes', but it's part of a longer answer. Let me start by telling you about The Gardner Group. TGG is what I like to call a virtual company. I'm the only employee of The Group but I have several Associates, senior people who work with me on a contract basis when something comes up that falls outside my own expertise. Some of them work with me so often that it looks as though they are employees of the Group, but they are all independent.

"We all have several things in common. All of us, for example, have had successful careers in the corporate world. We're all former executives who are used to high pressure situations and accustomed to delivering results. The reason my Associates choose to work with TGG, however, is more than just getting paid well. It's because TGG seems to be able to attract new clients and can therefore keep giving them challenging assignments. And one other thing; we don't think of ourselves as consultants.

"What I mean by that is that we don't just look at our clients from the outside and write reports or make recommendations. We help executives of smaller companies through periods of difficult change. Our clients are at either end of the growth curve; they are either imploding or exploding, and whatever the CEO has tried to do to fix the problem simply hasn't worked. If the business is falling apart or falling down, we help them through a turnaround. At the other extreme, if the company is doubling or tripling in size each year, then they are growing so fast that they need our help to put in more capital, internal controls, and better management.

"The way we accomplish our assignments is by becoming interim managers of the company. We can manage either just the department that's in trouble, or we can run the entire company. We're not looking for a permanent home; we put changes in place and then we leave. We measure our success by how much we add to the value of the client's company, which means low overhead expenses so profits are high. I run TGG the same way. We don't have a fancy suite of offices in a high-rise building downtown. We all work out of offices in our homes and do most of our work at our client's place of business.

"Our fees are aggressive, but we deliver results. Before we begin an engagement, we agree on compensation. While we prefer payment in cash, we are open to discussion about payment in the form of stock as well.

"Enough about TGG; let's focus on your business. My first question is this: who is already producing carrageenan in the Philippines, and why do you think you can leapfrog their position?"

"What do you mean by leapfrog?"

"Sorry, Romy. The point is this: someone is ahead of you and it isn't enough for you to simply get even with them because you can be sure they'll respond by moving ahead again. You have to do something to not just catch up with them, but put yourself in the lead."

Romy smiled. "I see. Yes, there are, in fact, a few large companies already producing carrageenan. Two of them are American companies that have large refining plants in the Philippines, but the biggest is a company called Hatori, which is owned by Japanese interests."

"Do you know which U.S. companies have facilities there?"

"Certainly. One is a conglomerate called HMC, and the other a large chemical company. Its name is Titan Industries, I believe."

Nick hesitated before responding, "Well, that doesn't sound like very good news. I can tell you that it is incredibly difficult to launch a successful marketing attack against companies their size. Put the Japanese company aside for the moment; I haven't heard of them before. HMC and Titan Industries, however, have billions of dollars in annual revenues and a marketing budget that's so big they could squash us like ants. We'd be crushed under the soles of their boots and they wouldn't know that they killed us."

Romy sat forward in his chair. "You said 'we' and 'us', Nick. Does that mean you've agreed to work with me?"

Nick chuckled. "Sorry, Romy, that's just the way I talk. It's easier for me to think about solving your problems if I assume that we're already on the same side. So, aren't you afraid of going up against the big guys? You should be."

"Part of what you say is true, Nick. We know that those companies led lobbying efforts with your Food and Drug Administration to keep our semi-refined carrageenan out of your market. In July, though, the FDA issued a ruling against them, and allowed our PNG product—Philippine Natural Grade—a regulatory status equal to their extra-refined version."

Romy noticed the favorable reaction on Nick's face and went on. "They are powerful. True. But they are not invincible. In addition, our company would have a significant advantage over them."

"Why is that?" asked Nick.

"The large processing plants that are already in our market have to buy their raw material from tens of thousands of independent native farmers, because they cannot grow enough themselves to meet the demand. Under Philippine law, foreign companies are restricted to operating only thirty hectares—that's about seventy five acres—of farming area apiece. As Filipinos, our production company wouldn't have any restrictions. We could establish as many of our own farms as we like, and have no limitations on their size."

"And what about the independent farmers? Won't the existing companies just continue to get their raw materials from them?"

Romy smiled. "No, Nick. In the first place, we can pay them an extra peso or two per kilo for their crops and still make all the profit we need. Besides, the farmers would prefer to sell their crops to a Filipino company. And," he added enigmatically, "our company will have several influential people on its Board of Directors."

Nick held up one of his hands. "Influential? In what way?"

Romy hesitated slightly, picking his works with care, "All of us have experience at the highest levels of our Government. Two of us are actually elected officials, and one of them, Luis Carino, is the Philippines' Minister of the Interior. He has a great reputation in our country, and is a master at making sure the right things happen."

Nick raised his eyebrows. "Really?"

"I told you, Nick, we have taken care of the Philippine production issues. The problem we have is on the U.S. marketing end."

Nick thought for a moment. "OK. That's right, but maybe not for the same reason you think. American customers who've been buying from a giant company like HMC aren't always going to be excited about buying from a small startup. The emphasis on managing quality requires a manufacturer to qualify its vendors, and that's a formal process that can take weeks or even months to complete. So even after we identify a prospective customer, it's going to take a while to gain their trust and prove to them that we can supply them with the right material at a competitive price. We still have to sell them."

"So how do we accomplish that?"

Nick reached for his water glass. He always told people that the reason for TGG's success was that they delivered results for his clients. He knew, however, that results were secondary. The real reason for the success of the firm was his ability to attract clients in the first place. Nick was a closer. He knew how to get clients. And in every selling situation, he thought, there was a single, critical point—a point at which the client was on the edge of saying yes. "Yes, I believe you understand my problem. Yes, I believe you can fix it. Yes, I am willing to pay you to do it."

This was, Nick knew, that juncture. The right words would mean a new client. New billings for TGG. New opportunities. The wrong words would send the prospective business away. Away forever. Nick took a few sips of water and let his instincts take over.

"Well," he began, "here's the way I see it. For starters, we need to find some potential customers and learn what it will take to get them to buy from us. In order to convince them of our viability, we've got to actually create a new corporate entity and establish a legal connection to the Philippine company. The formalities associated with setting up the new business are the easy part. We'll need to find the right people to put in a couple of critical positions, but even that shouldn't be too difficult. It's going to be a little tougher to perform the due diligence. That's going to take some time and money."

"What do you mean by 'due diligence'?" asked Romy.

"While you and I might be willing to work together on the basis of only a handshake, this level of business requires contracts, and those agreements will only be made if both sides take the time to properly investigate the other parties. I need to thoroughly examine your business plan, meet the other members of your production company, and take a look at your operations and facilities.

"We need to prove that we have a bona fide company, and that requires a certain level of inspection. It is entirely possible that a customer won't sign a purchase agreement with the new U.S. corporation until they themselves visit the production facilities in the Philippines. Knowing that, it only makes sense that whoever is going to be doing the selling needs to have seen for themselves what the prospective customer would see."

Romy nodded. "I understand, but I am surprised. Why do you say that it would not be difficult to find executives for the U.S. company?"

Nick looked directly into Romy's eyes. "Let me ask you something. I've enjoyed the time we've spent together so far. Do you feel comfortable working with me?"

"Absolutely."

"Good," continued Nick, certain that his firm now had a new client. "Because I think we've got a remarkable match. The truth is, the U.S. company can be started with only a handful of people. We'll need a technically-oriented marketing person, one good bean counter, and a CEO. If you're willing to give up the right amount of equity in the new corporation, I already know who they are."

"You must be kidding. Victor said that you worked quickly, but this is incredible."

"Here's what I have in mind. We need someone who is a world-class marketer and who also has the right kind of experience in the consumer food industry. One of my lead Associates is a guy named Keith Dickson. He got an MBA from Stanford and was at the top of his class there. More importantly, he was at Procter & Gamble for a number of years as a product line manager. He knows about carrageenan, and has technical skills and knowledge about the manufacturing process that we'd need. He'd be a combination V.P. of Marketing and of Research and Development.

"I've also got a couple of candidates for the CFO spot, people who have been involved in public companies before and can handle the investor community as well as the accounting issues. That one would be the easiest.

"Finally, I know someone who could manage this company on a part-time basis until the business was big enough and had a positive cash flow. This person would also lead the sales effort. I'm not talking about just managing a group of salespeople, he would personally find the customers and close the business. Are you with me so far?"

Romy nodded his head, but wore a look of concern on his face. "Yes, but I am afraid that perhaps I have not made myself clear. As you know, Asians in particular value the relationship aspects of business. Since it takes so long to develop the right relationships, we are reluctant to 'change horses'. I have already done, as you say, my due diligence on you and your firm. My sources have investigated the backgrounds of you and your Associates, and confirmed the quality of your work. I particularly liked what you did for the Pro-5 company.

"We have concluded that we want to hire you to set up our marketing company here in the United States. We have only two conditions, Nick. The first is that you must lead this personally. We want you."

"I'm flattered by your interest, Romy. What's the second condition?"

"We can't pay you anything up front."

Nick raised his eyebrows. "Excuse me?"

"We want to pay you out of the capital that you raise. We are more than happy to pay you for results, but we cannot afford to pay for mere effort."

Nick hesitated before responding. "I see. And you figure that if I invest my own time and money in setting up the business, then I won't have any excuses about delivering results when it comes time to manage it."

Romy nodded. "Precisely."

"And what happens if I uncover something during my due diligence that makes your plan unworkable?"

"If you decide to walk away after you visit the Philippines, we'll pay you your standard fees up to that point, excluding travel time."

"I'm curious, Romy, what's your understanding of our 'standard fees'?"

"I am told that, while your Associates are somewhat more reasonable, you bill your time at the rate of two hundred and fifty dollars an hour."

Nick sat, motionless. Romy had, indeed, done his homework. The figures were accurate. But that wasn't what was setting off the alarm bells inside his head; it was the reference to the company that went by the name of Pro-5. Nick had established that company a few months ago in partnership with one of his clients and was personally its largest stockholder. Pro-5 was perfectly legitimate, and while it was hardly a secret, it was not at all well known. What bothered Nick was that he simply didn't remember ever telling Victor Crenshaw about it. Since Vic couldn't have told Romy about Pro-5, how did Romy find out?

"OK, Romy. I take it then that when we establish our new company you won't object to market compensation rates for the executive positions and a twenty-five percent stake for the management team, as long as I'm involved?"

Romy nodded.

"And a fair equity position for any outside investors we may need?"

Romy nodded again.

"Then we're in great shape. I'm the third guy. If everything turns out well during our due diligence process, I'll be the CEO." Nick picked up a felt-tipped pen from his satchel and began to make a list on a pad of lined yellow paper. "Let's talk about what I'll need to see when I visit you in the Philippines."

Nick drove north along Highway 101 past Candlestick Park, heading into the city at just over the posted speed limit. He picked up his cell phone and made a handful of calls. First to Keith, and then to his office to retrieve the messages waiting on his answering machine. He returned calls, and completed conversations with four clients and two Associates by the time he reached the Golden Gate Bridge. Knowing he had nothing further on his calendar, he decided he was done for the day and headed home to spend the afternoon with his family.

That time of the day was generally a blend of controlled chaos, and today was no different. Both his boys had friends over; some were inside watching television and playing video games, while others shot hoops. There was plenty of noise, but the boys had their own space on the lower level of the house and could amuse themselves without disturbing their parents, who passed the day relaxing upstairs.

At about six o'clock, Nick fired up the Weber grill on their deck just off the kitchen and prepared to barbecue chicken and hot dogs. As he waited for the coals to heat, their older boy, eleven-year-old Sean, set the table for dinner while Laurie sat at the kitchen counter, where she could enjoy the view of San Francisco Bay through the redwoods and watch Nick at the grill. Occasionally glancing at the sailboats out on the water, she sipped from the sparkling water in her glass as they talked.

Their conversation flowed easily from one topic to another; their only interruption was the occasional thundering sound of their younger boy, ten-year-old Max, running up the stairs to inquire about when everything would be ready. As soon as the food was prepared, the boys seated themselves in their usual positions and attacked their dinners, devouring it in far less time than had been necessary to prepare it.

Nick and Laurie arranged their schedules for the following day, since dinner time seemed to be the only time when everyone could be together to figure out who needed to be where, and when. As the food vanished from the plates, the conversation subsided. Max, stormed back down the stairs to his favorite games, as Sean stayed behind to do the dishes. Nick and Laurie went upstairs to the peaceful isolation of their bedroom suite.

"So," she began, "what have you been waiting to tell me?"

Nick laughed. After fourteen years of marriage, he should have known better than to think that he could conceal a surprise from her. "Well," he paused, letting the suspense build, "I have a new client. It's going to require an investment on my part, but my gut tells me that it could be really big. And, there'll be some travel."

"Oh?" she said flatly. "And when do you have to leave?"

"Not me." he responded with a smile. "Us. We have to go to the Philippines."

As the roar of seasonal rains echoed around him from the tin roof above, Buddy Ripley looked at his maps for the millionth time. Sitting cross-legged on the woven mat floor of his tiny home on the island of Leyte, he was surrounded by them. Some were tacked to the walls and others lay opened on the floor. More maps were folded, accordion-style, and piled in stacks on the crude shelving that stood underneath the window, while still others were stashed out of sight, rolled up in the honeycombed rack of cardboard mailing tubes that was jammed in the corner.

An enormous, six-color representation of the Philippines was mounted on the largest wall of the room, completely dominating the space. Nearly six feet tall and eight feet wide, it had cost Buddy almost a week's pay. Smaller colored maps spread before him featured a major island group, a single island, or a single city, and black and white topographical charts showed the relative elevation changes of given areas. While each of the maps in the room were different, all were of the Philippines.

Although the arrangement might have looked haphazard to an outsider, it was anything but. Buddy had drawn an extensive series of horizontal and vertical lines on the largest map with finely-tipped colored pens. Patiently labeling each of the lines, the superimposed grid formed a detailed indexing system that linked to each of his other maps and charts. Using only the resources in this room, Buddy could instantly access and examine in detail the topography of any location within the Philippines to an accuracy level of a single meter.

Buddy's system for indexing his maps, was based on more than the latitude and longitude of the country's geography. It included a third dimension—a timeline of the movements of Japanese troops within the Philippines during the Second World War. An outsider would have been intimidated at the scope and complexity of the project, but not Buddy. His need to be systematic and methodical, he knew, were traits that he had learned from his father. His other primary characteristics were inherited.

From his mother, Marie, he had gotten his pigmentation: jet-black hair and smooth skin that was colored a rich, brownish tan. Everything else about him came from his father's gene pool. Like his father, Daniel, Buddy was six feet tall, weighed one hundred and seventy pounds, was lithely-muscled and graceful in his movement. Also like Daniel, Buddy was intellectually gifted and very well educated. At the age of twenty-two, Buddy had entered Princeton University, where he earned a degree in Religion and Philosophy. Both father and son had earned law degrees from Boalt Hall in Berkeley, and both had strong ties to the Philippines.

For Buddy, it was because he'd been born there, ten years after the end of World War II. For Daniel, the Philippines was where he had met the two people who would provide the major fascinations of his life. The second person was his wife, Marie, a beautiful and diminutive native Filipina from Manila. The first was General Tomoyuki Yamashita.

Daniel T. Ripley III was one of many American attorneys involved in the prosecution of Japanese war criminals. Sent to Manila in the fall of 1944, he helped prepare cases against eleven senior Japanese officers, and gained the death penalty for each of them. While he took no special interest in ten of the defendants, one of them, General Yamashita, captivated his imagination.

The elder Ripley spoke with the General—through an interpreter—only once, but he read every transcript of every interview and interrogation Yamashita endured during his three month imprisonment. On three separate occasions, Daniel observed the General speaking with other high-ranking Japanese soldiers, and each time—despite his own inability to speak Japanese—he understood what the General said. "Silence!"

Ripley had ordered that all prisoners be held in isolation from one another, and through his patient, exacting, and methodical interviewing process, pieced together the movements of Yamashita's troops during the war. Having assembled the facts and evaluated all the allegations, Ripley finally uncovered Yamashita's actual wartime objectives. He was the first Allied officer to know of the existence of Yamashita's gold.

After the Japanese officers were executed, Daniel remained in the Philippines, met and married Marie, and had a son. In the beginning, he searched cautiously for clues about the treasure but found only rumors; nothing concrete. Despite the fact that the trail should have been fresh, the clues, like the treasure, seemed to have disappeared.

He looked for fifteen years with little success, but would have continued his search for another fifteen, and another fifteen after that. Would have, that is, if cancer hadn't mercilessly invaded his body. The disease attacked his liver with such ferocity that the end came in a matter of weeks. Weak and emaciated, Daniel called for his son.

Even though the sound of rain plummeting down onto the roof over his head was deafening, Buddy could still hear the sound of his father's straining voice during their final conversation, which had taken place in this very room some thirty years before.

"Don't ever forget that the treasure is real. Bigger, more valuable than you can comprehend."

"I know, Daddy, you told me that."

Daniel gave his son's hand a squeeze. "It's well protected. Not buried in haste, but methodically, by a man whose genius will never be appreciated. Remember, son, he was a Jap, and those bastards are sneaky. Expect surprises. Be patient. They think they can wait forever, so you'll have to be patient. You might have to outlast the sonofabitches."

His father looked over at him, his eyes losing their light. He spoke again, establishing the path Buddy would follow for the rest of his life. "He had to leave some clues. There had to be some way that he could come back and get it. It's yours, Buddy. Find them, and it's yours."

Buddy, awakened from his reminiscence by the staccato sound of the deluge overhead, contemplated his next move.

When Nick first told her about their trip, Laurie had stayed up half the night thinking of all the things she needed to do. Her first priority was attending to the boys. While there was a lot of shuttling around to do, she knew that her mother would be more than happy to stay at their home with her grandsons while she and Nick traveled. The boys had, in fact, been ecstatic to learn that Grandma was going to be with them, and didn't give any indication at all that they might miss either her or Nick while they were gone.

Next, she had considered what she needed to do herself. What would they be doing? What should she wear? What should she pack? How many gifts would she need to bring? She had stared at the blank piece of paper for some time before she wrote down the first entry on this list. It had been so long since she and Nick had traveled outside the country that she almost didn't know where to begin.

In the first years of their marriage, they had traveled together constantly. At that time, Nick was racking up successes as a sales manager for a rapidly-growing computer software company in Silicon Valley, and he was on the road nearly every week. Whenever his trips took him to an interesting place, Laurie would take time from work and join him. In the beginning, of course, the excitement of seeing new cities around North America made each of his destinations of interest, but after a while she found herself only going with him when he went to a handful of specific places. Laurie took every possible opportunity to go to Canada, to Chicago with its shops and restaurants, or to Washington D.C. to visit the museums.

Their ability to travel together had backed off considerably with the arrival of Sean, their elder son, eleven years ago. And after the following year, when Max, their second child was born, Laurie rarely joined her husband on his business trips. Traveling became even more problematic three years ago, when Nick resigned from the computer company and started his own business.

Impatient with the increasing sense of routine in his work, and frustrated by the arrival of colleagues who saw in the company's success a means for high salaries with mediocre effort, Nick had taken his stake and gambled it on TGG. From that time on, Nick never felt he could afford the time away from his clients, much less the expense of taking the entire family somewhere on an airplane. Besides, the boys were at the age where it made the most sense, whenever time became available, to just grab some clothing, stuff everything into the Volvo wagon and visit the grandparents in Southern California. It was only a day's drive away, it was inexpensive, and it was relatively easy.

In any case, this trip to the Philippines, Laurie knew, could hardly be called a vacation. It was something very different. She was used to entertaining TGG's clients, but the way Nick had described the days ahead, they needed to do far more than merely humor some businessmen in Manila. They would be traveling with their host to some of the Philippine's more remote islands. Not only would they not know in advance exactly where they were going, they would be going to places that were unreachable by telephone. It was, she thought, simultaneously exciting and a little scary.

Because of the unknowns associated with their schedule, the challenges of packing for a two-week trip abroad were made all the more difficult. Nick had told her she only needed to take an evening gown, some walking shoes, and some grubby clothes in a backpack in case they went camping. Right, she thought; men had it so easy. Nick traveled so lightly that he typically carried everything with him in a single, carry-on Lark suitcase. Either he just didn't get it, or he chose to ignore the realities of a woman's world. A long, sequined gown required not only matching shoes, but accessories as well. To miss such facts was one of Nick's more pronounced shortcomings.

He'd also said they would be there during the monsoon season. Just what she needed. Going to strange and isolated places with people she didn't know in the middle of a drenching rainstorm. Nick had, of course, told her how delightful Romy was, and had repeatedly said that the Filipino had stressed the importance of her coming along on the trip. She was, in fact, excited enough about having the chance to go someplace new with him that she hadn't really objected. She just thought the whole situation was a little—well—odd. This project seemed somehow different from all the others.

If her husband felt any reservations or uncertainties, he certainly had not shared them with her. Far from it. Every night for the past week, Nick had become more and more optimistic about the potential success of this Philippine project, which was a bit of a relief. When he'd first told her about it, Nick had described the risks of the deal. Not only would he not get paid anything up front, he would have to use his frequent flier credits to keep their travel costs to a minimum. Worse still, the time that he invested in getting the new company going was time that he couldn't bill to another client, so their immediate cash flow would take a substantial hit.

She shook her head. He worked so hard, she thought. From her point of view, TGG was already a success. Nick was happy, he was appreciated by his clients, and there always seemed to be enough money on hand to take care of themselves. Still, this was a big gamble. While she was nervous about having to dip into their savings, she trusted Nick's judgment. If he felt this could be "the big one," she'd be only too happy to give him her support.

She continued to check off the items on the lists she had made in preparation for their departure, pausing at the entry marked,

"Gifts for the Hosts." Nick had told her about Luis Carino, a charismatic, cabinet-level government official who would play in important role in this venture. Based on what Nick had shared with her, she looked forward to meeting him. But what kind of gift would be appropriate for a man of such stature? What do you offer someone whose world is so unknown to you?

The morning after Nick told Laurie about their trip, he rose a little earlier than usual and started the day by rearranging his calendar. That, it turned out, was easier than he had originally expected. The only thing that couldn't be handed off to one of his Associates was a meeting in San Diego. Nick had been working with a company there and was a member of their Board of Directors. He would check with them to see if this meeting could be delayed a week until his return. The company's Chairman frequently adjusted the schedule of Board meetings to suit his own travel demands, so his own request shouldn't be too difficult to accommodate.

Satisfied that his client commitments could be handled, he sat back and looked out at San Francisco Bay. He loved being in or around water. He had always lived near water, and had first started to swim at the age of four. Then came bodysurfing and his first surfboard, followed by more swimming and sailing. He competed successfully in swimming and water polo through high school and later, at Indiana University. His summers were also spent on the water, life guarding when in high school, and sailing professionally during the breaks from college. Water gave him peace and replenished his energy. He felt similar satisfactions—the same tactile awareness and complete escape from the left side of his brain— when he worked with wood, down in the garage.

When his back injury had forced him to back off on physical competitions, Nick turned to the quieter satisfactions of cabinet making. Over the course of the past decade, he had accumulated an extensive collection of hand and power tools, as well as the skill to use them. With all of the demands on his time, he knew, he wouldn't be doing much woodworking any time soon.

Romy had told him the necessary arrival and departure dates, and had also given him the name of the hotel where they should plan to stay their first night. After that, said Romy, they would be off to other locales. Nick picked up the phone and dialed the toll-free number of United Airlines. When the agent came on the line, Nick asked several questions and then made his selections. They would need to make one stop on their way to Manila and would have to deal with the mental and physical issues associated with crossing the International Date Line, but other than that, it seemed pretty straightforward.

The return leg of their trip was a little more complicated be-cause of the range of alternative possibilities. There wasn't a direct flight from Manila to San Francisco, so they would need to make another stopover. After briefly considering his options, he decided to route them through Hong Kong. After all, he thought, it was only a few years before the Chinese would regain control over the British Territory, and now might be the only time they could ex-perience that city in the way it had been for nearly a hundred years.

He hung up the phone, moved over to his computer desk, and banged out a quick fax for Romy, which outlined another request for information. They would depart for the Philippines the fol-lowing week, and before Nick got on the airplane, he wanted what-ever details he could get about the specific growth rate of carrag-eenan, the status of their test locations, and the names of the people he would be meeting. During his early professional days, he had been satisfied with knowing only the most basic aspects of busi-ness issues. He didn't attain any real success with his career until he learned to embrace details.

He stayed in the office until the sun came up, and then show-ered, dressed, and drove into the city. He'd be on the steps of the main public library when their doors opened at eight o'clock to start doing his homework.

Nick's investigations at the San Francisco Public Library gave him a solid understanding of the food additive marketplace, its major companies, competitive structure, manufacturing capabilities, distribution strategies, and price points within a few days. The information he learned fascinated him.

His first impression was of how little he knew about so much of what went on in the world. Only a few days ago he had never heard of carrageenan, and now it seemed that the stuff was everywhere. Seek, and ye shall find, all right. Then, armed with several thick manila folders that were jammed with copies of articles, analyses and notes, he joined Keith Dickson the following Sunday for a lengthy discussion of the marketplace in general, as well as the more technical aspects of growing and refining seaweed. Their meeting, which began over breakfast, had lasted well into the night.

At the start of the day, they briefly debated the implications of the recent volcanic eruptions. Since the carrageenan test sites had not been affected, they concluded that the event was, if anything, slightly in their favor; it had resulted in a renewed focus on the Philippines.

That discussion out of the way, they focused on the three main questions for which Nick needed answers. First, he wanted to clarify the size of the worldwide carrageenan market. Secondly, he needed to understand what was special about the Philippine variety of carrageenan, and third, he wanted to know if there was any way they could gain any sustainable competitive advantage.

The two men started with the issue of market size, because they considered it the easiest. They had been able to find a considerable amount of information, and now triangulated every scrap of data they had gleaned from their various sources. They took certain facts contained in the Annual Reports and 10-Ks of the publicly-held companies like HMC, Titan Industries, and McDonald's. They had performed a computer search of press releases and product introductions, and checked out the reports published by the industry's various trade associations, and now summarized their findings.

Totaling up their columns of figures, Nick had learned that Keith's initial estimate was remarkably close. Well, he had thought, no real surprise there. When it came to facts and figures, Keith was always right on target. Just as Keith had said, the worldwide market was a little over a hundred million dollars a year. Half of that consumption was in the United States, with most of the rest being divided between Germany and France.

The numbers were misleading, however, because the only available figures were for the highly-refined versions of carrageenan. The semi-refined version of eucheuma, which Romy called Philippine Natural Grade (PNG), had not been classified as true carrageenan by the United States until recently, when the Food and Drug Administration removed a two-percent fiber restriction they had imposed in 1985. As a result, the numbers for PNG were not reflected in the market totals. Since both Korea and Japan were heavy consumers of PNG, the worldwide market demand could actually be well over two hundred millions dollars per year. It was plenty big enough for a new company to come in and make a name and a profit for itself.

More important than the market size was the rate at which the market was growing. The faster the rate of growth, the higher the return they could expect. Since the need for materials that could effectively replace fat in foods would continue to expand for at least the rest of the decade, and with McDonald's publicly leading the charge, the rate of growth could be perfect.

Their target rate was anything in the low double-digits. Anything over ten percent generally indicated strong profit margins, but if it was too high—approaching thirty percent or more—then it would attract too much competitive interest and was too difficult to manage. After massaging the numbers for a while, the pair concluded that the growth rate of the worldwide carrageenan market was somewhere between fifteen and twenty percent. So far, so good; but what was special about this Philippine eucheuma?

Once again, Keith's contacts proved to be invaluable. After making a few long distance telephone calls, he had found the answer. More good news. The Philippines simply had the most favorable conditions for growing carrageenan. A very fast-growing plant, carrageenan required a specific environment for optimum growth. A moderate current, for starters, was essential, because it provided not only sufficient nutrients, but also reduced the impact of any pollutants. Too strong a current, however, or the presence of constant waves, were damaging. Also critical for the plant's success was an unfluctuating mild temperature that combined with a uniformly high salinity index. If all that weren't enough, he had learned, the root system required a firm sandy bottom and a water depth of at least two feet at low tide.

The picture, Nick realized, was becoming a little more clear. Sure, most of the world was covered with water, and of course seaweed grew everywhere. Looking at these specifications, however, he understood why the number of places around the globe that provided this delicate balance of circumstances was so small.

The need for mild water temperature ruled out huge sections of ocean. Also eliminated were the mild temperate waters off the shores of Africa, Mexico and the Americas, which were either too deep, too rocky, or had too much current. When these factors were considered, the only place in the world where eucheuma would naturally thrive was in Southeast Asia. There were plenty of locations there that met most of the essential criteria, but there was a significant problem with the increasing pollution along the coastlines of Burma, Malaya and Indonesia. As far as carrageenan was concerned, the Philippines, it seemed, was the Gold Coast.

Things were looking good, very good indeed. They had a market that was perfect in size and growth, and an apparently exclusive product. It was a perfect situation if they could solve their next issue. Could they establish a sustainable competitive advantage?

If Nick could confirm Romy's information about the regulations limiting the size of seaweed farms operated by foreign-owned companies, then their Filipino company would have a distinct advantage. Both men were seasoned in the realities of marketing and realized that it wasn't enough to simply have a strategic edge. Marketing, they knew, was a battlefield. It was possible to defend against enemy attacks if you controlled the high ground, but considerably more difficult if your forces occupied only the valleys. If theirs was the only Philippine-owned company, then they would have exclusive rights to large-scale production capacity and could establish their position on the high ground, able to defend their market position indefinitely.

If, that is, they could come up with a way to leverage the Philippines' thousands of independent seaweed farmers. Nick instinctively concluded that this factor was the critical piece. Almost every strategy of every company could point to a single element that alone defined its success. At this stage of their investigation, it appeared that control of independent farmers was that essential ingredient. Still, they continued to look at all other aspects of the puzzle. Their years of experience had refined their perceptions and taught them the importance of looking at a given situation in its entirety. On they went with their process of discovery.

Buddy sat on the floor facing his largest map, the continuing downpour of rain on the roof overhead the only sound he could hear.
He focused not on any of the land forms it represented but on the
thin red lines he had drawn on it. Red was the color he had chosen
to indicate the timeline of Japanese troop movements during the
Second World War.

While most of the work of collecting the data on the map had
been done by his father, it was Buddy who had taken his father's
handwritten documentation and transposed it into the three-di-
mensional format that he now studied. He had refined it over the
years and now could tell at a glance not just *where* Yamashita's
divisions had been positioned in the Philippines, but *when*.

Long ago Buddy had learned to ignore most of the mass of data
and concentrate solely on the activities of a single Yamashita division, the one led by Colonel Teiichi Hara. When he had first studied the movements of Yamashita's forces, their complexity appeared overwhelming. Once Buddy had broken them down into
component parts, however, a pattern emerged.

While all of Yamashita's other divisions had moved in logical
and orderly directions, one of them had not. The normal movement of the General's troops had been in a straight line—or at least
a constant direction—from one island to the next, such as south
to north or west to east. Starting in August of 1942, however, Colonel Hara's division had not only completely separated itself from
Yamashita's main forces but also had moved in relatively haphazard directions and at apparently random intervals.

When he initially discovered this anomaly, he had concluded

that Hara's troops must have been responsible for transporting food, medical supplies, or top-secret communications from one post to another. Upon further analysis, however, he identified other, smaller units that had performed each of those duties.

Buddy knew that the Japanese military moved like a finely-tuned machine, with no wasted motion or counterproductive activity. Because Colonel Hara's division operated autonomously, completely independent of the rest of Yamashita's troops, Buddy believed that it must have had a unique mission, and using his father's hypothesis, had concluded what that was. The key to this conclusion was Buddy's discovery that whenever the Colonel had transported his own troops, he had also carried with him a large number of prisoners of war. There was only one explanation that fit the facts, Buddy realized. And, having eliminated all of the other possibilities, he concluded that it was Colonel Hara who had been ordered to hide the treasure.

Buddy could see on the map before him exactly where the Colonel's troops had encamped, from which he surmised where the treasure was hidden. But he also knew something else equally important. He knew how long Hara had stayed in each place and how many POWs he had taken with him. The longer Colonel Hara stayed at a location, he reasoned, the larger the treasure that was hidden there. Similarly, the greater the number of POWs involved, the more deeply the cache was buried.

Buddy's eyes were drawn to his favorite location. Based on the amount of time that Colonel Hara had spent there, Buddy believed that it must have been Teiichi's favorite spot as well. Lying north of the island of Palawan, it was the Calamian Island group. Closing his eyes, he visualized the terrain there, which he had visited long ago. It was an extraordinarily beautiful setting.

With the rain now hammering down on the roof over his head, traveling to the site anytime soon was impossible. For now, his memories would have to suffice. And even though the weather forced him to wait, he knew how to advance while staying still.

The Gardners sat down to dinner. The boys knew, with the acute perception unique to childhood, that this would be the last time they would see their parents for a while. Seated around the long wooden trestle table, the two preteens were simultaneously relaxed and excited.

Nick had marinated and grilled a flank steak and Laurie had made salad and garlic mashed potatoes. They took their time eating and talked about the next few weeks. Laurie began by reviewing, for what Max had insisted was the hundredth time, the rules of the house during their absence. When she had finished, Sean started in with his questions.

Probably the smarter of their two children, Sean was already reading novels intended for adults, and constantly irritated his younger brother by insisting they watch PBS instead of MTV or cartoons. His chubby face was accented by dark brown hair and blue eyes, and his large white teeth were concealed almost entirely behind braces. "So Dad," he spoke in his prematurely deep voice, "are you going to be President of this company you're working on?"

"It looks that way, sport."

"But you're President of TGG. Will you have to give that up?"

Nick grinned. "Nope. You can be President of as many companies as you want, as long as you deliver results. But I need to learn more about the Filipinos I'll be working with before I know exactly what my relationship with them will turn out to be. That's why we're taking this trip. It's entirely possible that I'll learn something on this trip that will make me not want to work with them."

His younger son looked at him. Barely ten years old, Max was taller than Sean, thin and athletic. Constantly active, his handsome face was highlighted by long, dark eyelashes that set off his blue eyes and short blond hair. He had on the same grossly baggy shorts and oversized tee-shirts that defined the local adolescent style, and said, with a mouthful of food, "Learn something like what?"

"I don't have any idea. Although everything about this situation looks positive, part of what I do is to look for things that are wrong. Sometimes things that are wrong can be fixed, but sometimes they can't. For example, I had a meeting with a friend of mine down the peninsula. He's what they call a venture capitalist, and his job is to buy into companies that are just getting started. He gives them a lot of money and they give him shares of their company. Later, when their company succeeds, the VC sells his stock, and sometimes makes an enormous profit."

"Yeah," interjected Sean, "they can get, like, ten or twenty times as much as they invested."

Nick turned to look at him. "You're right, Sean. Sometimes they make that much, or even more, and sometimes they lose all their money. Where did you learn that?"

Sean thought for a second, a far-off look in his eyes. "One of those Wall Street shows."

Laurie and Nick looked at each other across the table. Not surprising, was the thought they shared. Nick continued. "Anyway, this man said something that concerns me. He and his company have invested a ton of money in startup companies that work with Pacific Rim countries, and he warned me about the realities of corruption in the Philippines. According to him, companies consider bribes just part of their everyday business practice."

"What kind of bribes?" asked Max, suddenly curious.

"Well, suppose you have a business and want to send something to one of your customers. Here, you go to the post office or call a shipping company to pick up your package. In the Philippines, you not only buy the stamps from the postman, but you might pay him a little extra just to make sure your package actually gets delivered. The customer also pays when the package arrives because they know that if they don't, then maybe the next time some of their mail will mysteriously be lost or accidentally get damaged."

"That sucks!" proclaimed Max.

"Max!" interrupted Laurie. "Watch your mouth."

"You're right, Max," said Nick, "but that's just the way it works. It's the kind of thing that could make it very difficult for me to do business there."

Laurie put down her fork and sat back in her chair. "I told Isabel, the woman who helps me with housekeeping, that we were going to the Philippines, and she told me about what we can expect to see. I didn't realize it, but she was born in Manila and lived there until she was twenty.

"She described what it was like to grow up there. There are a few wealthy people, but most of the people are extremely poor. There is a middle class, but it's small, and evidently the lines between the classes are very clear. If you happen to be born poor, you have to be very lucky to make it into the middle class, and if you are born middle class, you stay middle class. Here, it doesn't matter so much who your parents are. What counts here are your own abilities and what you do yourself."

"That's not really true, Mom," commented Sean. "There are families here with tons of money. You know, like the Andersons. They've got megabucks. They've got a Porsche and a Ferrari, and they have that humongous house up at Lake Tahoe."

"That's right," answered Laurie, "but that's not the point. Their family may have a lot of money, but they still live, in many ways, the same as we do. Their daughter is on Max's Little League team. You and Derrick are getting the exact same education. In the Philippines, upper and middle class children go to different schools. It doesn't matter how smart they are, only whose children they are."

106

"Besides," offered Nick, "Terry Anderson didn't always have money. He didn't inherit it from his folks. He made it all himself. When he started his company—about ten years ago, I think—the only thing he had was an idea. He got some investors, worked his butt off, and made a fortune when the company went public."

"What does that mean?" asked Max.

Sean chimed back in, "It means that the company sells its shares on a stock exchange."

Nick nodded. "That's about right. The management of the company goes through a process which allows the general public to buy and sell its stock."

"What happens to all the money?" asked Max.

"Some of it goes to the company so they can afford to grow their business—by hiring more people, spending more on advertising, or doing research. Some of it, however, goes into the pockets of the people who sell their shares."

"So how much did Mr. Anderson make?" inquired Max.

"I'll give you two answers. The first one is that it's none of our business and it really doesn't matter. He did well enough to never have to worry about money again. I'll give you the second answer if you promise to not blab about it at school or with your friends, because it might embarrass the Anderson kids if they found out you were talking about their family."

"Nick. You're not going to tell them how much he made, are you?"

"Relax, Sweets. I don't know the exact amount, but it is a public company, and you don't have to be a rocket scientist to do the math. It's in the newspapers every day, and there's no reason the boys shouldn't know."

Laurie smiled. With that kind of buildup, she knew they had gotten their boys attention. She and Nick had long ago recognized that their family dinners were the best forum for teaching the boys important lessons. Not only was it the only time of day when they were all together, they knew that the things they discussed would be remembered.

She could only see the backs of her sons' heads as they looked at their father at the other end of the table. "Remember, boys, not a word."

Nick glanced at Laurie, letting both pairs of eyes remain riveted on him for another moment. "Fifteen million dollars. Not as much as Joe Montana or Barry Bonds, but enough to pay off the Anderson's house, buy a couple of toys, get the kids through college, and never have to worry about money again." There was a murmur of animated reaction from the boys and then Sean turned to Nick.

"Dad? The Gardner Group is a company, right?"

"Yep," replied Nick, anticipating Sean's line of questioning.

"Does it have stock?"

"Sure. It's a corporation, and it has stock."

"Who owns it?"

"Your Mom and I own it all." God, he thought to himself, I love the way he sets up his dominoes.

"Then why don't you sell shares in TGG and go public?"

"It's not the kind of company that would interest most people, Sean. TGG sells answers to very specific problems. We don't sell the kind of mass-produced things that would make the company appealing to investors."

"But you're going to make carrageenan into that kind of product, right? Even if you can't take TGG public, you can with the new company, can't you?"

"It's possible, sport, it's possible."

"Then you should get a Porsche! No, a Lamborghini!" exclaimed Max.

"You're missing the point. Less than a fraction of one percent of the people in the world—way less—ever make twenty million dollars. The real benefit of making that much money isn't so that you can buy fancy cars. Making twenty million dollars means that we'd never have to worry about money again. None of us.

"Not only would our future would be secure," he said, indicating himself and Laurie, "but so would each of yours, as well. And instead of just taking care of our own needs, we'd have enough to give to other people that haven't been as lucky. Instead of having to work just to keep our lights turned on, I'd have the luxury of spending my time doing things that I love. And the fact is that, even if that happened, I'd still choose to work. Not as much as now, for sure. The difference is that I'd only work with people that I really liked.

"Anyway, don't go off telling your friends about this. It's way too early to know how things will turn out. We need to go on our trip and learn a whole lot more about these people. I also need to find out everything I can about how carrageenan can be used."

Sean finished chewing his steak and took a swallow of milk from his glass. "I know the answer to that, Dad. That stuff is used in everything. I went up and down the aisles at the store today, looking at the ingredients of the foods. You wouldn't believe how many of them have carrageenan."

Max's eyes sparkled as he announced, "Yeah. I found it in Sean's favorite foods." He paused briefly for effect before delivering the punch line. "It's in baby food *and* dog food!"

"Moron." Sean kicked into high gear. "It's in a lot of stuff I like—cakes and pies, puddings and breads. Marshmallows, frosting, chocolate milk, yogurt, ice cream. It's in salad dressing, soups, jam, ketchup, mayonnaise—"

"They kept saying, 'Here it is again', " Laurie added. "I didn't believe it at first and checked some of the labels for myself."

And so it went, continuing through dessert. Afterwards, they cleared the table. Laurie wiped off the countertops and Max followed close by, shadowing her around the room. Nick headed downstairs with Sean, and plopped himself down into the overstuffed sofa that dominated the middle of the play room. A few minutes later, Laurie and Max joined him, and Max, snuggled between them, flipped through the pages of the latest *Sports Illus-*

trated. Max made comments about the athletes in the magazine, and generally made sure he kept both parents occupied exclusively with him, until he was satisfied.

Laurie and Nick lingered downstairs until both boys had received enough attention to last until they returned from their trip, and then headed to their master suite upstairs. There, easing into their respective recliners, they talked for a while before settling into silence. They enjoyed the quieting sounds of their home, and the view of the lights in the distance and the stars beginning to fill the skies to the east.

As the gentle hum of the house subsided, they rose and prepared for bed. They each brushed their teeth at their own separate pace, and never once said a word. Turning out the lights, Nick got to the bed first. Several minutes later, illuminated by nothing more than the moonlight, Laurie slipped between the king-sized sheets to join him.

Nestled comfortably in each other's arms, they chatted softly. Before long, words gave way to kisses. Nick always liked it when Laurie came to bed naked. And afterwards, she thought, so did she.

Laurie and Nick relaxed in the back seat of the limousine as their driver navigated through the traffic of 19th Avenue on the way to San Francisco Airport. The first part of their morning had progressed swiftly as they made their last-minute preparations. Laurie's mother had arrived just as they were pouring their first cups of coffee, and the boys had instantly herded their Grandma to their rooms downstairs, leaving the parents to finish packing without interruption. The airport transportation had arrived precisely at 10:00 A.M., and their good-bye scene had been cheerful.

Nick reached over to take Laurie's hand in his. "You doing okay?" he asked.

She squeezed his fingers. "Yeah, I guess so. I'm sure the boys will be fine, and it'll be nice to get away. I'm just sort of catching my breath." She looked up into his eyes. "The past couple of weeks have sure been busy."

"For both of us."

"Did I tell you about the rest of the conversation I had with Isabel?" inquired Laurie.

"I'm not sure. Was there anything special?"

"Yeah. A couple of things that I really didn't want to talk about in front of the boys."

"Oh?" replied Nick, his curiosity piqued.

"Well, it's probably nothing. Isabel went on and on about how bad President Marcos had been for the Philippines. About how he ransacked the country and took everything he could possibly get for himself. It sounds like he was a horrible man. She said that so many people there are incredibly poor, and it would have been easy for him to make their lives better. It sounds like they either can't get or can't afford even basic staples. That's one of the reasons that I brought all that fabric with us."

Nick nodded. When he had seen the huge pile of stuff that Laurie was planning to take with her on the trip, his immediate reaction had been one of incredulity. But she was right. It would be not only polite but appropriate to give the people they would meet thank-you gifts.

"There's something else Isabel said," Laurie continued, "that's been bothering me ever since. She said that Filipinos—even though they speak English—think and communicate like Asians, and not like Westerners. The way they talk to Americans is completely different from the way they speak among themselves. They will speak with complete honesty to each other, but have a different standard where we are concerned." She paused. "It's as if they're afraid they might offend us by telling us something we might not like to hear. So, rather than tell the truth, they might lie, and think they're being polite. Do you know what I mean?"

"I think so."

"I know that you trust Romy, and I believe in your judgment. But it's just that you haven't known him that long, and it—well—it bothers me."

Nick was silent for a moment before he responded. "Don't worry about it. The whole reason for us to go over there is to be able to see things for ourselves. I'll make sure that we look at all of the important aspects of this situation personally, so please don't worry.

"As far as Marcos is concerned, I don't know what to say. Whatever he did happened years ago. It's history. Besides, we've already heard about the graft and corruption—that's no surprise. I just need to make sure that our business is on the right track."

It was Laurie's turn to be quiet. "Maybe," she said softly. "Maybe you're right. You know how to take care of yourself."

A few minutes later they pulled up to the curb at SFO, stopped, and unloaded their bags. Nick paid the driver, and then, lifting carefully so he wouldn't hurt his back, picked up both of his bags and led the way into the terminal. Laurie, trailing behind, pulled the two stout leashes that were attached to her own suitcases, their wheels squealing in protest as she slowly progressed. Hardly a surprise, thought Nick as he heard the high-pitched and irritating squeaks following him. Her two overly-packed Lark suitcases were as big as small condominiums.

Nick was dismayed by the amount of stuff Laurie had chosen to take, since he had reminded her that they each needed to be able to carry their own bags. Normally, he would have hired one of the curbside porters to help them, but because he knew that they couldn't rely on assistance everywhere, he chose to have them hump their own luggage here.

Nick advanced to the roped-off check-in area and managed to place his larger suitcase on the scale beneath the countertop without getting too far ahead of Laurie. He turned to watch her complete the final few steps of her fifty-yard journey. He knew he had made his point clear, but if she was troubled or frustrated by her awkward and ponderous load, she was stubborn enough not to let it show on her face. She joined him, unhooked the leashes from the suitcases, and stored them in one of their zippered pockets. Not a hair out of place, nor a bead of sweat on her brow.

Buddy awakened to silence. The rain, which had been his constant companion for the past four months, had stopped. Rising from his futon and stretching, he walked a few steps to his front door and looked outside. The faint light of the pre-dawn sky showed patches of stars—the first ones he had seen since late May. While he knew that the rains would surely return, the stars above signaled to him the beginning of the end of the monsoon season.

Buddy knew how to read the weather, because it was the very rotation of the seasons that drove the pattern of his life. Since he always reserved the dry season for field research, travel and potential excavations, during the monsoons he furthered his preparation with things that could best be done indoors. He read from his extensive collection of books on geology and metallurgy and studied everything he could find on the subject of Asian art and history, and Japanese theology.

He also practiced law in his community, but the problems of the local people weren't very challenging, and, though he didn't earn much money, he didn't need to. The inheritance from his father had been enough to fund his education, allow him to buy his boat, and still have an adequate sum left over. When his Mother had died three years ago, she left him this house. Although the balance in Buddy's bank account was less than thirty thousand U.S. dollars, the interest it earned was more than enough to support a modest lifestyle in the rural Philippines.

Looking up at the welcome sight of stars, he thought back to the last time he had seen a sky full of them. It had been the end of May, and he had been in Indonesia investigating a legendary statue, the Birds of Cirebon. Known to be a fabulous carving of solid gold, the priceless piece was reputed to be both exquisite in detail and breathtaking in its grandeur. People who had seen it were enthralled by the mass of solid gold that stood over five feet in height, while others were mesmerized by the number, size, and cut of the precious gemstones arrayed upon it. Knowing what the work of art actually looked like was impossible because there were no pictures of the piece, only a few oral accounts that had been passed down for the past five decades.

Some people described the pair of nesting birds like swans or storks, while others swore the birds were pheasants. It had taken Buddy two years of research to determine the type of bird that the statue truly depicted. During his second trip to Indonesia, he had sailed his boat first to Jakarta, then to the port of Cirebon itself, and finally trekked to Semarang, interviewing as many elderly people as possible along the way. His language skills were passable, but his knowledge of their history and Muslim culture was thorough. With infinite patience and respect, he spoke with the oldest *Pak* and *Ibu* of each village, and those elderly men and women told him tales of the cultural riches of their past. He showed them pictures of birds from a book he carried and looked for signs of recognition on their faces.

Finally, in the small coastal village of Pekalongan he met an ancient *Pak* who solved the mystery. The old man's eyes had nearly popped out of his head when he saw the picture of the Demoiselle Crane. A proud and statuesque bird, its black feathers ran from the front and sides of its head down to its rounded breast. The rest of the feathers were white. The bird's most distinctive feature, however, was the triangle of white that ran from the back of the head to its eye.

The artist who created the golden Birds of Cirebon had chosen a different implementation. Blood-red rubies defined the crane's black feathers and sparkling diamonds represented the white ones. After his meeting with the *Pak*, visualizing the gem-encrusted work of art had been easy for Buddy, and every time he looked up into the nighttime sky and saw the sparkle of the stars, the vision of nesting cranes flashed through his mind again.

It was, he knew, one of the reasons that he would be able to find it. There were probably hundreds of other treasure hunters that were looking for Yamashita's gold, he guessed, but they were just looking for treasure. No matter how well equipped or funded the others might be, they hunted for the elusive treasure because they wanted its wealth.

Buddy was different, in two important ways. The first was that he wasn't looking for just treasure in general, but rather, for a specific piece—the Birds of Cirebon. He knew all too well that the process of achieving a goal began with a precise definition of the objective. The other thing that separated Buddy from other treasure hunters was that he didn't care about the money. He simply sought the satisfaction of being the one to find it.

PART FOUR

DUE DILIGENCE

N

LUZON

MANILA•

•LEGAZPI

CALAUIT
ISLAND

BUSUANGA
•CORON

•TACLOBAN

CEBU•

•CAGAYAN DE ORO
•MARAWI

MINDANAO

THE GREATER
PHILIPPINES

Even through the fuzzy veil of jet lag, Nick thought that passing through Philippine customs was a breeze. Maybe because it was twenty minutes after ten o'clock at night, and the airport was virtually empty. Maybe because of their image, which, despite twelve hours of confinement in a packed Boeing 747, was relatively respectable, or maybe it was their luggage, which looked nearly new. Nope, he realized. They're simply not worried about what we might be bringing into their country. Curious.

They stopped briefly at a currency exchange counter, then followed the arrows to the exit and schlepped their luggage outside, pleased to find a line of taxicabs there waiting. It was very warm—probably in the high-eighties—and raining heavily. Laurie got in the rear seat of the lead car and Nick helped the driver load the suitcases into the trunk and the passenger side of the front seat. He didn't do this out of courtesy, but because he knew that each of the bags weighed more than the driver himself.

Entering the late-model vehicle, Nick sat back into the rear seat next to Laurie. "Quezon City, please, the Sulo Hotel."

"Yes, Sir," came the reply in lightly accented English.

They rode in silence for a while, nearly falling asleep as they listened to the sound of the fat raindrops plummeting down on the car and the rhythmic beat of the flapping windshield wipers. Nick couldn't see much through the window, either because of the darkness or the rain, or, perhaps, because of his own weariness—he wasn't sure which. From the amount of water around, though, he judged that it had been raining for some time. The streets were not crowded, and they sped along at what seemed to be fifty miles per hour for several minutes before they entered the city limits. What city? he wondered, too tired to ask the driver.

They couldn't see the details of street signs or traffic signals, but were aware that the road now carried at least two cars abreast through an area with multiple-storied buildings and plenty of lights—most of them yellows and whites, with an occasional red. He couldn't make out what they said. It all passed by him in a hypnotic blur.

Suddenly their pace slowed, and the car veered to the right and down a hill. As their pace decreased, visibility improved. A large building on the right—was it a hospital? And something big over on the left, off behind a high, wrought-iron or steel fence. He saw a few people milling about on the dirt sidewalks, people wearing shorts and tee shirts, barefoot. Only a few had umbrellas. No groups or couples walking together, it seemed, just individuals.

They made another right turn at the bottom of the gentle slope, and immediately turned left into the hotel driveway. The driver pulled up under the structure's overhang and parked, the motor still idling. Nick and Laurie emerged from the vehicle, unloaded their bags and paid the driver in the pastel peso scrip.

As they walked slowly towards the entrance, Nick felt apprehensive. Dark and dingy, the Sulo Hotel looked as tired as he felt. The border of the circular driveway was mud. Tall weeds grew out of cracks in the pavement. No landscaping to be seen anywhere, only a couple of skinny, unimpressive trees. The building itself was an old, dreary gray cement structure, probably three or four stories tall. He saw large, twin glass doors leading to an open space with a countertop dead ahead. The carpeted lobby probably measured ten yards in width, five yards deep, and had one glass door on the right opening to a store of some kind, and another door to the left of the registration desk that probably led to the restaurant.

Stepping up to the antiquated counter, they were greeted by a short, smiling uniformed man whose name tag identified him as the Manager. "Welcome, Mr. and Mrs. Gardner. How was your journey?"

"Fine, thank you," responded Nick. How did he know it was us?

"I am certain that you would both like to get to your room without further delay. If you would please let me take an imprint of your credit card, and sign this." A piece of paper was thrust in his direction and a plastic pen, which Nick exchanged for his American Express card. With a conscious effort, he lifted his eyes to look at the manager who continued to speak.

"—in room 212. Take the elevator to your left, turn left on the second floor, and the room will be on your left. Would you like some assistance with your bags?"

Nick looked both left and right and then shook his head. He didn't see a bellman nearby. Their room was so close he could taste it. They were close to a bed, and he didn't want to do anything that would delay getting to it. He shook his head wearily at the uniformed manager.

They made it to their room in less than a minute. Opening the door for Laurie, Nick reached in, flipped on the light switch, and followed her inside. He glanced around. The door to the bathroom was opposite a closet with dirty mirrored doors that slid on tracks. Gray walls. Thin, nearly threadbare carpeting. Furnishings so old they looked like rejects from the Salvation Army. Clean, but with a faintly familiar, medicinal scent. A loud whir of the air conditioning unit on the far wall by the ratty curtains. There. The king-size bed.

Laurie went into the bathroom, but Nick simply stripped down to his boxers. He pulled back the lightweight, chintz bedspread and lay down, asleep before his head even hit the pillow. It was midnight.

N

· MINT
· QUEZON CIT
· MANILA

Manila
BAY

· AIRPORT

CORREGIDOR

SOUTH
CHINA
SEA

GREATER
MANILA

Nick's eyes popped open, and he looked over to his right at Laurie. She lay on her side facing him, with both hands tucked under her pillow cradling her head. Her beautiful green eyes stared back at him, and she broke into a wide grin.

"Hi. I was wondering when you were going to wake up," she said cheerfully.

Nick rolled over to look at the clock on the rickety night stand next to him. In the dim light of the room he saw the numbers, which read 6:10. It was morning, he guessed, and it sounded like it was still raining outside. He realized that he wasn't sure about either. He tested his voice. "How long have you been awake?"

"About an hour. I've been watching you. You sure slept hard—you must have been really wiped out."

He sat up on the edge of the bed and swung his feet onto the thin carpet, looking toward the bathroom. "I was toast. I don't even remember when you came to bed."

"Tell me about it. You were snoring before I even finished brushing my teeth." Laurie sprung up, raced into the bathroom and shut the door behind her. "Come on, I'm starving. Let's go get something for breakfast."

His brain on autopilot, Nick took his suitcase and began to unpack. When Laurie emerged a few minutes later, he quickly stepped past her and told her he'd be out in ten minutes. He was just beginning to rinse his toothbrush under the tap when Laurie called to him through the door, "Don't forget to use the bottled water I brought for brushing your teeth."

"Oh, right," he responded, sheepishly. His realized that his jet-lagged brain was not yet firing on all cylinders. He still didn't feel like his normal self.

He stepped into the shower, turned on the hot water and waited for more than a minute, as the slowly heating water splashed over his hand. He saw that most of the bath tiles were chipped and broken, and the metal of the drain itself was badly rusted. After a quick shower under the weak tepid stream, he dried off on one of the thin white towels, quickly combed his hair and dressed—a pair of beige Bermuda shorts, a white polo shirt, and sandals. He was, as he said he'd be, ready in ten minutes.

Laurie was waiting impatiently for him, dressed in similar attire. She held the door open for him, then led the way to the dimly-lit lobby, arriving at the glass door to the restaurant just as it swung out towards them. A petite lady wearing white and carrying menus under her arm greeted them with a warm smile.

"Come in, come in! We are just now opening for breakfast." She ushered them to a booth on the side of the room and handed them menus, covered with heavy clear plastic. "You must be Mr. and Mrs. Gardner. My name is Rita. Welcome to Quezon City. Can I bring you some tea or coffee?"

"I'll have tea, thank you, and he'll have coffee. Cream, if you have it, for both of us, please."

With a nod of her head and a broad smile on her face, the waitress turned and disappeared, returning a moment later with their order. They sipped from their chipped cups and glanced around the room. There were four booths along the wall where they sat and perhaps a dozen other tables arranged in loose rows around a buffet stand in the middle of the uncrowded space. Two men wearing grimy aprons wheeled a stainless steel dolly out from the kitchen and began to put large trays of food into the warming stands on the buffet. Several other diners—men wearing dark slacks, white shirts, and carrying newspapers—entered and, without any assistance from the waitress, seated themselves at tables on the other side of the room.

When the buffet had been completely assembled, Nick and Laurie walked over to check out the breakfast offering: white rice, steamed fish, some unusual fruits, and three trays of grilled meat, which were, to their eyes, of unidentifiable origin. They went back to their table empty-handed, and asked the waitress to bring them each a couple of eggs and some toast.

They were halfway through their meal when a familiar figure appeared at the head of their table. "Good Morning!"

Nick looked up. "Romy," he said, standing up and shaking the man's hand enthusiastically, "it's good to see you." With a sweep of his hand, Nick indicated his wife. "You haven't met Laurie yet."

Romy extended his hand towards her as she said warmly, "It's so nice to finally meet you, Romy. Please, join us."

Romy pulled a chair over from the table behind him and sat down at the end of their booth, grinning hugely, "I thought you might be awake, but I did not want to telephone your room and possibly disturb you. I have some things for you to read, and brought a copy of this week's itinerary." Romy handed Nick an oversized envelope and turned to Laurie. "You are even more beautiful than I expected, Laurie. How was your flight? Is your room acceptable?"

It was Laurie's turn to grin. "Thank you, Romy, how nice of you to say that. The flight was long, but everything here is fine. I love your shirt," she said reaching out to touch the soft, openly-woven, cream-colored fabric of his sleeve. "It looks very comfortable. What's it made from?"

Romy grin was so wide that Nick could not only could see the large gap in his upper right teeth, but thought the man's cheeks might crack. "Laurie," he began, pronouncing the name so carefully that every vowel was discernible, "thank you. It is called a barong, and it's our customary attire for business, or even formal occasions. This one is made from the husks of pineapple."

Laurie examined the fabric more closely. "That's amazing. It's very handsome on you."

Nick looked at the two of them as they continued to chatter. Remarkable, he thought. Not that Romy had been captivated by Laurie. That was hardly a surprise. It was that she'd managed to establish an unbreakable bond with Romy in less than a minute. Then again, he recalled, years before she'd captured his own heart just as quickly.

Nick refocused on what Romy was saying. "—be tired today and need plenty of rest. If it suits you, I shall return around one o'clock this afternoon and take you to lunch. We will be joined there by someone I want you to meet. Until then, I will excuse myself." Romy shook their hands, and then left just as quickly as he had appeared.

"Nick, he's adorable. I can see now why you've enjoyed working with him."

"Well, I wouldn't say he's adorable, but he seems like a good guy. Let's get out of here."

Finished eating, Nick signed the check and led the way upstairs.

"Did you notice the way everyone in the restaurant looked at us?" Laurie asked as they entered their room.

Nick nodded. "Sure. They probably don't see that many *haoles* around here," he said, using the Hawaiian word for white person. "And particularly knockouts like you." He sat down in one of the room's two flimsy chairs, opened the envelope Romy had given him and began reading Romy's file.

At 1:00 P.M. Nick and Laurie were in the hotel's lobby. True to his word, Romy arrived precisely on time, entering through the large glass doors and waving towards them. Following him outside, they got in the back seat of his car—a small, red, nondescript sedan— as Romy held the door open for them. It was a good thing that the car was parked underneath the protective overhang, Nick thought, or the heavy rain would have soaked them. A second later Romy settled himself in the front passenger seat and pivoted sideways, so that he could look at the two of them. Or, Nick thought to himself, so that he could look at Laurie.

With a nod of his head, Romy indicated their driver, a youngish man wearing an old and faded polo-style shirt. "This is Maynard," he said, and then to Maynard, "Let's go to Michael Jordan's."

Nick spoke up as they merged with the traffic that crawled along the rainy streets. "Is that the name of the restaurant? Is it owned by the basketball player?"

Romy swiveled even further around in his seat, now nearly facing Nick, grinning. "Yes and no, Nick. It is the name of a restaurant that belongs to a client of mine, and we chose the name very carefully. Although it is not connected with the NBA star, Mr. Jordan has definitely heard about it. In fact, he took us to court to stop us from using the name. We won. It was very good publicity for us. The restaurant has been busy ever since it opened."

"But Romy, people like that hire the best lawyers in the world and usually win. How did you do it?"

"Even though the restaurant's decoration does indeed have a sport theme, it was easy. You see, the owner has one son named Michael—"

Nick interrupted, "—and another son named Jordan."

Romy nodded appreciatively. "Exactly." He turned away to face the front of the car. "What judge would dare to rule against a man who named his only restaurant for his two sons?"

A short time later, they arrived at the restaurant, and the three passengers dashed inside, doing their best to stay dry in the downpour. They were warmly greeted by the owner himself, who immediately ushered them to an isolated corner where a solitary figure already sat at an expansive table, waiting. As they approached the immobile man, Nick noticed the eyes that studied them as they walked. Small. Heavily-lidded. Observing and judging. Boring right through them. Suddenly, in a single, fluid motion, the man stood up and extended his hand to Nick. "How do you do, Nick? Papa Villangca."

Although Nick kept the expression on his face friendly, he was almost shocked at the transformation he had just witnessed. Only an instant before, this man had appeared to be stiffly cautious and guarded. Now he was a different person entirely—friendly and engaging. "Papa? My pleasure. This is my wife, Laurie."

The man took Laurie's hand gently in both of his own. At five-foot-five, he had to look up slightly to look at her. Like Romy, he wore a barong, although the color of his was more yellow than white. Of average build, the fine features of his face made it difficult to judge his age with any accuracy. One or two strands of gray in his eyebrows contrasted with a jet-black, full head of hair. Probably sixty, guessed Nick.

"I am delighted that you are here, Laurie. While I am, of course, pleased that Nick agreed to work with us on this project, it was very important to me that you were able to join him. Families are very important to us here. We have so much that we want to accomplish, and it will be much easier for all of us with you participating."

"Papa, thank you. I admit I was a little nervous about coming, but so far, you've all made me feel at home."

They seated themselves around the table as the maître'd, as if from nowhere, produced a large platter of fried shrimp and some canned soft drinks. As everyone helped themselves to the finger food, Papa continued. "So, how is your hotel?"

Nick responded, "It's OK. It's not the Ritz, but it's clean enough and quiet. I assume you chose it because it's close to where you both live?"

Nick caught a momentary glance between the two other men before Papa spoke. "Yes, we live nearby, but that is not important. What matters more is that the Sulo Hotel is where people expect to see me. I have been going there for meetings for years and years, and if I were to suddenly change my habits and meet with you at one of the fancy hotels in Manila, people would be suspicious."

"Suspicious?" Nick asked.

Another look passed between the two men seated opposite him, and this time it was Romy who spoke. "They might think that you were another treasure hunter."

"What?" exclaimed Nick and Laurie, almost in unison.

With a slight shift of one of his fingers, Papa signaled Romy for silence. "What do you know about Yamashita's gold?" he asked, leaning forward and speaking very softly. He pronounced the name as if it did not have the letter 'i'. Seeing the blank expressions on their faces, he continued. "I'm not surprised. You were both born after the Second World War," he added with a dismissive wave of his hand, "and this all happened so long ago.

"As the story goes, Yamashita was one of the top Japanese Generals. During the early years of the war, he invaded the countries of Southeast Asia and robbed them of all their riches. Later, when our Allied forces prevented him from transporting the loot back to Japan, he buried it here in the Philippines."

Curious, Nick arched his eyebrows, as if to say, "So?"

Papa went on with his tale. "Yamashita surrendered, was executed for war crimes, and died without ever telling anyone where he had buried his treasure. Many people, over the course of the years, have searched for it, but the only one who ever had any success was Marcos."

Nick broke in, "Ferdinand Marcos?"

Papa nodded, "Yes. Marcos actually found a couple of the hidden stashes and recovered a great deal of gold. It's how he made most of his fortune."

Nick glanced at Laurie, and then spoke to Papa, "Excuse me. I don't mean to be rude, but I thought that Marcos got his wealth through—," Nick paused to pick his words carefully, "less exotic means."

Papa laughed briefly, as did Romy. "Good, Nick, very good. You'll do well here. That was very diplomatic. What you say is true, of course. 'The Old Man' did make a questionable fortune while he was in power, but the vast majority of his money actually came from these discoveries. He found billions of dollars of gold."

"Billions?" queried Nick.

"That's nothing, really. According to the legend, Yamashita buried his loot in more than two hundred places. Marcos claimed that he only found two of them. If you believe the rumors that have circulated since the end of the war, the total value of the treasure today is worth more than a trillion dollars."

"Good Lord!" exclaimed Nick. He looked over at Laurie. "But I still don't get it. What does this have to do with any of us?"

Papa leaned forward, "As you probably know, before Marcos died, he took everything he possibly could out of the Philippines and hid it in a maze of numbered foreign bank accounts and false corporations. As soon as Cory Aquino was elected President, our government began actively trying to recover his fortune from these sources, both through internal efforts here, and in the international courts. The government also suspects that Marcos didn't discover just the two treasure sites that he claimed to have found. They believe that he also had access to maps that identified the locations of the rest of Yamashita's gold."

It was Romy's turn to speak. "Papa worked for Marcos. People think that he knows what happened to the fortune and to the maps."

Laurie cut in, "You worked for President Marcos?"

"Yes, Laurie, for a number of years. I was one of his closest advisors, and last saw him in Honolulu just before he died. Because of my close association with 'The Old Man', I've been investigated more times than you can count, but no one has ever been able to prove that I know anything. I still live in my old home and drive the same car I've had for almost ten years." He took a small sip of coffee, briefly gauging their reactions. "If I had all that money, would I still work for a living?

"Still, people keep an eye on me," he shrugged as if it were nothing. "And I find things are easiest for me if I make it easy for them. So, the Sulo. Do you understand?"

Taking the lack of response from either Nick or Laurie for acceptance, Papa continued. "It does make some things more difficult, such as discussing our carrageenan venture. People know that
I'm involved in something new and are curious, but they don't
know any of the specific details yet. Since we will be seen having
meetings together, I have told everyone that you are my financial
advisor. That way no one will bother you."

Nick, his energy suddenly beginning to fade, felt as though his
brain was processing Papa's words in slow motion. "Why would
anyone bother us?"

Papa answered calmly, as if stating the obvious. "If you only
visit Manila, you haven't really seen the Philippines, and very few
tourists take the time to explore our country. If these people see
an American man traveling alone to our outer islands, they assume he is a treasure hunter. That's one of the reasons that we asked
you to bring Laurie along. If you had come here by yourself, it
might not have been so easy to convince them that you were only
my advisor."

Nick shook his head briskly, trying to clear the cobwebs that
were gradually overpowering his thinking. His brain, he realized,
just wasn't functioning properly today. He looked over at Laurie
and noticed her eyes starting to glaze over and eyelids beginning
to droop. The change in time zones seemed to be hitting them
both, and hitting them hard. He swallowed once, somehow found
his voice, and said, "I'm sorry, gentlemen," to his hosts. "I hate to
cut this short, but I'm afraid the jet lag is catching up with us."

Romy immediately asserted himself. "Certainly. You both must
rest. Come, I will get you back to your hotel immediately."

Nick and Laurie thanked Papa and followed Romy out of the
restaurant to the waiting car. Neither one of them looked back at
Papa. Neither one of them saw his sphinx-like, unblinking gaze as
he watched them make their way to the red vehicle waiting outside.

The telephone on the night stand next to Nick rang with shrill insistence at 7:00 P.M. He answered it on the second ring. "This is Nick."

"Nick? It's Papa. Did I wake you? I'm sorry. We thought you might be asleep, but this is important. I'm downstairs in the restaurant with someone I want you to meet. Can you join us for a few minutes?"

Nick said he'd be downstairs shortly and went to splash some water on his face. He glanced at Laurie's sleeping form on top of the bed covers and realized they both still had on the same clothing they had worn to lunch. A couple of strokes with his hairbrush later, Nick stuck his feet into his sandals and headed downstairs. What a drag, he thought, to have his body-clock so out of sync with his clients.

Sitting at the corner table with Papa was a small, handsome, very trim gentleman wearing a starched white, button-down shirt and a beautiful red silk necktie. As Nick approached, he could see a charcoal gray suit coat folded carefully over the back of the chair next to him. The man rose to greet Nick and they shook hands as Papa introduced the man. "My good friend, Alawi Sarip Dimakuta. Call him Alec."

Neither Alec nor Nick spoke for the next several minutes; Papa did all the talking. As the pair listened to their host talk about their schedule, they studied each other. Alec was forty-seven years old, Nick knew, and carried himself in a manner that suggested good breeding and intellect. Large, light brown, curious eyes stared back at him with a hint of a smile. Smooth, light brown skin that had a tinge of yellow. High and wide cheekbones. Despite his height, which was probably a full foot less than Nick's, Alec had a very commanding presence.

It was not surprising, thought Nick. One of the things that Romy had given him to read earlier in the day was Alec's *curriculum vitae*. Although Nick couldn't recall its details in his foggy state of mind, the highlights were impressive. Youngest Congressman in the history of the Philippines. Minister of Muslim Affairs for the past decade. Sultan of Sarip—the leader of nearly one million Muslims in Mindanao—for life, his birthright as an eldest son. An investor in their new carrageenan venture.

"So, Nick" concluded Papa, "we will meet again when you return from your inspection of our seaweed farms. I know that you need more rest, so we won't keep you any further."

Still in a slight daze, Nick nodded, shook hands with both men, and went back upstairs.

The driver of the black van pulled up in front of the dilapidated structure and stopped. It was well after midnight. Steady rainfall and the near blindness of his withered left eye made it difficult for him to see any identifying markings on the house. He called back to one of the men in the back of the vehicle. "Is this the place?"

One of the men grabbed the handcuffed prisoner by the hair and lifted his head to the window. "Is that where Ortega lives?"

With both eyes nearly swollen shut from the beating, the prisoner struggled to cooperate. Looking outside, he merely nodded.

One of the men opened the rear door and got out. He was joined by two more men while the others stayed behind with the prisoner. Not worried about making noise, the trio approached the front door and kicked it in. In the house for less than a minute, they emerged with their quarry—a frail looking gentleman, naked except for his soiled shorts and handcuffs. Two of the burly men held Ortega tightly by the arms as they dragged him to the rear of the van and tossed him inside. Ortega landed on the metal floor of the van next to his handcuffed brother. His eyes jerked open in recognition. "Raul! What's happening. Why are they doing this?" he asked, before a blow to the back of the head silenced him.

When Ortega awoke, he found himself tied to a sturdy wooden chair in a room that seemed like a warehouse. In the dim light, he could see Raul a few yards away, tied spread-eagled to a chain link fence. The driver bent down and spoke into Ortega's ear. "Did he find anything?"

"Who? Find what?"

The driver glanced at his men. In response, the largest of the group took up a four-foot length of pipe, gripped it like a baseball bat and slammed it into Raul's ankle. Raul's scream filled the room as the bones of his foot shattered.

"Did he find anything?"

"Mother of God!" shrieked Ortega. "Who?"

The driver looked back at his men again and his bad eye began to twitch. Another vicious swing of the pipe crushed Raul's kneecap.

"No! Stop!" Ortega cried out as Raul slumped, unconscious.

The driver picked up a shiny steel machete and pressed its blade against Ortega's genitals. He asked once again, "Did he find anything?"

Nick and Laurie, leaving their largest suitcases under the care of the hotel's Manager, checked out of the Sulo. Standing outside, but protected from the elements by the overhanging roof, they were rested and ready to go, even if the weather was uninspiring. The sky was the same gray overcast, the same light rain fell, and the temperature was the same humid mid-eighties as it had been since their arrival.

Romy's car pulled up in front of the hotel precisely at 8 A.M. Much to Nick's relief, the stout Filipino had the courtesy to be on time. Romy opened his door and bounded out to help them with their baggage, wearing casual clothing and his usual big grin. Shaking hands energetically with each of them, he waved them impatiently into the back seat of the car.

"Come, we must hurry! I have arranged something special for you."

"What's that?" asked Nick, as they packed into the car.

"You will see in just a minute," answered Romy excitedly, as Maynard pulled out of the hotel's driveway and onto the street. "Our flight is scheduled for noon, but it is best if we wait a little to allow the traffic going in the direction of the airport to settle down." The car turned left at the next intersection and then quickly veered right, into a private drive that was partially hidden by a dense stand of tall trees. After proceeding fifty yards or so, they turned a corner and saw a small stone guardhouse standing next to an enormous iron gate. Through the high black metal bars of the gate they could see, in the background, a low-profile gray building. "There it is," exclaimed Romy. "The Philippine Mint."

Nick and Laurie exchanged surprised glances as Laurie offered, "Really? I've never seen a mint before. Will we get to go inside?"

Romy turned to Laurie with twinkling eyes, and held up a hand to silence her. The car pulled up in front of the guardhouse and a heavy-set uniformed man emerged. Maynard rolled down the window as the guard approached the driver's side of the car. Bending down to look into the vehicle, the man said loudly, "Mr. Villanueva, nice to see you again. Mr. Emmanuel is expecting you."

With that, the guard signaled behind him and the iron gates swung open. As they slowly motored up the arching drive, Romy turned back to face Laurie. "Yes, Laurie, you will get to go inside. The Mint is not open to the public, but the Director is a friend of ours and has offered to give you a private tour."

They parked in the cul-de-sac that defined the end of the long drive. While Maynard remained in the sedan, the other three exited and quickly moved up the wide, gray flagstone walkway that led from the parking area to the building. Only from this vantage point did the scale of the building become evident. It was massive—probably sixty feet high and several hundred yards long. Huge blocks of polished stone tiled the building's solid exterior, which had no other distinguishing features. No columns, no cornice and no windows. That was it, Nick realized after a moment. It was the lack of windows that masked the scale of the building from a distance. Viewed from outside the iron gate, the building appeared relatively modest in size, but here, up close, it was gigantic.

They trotted up the wide stone steps to the entrance and heard a loud electronic clicking sound. In response, the tall metal entrance door swung open for them, and they went inside. Waiting for them was a trim man wearing dark pants, a barong, and bookish, round, black-rimmed eyeglasses. He looked vaguely familiar, thought Nick, as the man nodded to Romy and then extended his hand in greeting. "Welcome, Mr. Gardner, Mrs. Gardner. I am Roberto Emmanuel, Director of the Philippine Mint."

"How do you do Mr. Emmanuel?" began Nick. "This is an unexpected pleasure. I apologize for our casual dress; I didn't realize that we'd be given this opportunity."

Mr. Emmanuel smiled. "No matter, Mr. Gardner. I am aware that you are on your way to the airport. We thought you would both enjoy a brief look at our facilities. This way, please."

They followed the Director past a security checkpoint and down a long corridor as he recited the relevant structural statistics: two floors above ground, three floors below, nearly one million square feet of interior space, a work force of 320 employees. Administrative offices, including some for senior executives of the Central Bank, on the top floor, production on the ground floor, storage vaults underground. They stopped at the first door they encountered—a plain, unmarked door which Mr. Emmanuel unlocked with a single, silver-colored key. He motioned for them to follow him, and led the way inside.

The room was cavernous, with bare white walls nearly forty feet high that stretched for several hundred feet. Large enough to hold probably twenty full-sized basketball courts, thought Nick. Squarely in the middle of the room stood four large printing presses. Their host led the way towards the machines. "These," he said proudly, "are our specially modified Heidelbergs. When it is time to replenish our paper currency, we fit each unit with plates from our vault downstairs and produce everything right here. As you may know, we only print our pesos in six denominations; two, ten, twenty, fifty, one hundred, five hundred, and one thousand, and we dedicate each press run to a single denomination. This way, please."

They walked down another echoing hallway to another unmarked door, which Mr. Emmanuel unlocked. This room was identical in size to the first one, but appeared to be used more efficiently. At the near end of the expansive area were four large smelting ovens, each one measuring several yards across. Above them were broad copper hoods, which fed into a series of brick chimneys along the wall behind them. In the middle of the room stood several tall industrial machines, and rows of other machines were beyond them, at the far end.

Mr. Emmanuel led them to the ovens. "This, as you have probably guessed, is where we mix our raw materials. These electrical furnaces melt the metal, which is poured into molds to form ingots. We use a variety of metals, including aluminum, brass, steel, and cupronickel, and each furnace is dedicated to manufacturing a specific alloy." The group followed him as he began to walk the length of the room and continued his narrative. "The ingots are then brought to these machines, which use a succession of rollers to reduce them into strips of metal of the precise thickness required.

"The prepared metal strips are then fed into the next group of machines, which cut out the circular blank stock, or planchlets, for the various sizes of coins. The planchlets are then heated in the annealing furnace, washed, dried, and transferred to the final step of the process down here.

"These units perform the actual coining. They accept the finished stock and stamp the impression under pressure that ranges from four to twenty tons per square centimeter. The coins are then inspected, counted, rolled, and taken to the vaults below." He turned to his guests with a vague smile. "I would be happy to answer any questions you might have?"

Laurie jumped in first. "When do you actually make new money?"

"I am sorry, Mrs. Gardner, but the specific answer to your question is actually classified information. I can tell you, however, that the paper denominations are printed four times each year, and that coins are minted twice each year. We did produce some paper currency recently, but, as you can tell by the lack of heat coming from the furnaces, it has been some time since we minted any centavos. Those ovens get so hot that it takes them weeks to completely cool down."

It was Nick's turn. "If you manufacture just a few times a year, what do you do with your equipment operators when the facility is idle?"

Mr. Emmanuel smiled as he thought for a moment, then answered. "They work in other areas of the building, mostly in maintenance and security." He consulted his wristwatch and continued. "Let us go to the last of our manufacturing areas. If you please?"

Turning abruptly, he led them to another wing of the building, and past another security checkpoint. Waved through by a faceless guard, they walked down another long corridor before coming to a halt in front of another unlabeled door. This one, it seemed, as they watched their guide sort through his ring of keys, had to be unlocked with two keys—one silver, and one bronze.

Passing through the door and turning abruptly, he led them to another wing of the building and past another security checkpoint. Waved through by the guard, they walked down another long corridor before halting in front of another unlabeled door, which he unlocked with the same two keys of silver and bronze.

Once inside, Nick found the area similar to the second production room they had seen, but with only a single smelting oven and no specialized milling machines. Considerably warmer than the other rooms, it was every bit as quiet and clean. Instead of walking over to the furnace area, Mr. Emmanuel kept them near the door and then began to speak. "And this," indicating the equipment, "is used only on special occasions. It is where we process gold."

"Really?" inquired Nick. "I didn't realize the Philippines had enough mining to warrant a special facility like this."

Mr. Emmanuel looked at Nick impassively. "You are correct, of course, Mr. Gardner. That is definitely the case today. This facility, however, was built over twenty years ago, and designed according to the specifications of President Marcos. He didn't intend this plant to accommodate the country's mining production, he had other sources in mind."

Nick and Laurie exchanged looks. "Why was it built?" she asked.

"For the Yamashita treasure," their host said matter-of-factly. Without another word, he led them out the door and down the hallway, toward the vaults which held the inventory of finished currency.

The drive to the airport took less than an hour. Maynard dropped them off in front of the terminal, and they each grabbed their bags and headed inside. At Romy's suggestion, he proceeded to the ticket counter alone as Nick and Laurie waited some distance behind. Only a few yards away, they were close enough to be able to watch Romy's progress in the crowded line, but far enough away to be out of his earshot.

Nick spoke first. "So, what did you think of the Mint?"

"It was a great tour. I only wish the boys were here to see it with us."

"Yep, I was thinking the same thing," responded Nick softly. He looked at Laurie's face and sensed something bothering her. "What is it? Are you missing the boys?"

She looked up at him. "Sure I miss them, but that's not it. It's something else. Remember our meeting with Papa, when he first told us about Yamashita? I didn't believe it then, but, after seeing the Mint, I have to wonder. What do you think?"

Nick looked off in the distance and spoke to her in slow, carefully measured phrases. "I think Papa told the truth." He paused, then looked back at Laurie. "If you think about what we've heard, it all fits. Marcos finds some treasure, he believes he'll find some more, so he builds that facility." Another pause. "It's interesting. Before yesterday I'd never heard of Yamashita or his treasure. Now it's twice in two days."

They were deep in their own thoughts when Nick felt a tug on his arm. It was Romy. "Come," he said, "our plane is boarding." And with that, they grabbed their backpacks and followed him past the ticket counter and out a back door.

A few yards away stood a twin engine, twelve-seater airplane, its passenger and cargo doors open. Dashing through the drizzle, they boarded the plane. A handful of other passengers were already seated. Romy sat somewhere toward the back, while Nick and Laurie took seats in the front row, separated by the aisle. No sooner were they seated than the door was shut, the engines started, and the propellers began to spin.

They taxied to a nearby runway and took off. No flight attendants, no safety announcements—just load 'em and go. Airborne, the plane lurched slightly as it flew into the clouds. Nick glanced over at Laurie. Leaning back in her seat, she gave an extra tug on the end of her seat belt, closed her eyes, and tried to relax. Nick followed her lead.

Coron, The Philippines

An hour and a half later, their plane landed on the island of Busuanga, the largest of the Calamian island group, southwest of Manila. Nick looked out the window. No control tower, no hangars, and no baggage handling crew were anywhere in sight. For that matter, there were no other aircraft on the grassy field. The pilot left the cockpit, passed down the narrow aisle and opened the door and lowered the deboarding steps. The passengers followed, with Nick the last to leave the plane.

Looking around him, he was struck by four images in immediate succession.

The first was the weather. It was warm and overcast, but it was not raining. For the first time since their arrival in the Philippines, he was outdoors but not getting wet. Second, they had landed in a pasture. He spotted a number of brown clumps on the ground that his nose confirmed were animal droppings. Third, there was a delighted expression on Laurie's face as she looked over his shoulder and animatedly pointed. "Look, Nick, it's a water buffalo!" Fourth, Romy was gesturing at him emphatically, indicating the approach of the jeepney that would take them into town.

A hybrid vehicle which they had seen everywhere on the streets of Manila, jeepneys resembled their Chrysler namesake. The rear of the vehicles, however had low sides and an awning for a roof, and, inside, two long parallel benches which faced each other. Generally painted in bright colors, jeepneys in the city displayed gaudy lettering, and their surfaces were often covered with innumerable small objects—mosaics of tiny mirrors, tiles and plastic children's toys. Some of the results were strikingly attractive, and others so overdone they were eyesores.

The jeepney stopped to allow the aircraft's passengers to board. They piled into the back of the conservatively-painted vehicle, and it began to move. Not for long. They had only progressed a few hundred yards when the driver stopped and barked something in Tagalog, and the other passengers started to unload. Strange, thought Nick, as he and Laurie followed behind. Once he stood back outside the vehicle, he could see the driver's dilemma.

While a barbed-wire fence defined the perimeter of most of the pasture, the boundary on this side was a small river. The shallow riplet of running water lay ten feet below, at the bottom of a chasm that was about twenty feet across. Spanning the gap was a make-shift bridge that consisted of nothing more than two split telephone poles, each partially buried into the ground on either side. A couple of random boards helped control the spacing of the two timbers.

As Nick and Laurie watched in semi-disbelief, the driver rolled the front wheels of the jeepney onto the boards and, following the directional signals from someone on the other side, slowly drove across. The passengers stood behind and watched the vehicle creep over. When the jeepney completed its journey, the passengers burst into a brief round of cheers and applause. The driver responded by honking the horn—his signal for them to reload. They cautiously tight-roped across, and once again, piled into the bench seats in the back.

Nick glanced around him at the other people as Laurie chatted with the lady seated across from her. Four Filipino women sat on the opposing bench, three wearing cotton print dresses, and one in blue jeans and a tee shirt. Two men sat next to Romy, Filipinos as well, who were traveling with the women. Nick guessed that all of the other passengers were in their twenties or thirties. Two of the women were talking at the same time, firing questions at Laurie in English and then turning to their companions occasionally to translate into Tagalog.

Relaxing as well he could on the narrow aluminum seat, Nick

observed as his wife quickly connected with her audience. She introduced herself—first name only—and got their names. She was traveling with her husband—the women turned as one and appraised him, smiling—and his associate on a business trip. They had two preteen children—nods from the women—and were from California.

The informally clad woman interrupted, "Please, my friend asks if she can touch your hair. Do you mind?"

"Not at all." She reached up and swept her hair over the front of her shoulder, leaning forward so that the women could reach it more easily. They reached out and explored its texture as if caressing a newborn. They whispered to each other in their native tongue. "Yes," interjected Laurie instinctively, "it's my natural color."

The women were taken aback by her response, and Romy burst into laughter. "Laurie, they think you speak Tagalog!"

Nick laughed also, impressed again by Laurie's ability to bond with people. The group continued to chitchat as the vehicle lurched slowly along the winding dirt roads. From what Nick could see, there were no people, no farms, no fences and no buildings of any kind. The gently rolling hills on either side were lush shades of green, and tall trees with dark green leaves overhung the road. The lower-lying vegetation was jungle-like in its density. The air, though humid, was sweet and clear. He turned to Romy. "Why doesn't anyone live out here?"

"The people here depend on the sea for their livelihood. This island has two towns, Bintuan and Coron, and the only reason they exist at all is because they have natural ports on the coastline. There is no economic incentive to live out in the hills of the central areas, so no one does. The only reason it is used at all is because it has flat land for the airstrip.

"It is the same throughout the Philippines. We have over seven thousand islands, but only a handful of them have a population of any size. The vast majority of our islands are uninhabited. Those islands that are populated have only one or two towns. Look," he said, pointing over Nick's shoulder, "we are entering Coron."

The road flattened out as they came to the bottom of the hill, and as they emerged from the trees, they could suddenly see water. Good Lord, thought Nick, it was beautiful. Sparkling clean and crystal clear, the color, even beneath the overcast skies, ranged from a translucent aqua just offshore to a deep, royal blue in the distance. The horizon was dominated by the profile of a single island, perhaps three miles away, which appeared to be substantial in size. Accenting the skyline were scores of other, smaller, jagged outcroppings, which thrust through the surface of the water like stalagmites on a cavern floor.

The jeepney slowed as it rolled up onto the cement pavement of the town's main street. They passed a couple of wooden shacks and came to a halt by a two-story structure. Everyone exited and, with waves of good-bye for Laurie, Nick and Romy, the other passengers walked on down the road.

Once they stood outside the jeepney, the smell hit them with the force of a hammer splintering a dry piece of wood. Raw sewage. The source of the odor was obvious—running along the downhill side of the road was an open pit, probably two feet across and a foot or so deep. Roughly paved with cracked cement, it directed a stream of murky water and human waste towards some unfathomable destination.

On the other side of the gutter stood a two-story, wood framed building, which housed the town's bakery. It had a few rooms for rent upstairs, which Romy had reserved for them. Trailing behind him, Nick and Laurie nodded politely at the tiny woman behind the counter as Romy jovially exchanged staccato phrases of Tagalog. On the wall behind her was the inscription "L&M", which appeared to have been hastily painted decades before. Romy motioned for them to follow. Outside, a narrow wooden staircase led them to the upper floor at the back of the building, where four doors opened onto a small covered lanai. The view was marvelous.

Just below them was a deserted open-air market. Three white-tiled counters stood parallel to each other, adjacent to a small beach. From the hoses attached to spigots at the end of each counter, and the smell carried up by the ocean breeze, Nick realized it was the town's fish market. A short pier jutted out into the water; at its end was a pen covered by a thatched roof. Past the pier stretched a mile or more of single-story buildings, which lined both sides of a street that ran parallel to the water. All the rooftops were made of tin, and, although there wasn't a telephone pole in sight, there were hundreds of television antennas.

Turning his gaze back to the lanai, he found four rattan chairs and a low-slung rattan table arranged in the middle of the small space. A rickety railing and a shiny tin roof above them completed the enclosure. Laurie walked on ahead.

Peeking inside the first doorway, she found two single beds in a room that was barely big enough to contain one of them. The light fixture was a bare bulb dangling from the ceiling. She looked at Nick with a slight lift of her eyebrows. Proceeding to look into the other rooms, she found them all to be identical to the first. The last door opened to their communal bathroom. Seeing and smelling the crude facilities inside, she closed that door as quickly as she had opened it.

Nick stood in the doorway of the first room and tossed his backpack onto one of the beds. "Gee, Laurie, I guess they forgot the mints."

Joining Nick, Laurie turned to Romy. "We'll take this one. It'll be fine."

Romy's response was a smile so wide that Nick could see every one of his large, white teeth. "Laurie," Romy started, "I am relieved. I know that you are accustomed to much finer places, and I was concerned that you would not be comfortable enough here. This is the best this town can offer, and it will make the owner truly happy to learn that you will stay here."

"Romy, don't worry about us. It is a little rustic, but we'll just pretend we're camping indoors," she replied.

"Excellent, Laurie. I will pay you a compliment. Not only are you beautiful, you are a cowboy as well!"

Laurie laughed. "I like that, Romy, a cowboy. Come on, Nick, let's take a walk and explore the town. Romy, do you want to join us?"

"No, thank you. I think I shall try to find a radio. There are some people I need to contact about our travel arrangements for tomorrow. There are no telephones here, you see. Go ahead and look around. If you meet me back here before dark, I will arrange for our dinner."

Seated on the lanai, Nick and Laurie told Romy about the day's discoveries over dinner.

"Romy, I love this place. The people are all so warm-hearted and approachable," enthused Laurie between bites of fish and white rice. "We walked from one end of the town to the other, and everyone we saw waved or smiled at us. And the children, they followed us everywhere—first a couple of them, then a couple more, and finally a crowd. If one of us said 'Hello', they'd run up to us and practice their English. Every one of them must have said the same thing, 'What is your name?'"

Romy smiled broadly, somehow keeping the food in his mouth from spilling out. "Many of them have never seen a white person before, and I would be surprised if any of them at all had every seen someone with blonde hair like yours, or someone as tall as Nick."

Laurie continued. "We went by two schools and were invited into each of them. The teachers told the children where we came from, and I talked to them about our schools back home. The schools didn't have very much in the way of supplies and teaching materials, Romy. I copied down the teachers' names and addresses, and as soon as we get back to Manila, I'm going to send them each a package—you know, textbooks, paper and pencils. Would you please make sure that they get here safely?"

"Of course, Laurie," he replied. "It would be an honor."

Laurie waved her hand in dismissal. "And the basket factory. We walked by this two-story building and were sort of trying to see what we could see from the street. Someone saw us, came out, and offered to let us look inside. The upper floor was made of lengths of bamboo lashed together. You should have seen the expressions on their faces when Nick walked in. They kept looking at his feet as the bamboo flooring bent beneath him."

"I guess they don't see too many size thirteens around here," Nick. "The ceiling was so low that I had to crouch down, and I wasn't sure the floor would support my weight. I must have looked like a Great Dane playing in a pup tent. The workers seemed to get a kick out of it.

"You know, Romy, they must have had twenty-five people working there. They get a design from an office in Manila, and they spend the next few weeks making nothing but one type of basket. Every person there does just one part of the assembly process, and then hands the piece to the next person in line. It didn't look very stimulating, but they seemed to be enjoying the work."

Laurie had a question. "When we got back from our walk, I sat up here for quite a while and watched the action at the fish market. The boats pulling up on the beach, the fishermen getting out and bringing up their burlap bags full of fish. Then the women came out and walked along the tiled tabletops inspecting the catch. There were lots of different kinds of fish, and they can get bread and rice downstairs. But there doesn't seem to be much variety in their diet. Where do they get their fruits and vegetables?"

Romy put down his fork and folded his hands in his lap. "You are right, there is not much variety. Did you walk down to the end of the pier and see the pigpen? Once every week or so, they will butcher a pig, and all of the families that can afford it will enjoy pork for a night.

"As far as fruit and vegetables are concerned, I am sure that you saw gardens in some of the homes that you walked past. People here grow what vegetables they like, but only enough to feed their own families. No one grows crops for sale. Commercial fruit and vegetables would be so expensive that not many of the families here could afford to buy them."

He reacted to the quizzical look on her face. "Nearly all the money that is on this island changes hands every day. The fisherman sells his catch for twenty centavos, and hands the two coins to his wife. Today she takes those coins and buys rice. Tomorrow she will take the money he gets and buy more rice, or maybe some bread or pork. The fisherman only catches what he knows he can sell that day. There is no refrigeration. What he cannot sell, his family eats. There is no surplus catch, so there is no extra income. They have no savings. If the wife must choose between buying fruit and buying clothing for her family, they will do without fresh fruit."

For a long moment, Laurie looked out over the railing at the roofs of tin. "Nick, when this business takes off, you'll have to come back here a couple of times a year, right?" Nick nodded. "Well, I'll come back here with you, buy a couple acres of land, and start a community farm. A co-op. The people who help to work on it can share whatever we grow."

"If you want to do that, it's fine with me," Nick responded. "But I don't think it'll be necessary. Think about it this way: right now, this is a closed economy. People today can't buy things they might want because there isn't enough new money coming into Coron. We're probably the first people to rent these rooms in months, so we're the first people that have brought any new money into town for a while. When we start growing carrageenan, though, that will change. The townspeople will be our employees, and Romy and I plan to pay them very well. According to the numbers I've run, we won't just pay them enough for them to buy fresh fruit and veggies, we'll pay them enough to change their lives."

"I sure hope so, Nick. These people deserve better."

Their eyes met, and Romy waited a moment before interrupting. "I was able to contact the test site by radio. They will send a boat for us tomorrow morning. I suggest we all try to get some sleep. We have much to do tomorrow."

Nick and Laurie said their goodnights to Romy, and went back to their room. Closing the thin door behind them, they repeatedly bumped into each other in the cramped space as they prepared for bed.

"Welcome to the Ritz. Can I interest you in some room service?"

She rolled her eyes. "Good night, Nick."

Tacloban, The Philippines

Buddy always listened to the evening news on the radio, and the lead story on tonight's broadcast from Manila captured his undivided attention. Intermittent static occasionally interrupted the tinny sound of the newscaster's delivery:

"Also in the news tonight is the report of a gruesome discovery. Police have found the remains of two men within the ruins of Intramuros. The wounds on the bodies were so extensive that authorities could not immediately ascertain the precise cause of death. A police spokesperson, however, stated that the two men had been brutally assaulted and killed, apparently at a different location. Their bodies were then transported to an obscure part of the historic site, where they were dumped.

"The bodies, found by Japanese tourists shortly after noon today, have been identified as two brothers, Raul and Ortega Corpuz. This is the second time in less than a month that tragedy has struck the Corpuz family. Only two weeks ago their younger brother was accidentally killed by a cave-in that occurred while he searched for treasure in the hills of Mindanao.

"Turning now to the weather—"

Yeah, right, thought Buddy. Some accident. What had happened was obvious to him—the poor bastard in Mindanao had been caught poking around in the wrong place. The death squad that worked for the Chairman of The Committee then paid the kid's family in Manila a visit to make sure that none of Yamashita's gold had been retrieved.

Buddy knew that there were plenty of others looking for the treasure, and that the stakes were high enough to make some of them dangerous. The only people, however, who he believed represented a competitive or physical threat to him were those affiliated with The Committee. Most of the other treasure hunters operated on their own schedules and were easily distracted by their families or their jobs. Filipinos, after all, observed *jam karet*, or "rubber time," believing that rigid schedules were pointless.

Not Buddy. He stayed focused and kept his discipline. He was way ahead of most of the others, not only in searching for the gold, but also in protecting himself. Still, the report brought the truth home to him once again: he did not have all the time in the world.

Nick and Laurie awoke simultaneously to the sound of a dogfight in the street below. A crack of light under their door suggested that it was near sunrise, so Nick got up and, still groggy, padded off to the bathroom. He opened the door to the cramped room, and was knocked awake by a wave of foul odors. Looking at the rusty pipe that snaked up from the floor in the corner and ended, about waist-height, in a nozzle, he noticed a drain beneath it. He twisted the faucet that bisected the pipe, crouched down into the tepid stream, and did his best to bathe.

He was about to dry off when he heard a rustling sound. Reaching for his towel, a large black rat scurried out from beneath it and promptly disappeared through a crack in the floor. Disgusted, he didn't bother to use the towel, and stepped onto the lanai to air-dry.

Nick took a seat and looked out over the railing at the town. This morning, the humid overcast skies seemed a little brighter, so the hues of the water were simultaneously lighter and darker than yesterday. There was an armada of small boats making their way off to the east—dozens of them, maybe as many as a hundred. All brightly colored, they ranged from dinghies to outrigger canoes to multi-hulled craft. Most were between fifteen and twenty feet in length, although a few of them were much larger, and they popped along the surface under the power of small, noisy, two-stroke diesel engines.

As Nick watched them fade from view in the distance, Romy hurried up the stairs with the owner of the bakery in tow. She brought with her some biscuits, which she left on the table for her guests. Laurie joined them a short time later, and as the three of them washed down the still-warm pastries with cans of Coke, the throaty sound of motorcycle engines alerted Romy.

"Come!" he said energetically, "It is time to go."

Grabbing their backpacks and following Romy down the stairs, they were met by two motorcycles outfitted with sidecars.

"I get the front!" said Laurie,

Romy's cheeks spread wide in a grin. "That Laurie," he said to Nick, "what a cowboy!"

Nick sat down first in one of the low seats and Laurie piled in on top of him, settling in between his legs. Romy got in the other. They whisked along the streets all the way to the dock at the other end of town. They got out and, thanking their drivers, were surprised to see the vehicles rev up and speed away.

"Don't we have to pay them?" asked Laurie.

"No," replied Romy, "they just wanted to be able to tell everyone that they gave you a ride."

Romy led the way towards the dock, where a vessel awaited them. Nick looked it over with a sailor's eye. Fifty feet. Twin hulls. Weathered strips of teak for the deck. Five feet of freeboard, probably another seven feet below the waterline. Plenty of space below decks. Tired canvas awning over the small cockpit stretching from the single wooden mast. Yellowing sails of woven flax that billowed from the vertical spar. Over by the tiller stood a sturdy Filipino, barefoot, wearing ragged shorts and a tee shirt. Romy introduced the man as Bongo, adding that the man spoke no English.

They hopped aboard as Bongo brought the engines to life. Helping him release the mooring lines, they seated themselves on the forward deck as the vessel ponderously turned away from the dock. Quickly gaining speed as the powerful diesel churned, they moved out into the middle of the channel that separated Coron from the island to the south.

A few minutes later, Laurie nudged Nick. "Look at the water. It's so beautiful."

"It's deep, that's for sure. You can tell by how dark the color is, and also by the cliffs." He pointed. "See the face of that one? It must rise, what, maybe a thousand feet, almost straight up. There's a good chance that it continues straight down below the water for quite a ways.

The rugged craft moved through the modest swells effortlessly, passing the first of the drifting boats of the village's fishing fleet. Nick watched the fishermen on the tiny craft. They used drop lines, he noticed. No rods, and no reels, just the fishing lines in their hand. He turned to Romy. "Why don't they use nets or poles?"

"They only use nets to catch the smallest fish—the ones they use for bait. They can't afford fishing poles, so they fish the way they have for centuries."

Just then, over Romy's shoulder, Nick noticed a dark flash in the air followed by an enormous splash. He guessed by the size of the spume that the fish that caused it must have been a good six feet in length. There were only two things that made fish jump like that—they were either leaping because they were trying to catch something in their mouths, or they leapt to avoid being caught by the mouth of a larger predator below.

Facing the bow, Nick saw the faint profile of an island in the distance. It was impossible to miss. "Check this out," he said pointing straight ahead.

It was as if God himself was highlighting one of his most precious creations for them. An isolated break in the overcast skies allowed the sunlight to pinpoint its glory on this particular island. While everything around it faded into the relative gloom of the humid, gray skies, this solitary bit of land basked in sunlight. It was as if the island were the only part of the scenery which had been colorized in an old black and white movie.

They looked back at Romy. "That is our destination," he said. "The Old Man's Island."

Nick and Laurie stared ahead, captivated. Running north to south, The Old Man's Island was easily over a mile in length, with sandy beaches stretching out in both directions. The spine of the island rose to a peak of perhaps two hundred feet, very green, composed of a variety of trees and shrubs. To the east of the island, some five hundred yards away, a tiny islet pierced the water's surface, and surrounding that islet was a reef. They knew, from sketches they had seen previously, that the site was an atoll— the rim of a flat-headed volcano that lay barely submerged beneath water level.

Now approaching the midpoint of the larger island's length, the helmsman steered their boat toward a beach. Dropping an anchor about one hundred yards from the shore and cutting the craft's engine, Bongo paid the anchor line out off the stern until the boat gradually came to a gentle stop, it's bow arching out over the dry sand. A nifty piece of seamanship, thought Nick.

Laurie looked once over the side and, in a graceful movement, leapt overboard into the shallow water. Running barefoot toward the beach, she danced along through trailing splashes. Bending down to reach an object on the land, she turned to Nick and raised it like a trophy over her head. "Nick! Look at this!"

Nick joined her quickly on the sand. In her hands was the shell of a clam. It was wide open, and must have measured fully eighteen inches across its natural hinge, and was at least six inches in depth. Dotting the fine, white-white sandy beach were other shells, and each of them was at least as large as the one picked up by Laurie.

With a conscious effort, Nick looked away from the beach and up towards the palm trees that separated them from the interior part of the island. Three brown figures were waiting there at a simple encampment some fifty yards away, waving at them. Taking Laurie by the hand, he led her towards the others.

Romy introduced the older man as Pedro. A man of seventy, he had been born on the island, which had been first purchased by—and named after—his grandfather. He was probably five-foot-five, and had a full head of bright white, close-cropped hair and an engaging smile. Laurie reached into her backpack and produced a San Francisco Forty Niner tee shirt, which he accepted with childlike glee and put on immediately.

Romy next introduced Tony, Pedro's son-in-law, who asked in accented English if they were thirsty. Laurie told him that she had brought bottled water, but Tony either didn't understand or didn't care. He promptly climbed a nearby tree and harvested some coconuts.

While Tony picked and tossed five or six coconuts onto the ground, his wife, Pedro's daughter, was introduced. A thick-waisted woman of perhaps thirty, her name was Maria, and she had thick, long, black, curly hair that glowed in the sunlight. She stared at Laurie, who stepped forward and took Maria's hand. Laurie reached up to touch the natural waves of Maria's hair, and said, "Beautiful."

Maria responded, smiling, "Welcome to my home," and the two women hugged warmly.

Tony, meanwhile, had descended from his perch in the trees and, using his machete, opened the fruit, exposing the meat and milk. He instantly fashioned spoons from their husks, which he offered to the others. At Maria's insistence, they sat on the benches of a wooden picnic table that served as the major furnishings of their home. She poured some of the coconut milk into plastic cups and passed them to her guests, while continuing to stare at Laurie. Laurie pretended not to notice.

Nick watched a pig rooting in the underbrush, and a couple of chickens pecking at the sand. Sweeping his eyes around, he saw a three-sided lean-to which housed a bed, and a freestanding stone fireplace. He saw the outline of another primitive hut off in the trees, when something made his eyes return to the fireplace. It was, he realized, both functional and artistic. The hearth appeared to be made from a single, massive block of stone, which supported a heavy metal grill. Arching over the cooking surface was a rock and mortar enclosure, which served as their oven. Meticulously carved into the stone base was the snarling face of a tiger.

When he thought they had been seated long enough to not offend their hosts, Nick asked Pedro if it was possible for them to see the test site. "Of course," he said loudly. "Tony, the seaweed plantation."

With that, Tony patted his belt, and, feeling the handle of his machete, motioned for Nick and Laurie to follow. Into the jungle they went, close enough behind Tony to keep up, but far enough back to stay out of the way of the hacking blade that created their path. The temperature, which had been warm but unnoteworthy a few moments before, was suddenly stifling. It felt a good twenty degrees hotter here than it had by the water.

Thirty minutes later, a sweating Tony stood on the crest of the hill, and pointed to the view on the other side of the island. "Plantation," was all he said.

And there it was. Spreading before them in a three-mile-wide oval was the reef which defined the perimeter of their test site. Several segments of the curving reef were alive with foamy surf, caused by small waves that broke over the nearly exposed rim of rocks. The pastel turquoise water within the reef was the perfect depth, and the bleached sandy bottom was pristine, except for rows of faded buoys, which Nick knew supported the lines on which the carrageenan grew. A faint breeze comforted them, and the dark sapphire waters of the South China Sea beyond beckoned invitingly.

"Wow," whispered Laurie.

Gesturing to Tony, Nick pointed down at the shore. Tony nodded in understanding, and proceeded to hack a path down the overgrown gentle grade. In no time they were on the beach, a mirror image of the one only a few hundred yards away, on the other side of the island. Again, Laurie ran off, picking up seashells. Nick paced down the beach, checking the measurement between the rows of buoys as well as he could. When they had completed their walk along the length of the strand, an inflatable boat with an outboard motor approached them, with a smiling Romy perched at its helm. They took off their sandals, waded into the warm water of the lagoon, and hopped aboard.

Romy gave them a guided tour. First, he sped them around the perimeter of the reef, mindless of the impact the wake of the boat had on the seaweed, and then, slowing down considerably, pointed the craft towards the buoys. As they came alongside the first plastic white float, Nick saw that it bore the number one and was anchored to the bottom with a nylon rope. Stretching between this buoy and its partner, some twenty-five yards away, was another strand of rope, which floated on the surface. At evenly spaced increments along the floating line were red stubs of rubbery kelp. It was the first time Nick had actually seen carrageenan.

At Romy's instruction, Tony slipped overboard and dived beneath the surface. Quickly retrieving a length of the aquatic plant for their inspection, he hoisted himself back into the boat. Glistening in the sunlight, the seaweed felt sensuously soft and smooth to the touch. Their curiosity satisfied, they dropped it back in the water and cruised slowly down the line of floats. When they got to the buoy marked with the number twenty, Romy killed the engine and, reaching down by his feet, produced a cloth measuring tape and a notebook.

Once again, Tony was dispatched into the water to retrieve one of the plants. Romy turned to Nick. "As you requested, we began measuring the first plant in certain rows at least once each week, and have developed charts to record the rate of growth." He measured the length of the plant and noted the result in his booklet. After flipping through a few pages, he smiled. "Excellent, Nick. It seems that this particular plant has grown nearly fifty centimeters this week."

Nick nodded. "Romy, it looks like the plants are tied to the floating line every six feet. Is that right?"

"Every two meters," he corrected.

"Why so far apart?"

Romy shrugged. "I can only say that this is the way it is done by

160

our competitors. I do not know if there is a technical reason."

"Why don't you run another test with a few of the lines. See what happens to the carrageenan's growth rate if we put the stalks closer together."

"Of course, Nick. Good idea. What do you think, shall we try a spacing of one meter?"

"With a line or two, sure. You might also try them as close as every foot, just to see what happens. Another thing, were you able to get that topographic survey of the area?"

"Yes, I thought I had already mentioned it to you. It should be waiting for us when we return to Manila."

"Good." Nick pointed to the islet. "Would you mind taking us over there, please?"

"Not at all." In less than a minute, the water became so shallow that Romy had to stop the engine. Hopping overboard, they waded over to the tiny island.

Small enough to explore completely in less than ten minutes, it covered an area of three or four thousand square feet. Its profile was two rounded hills that rose thirty feet or so above the water. The beach, unlike those on The Old Man's Island only a five-iron shot away, was not sandy, but instead seemed to consist of small pieces of rock that crunched under the soles of Nick's sandals. Looking down at it more closely, he realized that it was made from broken clam shells.

Nick turned to Laurie. "How about a swim?"

She leapt at the chance. As their hosts discretely looked the other way, they took off their shirts and shorts, exposing their bathing suits. Reaching into his backpack, Nick grabbed a pair of goggles, and hand-in-hand, they waded out into the lagoon. Nick plunged in and powered through the water for a dozen strokes before stopping.

Standing on the fine sand in the chest-deep water, he flipped off his goggles and watched Laurie swim up to him. As she neared, Nick reached out his hand for hers, and pulled her towards him into an embrace. They clung together for a full minute, their arms wrapped around each other comfortably.

"Nick," she said, breaking the silence, "this place is just fantastic. It's like heaven."

He gave her a squeeze, and kissed her lips. "Yeah. It's unbelievable."

"How can we be doing this? Standing here in the middle of the South China Sea?"

Nick looked at her and grinned. "If you knew how deep the water was only a few hundred yards from where we're standing, you'd be even more amazed." He pointed to the east. "I'll bet it's five thousand feet deep over there. And we're not far from the Manila Trench, which is over fifteen thousand feet deep."

"This day is so perfect, Nick. I don't want it to end."

He nodded. "You mean you're not looking forward to another restful night's sleep at the L&M Bakery? Where the only thing thinner than the walls are the mattresses?"

With a shake of her head, they swam back to the inflatable boat, piled in and took one last look around the site. As Romy, slipping the craft through a gap in the reef, steered them back to The Old Man's Island, the sky began to cloud over noticeably.

During their absence, Maria and Pedro had prepared lunch. A small fire blazed away in the cooking stove, and thick slabs of white fish simmered on its grill. Maria ushered them to the benches at the table, which had been moved into the shade of an overhanging palm tree, and brought their meals over to them. Nick and Laurie each received a plastic plate of fish, some rice, and a slice of coconut. Maria served the others similar servings, but used thick, brown, woven mats instead of plates. Nick and Laurie accepted her offer of chopsticks, while the others ate with their fingers.

"Maria, this is, without a doubt, the best fish I have ever tasted. What is it?" asked Laurie.

Maria blushed. "Lapu Lapu."

"Grouper." chimed in Romy. "Not as good, perhaps, as your

American salmon," he said, pronouncing the 'l', "but delicious." They finished their meal in silence, each one alone with their thoughts. Well before they were ready to let go of the moment, Romy announced that it was time to leave.

Laurie reached for her backpack, and, looking at Maria, said, "Thank you for your kindness. It would mean a lot to me if you would accept this as a reminder of our visit." From under the flap of the backpack, Laurie produced two small bolts of fabric. Each was a simple cotton print, but Maria's eyes widened with pleasure as she accepted the brightly-colored cloth.

"Thank you," she whispered, and pivoting, raced back into her shack. Returning an instant later, she held something small and shiny, which she gave to Laurie. "For you."

Laurie inspected the thin article. About two inches across, it was a flat, white piece of heart-shaped shell inlaid with bits of silver-and-rose colored mother-of-pearl. Wrapping her fingers gently around it, she brought her hand to her breast. "It's lovely. Did you make it?" Maria's expression indicated that she had. "Thank you so much."

Laurie looked at the piece of jewelry for a moment longer and then tapped at her eyelids with her finger. "Nick." she whispered, "Your goggles."

Nick grabbed his goggles from his backpack and, rising to his feet, presented them to Tony. "Thank you for your help, Tony. I hope you will enjoy using these."

Tony's eyes bugged out so far that, for an instant, Nick wondered if the goggles would be big enough. They said their goodbyes and shook hands all around. Maria and Laurie hugged again. As they began to move down the beach towards Bongo's boat, they turned and waved back at their hosts. "Romy," asked Laurie, "was that OK?"

Reaching up, he patted her on her shoulder. "It was perfect. The gifts were things that they will use everyday, but not too extravagant. If you had given them something more valuable, they would have been embarrassed because they could not give you something equal in return. They will tell everyone in the town that you are not just a beauty queen, but a practical woman as well."

They climbed aboard the waiting boat and were soon underway. In the distance, they could see that the sky was not just cloudy and gray, but that they were heading back into rain. Their reprieve from the gloomy weather was at an end. Nick and Laurie both grabbed their backpacks, withdrew their ponchos, and hurriedly put them on. No sooner had they covered themselves than the first drops of rain hit them.

And then came the wind, and the rain began to fall harder. In a matter of seconds, they were in the middle of a squall, where the combination of the driving rain and the forward progress of their boat made it appear that the rain was falling not vertically, but horizontally. They felt the heavy points of rain pummel their protective ponchos as the boat drove through the gentle swells, and snuggled together, feeling completely safe and dry. Nick turned to look back at the helm and saw Bongo and Romy wearing hooded rain slickers.

Exchanging a glance with Nick, Romy gave him a thumbs up sign, pointed at Laurie, and yelled up to him, "Cowboy!"

After twenty minutes or so, they had passed through the heart of the storm and the intensity of the rainfall slackened perceptibly. They were in the middle of the channel that led to the pier on the eastern end of Coron. Bongo slowed the boat, and in a smooth, arching approach berthed his vessel precisely at the end of the dock. The rain was now falling gently, and the three travelers got off, waved their thanks, and walked back to their rooms at the other end of the village.

By the time they reached the bakery, the rain had stopped and the sky had cleared a bit. The afternoon's rainfall was a blessing, Nick thought. It had flushed the raw sewage from the gutters and the stench had subsided considerably. They went up the stairs, put their rain gear over the backs of the chairs to dry, and headed to their rooms to towel off and change clothes.

Feeling refreshed, Nick grabbed his notebook and returned to the chair on the lanai. He made a series of notations and lists of things he needed to learn or accomplish. He was soon joined by Romy and Laurie. Romy informed them that he had arranged for dinner to be brought upstairs to them, and Laurie announced that it was time for a game of scrabble. Spreading the travel-sized version of the game on the table, they settled in for a leisurely couple of hours.

They talked as they played. About The Old Man's Island. About the other seaweed farming sites that Romy had secured under option. About what Maria might sew with the fabric Laurie had given her. About their own children. About Romy's childhood.

As Romy talked, Nick glanced at the score sheet. He and Romy were tied, and Laurie not far behind. Well, he thought, not really tied. They had allowed Romy to use a couple of words in Tagalog, and who could be sure that *bilog* was really a word for round, or that *ngongo* really described someone with a sinus infection?

Late afternoon blended into evening, and they became aware of foot traffic on the streets below. Peeking through the railing, Laurie noticed dozens of couples and families walking by, looking up at them. Looking down, Nick waved, and a few hands waved back at him. Laurie stood up, smiled and waved. Every hand shot up in response.

Laurie stayed at the railing, exchanging waves and brief greetings, until the shopkeeper arrived with their dinner—again, grilled fish and white rice. As they ate, Laurie seemed lost in her own thoughts, while Nick and Romy talked more about the test site. They had already agreed that a certain amount of construction would have to be completed to make the site viable for industrial levels of carrageenan processing, but Nick, having seen the beauty of the place, now had other ideas.

"Yesterday, I had assumed that we'd put in a big dock, dredge out a channel, clear a level spot on the island, and build a bunch of cinder block storage and drying facilities. I've changed my thinking. I don't want to do any more to disrupt the site than we absolutely have to. Instead of constructing buildings and warehouses on the island, we'll use floating platforms out in the water." Seeing Romy's nod, he continued. "We need to look at the survey maps to be sure, but my guess is that the water on the northwestern end of the reef—right where it connects to The Old Man's Island—is deep enough to allow access for a barge.

"If that's correct, we won't have to build any permanent structures. We could moor a couple of houseboats in the lee of the cove on the other side of the channel for workers that don't want to make the trip back into town at night. We could have another floating houseboat out by the lagoon with eating and sanitation facilities. We might have to lay in an underwater cable for electricity, but that wouldn't be too big a deal."

"We can get all the yield from that site that we need, and still keep it beautiful," he said, looking first at Laurie and then at Romy. "What do you think?"

Romy replied in a soft voice. "Yes." He blinked his eyes, looked over at the couple, and then spoke again. This time his voice was strong, and the smile returned to his lips. "Yes. And in response to that example of your business leadership, our partners will want to repay you. You know the islet by the reef?" Seeing the nods from both of his companions, Romy continued. "It does not have a name, and we will give it one. We will call it Laurie's Island."

Nick looked over at Laurie just in time to see her mouth open in amazement. A moment later, she recovered, breaking into a shy grin. "Really?"

They took their drinks in their hands, and clinked the cans of soda together. "To Laurie's Island!"

Nick and Laurie were awakened again by the sound of fighting dogs. Stepping outside for a look at the commotion, Nick found Romy already seated in one of the chairs on the balcony.

"Good Morning, Nick"

"Morning, Romy. Did the dogs wake you up?"

"No, I have actually been up now for some time. I was about to come and knock on your door. We have much to accomplish today, so we should leave as soon as possible."

Nick and Laurie were dressed and ready in fifteen minutes. Romy met them downstairs by the bakery and led them to the nearby dock. They munched on day-old biscuits in silence and sipped from cans of soda as they waited for Bongo to motor up to them in his boat. Hopping aboard, they soon found themselves headed to the west, traveling around the side of the island they had not seen the day before.

According to Romy, the day would be spent looking at other potential locations for company farming sites. Romy and Bongo alternately looked out at the horizon and checked their heading with the enormous map that lay unfolded at their feet. They didn't bother to use a compass, Nick noted, suspecting that Bongo either knew these waters so well that he didn't need one, or the boat didn't have one. Maybe both.

They plowed through the still waters, their wake streaming behind them, with Nick and Laurie lounging in the cockpit, enjoying the view. The blue, clear depths they slid through were interspersed with islands. Busuanga, with its gently rolling hills, dominated the view off their starboard side, but the port side faced dozens of rocky outcroppings that rose to impressive heights.

Passing one particularly impressive vertical cliff, Romy called out to them. "See those birds?" he asked, pointing to some tiny dark shapes that were high above, flitting in and out of a crevice on the sheer face. "Those are sea swallows. Their nests are used to make Bird's Nest Soup."

Nick and Laurie turned around to face Romy. "It is a delicacy that is enjoyed throughout much of Asia. The birds live in small caves full of bats, and build their nests out of seaweed. Their saliva mixes with the spawn of tiny fish to form a sort of glue that binds the nest together. The Chinese believe it to be a great aphrodisiac. They pay up to fifteen hundred American dollars for a single kilo of the finest nests."

Nick grinned at Laurie. "With China's overpopulation, an aphrodisiac is the last thing they need."

Laurie shook her head. "Give me a break. Romy, those nests are so high up I can't even see them. How on earth could anyone collect them?"

"It is an interesting story. If a young man from Coron wants to buy himself a boat, or move to the city and buy a jeepney, he cannot turn to his family for the money. He must earn it himself. There are only two ways that he can do that, and the only way that is quick is by harvesting the nests of the sea swallows.

"If a boy decides to go after the nests, he rarely tells his parents. One day, he simply goes off by himself with nothing more than a net basket and climbs the cliffs. If he is lucky, he can find enough nests in just a few days to earn all the money he needs." Romy paused, a somber expression on his face. "The cliffs, as you can see, are quite rugged, and the boys climb in their bare feet. They do not have any ropes or special climbing equipment. Many—if not most of them—fall and die."

"My God." Laurie craned her neck up at the immense wall towering over them and tried to visualize someone clinging to its surface and climbing up five hundred feet or more. It looked impossible. "That's terrible. You said there was an alternative. What is it?"

"They fish for it. Do you remember the floats in the middle of the channel in Coron, the ones you thought were houseboats? Those floats actually have net cages beneath them. If a fisherman hooks the right kind of grouper, and is skilled enough to land it unharmed, he will put it into one of the cages and sell it to Chinese traders. Live pink and white Lapu Lapu are delicacies that command a high price. If all members of the family put their catches together, then a boy can make enough money to buy what he wishes."

Laurie said, "That sounds so much easier—and certainly much safer—than climbing those cliffs."

"It is, but things can go wrong with the Lapu Lapu. They are very fragile. They soon die in captivity, and often escape from their cages. It is a lucky family that can keep good specimens alive long enough to sell them. Ah, here we are."

Bongo responded to Romy's pointing gesture by slowing the boat and veering in a wide arc between two modestly-sized islands with low, hilly profiles and white sandy beaches. They coasted towards the larger of the two, aiming for a place on the sand where a small boat lay beached.

Bongo killed the engine and Romy, telling them to remain in the cockpit, went forward to the bow and called out a greeting. An ancient man immediately appeared, parting the dense vegetation that bordered the beach, and walked in smooth, effortless strides towards them. He was short and wiry, with a full head of very thin, long white hair, which made the rich, brown color of his deeply wrinkled skin appear nearly black. Barefoot and shirtless, he wore a simple loincloth around his midsection. Romy attempted a few phrases, evidently trying to decide which of the many dialects of Tagalog the elder man spoke. The man finally said something to Romy, and the two talked to each other for several minutes before Romy gestured back to the cockpit.

Laurie raised her eyebrows to Romy in an unspoken question, to which he responded with a slight shake of his head. "Nick," Romy called back, "just you, please."

Nick went forward to the bow of the boat and climbed down onto the beach as Romy maintained a steady stream of speech. It was another few minutes before the ancient man turned his attention to Nick, looking at him from head to toe in a careful inspection. He seemed to be both blatantly curious and gracious, thought Nick.

"He has never met a white man before. His name is Felipe," said Romy, placing the accent on the second syllable. "He farms carrageenan and has agreed to answer some of our questions."

Nick introduced himself and extended his hand in greeting. The native appeared to ignore the gesture, and responded with a slight bow of his head instead. Nick brought his arm back to his side and, with a slight smile on his face, returned a nearly imperceptible bow.

Romy appeared to ask a question and Felipe began to talk at length. Another query by Romy was followed by another extended response from the native, and so on for about ten minutes. Finally, Felipe turned to Nick and spoke directly. Romy began to translate.

"He wants to know how you got here," said Romy. "I could tell him, of course, but he wants to hear you speak."

"We came in from the United States earlier this week by plane," said Nick, pointing back in the distance, "and ultimately landed on Busuanga." Romy immediately spoke to Felipe; the only word recognizable to Nick was "Coron."

Felipe spoke again, his words coming back to Nick through Romy. "I saw the airport there once. The road that leads to it did not exist when I was born. The Japs put it in during the war."

"Did you live here during the war?" asked Nick.

"Yes, but no one bothered me. I have lived here all my life."

Nick turned to Romy, torn between learning more about the

man's background and wanting to get to the point of their visit. "Would you ask him if we could take a look at his carrageenan crop?"

In response to Romy's request, Felipe led them a short way down the smooth, white sandy beach where he stopped, pointing to a couple of faded buoys that floated a few yards offshore.

Nick asked Romy, "Did you ask him how far apart he ties his plants?"

"Yes, I did, but it is best if you ask him yourself."

Nick turned away from the water, faced Felipe directly, and repeated the question.

"About every two meters," came the interpreted response.

"Why? Is there any particular reason?" asked Nick. "Does it have something to do with the nutrients in the water?"

"No," said Felipe through Romy. "Sometimes I put a couple of extra plants closer together at the end of the line by the buoy. They seem to grow just as well as the others."

"Why don't you plant them all that way?" Nick inquired.

"If I put them all that close together, then a few weeks later, when they have grown, they get so heavy that they sink the line."

"Why not just put more buoys in the middle of the line?"

Felipe looked at him as if he were from another planet. "Buoys are so expensive. I only have enough of them to put one on each end of the line."

"Are you saying that the reason you don't tie the plants closer together is that you don't have any way to keep the line from sinking when the plants mature?"

"Yes."

Nick glanced at Romy, and then spoke again to Felipe. "If you had as many buoys as you wanted, how close together would you tie the plants?"

Felipe put his hands about a foot apart. "Probably this far, but it would take so many buoys that I cannot even imagine doing that."

Nick looked at Romy again for a long moment before turning back to Felipe. "If we give you all the buoys you need—for free—would you agree to sell your crops only to us?"

Felipe's body language changed instantly, and he looked at Nick in a new light. "How much would you pay me for the crop?"

"How much do you sell it for now?"

"Usually four or five pesos."

Nick eyebrows shot up. Had something been lost in the translation process? "Did he say four or five pesos, Romy?"

Romy nodded, knowingly. "I already asked him the same thing. He told me that he haggles with the Chinese traders who stop by here from time to time to buy his crop. According to Felipe, the price he gets depends on what the trader has been able to get from the other farmers. If his boat is almost full when it gets here, the trader only offers two or three pesos. If he has more space to fill, Felipe is sometimes able to get as much as six pesos."

Nick turned to Romy. "That's all? You know our projections assume that we'll pay twelve or thirteen pesos per kilo. Does the trader take the difference?"

Romy answered, "That is correct. If we buy from the traders who collect the crops, we expect to pay them the twelve or thirteen pesos. We knew, of course, that they took a profit, but I did not expect it to be as much as ten pesos."

"That sucks," said Nick. He turned back to Felipe. "What would happen if you insisted on getting more?"

Felipe responded, the expression on his face indicating that he was warming to their discussion. "I never ask for more because I am afraid that if I did, then he wouldn't stop here the next time and I would get nothing."

Nick changed the focus of his questions from price to volume. "Could you grow a larger crop?"

"I am lucky. I have the space along the beach to grow much more."

"Then why don't you grow all you possibly can?"

"Because if I grow too much, the Chinese lower the price they will pay me."

Nick slowly shook his head. There it is, he thought. It's always the little guy who gets screwed. Well, not anymore.

"Felipe, I want to buy your crop. This is the way it will work: when our barge arrives to collect your harvest, we'll tell you then what we'll pay you the next time. That way you will know in advance what to expect."

Felipe nodded. "And what will you pay?"

"I will pay you ten pesos per kilo for as much as you can grow."

When Romy translated, Felipe simply stared at Nick with his mouth open. He didn't have any teeth. Nick continued. "There is only one condition. Whatever you grow, you only sell to us."

Felipe nodded again, vigorously. He and Romy exchanged bursts of speech in a barrage that lasted for at least a minute. Romy turned to Nick, one of his grins beginning to form. "He agrees. He cannot wait to tell the traders that he has new partners."

"Romy, there's something I need you to do for me. Do you see those small fenders tied to Bongo's boat? The ones that look like white balloons? Ask Bongo how much he wants for them. I'll buy a couple of them from him right now."

Romy grinned hugely. Asking Felipe to wait, the two men walked back to the boat and spoke to Bongo. Only too happy to oblige, Bongo handed over to Nick half a dozen of the rubber floats in exchange for five hundred pesos. Carrying the fenders by their short ropes, the men returned to Felipe.

Nick placed the fenders in the sand next to Felipe, held out his right hand, and raised his eyebrows, saying, "Do we have a deal?" The ancient man looked directly at Nick for a long moment. He slowly extended his own weathered and wrinkled hand and shook Nick's in a surprisingly strong grip. "Yes," he said, in English.

Buddy was at the helm of his forty-five foot ketch *Makatà*, which sliced through gentle swells, heading south. Large enough to be comfortable for months at sea, and still small enough to be sailed single-handedly, the *Makatà* was perfect for cheaply transporting him and the tools of his trade around the Philippines.

Leaning against the wall of the cockpit, his hands resting on the wheel, Buddy listened to the sound of breezes as they passed through the rigging. A human autopilot, he was capable of maintaining his position at the helm for up to eighteen hours at a stretch before bringing the craft into the lee of an island and napping for a couple of hours. He sniffed the air. Another squall coming in, he sensed. Deciding to continue to sail for another hour before seeking shelter, he reflected on what his research had uncovered yesterday in Manila.

Long ago, Buddy had found that the library of the university was a rich source of information about the art and folklore of Southeast Asia. Although there were no pictures or diagrams in the earliest historical sources, he had learned to compare their descriptions of precious artifacts with fictional works of the same period. Just as his legal training had taught him that the best deceptions were at least partially rooted in fact, he believed that even the most fabulous legends were based upon some amount of truth. By studying countless volumes of myth and history, Buddy was piecing together the genealogy of many of the works of art that had ultimately fallen into Yamashita's hands.

What he found fascinated him. Centuries ago, ancient works of art in eastern Asia were rarely displayed in museum settings or private galleries. They were transported from place to place among the royal luggage to be exchanged as gifts, or as objects of trade. And so it was that nuggets of gold from Siberia were transformed into delicate, ornamental bowls in China, which later found their way south to New Guinea. Enormous rubies from Thailand traveled the spice routes and ended up among the crown jewels of Borneo.

Information about an artifact's existence would be passed on through local word of mouth. Miners who had found the gemstones and craftsmen who had actually worked on individual pieces told their families who, in turn, told friends. Generations of such stories created legends, which eventually were committed to paper. It was through such folklore that Buddy had discovered the existence of the Birds of Cirebon, and followed the travels of the Chavet Pearls to their source.

Indispensable to this effort was his knowledge of *Kungi*. While legends of fabulous artifacts were spread throughout the area, the finest historical documentation had been preserved by Japanese scholars in this ancient academic script. Buddy had developed a working knowledge of the language as an undergraduate, and over the past few years had mastered it, sifting through library volumes for records that gave shape to his plan.

The rhythmic rocking of the hull suddenly reminded him of Jenessa, the only person in the world with whom he had shared his dreams. A native Filipina, she was a flight attendant for Philippine Air Lines, based in Manila. In her late twenties, she was gentle and intelligent, with silky dark hair, flashing brown eyes, and skin without blemish that covered her angular face and lean body.

He thought about the games they played when she visited him on the boat. The rules of their games were simple. Clothing and use of hands were forbidden. He smiled, almost able to hear her laughter and see her naked figure running towards her favorite hiding place in the *Makatà's* small, forward cabin. Its built-in berth followed the form of the bow and was shaped like a capital letter

"A." He'd always find her in the same position, with her torso situated in the center of the padded bunk and her head pillowed at its pointed end. Jenessa's beautiful legs were spread completely apart, each one resting comfortably on the extended sections of the cushioned mat.

Finding her lying before him there, he always enjoyed his choices. Sometimes, when the seas were calm, he would begin by kneeling down on the wooden floorboards between her legs. When the rocking of the boat was more pronounced, he would stand. Bracing his feet, he would grab hold of a narrow beam on the ceiling, bring his hips between her thighs and guide his erection to her wetness and warmth. The motion of the boat as the bow plowed into an oncoming wave would plunge him inside her, and the movement of the stern settling into the wave's trough would rock him slightly back.

An experienced sailor, Buddy knew that he should never fight the ocean. He'd simply go with its flow, and let its motion control their pleasure. He also knew that there was an endless supply of waves.

As Bongo's boat motored along, Nick and Romy told Laurie what they had learned during their visit with Felipe. Hearing the details of their conversation, Laurie became incensed.

"So the farmer does all that work for only a couple of pesos? That's not fair!"

Nick responded, "That's why I offered him ten."

"You can afford to do that?"

"It seems counterintuitive," Nick explained, "but the fact is, the higher the market rate for the crop, the better. You see, the other companies with processing facilities here in the Philippines are limited in the amount of carrageenan they can grow, so they have to rely heavily on traders to collect the raw materials they need. Naturally, they want to pay the lowest amount possible.

"We, on the other hand, aren't limited in the amount we can grow at our company locations. The way it looks to me now, most of our production will come from our own farms. I need to understand a lot more about the process, but I think the overall equation is pretty simple. I can't believe that it will cost us much more than two or three pesos per kilo to grow the seaweed in our own farms.

"We know that the price the traders receive from the processing plants is twelve to thirteen pesos, so the profit margins on our own production will be huge. If eighty percent of our production comes from our own internal sources, then we can easily afford to pay a lot more for the crops of the independent farmers. When we average it all out, it means our average cost will be something like," Nick did some quick math in his head, "four or five pesos per kilo."

"We can't lose. The more the farmer gets, the tougher it will be on our competitors, and ultimately, the higher the price we'll be able to command."

"Why do you say that?"

"It's just supply and demand. If we get the word out that we're willing to pay independent farmers ten pesos, what do you think will happen? Is any farmer is going to be willing to sell to the traders for less than half of that? No way! The traders can either match our price or get out of the business.

"If they choose to match our price, they'll have to charge our competitors a lot more to make it worth their while. The more money our competitors pay them, the higher the ultimate selling price. Since we will be selling to our customers at the same market rate as our competitors, our profit on the selling side increases as well.

"The farmers win and we win. The only person who gets hosed is the trader, and it won't be long before they find something else to transport in their boats. If I'm right, we have a chance to corner the market."

The three of them continued their discussion for a while, nearly oblivious to the scenery passing by on either side of them. Bongo said something to Romy, who responded by looking at the map, then turning toward the horizon. "Yes," he said, "we have arrived." Pointing to the rapidly approaching island, he said to Nick and Laurie, "There it is, Calauit Island."

The island was one of the larger ones they'd seen that morning, perhaps a mile or more in length and indeterminate, from this angle, in its width. What made the land form impressive, however, was its profile. The entire perimeter of the island was defined by a sheer vertical face that rose some three hundred feet into the air. At the top of the cliff, there appeared to be a mesa with gently rolling hills in the island's interior.

"How are we going to get up there?" said Laurie.

Romy smiled. "Just out of sight, at the southern end of the island is a tiny landing area. There is a dock. Did you think I was going to make you climb the cliff?"

"Yeah, and pick up some nests for soup while we're at it."

As Bongo steered the boat towards the stubby wooden pier, Romy told them the history of the place. The island had been acquired by Marcos in the early years of his presidency to function as his private game preserve. Because of the topography, Marcos saw it as an ideal place to let wild animals roam in a natural setting.

Looking up at the island, Nick had to agree. At the foot of the pier, on the only usable shore land, stood a two-story building and a small Quonset hut. Immediately behind the structures was an extremely high fence made of stone and iron that stretched the few hundred feet between the sheer cliffs on either side. A short roadway ran from the pier to a tall gate in the middle of the fence. As if standing guard, the large stone pillars that formed the sides of the gate were carved in the image of panthers rearing on their back legs. Beyond the gate, the road quickly rose to the top of the island in a series of tight switch-backs.

Waiting on the dock as they approached was an animated figure, who waved wildly at them. "Romy," the man called, "Romy!"

The man kept talking to Romy, even as Bongo brought the boat gently to a stop and began to tie the boat securely to the pier. Excitedly shaking hands with his friend, Romy introduced Nick and Laurie to Franco, who continued to babble on in a mixture of English and Tagalog as he shook hands all around. Romy stopped Franco's rambling every now and then to translate his comments as they walked up the pier towards the shore.

Franco had been a student of Romy's at the university, and had accepted the posting at Calauit Island only a year before. He lived on the island alone, which, Nick thought, explained why he was so happy to have company. His job was to monitor the animals and keep a natural balance between prey and predators. A family of tigers roamed the island, and Franco rode into the center of the island every day to make sure that the grazing herds of smaller animals were not being depleted.

"Come," said Romy, "let us go and have a look."

With that, the threesome followed the still chitchatting Franco to the rear of the building. Romy explained that the modified truck parked there had been purchased from a company in Africa that equipped vehicles for use on safari. Built to hold eight passengers, it had steel bars welded at close intervals over the windows.

They entered the vehicle, which Franco started easily, and rolled slowly toward the iron gate. As Franco pressed a button on his dashboard, it swung open, and in less than five minutes, they had negotiated the steep roadway and emerged on the top of the island. The next half hour was spent creeping along the smoothly paved road that snaked its way in a single, enormous circle around the plateau of the island, and listening to Franco talking in his breathless, nonstop prattle.

In another time, in another place, Nick would have been irritated and frustrated by the constant monologue of his host, but not now, and not here. Golden bands of brilliant sunshine filtered through the clouds that were beginning to gather in bunches in the sky above. The thick, lush greens of the gently rolling, grassy meadow seemed to flow with the brush of the wind. It wasn't just the richness of the colors surrounding them that Nick found so bewitching. It was as if the setting itself displayed its abundance of animal life like a pendant on the plunging neckline of a beautiful lady.

They saw many different types of small, sleek deer and a few large pigs. There were hordes of gray monkeys, screeching noisily high above in the treetops, and dozens of species of multi-colored birds. At the northernmost end of the island was the only caged area to be seen. Romy interrupted Franco's narration long enough to mention that, when any work needed to be performed on the island's interior, the predatory animals were injected with drugs shot from dart guns and placed in this enclosure for their later release. Continuing their progress in a counterclockwise direction, they finally rolled to a quiet stop.

Looking back at them from less than twenty feet away was the prone figure of an enormous female tiger, guarding its recent kill. The tongue of the tigress, red with the blood of the disemboweled deer that lay broken beneath its front paw, licked at its long, white whiskers, its wide-set eyes staring at them intently.

They stayed there long enough to watch the tigress return to its kill and resume eating before Franco again fired up both the engine of the vehicle and the motor of his mouth. They completed their circuit of the high plateau, struck not only by the beauty of animals active in wild surroundings, but also by the vistas from the island itself. At their back were the deep blue waters of the South China Sea, and in front of them, backlighting the emerald leaves of the island's vegetation, were the translucent tones of the Sulu Sea.

Suddenly coming to the end of the plateau, the vehicle navigated the downhill switch-backs and, passing between the stone panthers at the gate, exited the compound. Romy turned his back on Franco and spoke to them. "Franco says that he is sorry to rush our visit, but he has heard from his radio that a storm is approaching. It is best if we return to Coron before it hits."

Nick and Laurie shook hands with Franco, who then darted inside the building and returned with a large plastic bag. Walking them to Bongo's boat, he gave the bag to Romy and stood on the pier, waving occasionally, as the mooring lines were released and the boat powered off into the distance.

Romy told them more about the island's history as they headed back for their final night on Coron. While Calauit Island had originally been envisioned as a tourist destination, the thinking had recently changed. The powers that be—whoever they might be, wondered Nick—had decided that all visitors must be closely supervised and monitored. The construction of lodging facilities for visitors on the island was out of the question, and since the closest existing hotel was quite a distance away, the logistics of providing public tours of Calauit were daunting.

Romy opened the bag that Franco had given him and produced cans of soft drinks and a few small bundles of *Dim Sum* wrapped in white paper. While they ate the fragrant, meat-filled pastries, they discussed the findings of the day.

No new sites had been found that fit the desired profile for company-owned farms, but they had learned a great deal from their interview with Felipe. Nick was more optimistic than ever about the business math that would drive their success. Usually, he pointed out to Romy, a due diligence process revealed that costs would be higher than anticipated. Everything they had learned from Felipe, however, was overwhelmingly positive. Almost too good to be true.

Nick prodded his brain awake and realized the gentle tapping that had shaken him from sleep was the sound of fingers on wood and not the ping of raindrops falling on the tin roof. Pulling on his shirt and shorts, he felt his way to the door.

"Miss Laurie, Miss Laurie," came a small voice outside.

Nick slowly opened the door. Although the sun had not yet appeared, there was enough light for him to see the smiling face of a young girl. Holding up his hand, Nick smiled back and then called to Laurie, "Wake up. You have a visitor."

"Over here," he said softly to the child as he stepped out and led her towards the chairs. "Please, sit down."

"I'll be right back. Don't go away," came her reply, as she spun on her heel and raced down the stairs. Laurie joined Nick on the balcony, rubbing the sleep from her eyes. "What is it?" she asked.

"I'm not sure. Have a seat."

A moment later, they heard footsteps coming up the steps, and turned to look. Nick saw the girl walking towards them, beaming, and carefully holding a large, covered wooden tray. "I made you breakfast," she said proudly, placing the tray on the table in front of them.

Laurie reached over to touch the girl's wrist. "I don't know which I like better," she said, "the breakfast you brought or the dress you're wearing. Turn around. Let me look at it. Did Maria make that for you?"

The expression on the girl's face was a mixture of pride, excitement and joy. She spun around several times, holding the hem of her sleeveless dress out to display the sash which gathered the pleats at her waist, ringlets of her long, dark hair shining even in the dim light. "What's your name?" asked Laurie.

"Rose Marie Escador," she answered. "My Aunt Maria made it for me. Do you like it?"

"It is just as beautiful as you are." said Laurie. Only then did Nick realize that the dress was made from the fabric Laurie had given to Maria barely a day before.

"How old are you, Rose Marie?" asked Laurie

"Seven," came the singsong reply.

"You speak English so well."

Rose Marie blushed. "Thank you. I'm only in third grade, but I try really hard. I won't wear this to school, though," she said, indicating her dress. "Only on special occasions." She gestured toward the tray on the table before them. "I made you breakfast. I wanted to thank you."

"And thank you. What did you bring?" asked Laurie.

Rose Marie lifted the cover off the tray, exposing two plastic plates. One of the plates held two barely cooked eggs, and the other six more. Nick looked at the eggs closely. The whites, still translucent on top, were hardly gelled at all, and the yolks slumped dully in their centers. Covering the entire surface of each egg were chunks of salt. He could tell that they were cold.

"These are all the eggs our chicken made this week. I didn't know how many of them you would want, Miss Laurie, so I gave most of them to Mr. Laurie." She paused for a second, and then, bringing her hand to her mouth to hide her whisper from Nick, "I bet he could eat all the eggs himself."

"Sweetie," Laurie said softly, "this is so nice of you. Why don't you sit on my lap while we watch him eat. He loves to eat eggs, and I'm sure he'll want them all." With that, Rose Marie leapt up onto Laurie's lap, and the pair watched as Nick picked up the spoon and began to eat.

Erasing from his mind any thoughts of salmonella, he attacked the eggs with gusto. The glance from Laurie as she wrapped her arms around Rose Marie was all it took. Laurie's eyes communicated the thought that echoed in Nick's mind—if Rose Marie's family cared enough to offer them food that they could almost certainly not afford to share, the last thing he would do is decline to eat it.

He had almost cleaned his plate when Romy appeared, his eyes instantly taking stock of the situation. "I see you have made a new friend, Laurie."

"Yes. This is Rose Marie Escador. She is Maria's niece."

Romy smiled and turned to Nick. "I have been on the radio. If the jeepney comes in the next hour or so, we will be able to leave for Manila."

Nick looked up at him, startled. "What do you mean, *if* the jeepney comes?"

"Well," began Romy, pulling up a chair, "as you can see, this is not the best weather for flying, and the inter-island airplanes operate on their own schedule."

"What do you mean?"

"The plane that will take us to Manila comes from Cebu. It will not land here in Busuanga unless they think they have enough passengers to make a profit."

"But what about the people that need to get picked up here?" asked Nick.

"There is another flight on Tuesday."

"But this is Sunday and we've got meetings tomorrow in Manila. What are we supposed to do here for the next two days?" asked Nick in a tight, but quiet voice.

Romy shrugged. "Things will work out. They are just uncertain." Nick nodded, struggling to adjust his expectations to fit the new reality.

Rose Marie chatted with Laurie for a few more minutes. When Nick was done with their breakfasts, she climbed reluctantly down from her perch and returned the cover to the tray. With a hug for Laurie, she picked up the tray and trotted off down the stairs.

"I love these people, Nick. I love this place."

"I can see that," he replied. He looked out at the town and watched the constant drizzle drift down from the overcast skies, repeating, "I can see that." He looked back at Laurie, "Come on. Let's get ready to go. Maybe we can get the plane to land here through the sheer force of our will. I'm going to get cleaned up and pack."

Within the hour, his hopes were realized. The jeepney arrived at the bottom of the stairway and honked its horn until the trio came down. They piled into the back and, as it started to pull away, took one last look around. As if from nowhere, dozens of towns-people appeared from doorways and windows and called out to them in a chorus of good-byes. Laurie waved back almost franti-cally, as a few tears mixed with the drops of rain on her face.

They came to a stop just outside the grassy meadow, the driver not attempting to negotiate the crude bridge in the driving rain, and waited in the jeepney until the plane landed. It taxied fairly close to them before shutting off its engines.

They were no sooner in their seats than the engines roared back to life. Nick looked out the window of the twelve-seater as it rolled down the rain-slicked pasture, gathering speed for its takeoff. The wheels lifted off with a perceptible thump as they cleared the tree-tops at the end of the meadow. Just as he was about to sit back in his seat and relax, he saw what looked like a yak standing motion-less in the pasture, just below their flight path. He wondered why it didn't move away from the motion or noise of the airplane.

Given the speed of the aircraft and the poor visibility through the dirty window and the falling rain, Nick couldn't tell that the muddy image he had just seen was not a living, breathing animal. It was a statue carved from stone.

Their cab came to a halt under the welcoming roof of the Sulo Ho-tel. Romy explained that he was taking the taxi home, and that he would see them there the next morning for breakfast. Saying brief good-byes, Nick and Laurie headed into the lobby. After three nights at the L&M Bakery, the Sulo Hotel felt as luxurious to them as the resorts back home on the Monterey Peninsula.

Walking through the glass door and striding towards the registration desk, Nick's peripheral vision caught the glimpse of a familiar figure, seated on a sofa in a shadowed corner of the room.

"Papa!" he said, veering toward the seated man, "I didn't expect to see you this afternoon. How are you?"

The man rose, somewhat stiffly, and extended his hand in greeting. "Nick, Laurie. Good to see you. It appears that you did not get my message. We have an important meeting downtown at seven o'clock," he checked his wristwatch, "which means we need to leave here in ten or fifteen minutes."

Nick and Laurie looked at each other, scarcely able to hide the look of dismay on their faces. Papa continued, evidently choosing to ignore their unspoken reaction, "I realize that you will need to get cleaned up and change your clothes, but please hurry. This is a very important dinner, and these people are expecting to meet you tonight."

"Of course, Papa, I can be ready shortly," began Nick. "Laurie, how about you? Would you like to join us, or would you rather just relax and get a bite to eat in the restaurant here?"

Papa interjected, "I'm sorry, Nick. I didn't make myself clear. You are both invited. It would be best, Laurie, for you to join us as well."

Laurie had been studying Papa while he spoke and was one step ahead of Nick. "No problem. We'll be back downstairs in fifteen minutes or so."

Papa's face broke into a wide smile. "Excellent. I realized that you would be in a hurry, and took the liberty of having the hotel manager send your bags directly to your room. He will give you your key."

And with that, Papa returned to his sofa, and Nick and Laurie, after a brief stop at the front desk, bolted upstairs to change. Their suitcases stood in the center of the room, unopened, and a small bottle of wine stood on the table, along with a note. As Nick stripped down and headed for the shower, Laurie picked up the simple card and scanned it. A moment later, she joined Nick.

"We got a 'Welcome Back' bottle of wine from the hotel," she said as she pulled aside the shower curtain and stepped into the tub next to Nick. "You know, this place isn't so bad. The building itself is a train wreck, but the people have their hearts in the right place."

"You sure you don't mind going to this thing tonight?" he asked.

She rinsed her body and began to shampoo. "Nick, we're not here on vacation, we're here for business. I'm surprised you missed the expression on Papa's face. I don't know who it is we're supposed to meet with, but whoever it is, he thinks it's important."

"I guess so. I appreciate your attitude. I know how much you were looking forward to a full-sized bed and a decent night's sleep."

"You're right about the bed, but who said anything about sleep?"

Twenty-two minutes after they had walked into the hotel, they were back downstairs in the lobby. Nick wore a suit and tie, Laurie a sleeveless black dress. Her hair was still slightly damp, but since it was still raining outside, no one was likely to notice. Papa stood up as they entered, a broad smile on his face, appearing much more relaxed than he had earlier. "Thank you for being so quick. Laurie, you look marvelous."

"Thank you," she replied, as Papa directed them outside to a waiting vehicle. They got in the spacious back seat of the large sedan, and Papa sat in front with the nameless driver.

"Well, Papa, the last few days have been very productive," began Nick as the car pulled away from the hotel.

"Excellent," said Papa. "I shall be joining you and Romy at your meeting tomorrow. I look forward to hearing all about it."

"So, where are we going tonight?"

"The Holiday Inn," replied Papa. "You may not realize it, but in Asia, the best restaurants are often found in the fancier hotels. This one is no exception. We shall be treated to a special buffet by some men that I have known for a number of years."

"Oh?" responded Nick as the driver aggressively darted in and out of the dense traffic. "And what is the purpose of this meeting?"

"They know that I am getting involved in a new business venture, and that you are working with me. They want to meet you and make sure there is no connection to their own interests."

"Are they with one of the competitive companies?"

"No, Nick, they are members of our government."

Nick looked quickly at Laurie, a puzzled expression on his face. "Why would they want to talk to me? Is it because I'll be on the Board of Directors of our Philippine subsidiary?"

"Not directly, no." Papa swiveled in his seat so that he could face Nick. "The men we are going to meet run the Philippine Committee for Good Government. When Corazon Aquino was elected President, her first official act was to create 'The Committee,' as it has come to be known. The charter of The Committee is to locate and recover all of the Marcos funds, so that they can be rightfully returned to the people of the Philippines."

"Fine, Papa. And what does it have to do with us?"

"I told you, Nick. I worked closely with Marcos for a number of years. When The Committee was created, I was one of the first people they questioned about 'The Old Man'. Ever since then, whenever I get involved in something new, they make a point of meeting with my associates. It's their way of knowing that I haven't been withholding information."

Nick glanced again at Laurie, and then spoke to Papa. "Let me make sure I understand this correctly. These men are senior executives of your government, right? Is this an official meeting, then? Should I have an attorney with me?"

Papa chuckled. "No, Nick, that is the last thing you should do. The reason we are meeting over dinner is to keep the meeting as informal and social as possible."

Nick digested the information. "And what if they ask me questions about the carrageenan business? How specific should I make my answers?"

"Tell them whatever you want, Nick. I'm sure it will be fine."

"Let 'em ask away, then. I have nothing to hide."

"I know, Nick. I know."

Entering the lobby of the downtown Holiday Inn, Nick saw in an instant that it was identical in design to many of the hotel chain's high-rise facilities in the United States. Papa directed them to the main restaurant, where they passed a gauntlet of Asian men wearing dark suits who seemed to be standing guard. They looked like something out of an old Robert Ludlum novel, Nick thought. While a few of the men were small and thin, many were heavily muscled, and most seemed to have scars on their faces.

With Papa leading the way, Nick ushered Laurie ahead of himself, and they walked into the dining area. A small man was seated alone at a table in the center of the large room. Strange, Nick thought. The only other tables that were occupied were along the outside perimeter of the room near the walls; the only other diners wore same the dark suits, white shirts, and narrow neckties as the men standing guard at the door. As they approached the seated figure, Nick appraised him. Longish, slicked-back hair, and a black, highly-polished cigarette holder held between small, almost delicate fingers. A double-breasted, navy blue, pinstripe suit with broadly padded shoulders. A pastel paisley tie, and a matching, but overly extended foulard. Gold cuff links, and a gold collar pin. Nick knew instantly that he wouldn't like the man.

Only when they stopped at his table did the little man stand up. After a quick nod at Papa, he weakly shook Nick's hand. "How do you do, Mr. Gardner? I am Commissioner Ramierez."

"How do you do, Commissioner?" replied Nick courteously.

The man smiled smugly. "I must say, Mr. Gardner, I love the fabric of your shirt. Egyptian cotton, is it not?"

Nick thought for an instant. "Yes, as a matter of fact, it is. Please, call me Nick. And this is my wife, Laurie."

The little man turned to Laurie, took her hand and kissed it, continental-style. "And you, Madame Gardner, you are even more beautiful than I was told. Please, be seated."

As Papa and Nick took seats across from each other, the Commissioner held the chair opposite his own for Laurie, allowing his fingers to linger next to her shoulders just a little longer than necessary. Laurie looked at Nick. She didn't like the guy either.

The Commissioner then seated himself, taking a few extra moments to straighten the crease in his trousers and pluck some imaginary lint from his sleeve. "Drinks, everyone?" he said, looking in Laurie's direction. Or rather, noticed Nick, looking in the direction of Laurie's breasts. The Commissioner didn't wait for an answer, he raised his hand over his shoulder, exposing the heavy gold band of a Rolex, and snapped his fingers.

A tuxedoed waiter appeared instantly and took their orders— champagne for Laurie, ice water for Papa, a vodka martini and a bottle of sparkling water for Nick. As they waited for their drinks, the Commissioner described the food waiting for them at the buffet at the far end of the room. While he talked, he never smoked his cigarette, but kept it in his fingers and looked at it idly, as if to see if it were still lit.

The waiter's timing was perfect. No sooner had the Commissioner finished speaking than their drinks arrived. The waiter made eye contact with their host, exchanging a signal of some sort, and disappeared.

"So, Mr. Gardner, what brings you to the Philippines?"

Nick glanced briefly at Papa before looking at Ramierez. Nick was used to dealing with people like this. While he wouldn't be rude to their host, he certainly didn't want to spend any more time here than was absolutely necessary. The sooner they could all get out of there, the better.

With a smile that was almost genuine, and without impatience in his voice, Nick looked at Ramierez. "Well, Commissioner, I'd be disappointed if you didn't already know. I'm here to evaluate the possibility of establishing a successful export business."

The little man blinked. "Yes. Just so. And how have you enjoyed your stay here so far?"

Nick took a sip of his martini and sat back in his chair, crossing his legs. "I presume you have some idea about what we've been up to since our arrival?" He sensed Laurie stiffen slightly.

"Yes. I am familiar with your movements."

"Well then you know that, other than our hotel, we haven't seen too much of Manila. We did enjoy the other islands a great deal."

"I see. And what did you think of your tour of our Mint?"

Interesting question, thought Nick. Ramierez must have had us followed. "It was terrific. Very impressive. We only wish that we could have been there when it was actually in operation."

"Yes. Quite so. Why don't we all get some food so that we can eat while we continue our conversation?" With that, he rose and walked around the table to help Laurie with her chair. "Come, Madame," he said offering her his elbow. "Allow me."

Laurie cast him a cool smile, "Of course, Commissioner."

Several minutes later, they were back at their table, their plates piled high with food. As the others began to eat, Nick speared a shrimp with his fork. He had nearly placed it in his mouth when Ramierez asked his first question. Returning the shrimp to his plate, Nick answered. When he again tried to eat the same forkful of food, Ramierez asked another question. Again Nick set down the shrimp and responded. He remained motionless for several moments before once again attempting to eat. Only when the shrimp neared his open mouth did Ramierez ask his next question.

Nick placed the food in his mouth and took his sweet time chewing on it. If that was the extent of the Ramierez' aggravation techniques, he needed to learn some new tricks. "This is delicious," began Nick, with his mouth still full. After swallowing his food, he answered the question.

The evening wore on for another two hours. The Commissioner asked increasingly pointed questions about Nick's company and his reason for coming to the Philippines. Nick was candid in his responses to questions about The Gardner Group, but considerably more vague when talking about their exporting business. If Ramierez noticed the difference, it didn't appear to bother him.

Apparently satisfied with what he had heard, Ramierez suggested to Papa that he take Laurie back to the buffet and get some dessert. As soon as they were gone, he shifted the focus of his questions. "So, Mr. Gardner, you have many other clients, right?"

"Of course."

"And many of them have an interest in expanding into the economies of the Pacific Rim?"

"Some of them, sure."

"And they follow your advice, correct?"

Nick looked at him, seeing exactly the direction he was taking. "When they feel that it's sound, yes."

"Well, then, when one of them—any of them, actually—needs a Director for their Board, someone mature and seasoned in the ways of international business, I suggest you could do far worse than to select me. If you do, then I'm sure things will go much more smoothly than you might otherwise expect."

"Really? I shall have to keep that in mind."

Papa and Laurie returned to the table with their desserts.

"Commissioner, do you mind if I ask you a few questions?"

Ramierez looked suddenly puzzled. "No. Certainly. Go ahead."

"How long have you been in charge of The Committee?"

"I am nearing the end of my two-year term."

"I see. And how much of the Marcos fortune have you recovered during your tenure?"

Ramierez lit another cigarette in his holder. "Nothing as of yet, but we do have some promising leads."

Right, thought Nick. Billions of dollars had been looted, and not a single cent had been returned to the country's Treasury. How much money had found it's way into the Commissioner's personal bank accounts?

"Interesting. Well, if you don't mind my changing the subject a little, you're in a unique position to help me with my own due diligence effort."

"Excuse me?"

"Yes. Part of my objective during my stay here is to learn as much as possible about my new associates. If I'm going to raise capital for this venture in the United States, it is critical that our Philippine investors be thoroughly checked out.

"You say that you have investigated every possible source of Marcos' fortune, correct?" Ramierez nodded. "Have you learned anything—about any of the gentlemen who will serve with me as Directors of our company—that in any way implicates them in illegal actions?"

The Commissioner looked down at the smoke rising from his cigarette, cleared his throat, and quietly answered, "No."

Nick momentarily studied Ramierez, then pushed back his chair and stood up. "I see. If you'll excuse me for a moment, I'd like to get some dessert."

Nick fidgeted in their room at the Sulo Hotel as he dressed for dinner. For Nick, the first half of the day had flown by and every-thing—almost everything—had gone well.

He had gone downstairs for his breakfast meeting and Laurie had taken a taxi downtown to do some shopping. While he waited for Papa and Romy to arrive, Nick had flipped through the local newspaper, *The Philippine Reporter*, and noticed an article in the business section about the price of carrageenan. While his initial plan was based on an index price of twelve pesos per kilo, he had been astounded to find that the current price was seventeen pe-sos. He couldn't wait to get back to his office and run the new fig-ure—an increase of forty percent— through his spreadsheet pro-gram.

When his associates had arrived, they had brought with them a tailor who took Nick aside and measured him for a barong. The tailor had finished that task in no time, and the men had seated themselves at one of the corner booths in the hotel's restaurant, where they worked into the afternoon.

Papa had brought with him a large map of the Philippines, and the three of them had pored over it, marking locations that could be suitable for company-owned farming sites. It had been an in-teresting discussion, because the two other men had already marked hundreds of locations on the map, giving various reasons for their selections. Because there were so many sites, one of their main challenges would be to manage the negotiation process with so many different sellers simultaneously. Nick had suggested that what they needed to do was not negotiate individual purchase terms with each seller, but rather secure options to purchase the sites instead, since that could be done more quickly and for far less money than an outright purchase. They had agreed.

Nick had then looked at Papa's topographical surveys of The Old Man's Island and its surrounding reef. His initial instincts were confirmed. There would be no problem with using barges and floating work spaces. Moreover, the surveys had convinced Nick of the desirability of getting the rights to the land on the island of Busuanga that lay directly across the narrow channel. Nick did not, however, want merely an option on those particular properties. The Old Man's Island would be their main growing facility, making Busuanga a desirable site for their future headquarters. He wanted to purchase the land there outright, and Papa and Romy had agreed.

They had moved on to the subject of personnel, and Nick had suggested that they get the names of the plant managers that led daily operations at the competitive processing plants. It was probable, he had pointed out, that they would want to recruit one of those managers to work for them. Romy had made a note to follow up on the idea.

Their next major discussion point had centered around two interrelated issues—staging the freshly harvested raw material, and where to locate the site of their own processing plant. As Nick looked at the maps, he needed to remind Papa and Romy that the distances involved were not insignificant. From his travels to the islands, he knew that he had grossly underestimated the number of shipping vessels they would need to solve the logistical issues.

For example, no matter where they located their processing site, they would have to transport their harvested crops to it from the Palawan, Visayan, and Mindanao island groups. According to his logic, it would make more sense for them to have a collection point in each of those major island groups than it would to receive harvested crops from every individual farmer in a single place. They quickly accepted his point, and Papa had indicated on his maps the best sites for them to consider for staging warehouses.

There was another reason his idea made sense. If they were going to collect the crops from each of the farmers, they would have to pay for the harvests on the spot, and that meant that their collection ships would also have to travel with a lot of cash. Sooner or later, the presence of cash and the isolation of the area would prove to be too tempting for thieves, and none of them wanted to risk either the safety of their employees or their money. If their company created, instead, a series of collection sites, then they could use the existing commercial banks in each of those areas to handle the money.

The final point of their discussion had revolved around their need for access to the Philippine customs facilities. Unfortunately, as Nick had pointed out to them, none of the existing customs offices were in places that were convenient for their purposes. As a result, they would have to load shipping containers at their collection sites and transport them to a customs inspection office. Although Nick wasn't worried about the extra time involved, he was certainly concerned about the expense. Papa had suggested to Nick that he mention it at his dinner meeting tonight.

Nick had left that extended session with Papa and Romy full of optimism. The pace of their trip, which had seemed to start so slowly, was now accelerating. Nick had returned to his room an hour ago and had sat down to flesh out the notes of his meetings, study the maps, and make lists.

Then Laurie had returned. Only thirty minutes earlier, she had burst into the room, looking terrible. She was completely drenched, trembling, and wore a horrified expression on her face.

"What is it?" he had asked. "What's wrong?"

She had nearly run into his arms. "Nick, it was terrible! I went into town to do some shopping for the children in Coron. Everything was fine until I was on my way back here."

She wrapped her arms even more tightly around him. "It took me forever to get a taxi, and, when I finally got one, it had almost no rear floor. There was just a gap between the back of the driver's seat and the rear seat. You could actually see the road under the car. I had to swing my legs up onto the seat, and because of all the rain, the water splashed up and soaked me."

Nick held her while she continued.

"But that wasn't the worst part. The traffic was so heavy that the driver started to take shortcuts. I had no idea where we were or where we were going. He took us down a narrow back street and, all of a sudden, stopped and started laughing. It was a sick sounding laugh, and I turned to see what he was looking at. On the sidewalk next to us—right out in the open—was a group of men—five or six of them—standing in a circle. Kneeling in front of each of them was a little girl—giving them blow jobs. The men acted as if nothing was happening. They just stood there having a normal conversation while the children sucked on them.

"One of the men turned and saw me watching. He grinned—it was horrible. Then he grabbed the girl by the hair, spun her around and bent her over. I just sat there, helpless, and watched as he lifted up her skirt and forced himself into her. He never let go of her hair, and he never took his eyes off mine."

"The way the driver laughed was so—ugly. So evil. It was terrifying. I was so afraid." Her voice drifted off as she started to cry, the sobs wracking her body. Nick had kept his arms tightly around her for a long time and comforted her until the tears had stopped.

"Good Lord. I'm sorry. It must have been terrible." They rocked gently back and forth for more than a minute before he said, "You're OK now, and that's what matters."

"Look, we're going home in less than two days, and until we're on the plane, I'm not letting you out of my sight. I can change my schedule for tomorrow, but I'm afraid there's nothing I can do about our meeting tonight. I need you to join me for our dinner as we planned. I'm sorry, but at least I know you'll be safe."

She had stayed nestled in his arms for another long moment before responding. He had felt her arms squeeze him as she wiped her eyes and nose on his shirt and then looked up into his face. "This is the big night, isn't it? This is the really important meeting."

He nodded.

Freeing herself from their embrace and shaking her shoulders in an effort to shrug off the nightmarish memory, she silently stepped into the bathroom and closed the door behind her.

He had immediately telephoned some other hotels and revised their travel arrangements. The Sulo Hotel was clean enough, certainly quiet, but dingy and depressing nevertheless. After their stay at the rustic L&M Bakery, and Laurie's shock in the back streets of the city, they were due some upgraded accommodations.

Now, as he straightened his tie in the mirror, he looked forward to the evening's events. In less than half an hour, he and Laurie would meet Alec Dimakuta, who would take them into Manila for a tour of the Philippine Senate Building. Nick had already explained to Laurie that Alec's birthright bestowed upon him the title of Sultan—a combination of judicial, legislative and religious authority over more than a million Muslims. Their tour of the Senate chambers would be followed by dinner with the Philippine Minister of the Interior, a man by the name of Luis Carino.

Romy had briefed him on Luis's background, and it was impressive. Not just a statesman but a scholar, Luis Carino had mingled with world leaders and addressed audiences in international settings that ranged from commencement at Oxford University to the United Nations. It would be a fascinating evening.

In spite of her shake-up, Laurie proceeded to make herself look spectacular in about fifteen minutes. She now wore her hair up and had put on her blue-sequined evening gown.

"You look fabulous, Laurie. Are you sure you're up for this?"

She simply smiled. "As long as you're never out of my sight, yes." As they were ready to leave their room, she opened the sliding door of their closet and pulled out a huge, oversized canvas shopping bag, filled to the brim with packages. By the way she lifted it, Nick could tell that it was very heavy.

"New purse?" Nick asked.

"Don't even start." They went downstairs, where Alec stood, waiting for them. After exchanging pleasantries and introducing Laurie, Alec led them outside to his vehicle.

Nick had not seen this particular type of car before. A Japanese four-door model, it seemed to be a cross between a truck and a car, with the body of the former but the interior of the latter. Nick liked it and wondered why the vehicle wasn't sold in the states. He also noticed something else: unlike their other hosts, Alec preferred to do his own driving.

To say that he drove aggressively would be an understatement. His eyes constantly moved, always searching for an opening that would allow him to press forward. He spun the steering wheel decisively, cutting in and out of traffic, but without ever giving his passengers the feeling that they were in any danger—he was completely in control. "So, Laurie," he began, "what did you think of Busuanga?"

"It was beautiful, Alec, and the people were wonderful. But there is so much that they need. Sewers, for instance. And all those rats!

"Do you know what else hit me today?" She turned to look at Nick. "We didn't see a hospital while we were there. What happens if someone gets injured or really sick?"

Alec cleared his throat. "You are right, Laurie, those are very real problems. Most of the smaller islands lack medical facilities, and none of them have underground sewage systems. I do not know the statistics, but many children die each year from the bites they suffer from rats."

Laurie shuddered. "Are the conditions similar in Mindanao?"

He nodded. "Similar, yes, but better than what you saw in Coron. We have a hospital. We also have hydroelectric power facilities. They do not produce quite as much as we need, and they are not completely reliable, but it is far better than the rest of the Philippines."

"I'm glad to hear that. You know, what affected me the most, Alec, were the children. We had a chance to visit their schools and talk with the teachers. I told them I would send them some things for their classrooms. Today, when I went into the city, I found a bookstore that had a decent selection of children's books. I bought a couple of cases of them. They're being delivered to our hotel in the morning."

Alec shot a glance at her in his rearview mirror.

"I also found a store that sold art supplies—pencils, construction paper, water colors— that kind of stuff. I got a bunch of those, as well. Tomorrow, when you're in your meetings, I'll box it up and get it ready for the schools. Romy said he'd make sure it gets to Coron."

"That is very kind of you, Laurie. Thank you."

"It's nothing, Alec. I only wish there was something more I could do. The fact is that if this company of yours is successful, you can really help these people. I assume that's why you're involved with this." She saw the back of Alec's head nod.

Nick was about to comment when Alec's driving suddenly distracted him. A moment before, they had been in the left-hand lane of a major boulevard, stopped in the front row of a long line of cars who waited for a red light to change. Up ahead, on the other side of the intersection, had been the tail lights of another mass of motionless vehicles. Only a couple of cars away from gridlock, Alec accelerated through the red light and steered into the oncoming traffic on the other side of the median. As Nick gripped the armrest on his seat, he heard Laurie gasp. The oncoming traffic was sparse; most of the headlights they now faced were parked behind a stoplight at the end of the block. As they reached the next intersection, Alec veered to the left, once again rejoining a group of vehicles headed in their same direction.

"Counterflow," said Alec.

"Excuse me?" asked Nick, straining a little to keep his voice normal.

"We call that 'counterflow'. It is the best way to make a left hand turn when the traffic is heavy."

"The traffic is always heavy," said Nick.

"Exactly," returned Alec. He was silent for a few moments, and then asked Nick with a smile on his face, "I am curious, what is the price per centare of real estate in California?"

Nick laughed. "That's a good question, Alec. I've never thought about it quite that way. Let's see. The typical rate for new construction is around a hundred dollars per square foot. With about ten feet per square meter, and given the current exchange rate for Philippine pesos, the answer would be something approaching thirty thousand pesos. That's for the building. The price of the land itself would vary. In rural areas, the price per square meter could be only," he stopped for a moment, doing some quick calculations, "a peso or two. In the major cities, it could run into the millions."

Alec nodded, absorbing the information. He asked a series of similar questions about the price of electricity, fuel and water, and then wanted to know how much Nick paid in taxes. Nick answered each question as best he could, translating back and forth between dollars and pesos, the Philippine's metric system of measurement and their United States equivalents. As Alec listened closely, Nick walked him through an overview of the economics of his business, and Laurie gave a similar explanation of their typical household expenses.

The subject shifted from economic comparisons to their families, and Alec spoke at length about his Muslim faith. Nick and Laurie were fascinated by his summary, and as the discussion progressed, a couple of things became apparent to Nick. The first was that Alec was an extremely intelligent man, and the second was the strength of the bond that he felt was being formed between them. Although Nick didn't yet know Alec well, he knew that he and Alec had more similarities in their lives than they had differences. The conversation came to an abrupt end as Alec pulled the vehicle into a gated area and came to a halt.

Ushering them past a row of massive columns into an ornate, white stone building Alec directed them down the spacious corridors of the Philippine Senate. Leading the way a few steps in front of them, he marched along so swiftly that Laurie, in her full-length gown, held on tightly to Nick's hand in order to keep up. Well, thought Nick, at least she wasn't schlepping her canvas shopping bag along with her. Alec looked at his wristwatch. "We must hurry," he called back to them over his shoulder, "they should still be in session."

Nodding to the pair of uniformed guards who opened a very large wooden door for them, Alec turned to them and put a finger to his lips, and they walked onto the small balcony which served as the observation area for the Senate chamber. From their vantage point at the rear of the enormous, wood-paneled room, Nick saw immediately that it was as impressive in structure and decoration as anything he had seen in Washington, D.C. They took front-row seats to watch the action on the floor below.

As they sat down, most of the Senators turned to look up at them. Hardly surprising, thought Nick. How often does a blonde in a low-cut evening gown enter this room? As the discussion on the floor resumed, it was several minutes before it dawned on Nick that the language being spoken was English. It didn't take long for him to understand the gist of the debate.

Here they were, at a profound juncture in world history—Gorbachev was coming back into power in the Soviet Union, and the United States was negotiating with the Philippines about its future commitments to Subic Bay—and yet the subject under discussion was the rate at which certain postal employees should be paid. No matter how urgent global events might be, he thought, the role of governments around the world focused on managing minutiae.

Alec, meanwhile, had walked down onto the floor to talk and shake hands with a number of representatives. It was evident from Alec's gestures that everyone wanted to know about the visitors he had brought. Alec stayed on the floor below for twenty or thirty minutes, socializing with his peers, and then returned to the balcony. "We must go," he said. "It is time for dinner."

They pulled up in front of an expansive, brilliantly-lit building that stood across the street from the waters of Manila Bay and on the edge of Rizal Park. It was the Manila Hotel, and it once served as headquarters for General Douglas MacArthur. As their vehicle was entrusted to the hotel's parking valet, they approached the hotel doors, and saw a small army of uniformed men.

A pair of the men bowed and opened the door. Another gestured for them to pass through an airport-style metal detector under the watchful gaze of another group. One of them came forward and bowed to Laurie, indicating her ponderous canvas bag, and said, "May I assist you, Madam?"

He placed it on a conveyor belt so that it could be examined by the x-ray machine. Nick turned his attention to the lobby, which was, by any standard, majestic. High, vaulted ceilings gave the feeling of luxurious spaciousness, and the hardwood panels above shone in the light of huge chandeliers. A small orchestra, positioned on the far end of the lobby area, played softly in the background, and a handful of expensively dressed people relaxed with cocktails nearby.

Laurie walked arm in arm with Nick, with Alec on her other side. As they progressed, every head in the room turned to watch them. Nick turned Laurie and spoke softly. "Psst! They're staring at your bag. They all wish they'd thought to bring one just like it."

If looks could kill, her glance would have dropped him.

They proceeded to the hotel's main dining room. "Mr. Sarip Dimakuta," said the uniformed *maître d'*, who recognized him instantly. "So good to see you again. Mr. Carino telephoned to say he would be a few minutes late. Your table, however, is waiting. Would you follow me, please?"

The three of them were led to a large table by the window, which enjoyed a view overlooking the lights of the harbor. No sooner were they seated than a commotion occurred at the entrance to the restaurant and they turned to see what was happening. A man had walked through the doorway and the room had immediately hushed in response. Escorted by the *maître d'*, diners rose to greet the man, shake his hand, or simply get a better look at him. Tall for a Filipino, he stood perhaps five-feet-nine and possessed a sizable girth, which was partially hidden beneath his tailored dark suit. Balding and bespectacled, there was nothing particularly distinctive about his features, but he had an unmistakable presence, carrying himself in a way that commanded attention.

Watching the man approach their table, Alec said, "Here he is." He rose and shook the elder man's hand. Nick and Laurie both stood to greet the newcomer as well, the last people in the room to do so. The gentleman extended his hand to Nick, saying in a booming baritone, "Hello, I'm Luis Carino. I understand that you prefer to be called Nick. It's nice to meet you."

"Luis, it's my pleasure," returned Nick. "I'd like to introduce my wife, Laurie."

Luis took her hand in both of his. She beamed at him, obviously responding to his charm. "How do you do?"

Luis boomed back, all the while gently shaking her hand. "I've heard so much about you, Laurie. This is indeed a pleasure. Please. Have a seat. Let's have a drink. No, let's have several!"

Nick looked at the two of them and laughed. It was going to be a fun evening.

For the next hour or so Luis dominated the conversation. Without interrogating either one of them, he learned everything he wanted to know about their backgrounds and beliefs, their positions and their passions. Nick, Laurie, and Luis enjoyed a round of drinks—and a second—while Alec sipped on his glass of sparkling water. During his chat with Laurie, Luis seemed to be particularly interested in the amount of time she spent doing volunteer work. He was intrigued by the notion that someone could have her level of family responsibilities and still work without pay for several days each week.

When their dinners arrived, Luis focused his attention on Nick. He asked only a handful of questions, each of which seemed based on discovering Nick's motives and opinions. Nothing he asked seemed to center on an item of fact or history. Nick had the sense that the man already knew everything there was to know about his academic and professional career. Luis was completely disinterested in *what* had happened, and instead was intensely curious about *why* things had happened.

Finally, Luis asked the question Nick had been waiting for. "So, Nick, tell me. Is there anything special you need to ensure the success of your new company?"

"Yes, there are a couple of things. The first one that comes to mind is that we need some technical assistance. We need to find chemists with access to laboratory facilities so that we can perform some critical tests on our plants.

"Our product will have to pass through the inspection filters of our Food and Drug Administration, and their standards are high. We need to find a way to certify and grade our materials, and it has to be done as close to the growing source as possible. We will repeat the testing back in the States, but we have to get a set of baseline figures here in the Philippines."

Luis nodded his head. "I understand. Ask Romy to contact my office. We'll get our State engineering staff involved."

Nick raised his eyebrows briefly in surprise. Was it that easy? He pressed on. "A more difficult problem is a logistical one. We're just beginning the process of securing the rights to the best locations for growing our crops. It's too early for specifics, but I'm worried about access to a customs office. It looks like we'll need to gather the farmer's harvests in two or three different staging areas, and then ship them in containers to our processing facility."

"That makes sense. What is the problem?"

"Well, Luis, we won't know the best place to locate our processing plant until we have a better understanding of where the independent farmers will be located. We want the main facility to be in the most central area, but it still isn't clear to me just where that will turn out to be. I only know this: there isn't an existing customs facility anywhere near our targeted locations, and that means we'll have the added expense of shipping our material twice. What we need is a customs officer to travel to our facilities to perform the necessary inspection, at least until we have enough volume to be able to afford the additional expense."

Luis studied him carefully for a moment. "Nick," he began, "when you get past the startup stage of your business, what do you think your annual sales volume will be?"

"We could easily be talking about tens of millions of dollars—U.S.—in only our second year," responded Nick instantly.

"I thought so," boomed Luis, "and if that is the case, then it doesn't make sense to have one of our customs officials travel to your facilities." He looked at Nick, pausing to gauge the impact of his words. "It makes much more sense to simply build a customs office next door to your processing plant, don't you agree?"

Nick blinked. "It sure does."

"Consider it done. We'll put it wherever you want it."

Almost in disbelief, Nick continued. "The other big issue is how to marshal enough of the independent farmers. I need to come up with a way to motivate and control a huge number of people who will be spread out over an enormous area. Any suggestions?"

Luis looked first at Nick and then at Alec. He turned back to Nick. "I think you need to talk more with Alec. He can help you on that one."

Alec interjected. "There is no need for further conversation, Luis. I would be honored to help in that area. I have already made some plans for tomorrow."

Nick pressed on, not understanding what Alec meant, but knowing he'd be able to talk with him later. "Luis, there is one final thing. Although I haven't come fully up to speed on your tax code, I know that our first year is going to produce a significant operating loss. Coupled with the investments that we're going to have to make in the U.S., I'm looking for every possible way to keep the financial bleeding to a minimum. If you have any ideas in that area, I'd love to hear about them."

Luis nodded. "Nick, if you look at the situation from a politician's perspective, I think you'll find that it is relatively easy to create a meaningful contribution." Seeing the questioning look on Nick's face, he continued. "Look at it this way: how many of our people are you likely to employ?"

Nick got it. "Oh, right." He thought for a moment. "Well, the number of company employees might only be in the hundreds, but, if you consider the independent farmers, the number of people we will be paying will certainly be in the thousands—maybe even ten of thousands."

"Precisely. Let me work on it. I can't promise you anything yet, but I wouldn't be surprised to discover that your company qualifies for one of our national investment incentives. I don't see any reason that you couldn't expect tax relief for the first five years of operation."

"Excuse me?" said Nick.

Luis smiled, nodding his head. "It is a fairly common practice, and certainly one that is deserved if you are going to impact as many of our people as I believe you will. Your company would have no tax obligation whatsoever for the first five years."

Nick took a sip of his sparkling water, digesting the information. "That would be incredible," was all he said.

Luis turned to Laurie, "I think I'd better change the subject, before your husband asks me for something else," he began, "and besides, you haven't yet told me about the materials you are sending to the schools in Coron."

"How did you hear about that?" Laurie asked.

Luis laughed. "This is my city, Laurie. There isn't very much that happens here that I don't know about, particularly when it involves a beautiful visitor from America. The stores that you visited today are owned by a friend of mine. When you told me about your volunteering activities, I put two and two together."

Laurie smiled in amazement. "I'm going to pack up a bunch of stuff and send it to the teachers there. It really isn't much, I'm afraid, but it might make a difference."

"Laurie, our world needs more people like you. I am certainly impressed with your husband, but I have to tell you something." He reached over and put his hand on top of her own, which was resting on the tabletop. "The thing that got me involved in politics, nearly fifty years ago, was my concern for the future of our nation's children. I can't tell you what it means to me to learn that you share my passion." He turned and gave a signal to the *maître d'*.

"I can, however, do something to express my thanks." The *maître d'* suddenly appeared, with three waiters in tow. The first waiter quickly whisked away all of their empty plates and glasses. Flutes of champagne were produced by the second uniformed man—with a flute full of sparkling water for Alec—while a round, multi-layered cake was placed in the center of their table by a third. The waiters quietly disappeared, and the *maître d'* leaned forward to light the candle which stood in the center of the cake. Although the decoration faced towards Laurie, Nick had spent enough time looking at topographical maps to recognize it instantly. Etched onto the white frosting of the cake was an image of The Old Man's Island, its surrounding reef, and, marked by the placement of the tall, blue candle, the tiny islet.

"One of the special privileges of my position," Luis began, "is the ability to influence what we call some of our smaller islands."

He stood up, and proposed a toast, "To what is now officially known as Laurie's Island," he said, in his deeply resonating voice.

As they clinked their glasses and took their sips, Laurie's eyes moistened.

"You named it after me?" she whispered, looking at Luis, almost in disbelief. "Thank you."

"Nonsense." he boomed, "Thank you. And Nick. Here's to your success as well, although something tells me you already have things well under your control. To success!"

After they clinked their flutes again, Laurie dabbed at her eyes with her linen napkin, trying to prevent mascara from staining her cheeks. She quickly composed herself, and reaching under the table for her canvas carryall, spoke to Luis. "I certainly can't match your gift, but I do have a little something for you to remember us by." "Here," she reached into the bag and took out several gift-wrapped bottles, "is some of our California sunshine. It's wine, but it will make you feel like sunshine."

"Thank you, Laurie." Luis raised his eyebrows conspiratorially, "Should we open some now?"

"Oh, no. Save it for later. And these," she said, digging deeper into her bag and producing several other wrapped packages, "should last you a little longer than the wine."

Luis accepted the gifts almost greedily, and immediately tore open the wrapping. "Oh, thank you," he said, as he glanced at the first book cover, and then, in rapid succession, at the others.

Laurie pointed to the book he held in his hands. "That's a collection of some of the works of Ansel Adams, one of California's most famous photographers. I hope you like it." Luis listened attentively to the explanation before he responded, "My favorite way to spend a rainy night is with a good book and a good bottle of wine. Thank you both."

Had the *maître d'* not appeared at Luis's shoulder, the evening might have continued on for some time. As it was, however, the man handed Luis a folded piece of paper, which he quickly opened and read. "I am sorry," he said, almost quietly, "but duty calls to me."

He rose to his feet, and they all stood to say their good-byes. "This has been a most pleasant evening," he said, more loudly now. "And I must say this: not only are you the most handsome couple I have met in a great while, you also have the biggest hearts of anyone I've come to know in a long time. I thank you for your gifts, and I look forward to hearing of your progress."

Shaking their hands warmly, he swept up the gifts on the table, turned, and strode out of the room.

The waitress brought Nick's coffee without his having to ask for it, a simple act that brought a smile to his face. All right, he realized, the Sulo Hotel might be run-down and shabby, but there was nothing wrong at all with the people who worked here. "Good Morning, Rita," he said, "and thank you."

She beamed back at him. She was so short, he noticed, that they were almost at the same eye level, even though he was seated and she was standing. Rita appeared to linger at the head of the table, and he wondered why. "Yes?" he asked.

"Mr. Gardner," she started excitedly, "I saw you and Mrs. Gardner on television last night."

Nick stared blankly back at her for a moment, not quite sure that he heard her correctly, when Laurie suddenly appeared and slid into the booth seat across the table from him. Laurie glanced at Nick and the waitress, sensing that she had interrupted something.

"What is it?" she said. "What's up?"

Nick let the waitress continue. "I was just telling your husband that I saw the two of you on television last night. You were on the eleven o'clock news."

"Really?"

"Yes! Yes! You were at the Senate, and you were wearing a blue evening gown. You looked just like a movie star."

Laurie laughed, and reached out to touch Rita's arm. "Nick, did you realize we were being filmed?"

Nick shook his head.

"You looked very handsome, too, Mr. Gardner," said Rita with a sheepish smile. "The newsman was talking about something that the Senate voted on yesterday, and as the camera moved around the room to show their faces, there you were. They zoomed right in on you."

Nick and Laurie looked at each other as the waitress kept on talking. "Would you like your tea, Mrs. Gardner? And the morning paper? I'll be right back."

"That's strange," Nick said. "I wonder why they even took that footage, much less showed it on the air?" He rose to give Laurie a quick kiss. "Anyway, good morning."

"Good morning. Just after you left the room, Nick, there was a knock on the door. I thought you'd forgotten your key. We got a package. Luis sent us a beautiful linen tablecloth and some matching place settings. And there was a really nice note inside thanking us for the gifts and 'the pleasure of our company.' Pretty nice, huh?"

"I guess he thought naming an island for you wasn't enough."

She shook her head. "I know, can you believe it?"

The waitress brought Laurie's tea and the newspaper, and they talked about the previous day.

"You never told me what else you bought when you went into town."

"Just a couple of little things for the boys. You know, Nick, some of the stores here are as big and modern as anything back home, but the number of salespeople they have is unbelievable. Instead of a handful of clerks hanging around at the checkout counters, every single rack has its own salesperson. It's amazing."

"I'll bet you got tired of repeating 'No thanks, I'm just looking.'"

"Anyway," he continued, "we've got another big day ahead of us. I've got a couple of meetings here in about an hour, and then Romy will be by to pick us up around noon. That should give you plenty of time to pack up the stuff you got for Coron and have it ready for him when he comes.

"Sounds like a plan."

They went back downstairs to the lobby at twelve o'clock sharp, and were not surprised to find Romy already there, waiting for them. "Look at you." exclaimed Romy, indicating Nick's barong. "It fits you perfectly."

"Thanks, Romy. It's very comfortable. I can see why everyone wears them."

They stuffed Laurie's shipping cartons into the trunk and back seat of Romy's small red sedan. The driver, it seemed, had been given the day off.

"This is great," Romy said indicating the neatly labeled boxes. "I know it will mean a lot to the schools to get them." They all squeezed into the front seat of the car and headed off to Alec's house in Manila. "How have your meetings gone, Nick?" asked Romy.

Nick summarized last night's session with Luis, concluding, "We've made a whole lot of progress. Luis has given us every advantage we could hope for. Something tells me, though, that we want to do everything possible to keep him on our side. He could be a formidable enemy."

Nick continued. "I also met this morning with the guy you sent over with the personnel business."

He turned to Laurie. "The first time I met Romy, he wanted to start a business providing contract laborers to the United States. I didn't think much of it at the time, but after this meeting, it looks like there is some potential. Not as much as there is with carrageenan, but still worth a closer look. Once we get the primary business launched, we'll meet with him again.

"I also had a chance to meet with the attorney, and he answered my questions about the taxes and regulations that will affect us. From what I can tell, we're in great shape. Everything I was told back in the States was essentially correct. I also asked him to get started on the paperwork we'll need to set up a cooperative."

Laurie shot him a curious glance, and Romy turned around to face him. "It came to me the other day, but I didn't want to mention it until I found out whether it was a legal structure here in the Philippines."

He turned to Laurie. "I've been trying to think of ways that we could lock up the production of the independent farmers. Once we set up our own company farms and start buying from the independents, the price we'll have to pay is bound to go up. Although I don't care if it goes up a little, I don't want to have to compete on price alone to ensure that we get the crops we need. If we set up a co-op, then the farmers will have an incentive. They won't be selling just to us; as members of a cooperative, they'll sort of be selling to themselves as well."

Romy nodded his agreement. "That is a truly great idea, Nick. No one has ever tried it before, but I believe—particularly after today—that you will be able to make it work."

"What do you mean?"

Romy gave him one of his broadest smiles. "Alec has a surprise for you. I will let him tell you himself."

Nick wasn't overly fond of surprises, but chose not to pursue the matter further. Laurie, whose curiosity was also piqued, let it pass. They drove through the crowded streets, a light rain falling, as Romy told them about his own plans for the afternoon.

"You won't be joining us?" asked Laurie.

"No," replied Romy. "I am sorry, but I have other plans. I received a telephone call from someone in Luis Carino's office this morning. I have to meet with chemists over at the state building. They are going to help us analyze the qualities of our seaweed."

Romy looked over at Nick, "Whatever you and Luis discussed last night certainly produced some action. They called me at five o'clock this morning." He pointed to a large stone wall ahead of them and steered into the driveway. "Here we are."

Pulling up next to an intercom in front of the wide iron gate, Romy rolled his window down and pushed the button. From the speaker came the sound of a metallic voice in Tagalog, to which Romy responded, and the gate clicked and then swung open.

Beyond the gate was a two-story structure made of stucco. Large but unimpressive, its few windows on the ground floor were covered with iron bars, and the landscaping inside the wall was plain and uninspired. The driveway extended beyond the gate perhaps twenty-five yards, and Romy came to a stop at the end of it, next to Alec's vehicle. As they exited the car, Nick saw the iron gate swing shut and, simultaneously it seemed, the front door of the house open. Alec stood in the doorway, wearing casual clothes and a smile on his face, and waved at them.

Nick and Laurie exchanged greetings with him on the doorstep, while Romy, explaining his schedule to Alec, returned to the car and drove away. Alec stepped aside, gesturing for them to come in. Juxtaposing the impression created by the building's outside, the interior of the home was elegant. The entry-way was wide and spacious, and opened onto a very large, formally-decorated living space. The polished marble tiles of the floor gleamed brilliantly, and thick, intricately-woven Persian rugs lay over them. The white walls featured several enormous tapestries, and there were interesting looking tribal artifacts everywhere.

In the middle of the room stood an attractive woman in a red silk sari, her hair completely covered by a matching silk scarf. She had large, expressive brown eyes and smiled broadly at them as Alec introduced her. "This is my wife, Eleanor," he said proudly.

Nick and Laurie shook hands with her as she said to each of them, "Welcome."

Eleanor examined Nick from head to toe, and then looked at Laurie. She spoke to them again in a softly melodic, soothing voice, "You look very handsome in your barong, Nick. And you, Laurie, I have heard so much about you. I am very pleased that you could join us. Come, please be seated."

They sat in comfortable chairs in the living room and began to talk. This was, it turned out, not their primary residence—that was in Mindanao. It was a second home for Alec to use when business required him to stay in Manila. A maid silently appeared and

YAMASHITA'S GOLD

brought a service of tea for them as they conversed. Eleanor wanted to know all about their children, and Laurie leapt at the chance to show off snapshots of the boys.

Eleanor then talked about herself, sketching a picture that both Nick and Laurie found extraordinary. She had been born and raised in the mountains of Mindanao, the eldest of eleven children of a *Hadj*. Her father was the third highest ranking member of his Muslim tribe, and it was he who had arranged her marriage to Alec at the age of fifteen, some thirty years before. Nick and Laurie exchanged surprised looks when they heard this, partly because they found it so beyond their own experience, but mostly because they found it hard to believe that the woman was that old. Her skin was flawless, and her movements as graceful as those of a ballerina.

Alec had apparently told Eleanor everything from their previous conversations. She didn't ask any of the questions he had posed previously, and she also knew of Laurie's interest in the schools of Coron. Nick and Laurie told her their impressions of the Philippines, which were positive, with only a few exceptions, including their dinner with the Chairman of The Committee.

"That's right," said Eleanor. "You met with him. What did you think?"

Nick and Laurie looked at each other and laughed. Nick only shrugged. Laurie said, "I don't like him at all. Part of him scares me, but mostly I think he's just an incredible jerk," which brought a great laugh from their hosts.

Eleanor looked back at her. "You are absolutely right, of course. Ramierez—by himself—is harmless. But the men he commands are a different story. Ramierez might get lucky and find some of Marcos' money, but he doesn't stand a chance of finding any of Yamashita's gold."

"So the story is really true?" said Laurie, still a note of skepticism in her voice.

Eleanor and Alec exchanged an amused glance, and then she

leaned forward to touch Laurie's arm. "Of course. Even though only a few of the sites have been uncovered, it is only a matter of time before the right person finds it."

"I thought no one had any clue about where it was buried."

Eleanor leaned back in her chair, resting her elbows on the armrests, and began to tell her story, "When General Yamashita was in prison awaiting his execution, he confided in one of the men who brought him food. He didn't reveal very much, evidently because he hoped his own countrymen would one day recover the treasure. But he did tell a guard where to find at least one of the burial sites. Yamashita wanted to make sure that his wife would not be penniless, so he made a deal and arranged for the guard take care of his widow.

"The guard was very clever about the way he handled his discovery. He did nothing with the information for nearly twenty years, so that most of the people who knew he had been one of Yamashita's captors had died. Then, when he recovered the gold, he hid it again in a different location, and had his son claim that he had found it. One of them then returned to the original site and blew it up to cover their tracks."

"Yamashita had rigged each of his burial sites with booby traps. You may have seen pictures of the bombs the Japanese dropped from their airplanes? Well, he used the biggest ones he could get, and sometimes canisters of poison gas, to prevent the wrong people from getting at his gold. If someone didn't have exactly the right information, they'd be blown to bits or gassed to death when they dug too deeply."

"That's terrible," said Laurie, now hanging on Eleanor's every word.

"That isn't the worst of it. Yamashita used prisoners of war to dig elaborate tunnels for his hiding spots. When the tunnels were done, he killed the workers and put their bodies on top of the boxes filled with gold. They say Yamashita did it because he thought someone might find the bones and, out of respect for the dead, stop digging."

"How do you know all of this?"

"When the son claimed he found the gold, Marcos got to him. It wasn't long before the son implicated his father, the one who had been Yamashita's guard. Marcos and some of his men found the old man and tortured him until he told them everything he knew. Marcos used that information to find treasure in a couple of places, and some of the details that they learned leaked out before Marcos could silence the men who were talking. They had some coded maps and descriptions of the markers that identified the treasure sites."

"The treasure sites are marked?" asked Laurie.

"Yes. Yamashita had some of his men carve large stones into the shapes of animals and animal heads. Although only Marcos knew what each of them meant, each location was marked by the likeness of a panther, a tiger, an ox or a dragon."

Something clicked in the back of Nick's mind.

Eleanor went on to describe the amount of gold that Yamashita had hidden, as well as the legendary details of some of the gems that were included in the treasure. She spoke of an ancient jade bowl that Yamashita's men had taken from the Chinese even before the war began, inscribed with a poem written by one of their Emperors. She told them about a set of earrings that had been presented to the Siamese Princess—flawless, four carat rubies from Burma, set in gold. She told them an amazing tale of a golden Buddha, explaining that many of the countries Yamashita ransacked had temples that displayed sacred statues made of gold, but one of them in particular was enormous, hollow and filled with diamonds.

Through the majority of this story, her narration was spellbinding, but somehow detached. Her eyes came alive, however, when she told them about a pearl necklace. The Chavet Pearls, a string of seventeen perfectly-matched black pearls, each more than three centimeters in diameter, had been taken from the royal vaults of

Singapore. With the gestures she used to describe the necklace, Nick could almost see it draped around Eleanor's shapely neck.

Eleanor seemed as if she could go on forever, but a faint chime sounded, and she abruptly stopped. "I am sorry," she said graciously, "but you will have to excuse us. It is time for our prayer. Please, feel free to look around. When we return it will be time for supper."

And with that, she and Alec stood and walked out of the room.

"Wasn't that incredible?" asked Laurie.

"It makes you realize," said Nick, "just how small our corner of the world back home is, doesn't it?"

They took advantage of Eleanor's invitation and looked around the downstairs of the house. Not overly decorated, the furnishings were enough to make each of the rooms they saw comfortable, but not cluttered. They went through the entire downstairs room by room—a study, a large 1940s-style kitchen, and what they believed was the dining room. They saw no table or chairs, but rather a series of pillows, which were arranged upon a solid-colored rug. In its center was a tall silver serving piece that reminded Nick of a three-tiered wedding cake, and some low-slung cabinets positioned around the walls. There were napkins and glasses already set out, but there was no cutlery or silverware.

They were looking at the artwork in the front living room when Alec and Eleanor reappeared twenty minutes later, and led them to the dining area. As soon as they were seated on the pillows, the maid entered laden with small silver trays of food. She arranged them on the central serving platform, and placed a large, pale yellow china plate in front of each of them.

One of the trays contained steaming white rice, another held small pieces of dark-skinned fish, and a third a curry dish. It all smelled delicious. Condiments were on the top level of the serving piece—chopped nuts and raisins. A large silver spoon was used to take food from the trays to their plates, but they would, as Nick had expected, eat using the fingers of their right hand. A bottle of sparkling water was produced, their glasses filled, and they began to eat.

Sampling a few bites, Laurie proclaimed, "I thought the meal we had last night was good, but this is even better."

They continued to converse during the relaxed meal. Finally, dinner came to an end, and with it, a subtle shift in Alec's mood. The maid produced a finger bowl and clean linen napkins, and then cleared the dirty plates from the room. Alec and Eleanor were quiet for a moment, and then Alec spoke, a serious look on his face.

"Nick," he began, "Romy told us that we would like you, and Papa told us we could trust you. We have not known you long at all, but I feel that we know you well. You have made a favorable impression on us, and on our people," he turned to include Laurie, "that will last for a long time."

"We understand that we come from very different backgrounds, but we understand your values, and we accept them. We believe that you can benefit our people."

Alec, sitting cross-legged but very straight and tall, looked into Nick's eyes and spoke in careful, measured, formal tones. "I can help you to help us. You need the respect of my people. You already have mine. I shall give you the gift of rank. Your title will allow you to travel around the Philippines safely, and without escort. You shall only have to express your wishes and the tribal farmers shall obey without question."

Alec looked away for a moment, as if visualizing something before continuing. "A ceremony. We shall have a ceremony."

His gaze returned to Nick and Laurie. "Yes. You will have to come back. You will bring your children. We will have the ceremony near our home in Marawi City, so that everyone in the tribe can attend and bear witness to the event. We shall have our best dancers, our best musicians, and we shall make sacrifice to Allah." Alec sat back and looked at Nick with satisfaction. "We shall be brothers."

"Alec?" asked Laurie, "I'm afraid I don't understand. What is the ceremony for?"

Alec's face glowed. "I shall make Nick a Sultan. And you, Laurie, you shall be a Sultana."

Nick and Laurie both woke up early. The excitement of the previous evening, coupled with the knowledge that today they would be leaving the gloominess of the Sulo Hotel made sleeping difficult. Alec had driven them back to their room early enough, but they had stayed up for quite some time, talking about their return trip to the Philippines.

They went downstairs for their morning tea and coffee, arriving in the lobby a few minutes before the restaurant opened. The hotel manager waved to them as they walked by. "Mr. Gardner, Mrs. Gardner, good morning. Could I please have a word with you?"

"Yes?" asked Nick.

"You will be checking out today, sir?"

"Probably around noon," replied Nick.

"And everything has been acceptable to you during your stay here?"

Nick responded warmly, "Yes. Everything has been just fine, thank you."

The manager looked slightly uncomfortable, as if his collar was too tight. "I am glad to hear that," he said, not sounding like he really meant it, "because I have a small favor to ask of you."

Nick and Laurie glanced at each other. Nick raised his eyebrows, "Yes?"

The manager cleared his throat. "We are making a television advertisement for the hotel today. There will be a crew here this morning with lights and cameras. I have been asked to ask if you would please consider allowing us to film you here in the lobby."

Nick was surprised. "You want us to be in your commercial?"

"No, sir, not exactly," he said sheepishly. "Just Mrs. Gardner."

Nick laughed. "Well, I don't blame you for that. Laurie?" he said, turning to her. "What do you think?"

Laurie laughed as well. "Sure. When do you want to do it?"

The manager, almost sputtering with relief, glanced at the large clock on the wall behind him. "They should be here at nine o'clock. Will that be convenient for you?"

"That'll be fine," said Laurie. "I'll see you then."

"Thank you, ma'am. And you, too, Mr. Gardner."

They walked over to the restaurant, its door just now opening, and took their usual booth in the corner of the room. Settling in, Nick said, "It's nice of you to help them out. Given the way we feel about this place right now, lending your endorsement to it is a little like me becoming the poster boy for The Committee."

They finished their breakfast and headed back to their room to pack. Nick gathered his paperwork and returned again to the restaurant for his final meeting of the week with his partners. "I'll be back in a couple of hours," he said, giving her a quick kiss. "Remember I'll be right downstairs. Come get me if you need me. Have fun with your commercial."

Papa and Romy were waiting in the restaurant. They exchanged warm greetings and congratulated him on his sultancy. Nick produced the dog-eared map of the Philippines that Papa had given to him and set it in the middle of the table.

"Papa," he began, "I've studied this map carefully, and I'm not sure I understand your interest in a lot of the places you've marked."

Nick pointed to two of the encircled spots. "These, for example, don't fit our profile."

Papa glanced down at the map and then back at him, his face expressionless.

Nick continued. "Look, they are much smaller sites than we'd like to operate, and they're both far away from any towns. Without a nearby source for workers, we'd have to provide housing facilities." Papa didn't seem to be listening, and Nick pointed to another area that was circled in red ink. "These others—they must be mistakes. They're completely landlocked, and they're in the middle of nowhere. They don't have access roads, so they couldn't even be used as warehousing locations. Why should we buy any of these?"

Papa looked over at Romy, who responded, "You are right, of course. Those locations do not fit the profile we developed. The reason we marked them is because the people who own them also own properties that we actually want. They wouldn't agree to sell us the prime locations unless we agreed to also purchase some of their less desirable lots."

Nick nodded, skeptically. "OK, as long as we don't have to pay a premium for them. I mean, look over here—this one is really isolated. Can we find anyone who will buy it from us?"

Papa spoke, softly. "Don't worry about them, Nick. They aren't expensive, and, who knows? Maybe someday they will be prove to be valuable."

"Well, as long as we can get control of all of the other sites that we want, I guess it's no big deal. Now, there are two things we need to take care of right away. Romy, you need to work on the first one, and Papa, you're the perfect guy to handle the second.

"Romy, it looks like I'll be coming back here in about six or eight weeks. What I need to have you accomplish while I'm gone is to prove that the growth rate of our crop is sustainable on a large scale. You'll need to take a bunch of baseline measurements at two—no, make that three different test sites. Pack the tie lines close together, like we discussed, and let's see what happens." He pointed to the map. "We should plant identical lines—tied with seedlings from the same source plant, if possible—here, here and here. That way, when we take our measurements, we can see if the different water and tidal conditions have any impact on the growth rate. Any questions so far?"

Romy shook his head. "Good," continued Nick, "you can also keep an eye out for people who will be able to manage locations for us."

Nick went on. "Papa, you've got the other critical piece. Since our attorney is going to be working on securing the options to all of these locations, you should have plenty of time to work on setting up the farmer's cooperative. Alec and I talked about it at length last night, and he's ready to take you with him down to Mindanao. He doesn't know for sure just how many Muslims farm seaweed, but evidently there are a lot of them.

"Go down there with him and figure out a way to get them organized. You know our basic price points, so cut the best deal you can. Locking them in—making sure that they sell their crops only into the co-op—is much more important than how much we have to pay them."

Papa responded with a nod of his head.

"Good. Here's what I'll be doing. As soon as I get back to the States, I'll file the registration papers and get the parent company incorporated. Remember that guy I told you about—the associate of mine with the background in marketing and food? Well, I'm going to get him working with me closely on this.

"We'll fine-tune the business plan and target a couple of potential customers. With any luck, we'll be able to meet with them and get them interested in our capabilities before I come back. When I've got a better handle on how much revenue we might bring in in the first year, I'll know how much capital we'll need to raise.

"Once I know how much money we'll need, I'll spend my time looking for the right venture capitalist." Nick looked across the table at the two men. "I have to tell you this. From what I have seen so far, getting an investor to put up a couple of million dollars shouldn't be too difficult. If you can prove our large-scale growth rate, and you can sign up enough farmers, I'll find someone to fund us. All of the pieces are falling nicely into place, and everything looks good. Really good."

They spent a few minutes looking at their calendars, working out some preliminary schedules, and then Nick went back upstairs to his room while the two of them waited behind.

"Laurie?" asked Nick as he entered their room, "How was your shoot?"

She was seated in the small chair by the window. "It was fine. All they wanted me to do was to walk through the lobby and stop to talk to the manager at the front desk. We walked through it a couple of times, filmed it three or four times, and that was it."

Nick looked at her in her emerald green blouse and matching skirt. "If anyone could make this dump look good, it's you.

"Come on," he said. "Papa and Romy are waiting downstairs, they're going to give us a ride into Manila. Let's get our stuff and get out of here."

As she started to gather her belongings, she asked, "Nick, tell me again why we're changing hotels. If it's just one more night, I really don't mind staying here."

He turned and walked over to her, taking her into his arms for a long moment. "I know you don't. But after your taxi ride yesterday, I don't want you to have any worries about your personal safety. Besides, our flight tomorrow is at 6:30 A.M., and we have to allow extra time for customs. You know what traffic is like, and I really don't want to have to leave here at three in the morning. The Manila Hotel is only fifteen minutes from the airport, and—hey, we've had a successful trip. We can afford to splurge a little and enjoy ourselves."

"OK, Nick. I have to admit, after seeing the place last night, I can't wait to see what the rooms are like."

The midday traffic was light, and they arrived at the Manila Hotel in less than an hour. Pulling into the driveway and gliding to a halt, they were immediately greeted by a bellman, who piled all of their baggage onto a brass cart and disappeared with it inside.

They all got out of the car, and both Romy and Papa shook hands with Nick. Papa spoke first, slowly and almost formally. "Nick, we have managed to accomplish a great deal this week, and I want to thank you for your leadership and contribution. We would not have made nearly this much progress without you."

"I'm pleased with our progress as well," replied Nick, trying to read the impassive expression on Papa's face. "Thanks for your hospitality, and also for the opportunity to work with you."

Papa turned and shook Laurie's hand. "And you, Laurie, were a big help. We have chosen well."

Romy came forward and started to shake Laurie's hand, but happily accepted her hug instead.

"Romy, thanks so much for everything you've done. It was so nice getting to know you. I'm looking forward to introducing you to our boys. Take care of yourself, and, really, thanks again."

Romy's smile was so big that the corners of his mouth seemed to nearly touch his ears, the gap in his upper teeth prominently displayed. "Thank you, Laurie. I have enjoyed our time together as well." He reluctantly disengaged from her hug, "You look like a glamorous lady, but you don't fool me—you are a cowboy!"

Laurie laughed loudly in response and gave him another hug. Nick and Laurie watched as the pair drove away, waving, and then walked into the hotel. The Manila Hotel, Nick noted as they breezed through security, was just as luxurious in the daytime as it had looked a couple of nights before. As Laurie looked around, Nick took care of registration, then a bellman appeared at his side as if from nowhere, and gestured towards the elevators.

The bellman led the way, describing the hotel's five restaurants to them as they rode to the second floor and made their way down the wide hallway. Inserting an old-fashioned brass key into the lock, the bellman held the door open for them and they went inside.

The room must have been twenty feet in width and considerably more in length. A huge, highly polished four-poster bed with a billowing silk canopy dominated the right wall, and twin six-drawer dressers stood on the opposite side. The far wall was covered with rich fabric curtains, parted in the middle slightly to show the view of the nearby harbor. A heavy armoire stood in the corner of the room, its doors open to display a large television.

Nick turned to the bellman, as another uniformed man appeared with the baggage cart, delivering their bags. Nick tipped each of them, they wished him a pleasant stay, and, with a short bow, exited. As the door closed behind them, Nick turned to Laurie. "Well? What do you think?"

She turned to look at him, and they both burst into laughter. As if reading each other's minds, they both leapt into the bed, luxuriating in the feel of the firm mattress and clean, fluffy bedding. They kissed, and Laurie asked, "And what do you want to do this afternoon?"

"Well," replied Nick, "afterwards, I thought I'd go check out the pool and the gym, and then maybe get a massage."

"Afterwards?" she asked, reaching up to his neck and pulling him towards her for another, longer, kiss. "After what?"

"After this," he said, reaching down and unbuttoning her blouse.

They sat at a quiet table for two in the corner of the same restaurant where they had eaten a few nights before with Luis Carino, Laurie in an elegant, sleeveless black dress, Nick in a dark blue suit. Music from the orchestra in the lobby drifted in the air, and as their drinks arrived they sat in silence, enjoying each other's presence.

Nick raised his glass. "To an incredible trip."

She responded, "And to you."

"This trip has been amazing," he continued. "The way the week started out—with the dinginess of the Sulo Hotel, all the rain, and the jet lag—I was afraid that this was going to turn into a big waste of time. But I've done everything that I needed to get done.

"You've heard me say it before. Usually a due diligence pro-cess uncovers something wrong. I've looked at more than a hun-dred situations, and there's always *something*. I keep thinking that maybe I've missed it, because I just haven't found anything out of place here at all. In fact, it's been just the opposite. The news keeps getting better.

"The way it looks to me now, there are only a couple of things that have to happen for this to be big. Really big. We could make enough money to do anything we want for the rest of our lives."

Their waiter came, and after ordering their meal—Steak Dianne for Nick and Pasta Primavera for Laurie— they continued their conversation.

"And it isn't just the money, you know? This is one of those times when there is a larger opportunity. We can make a differ-ence in the lives of a lot of people."

"I know. I'm proud of you for that."

Nick shook off the compliment with a shrug, "This hasn't been a bad week for you, either."

The waiter brought the wine, which was ceremoniously opened, tasted, and poured. Nick proposed another toast, "To the Sultana and her island," and Laurie clinked her glass with his.

A man in a starched white chef's coat rolled a cart up to the side of their table and began to prepare Nick's meal. While the chef went through his motions, Nick and Laurie talked about their af-ternoon, and their travel plans. When the chef had finished cook-ing, he signaled someone behind him, and Laurie's plate was pre-sented simultaneously with Nick's. They ate unhurriedly, savor-ing the evening.

Maybe it was because Nick had grown accustomed to the way that people openly stared at Laurie, or maybe it was because he was so focused on enjoying the moment. Whatever the reason, he didn't notice the man with the withered left eye who sat alone on the other side of the room, watching the two of them intently.

PART FIVE

BOXES INSIDE BOXES

Buddy steered the *Makatà* through the choppy waves. Approaching the port of Cebu, he lowered the mainsail and jib and cranked up the diesel engine as he entered the outer channel. For the time being, he kept the mizzen aloft. Although the trailing sail wouldn't add much power, it might make him more visible to the oil tankers in the early morning half-light. Glancing up, he made sure that the running lights on his mast were still on. Now that he was using his engine, he wouldn't have to worry about draining power from his batteries.

Because virtually all of Buddy's sailing was done within sight of at least one of the Philippine's thousands of islands, he usually navigated by dead-reckoning. Given his knowledge of the geography, his instincts usually told him where he was better than any chart could. Even so, he frequently sailed on the open seas, and, like most blue-water sailors, he used a hand-held global positioning system to verify his position. Originally, Buddy had purchased the device not to tell him his location at sea, but to help him locate the Birds of Cirebon. He had learned the inadequacies of even the most detailed topographical charts, and had bought the satellite navigational system to verify his position on land.

Once he started using the GPS, Buddy discovered the leverage of modern technology, and invested next in a portable ground penetrating radar system. His 50 Mhz GPR consisted of two compact pieces—a transducer, which was placed, or dragged, on the ground, and a digital control unit. The ground equipment transmitted ultra high-frequency radio waves into the earth that bounced off underground objects and reflected the signal back to the system. A small black and white monitor on the control unit provided a visual image of what was below.

Depending upon the type of soil, the GPR could be used effectively at depths of up to a hundred feet. It could not only detect the size and shape of buried metallic objects, it could also identify and locate voids. And voids, Buddy knew, meant tunnels. While efficient at finding tunnels and metals, the GPR couldn't differentiate between gold and silver. To accomplish that task he needed a resistivity detector, and he was on his way to Cebu to buy one.

Once he had this new piece of equipment, he would return to the site. Several weeks ago he had determined where the Birds of Cirebon statue was buried, but only within an area of several dozen square meters. Since he'd be digging with only a shovel, he needed to pinpoint the location precisely.

Standing at the helm and resting his hands on the spokes of the wooden wheel, he reviewed his plan for the day. He'd berth the *Makatà* at the dock of the industrial salvage company that would sell him the equipment, then nap for the rest of the morning. He had sailed all night and wanted to be rested enough to make the most of his evening.

He had timed this particular trip so that he could see Jenessa, who normally worked the international flights for Philippine Air Lines, but tonight had a layover in Cebu. Thinking about her, as always, brought a grin to his face. He couldn't decide what he liked most about her. In public, he enjoyed watching the way her mind worked. When they were alone, he preferred to lie back and watch the way her mouth worked.

Nick and Laurie had taken a quick flight from Manila to Hong Kong, where they enjoyed a whirlwind day of sightseeing and shopping. Elated with the prospect of success, Nick had pulled out all the stops. From the moment they arrived in Hong Kong, when a limousine met them at the airport and whisked them to a suite at the Peninsula Hotel, to their dinner in the hotel that evening, they had lived luxuriously.

They had departed on a pre-dawn flight the following day, and had actually been able to get some sleep on the plane. Two sunrises later, their plane landed in San Francisco. It was early Friday morning and they were eager to get home and be with their boys. They found the boys waiting outside customs with their grandmother, and after a brief reunion, they all jammed into the car and headed towards Tiburon. Both boys talked at the same time as they shared news of the past ten days.

When they arrived home, the boys helped manhandle the baggage upstairs to the master bedroom, where they gathered around Laurie's enormous suitcase, waiting to see what their parents had brought them. Max got a new snowboarding jacket, some new video games, and a fake Cartier wristwatch. They brought for Sean an abacus, a snakeskin knife, and a Casio wristwatch with about a million different features.

"So, what was it like in the Philippines?" Sean asked.

Nick and Laurie took turns sharing their perspectives. Laurie told them about the people they met, the schools, and the islands. Nick told them about the rain, the mint, the jeepneys and the seaweed plantation. Then he looked at Laurie. "Do you want to tell

235

them or should I?"

Laurie sat back in her chair. "You know that the Philippines is really a nation of islands." Seeing their nodding heads, she continued. "Well, it's a long story, but you'll never guess what happened." She paused, waiting for silence. "They named one of the islands after me."

While both of the boys reacted with surprise, it was Sean who asked, "Can I see it on a map?"

Nick went into his office to get his atlas. Coming back a moment later, he flipped open the huge book and showed them first the island of Palawan, then the Calamian island group, and then Busuanga and the town of Coron. "Here," he said, pointing to a little brown dot. "That's it."

The boys looked slightly disappointed, and Nick asked, "What's wrong, you wanted a bigger island?"

"No," answered Max. "I wanted to see her name on the map."

Laurie patted his shoulder. "I'm afraid you'll have to wait a while for that to happen, Max." She looked over at Nick and, raising her eyebrows, received the signal she was looking for. "There's something else we need to tell you. The people Nick are working with are giving him an extremely special honor."

Their heads turned in unison from her face to Nick's and then back again. "Because your dad's business is going to involve many of the Philippine people, he's being given a title. One of his business partners is a Muslim, and he is going to make Nick a Sultan."

Sean turned to look at Nick. "You mean you're going to start wearing a turban?"

Nick laughed as Laurie continued, "There's more. This is all going to happen in a big ceremony, and we have to go back to the Philippines for the event. You'll get to see it for yourselves. We're going to take you with us."

A cacophony of whoops, hollers, and high-fives erupted between the boys. They all continued talking for another hour or so. Then Max went to call friends, and Sean picked up the atlas and studied the pages that showed the Philippines. Nick lingered for a few more minutes, then headed into his office.

He sat at his desk for the first time in ten days and looked at the mass of mail and paperwork in front of him. Tomorrow, he thought, he'd start to deal with it. For now, it would be enough to make one quick telephone call.

His finger punched in a number as if it had its own memory, and Nick left a message on the answering machine. "Keith, this is Nick. I'm back, and we need to talk. Everything in the Philippines went much better than I expected, and I've got a bunch of stuff that has your name all over it. Do me a favor and give me a call in the morning. I'm not sure what time I'll be in my office, but let me know on my machine where I can track you down if I don't pick up the phone. I'm looking forward to spending some time with you, partner."

Buddy berthed the Makatà at the industrial salvage company's dock just before noon. After tying the craft securely, he headed for the office, striding up the narrow pier on legs still accustomed to the movement of the sea. He entered the corrugated metal building and approached the cluttered counter of the service area.

"Buddy! Good to see you," came the Tagalog greeting.

"You, too, Reynato. I got your message a couple of days ago. What's going on?"

The clerk looked around, as if making sure no one could overhear them. "Something's come up. You know that last piece of equipment you ordered? I don't know exactly what's going on, but there's some kind of a problem with the factory."

"Oh?" replied Buddy neutrally, even though his professional paranoia came alive like a sixth sense.

"They sent us a fax. It seems they need more than just the usual deposit. They won't ship the equipment unless the order is pre-paid." He scratched his armpit absent-mindedly. "I don't know why—it's the first time they've ever asked us to do this—but that's the way it is. Sorry. Do you still want to go ahead with the order?"

Buddy assimilated the new information. There were plenty of other things he could do to make good use of his time, but, without the resistivity detector, he wouldn't be able to do any digging. The pre-payment request was a little irregular, but Buddy figured there was probably a legitimate reason.

He nodded at the clerk. "Yeah. I can go to the bank here in town and have it for you in the morning. Will that be OK?"

"Sure. I'll tell the boss. Sorry for the hassle."

"Right. See you tomorrow."

Jenessa was sitting at one of the tables in the bar, facing the other way.

"Hey, Babe," Buddy said softly, kissing her on the back of the neck. "You look fabulous. Have you been waiting long?"

Turning to him, she put her hands on the back of his neck and pulled him toward her for a kiss. "Mmm," she sighed, as he reluctantly pulled away and sat down. "It's been too long," her eyes sparkled, "since I've seen my Buddy."

He sat down into the low chair next to her, his eyes focusing on her straight, white teeth, and soft, pouty lips. A waitress came by and he ordered a Campari and Soda for her and a beer for himself.

"So what brings you to civilization?" she asked.

"You, of course."

She grinned, showing a flash of white. "No way. The only time you come to see me is when you need to buy books or equipment."

It wasn't quite true, she knew. They'd known each other for five years and saw each other about once a month. There had never been any talk of marriage, but she knew that Buddy cared about her and she found their relationship completely acceptable. She wasn't yet ready to settle down, and, besides, Buddy was by far the most fascinating man she had ever met. She called him her modern-day Renaissance man. He was also the best lover she could imagine.

She smiled at him and flicked the tip of her tongue across her lips, knowing full well the image it would project, and Buddy hesitated before continuing. "Since I was going to be here anyway, I thought I might as well pick up something that will indicate the type of metal that's buried."

The waitress brought their drinks. Jenessa picked up her glass, and with a glance at the retreating waitress to make sure she was out of hearing range, asked, "And will it show where the bombs are buried?"

He shook his head, "You know my answer. There aren't any bombs."

Taking a swallow of his beer, he leaned forward. "Think about it. For starters, there was no suggestion of any buried ordnance in the transcripts of interviews with the Japanese officers. Second, people—thousands of them—have been digging around possible burial sites for decades. If any of the locations were booby-trapped, someone would have set off an explosion by now. There's only been one documented discovery—the Golden Buddha that Roxas found up in Baguio City—and there were no explosives found there.

"The booby-trap story, like so many others, was fabricated as misinformation. Besides, even if there are any bombs, they're fifty years old. I was in the Marines, remember? The only reason I enlisted was to become an expert in explosives."

He reached over and took her hand in his. He brought it to his lips and kissed the back of it. Looking into her dark eyes, he turned it over and kissed the palm. "OK?"

She kept her fingers on his cheek for a moment, then ran her hand down his neck to his chest. She let it linger there, the tips of her fingers toying with his nipple over the fabric of his shirt. He reacted with a shadow of a flinch and she put her hand back in her lap.

"So tell me," she said, "have you come across any tens lately?"

Buddy had created a system to evaluate treasure hunters that used a scale of one to ten, indicating how serious someone was about finding Yamashita's gold. He called it the greed meter. He assigned ratings of one to five to people that knew little about the treasure, or who only talked about things that were repeated in the occasional newspaper accounts. Higher ratings were given to people who spoke of a specific piece, such as the Birds of Cirebon or the Chavet Pearls, or referred to specific locations or dates that he knew to be correct.

The highest scores were given to the handful of people that knew about Colonel Hara's carved markers, or had developed a realistic method of converting the treasure into cash. Anyone who knew about the markers and had figured out how to launder the gold was a ten.

"No one that's even close. So how have things been going with you?" He listened to her response, watching her mouth form the words. Occasionally he interjected a comment, but generally he stayed silent, completely absorbed in the rhythmic movements of her red lips. Sometime later—he didn't really know how much time had passed—he realized that she had finished both her story and her drink. He glanced down at his beer. It was still half full.

"Want anything else?" he asked, indicating her empty glass.

She looked squarely at him, and slowly stroked her lips with her tongue, catching the last bitter traces of Campari.

He looked at her for a long moment before turning to find the waitress.

"Check, please."

August 27, 1991
Tiburon, California

Sunrise found Nick in his office, wading through the stack of work that had accumulated during his absence. The mundane obligations out of the way, he then called each of his clients, letting them know that he was back in the country and checking in on his projects. The last telephone message he'd received had been from Keith Dickson; he'd be able to stop by and meet with Nick sometime after noon.

It was nearly one o'clock when Keith rang the doorbell to the house and let himself in. "Honey! I'm home!" he called, and walked into Nick's office, unescorted. Nick rose from his desk to shake hands. Just under six feet tall and a well-muscled hundred and ninety pounds, Keith wore his usual non-client attire—pleated cotton slacks, a polo shirt, and his trademark, blindingly bright white sneakers. "Good to see you, Keith. Thanks for clearing your schedule so we could get together this quickly."

"No problem. Welcome back. From the look of it, everything on your trip went well."

"Better than that, actually." Nick led the way first to the refrigerator, got them each a bottle of sparkling water, and then to the patio chairs out on the deck. He launched right in. "I'll give you the headlines first.

"We've already set up a Philippine company to grow and collect carrageenan. That company will be a wholly-owned subsidiary of another company that I'll set up here, which will have the exclusive rights to all of the sub's production." Nick glanced at Keith, noting from his expression that he followed the explanation.

242

"Since you already know more about carrageenan than I do, I won't bother you with a bunch of details, but I will tell you that I've gotten a lot smarter about it. Forget about carrageenan's water-protein bonding characteristics, I've seen and felt this stuff personally, and I can tell you everything you *really* need to know about it. It's purplish red, really slippery, and smells just like seaweed."

Keith laughed. "You're one up on me. I've never actually seen it."

"Just as you said, there are a couple of major players—HMC and Titan Industries—that already have big facilities in the Philippines for processing carrageenan. The key point, however, is that Philippine law limits the amount of seaweed those companies can grow themselves. Our subsidiary, because it is majority-owned by Philippine nationals, will have no such restrictions.

"That turns out to be a critical distinction. It means that the existing producers have to rely on independent farmers for their raw materials." Nick looked at Keith while he took a sip from his bottle. "We think we've come up with some ways to persuade the independents to sell exclusively to us. That means that the current players will have to either find new farmers to buy from, or be forced to buy from us at whatever price we ask. Either way, we have an opportunity to corner the market."

Keith countered, "Won't HMC and Titan just respond by having some locals form their own farming companies that agree to sell to them?"

"You mean what is to prevent them from basically copying our strategy?" Nick was pleased at Keith's question. "Do you remember what you told me a few weeks ago about the conditions most favorable to growing carrageenan? Well, while I was there we did an analysis of all of the places that fit the profile you described. It turns out that there aren't thousands and thousands of practical sites for seaweed farms after all. There are, actually, only a couple hundred of them."

Nick waited several seconds before continuing. "We're securing the option rights to purchase every single one of them."

"Great idea," exclaimed Keith.

"I thought you'd appreciate it. By the time HMC and Titan Industries wake up to what's happening, we'll have preempted their only natural response. There won't be any good sites left to buy. The fact is that we'll use the best ones we acquire as production sites and just leave the others alone, ready for use in the event that market demand picks up."

"Sweet," said Keith.

"There's more," continued Nick. "I think we've found a way to increase the production capacity of each of our sites. I'm not talking about an incremental improvement of five or ten percent. I think we can double, and maybe even triple, our original estimates."

"You're kidding. How?"

"Well, just like you said," said Nick, using his hands to demonstrate. "The way they grow the stuff is by taking a cutting from a mature plant, tying it on a string—they call it a tie line—and then suspending it in the water from a longer piece of rope that's called a stretch line. The stretch lines are marked by buoys at both ends. Everyone over there attaches the tie lines to the stretch lines the same space apart—about two meters.

"When I first saw that, I assumed it was because the plants needed plenty of distance separating them in order to have room to grow, but that's not true. They can probably be tied much closer together, without impacting the growth of the plant in any negative way. The only reason they don't put their tie lines closer together is that as the plants grow, the stretch ropes holding the tie lines get heavy and start to sink, and that creates problems with the harvesting process.

"It sounds too simple to be true, but we should be able to increase our production capacity dramatically just by putting a series of buoys in the middle of the stretch lines to keep them from sinking. We're running an experiment on this right now."

"Why don't they do that already?"

"Because of the price of buoys. They're too expensive for the independent farmers to use any place but at the end of the stretch lines. Remember, these guys are out in the middle of nowhere, and don't have any contractual limitations on how much space they use. The way they see it, if they want to grow more, all they do is walk another few yards down the beach and put out another stretch line. That's a whole lot easier than worrying about one of their lines sinking."

Keith laughed. "TGG strikes again. Only a month ago, you didn't even know what carrageenan was. Now you're tripling capacity."

"Well, I'm sure it's no big deal. I just brought a fresh set of eyes."

He continued. "Our point man, a guy named Romy—he's the one I met here at the bank—is running the experiment. I'll be in touch with him pretty soon to get the initial results, and I'll plug his information into my business model."

"I also found out that our original pricing assumptions were wrong." Nick paused, knowing that Keith would be expecting the worst. "Our selling price is actually going to be forty percent higher."

Keith raised his eyebrows in semi-disbelief. "No shit!"

"I couldn't believe it myself. I was flipping through a Philippine newspaper one morning and read that the price per kilo for raw carrageenan was seventeen pesos."

Keith responded seriously, "I was afraid that you'd get over there and find out that the selling price was only six or seven pesos."

"Well, you're partly right. The farmer actually *does* usually sell his crop for only six pesos or so, but we missed an important link in the distribution process. It turns out that there are a bunch of middlemen—guys who have the right kind of boats, mostly Chinese—who collect the harvests and deliver them to the processing plants. The price the traders get is seventeen pesos."

"So you'll be able to take the spread?"

"No, and I'm not sure that's what we want to do. I haven't had time to run the numbers yet, but my current thinking is that we'll buy from the farmers at ten pesos, and sell to the other processing companies at something higher than seventeen."

"Why pay ten pesos? Why not less? If the farmers are only getting six or seven now, won't they think that eight pesos is a great deal?"

"A couple of reasons. First of all, they need the money. You wouldn't believe the way they live, and I'm committed to giving them as much of a break as we can. This isn't money we're leaving on the table, it's an investment we're making in our partners. Second, think about the ripples it creates. What will ultimately happen to the market price of carrageenan?"

Keith hesitated, instantly processing the information and calculating the impact of supply and demand. "I get it. It'll go up. You'll just take the money on the other end."

Nick nodded. "Right. And don't forget our company-owned farms. For everything we grow ourselves, we'll be able to have it both ways. Our cost to grow it ourselves will be one or two pesos per kilo. We'll make a killing.

"Anyway, that's what I think now, and it's all based on my original projections. They looked very strong ten days ago, but I need to recheck them. That's what I'll be working on this week.

"OK. So it's safe to assume that we won't have a problem growing the stuff. Now I need to get a handle on how much we can sell. That's where I need your help. We need to find some prospects and get in front of them. Any ideas?"

Keith reflected for a moment, taking a long swig of his bottled water. "Finding a list of current users should be easy," he began. "I know a guy who maintains an industry database that should be helpful. But before I talk to him, let's come up with a profile of the type of customer you'd like to have.

"If you think about it, the number of characteristics that define your perfect customer is pretty small. You don't want any really big users. One, they might need more than you can initially produce, and, two, if you start talking to them, the competition will hear about it. It's too early for that. You still want to keep a low profile, right? So we're really looking for a very specific type of customer, one that's small enough to target, contact, and possibly even close, but whose volume is significant enough to prove that we've got a business."

Nick nodded. "That's what I had concluded as well. We need to launch a quick guerrilla marketing campaign and find out what it takes to sell these guys. Let's find a couple of them, and see if we can interest them in a brainstorming session about 'improving vendor relationships' or something. Get them in a free-flowing conversation where we can all think outside the box. We don't want to simply match what the other guys are doing, we have to figure out how we can add some tangible value to the equation."

"No problem, Nick. I'll make some calls this afternoon." He glanced at his watch.

"I thought that was what you'd say. That's why I think you're the right guy for the job."

"What job?"

"Let me ask you, Keith. When I asked you to join TGG, one of the reasons you accepted was so that you and I would have a chance to work together, right?"

"Right."

"Look at what's happened. While we've worked together on several projects a year, we've always had to be in supporting roles as advisers. It's been all right, but it hasn't given either one of us the chance to flex our management muscles, much less leverage the synergy that comes from working together in an extended relationship, has it?"

Keith nodded in agreement.

"We have an opportunity here that is unique on several levels.

I mean, what we're talking about is setting up a company, with a very small group of principals, whose sole mission will be to market the natural resources of one country into another. Think about it. If you could wave a magic wand and create any job in the world for yourself, do you think you could create a position that uses your background better than this one?"

The smile on Keith's face showed that Nick was successfully reeling him in.

"OK, but what about the dollars?" asked Keith.

"What about the dollars?" blasted back Nick. "You'd have so much fun doing this that you'd probably do it for free! Besides, I'm gonna be the CEO, so you'll be working for a pussycat."

That brought a skeptical smile to Keith's face. "OK, Nick. I'm with you."

Nick took a deep breath, and exhaled loudly. Not a sigh, really. It was a mental and physical transition. "Good. Now, what is the going market rate for a Vice-President of Marketing for a technology startup in the Bay Area? Let's take the annual compensation first."

Keith thought for a moment. "OK. It depends on several things. Let's assume that the company is expecting to go public, right? It will hit an annual revenue in the first couple of years of what, twenty million? A double-digit market share, and profits of at least twenty percent, pretax?" Seeing Nick's nod, he went on. "Well, then, for the absolutely perfect candidate—a one-of-a-kind candidate—the compensation would probably be in the neighborhood of a hundred and fifty, maybe as high as two hundred thousand. Assuming, of course, that the stock options were at the right level."

"Naturally," replied Nick. "And what do you think the 'right level' of equity participation would be for this ideal, hypothetical, V.P. of Marketing?"

"One or two percent of the company."

Nick nodded. "You're right about the current market rates." He looked Keith right in the eyes. "But you're wrong about the value the perfect candidate would have on the success of this business. You are the perfect candidate, Keith, and I'm not only *willing* to pay you the market rate, I'm able to *afford* to do it as well.

"Here's what I have in mind. I'll give you a salary of one hundred and fifty thousand, plus a cash bonus equal to that amount if we can hit our profit and market share objectives. I don't know what those targets are yet, but don't worry. You'll help me figure out what they should be.

"On the equity side of the equation, your number is too low. The fact is, in this company, your role is actually greater than just marketing. Your experience would make you the head of Research & Development as well. Since I won't have to pay for an R&D V.P. I can raise the ante on your stock options. I'm going to suggest that you get an equity stake of five percent."

"Jesus Christ!"

"No, it's only me."

Keith smiled. "You know what I like about you, Nicholas? All you had to do was say please, and I probably would have done it. Still you went to all the trouble to walk me down the path."

"No trouble at all. There's just one little thing. Neither of us gets paid until we've raised the necessary capital. Not even for expenses.

Nick paused, giving Keith time to absorb the news. "I've already spent over six grand on travel so far, and it'll be at least twice that before we can fund this puppy. If I wasn't using my frequent flier miles, it would be a whole lot more.

"That's the downside. Oh, yeah, plus the loss of billable time. But think about it—it's only going to be a couple of weeks. At any point along the way, if things go wrong, you just walk away. On the other hand, if we can make millions, who cares if we run up a couple of thousand on our credit cards?" He leaned forward, the expression on his face intense. "This is the one I've been looking for. I can smell it."

It took Keith only a moment to come to a decision. "Thanks

for your confidence, Nick. I appreciate it. And," he added, lifting his empty bottle of sparkling water, "I accept."

They clinked bottles, and Keith continued. "You said you'd be the CEO?"

"Yep," nodded Nick, "and I'll be on the board of both the parent and the sub. So, let's have our first official meeting. I'm going to head downtown this afternoon to file the incorporation papers. I can submit three potential company names for the Secretary of State's office to check out. I'm pretty sure that the last part of the company's name should be 'Marketing Company'. Any ideas about what the first part should be?"

Keith looked out over the bay. "Well," he said, "it can't be 'Carrageenan' for sure. It's too specific. If this thing works, we could start exporting a second product right away."

Nick watched Keith's thought process unfold, a mirror of his own mind.

"For the same reason, we don't want to use the word 'Philippines', either. Look," he said, "why not Pacific Resource Marketing Company?"

"Sure, that works. It's direct and it's descriptive."

Keith immediately produced a pen and started to make some sketches on his pad of paper. "If it's available, we can do some fun stuff with the logo. See?" he started. "And even if it's not available, I like the initials, PRMC. We can play with either 'Philippine Resource' or, 'Pacific Rim' Marketing Company. I like it."

Nick nodded. "We're under a lot of time pressure. We need to work as quickly as possible, because we don't have much time before we have to go back."

"To the Philippines?" asked Keith with no small amount of surprise. "Laurie liked it so much she wants to go back?"

"She did, but that's not why we're going," said Nick. "You need to come with me and see the place for yourself. Besides, we have a ceremony to attend."

Keith was silent, so Nick continued. "Do you remember my

mentioning that we have a strategy to lock up the harvests of the independent farmers? Well, I want to do that by organizing a seaweed grower's cooperative."

"Yeah! That's a great idea," interjected Keith. "So it's definitely in their interest to sell only to us."

"They'll also have another, and in this case, far more important motivation. It turns out that most of the seaweed farmers are Muslims, and they'll want the honor of doing business with their Sultan."

"Wait a minute. Are you telling me that you've recruited a Sultan to be part of our Philippine company?"

"Yes and no," replied Nick enigmatically, traces of a grin beginning to form on his face, "One of the Directors and investors of our Philippine sub is, in fact, a Sultan, and it's he who will be performing the ceremony anointing a new one. The new Sultan, Keith, is not only another Director of the subsidiary unit, but also Chairman of our new Pacific Resource Marketing Company."

"That's fabulous," exclaimed Keith. "Who is it?"

Nick waited another few beats before answering, and raised his eyebrows twice. "Me."

The sight of the black Mercedes limousine in the salvage company's parking lot confirmed Buddy's suspicions. Walking confidently into the office, he again found Reynato standing alone behind the counter. They nodded at each other, but neither man spoke. Buddy handed over a bank draft, and watched the clerk take a thin file from a rusted metal cabinet and scan the papers inside. Even from a distance of several feet, Buddy could see a slight tremor in his fingers. Avoiding eye contact, Reynato quietly said, "Everything appears to be in order. We should receive the equipment within a month."

"Right." He turned to leave.

"Buddy. Be careful. Watch your back."

Buddy looked back and smiled. "Don't worry, I can take care of myself. But thanks. See you later."

Leaving the store, Buddy headed not toward the dock and the *Makatà*, but directly to the idling stretch limousine. As he approached, a uniformed chauffeur exited the vehicle, walked around to the passenger side, and held the door open for him.

"Please, Mr. Ripley, come in and have a seat," called an almost child-like voice from within.

Ducking inside, the chill of the air-conditioning engulfed him with the force of a wave breaking on the shore. He sensed, rather than heard, the door behind him close as he eased himself onto the leather seat and faced the lone occupant waiting for him at the far end of the space. Though normally impervious to surprise, Buddy found himself stunned by what he saw.

Wearing a vested suit made entirely of white was the smallest man Buddy had ever seen. The fine tailoring of the silk fabric he wore made no attempt to disguise his proportions, and, despite his lack of physical size, the man exuded an almost regal aura. The tiny figure's dark brown eyes twinkled back at him through impossibly thick glasses.

"I apologize for not making a proper appointment, Mr. Ripley, but my employer has requested that I take a few minutes of your time." There was a moment of silence before the high-pitched voice continued. "I have a business proposition for you."

"Concerning?"

"Yamashita's gold, of course. Or, to be more precise, a certain artifact of immense value to us."

Buddy took a deep breath and exhaled audibly. "You've got my attention, Mr.—?"

"You may call me Hassonal," came the reply, accenting the last syllable. "I have come directly from the Istana Nurul Imam as the personal agent for the Sultan of Brunei Darussalam. We have been following your actions for some time now, and are most impressed with your progress."

Buddy responded with a nod.

"One of the Sultan's many passions is the study of ancient art. He has, as you might imagine, amassed an impressive collection, and always bids for new pieces as they become available. It has come to our attention that you may soon be in possession of the Birds of Cirebon."

Buddy's felt his heart skip a beat. "I see. And just how did you arrive at this conclusion?"

"In addition to tracking more legitimate trading channels, we have been monitoring all treasure hunting in the Philippines for many years. We didn't become aware of your efforts until last May, when you visited Indonesia. Very few foreigners take the time to journey to the villages beyond Jakarta, and our sources confirmed that you carried a picture of a Demoiselle Crane.

"Tracking your customs paperwork was easy, and the technical equipment you have purchased left paper trails as well. Discovering your father's connection with General Yamashita was a little more difficult, but quite fascinating. We are delighted that you've chosen to follow in his footsteps."

"All right. You've done your homework. Why contact me now?"

Hassonal waved dismissively. "We know what you have been looking for, but could only guess as to when you would try to reclaim it. When you ordered your latest piece of equipment, we thought you might be ready to begin excavation."

Hassonal calmly observed Buddy, who had made no attempt to deflect or deny any of his assertions. He leaned forward slightly and continued, "You know where the statue is hidden. What do you plan to do with it once you've unearthed it?"

Nick and Keith sat in comfortable chairs just off the main lobby of the downtown Hyatt Hotel. The white china coffee cups on the table in front of them were empty, and the pair sat momentarily in silence, contemplating the meaning of the papers that lay scattered about.

"So, Keith, that's the overview. What do you think?"

Keith glanced down at the papers and then looked Nick in the eye. "It's a first draft. A little rough, but I like what I see. I assume by the format of Appendix One that it's a master list of all the plan's variables?"

"Right," confirmed Nick. "All of the spreadsheets and supporting schedules refer to it, so if I change any of the numbers on that page, they ripple through the rest of the plan automatically."

"Good," nodded Keith. "Have you tested the impact of a change in the exchange rate of pesos to dollars?"

"Not yet. But it's one of the first entries on the table. The current rate is right at twenty-seven Philippine Pesos per U.S. Dollar. If the exchange rate goes up a half a peso, all I have to do is plug in the new number and it updates all the other pages."

"I understand. But what I meant was, have you had done a sensitivity analysis to see what happens to our profit percentage—and therefore, the price of our stock—if the exchange rate goes up a point?"

"Well, yes and no. I've made a list of analyses that we want to do, including that one, but, I haven't bothered to do them yet. I wanted to focus first on making sure that the model was right, and that our assumptions were as bombproof as possible.

"That makes sense," agreed Keith.

"Let me give you a better answer," Nick continued, picking up his notebook and flipping through its pages. "Here is my initial list of analyses we need to run. A lot of them are routine, such as what the profit impact is of percentage point variations in sales, costs, production capacity, and so forth. There are others, however, that are a little more esoteric." Nick looked over at Keith with a smile in his eyes. "The 'green to dried' conversion rate, for example."

Keith thought for a minute. "Let me take a whack at it. When we initially harvest the plants, they're green, but we don't sell them until they're dried, right?" Nick nodded, so Keith went on. "How long does it take for the saltwater in each plant to evaporate? When is a plant considered dry? What percentage of moisture content must it have?"

"Bingo. That's the kind of stuff we still need to nail down. For purposes of our first pass on those 'nums,' I've used a moisture content of ten percent as my assumption that drives the model. I was told when I was in the Philippines that it only took a week or so for the crop to go from green to dried, and Romy is checking on all of that. But it'll be interesting to see what the changes in seasonal weather do to the drying time."

Nick sat back in his chair and sighed. "I'm afraid I didn't ask the right question when I was talking to the carrageenan farmer, and it didn't hit me until I was on the plane coming home. The question I asked was, 'How long does it take for your crop to dry to market weight?' I should have had him base his answer on the season of the year."

Seeing the questioning look on Keith's face, Nick kept on talking. "I've seen what it's like there in the monsoon season, and there's so damn much rainfall, and so much humidity in the air. There's no way the plants are going to dry quickly—if at all—if they're left outside. On the flip side, it gets so hot there in the summer months—it's like a sauna. I wouldn't be surprised to find out that, in the sizzling heat of the summer, the time it takes for carrageenan to dry is measured in hours and minutes."

Nick looked at Keith, who was connecting the dots of information and processing some calculations in his head.

Keith asked, "That could make a real difference in the price we pay per kilo."

"That's right," approved Nick. "And it has a significant impact on our cycles per year, as well. As I explained earlier, the plants reach their optimum maturity in seven to eight weeks. When you add to that the assumed average drying time, the number of times each tie line produces a plant could range from just under four, to as many as six times a year. That's a huge swing in our potential capacity."

Keith nodded. "Let me change gears a little. What happens if we take the green plants and just stick 'em in an oven? How long would it take for them to dry that way? Would we change the chemical composition of the plant, or somehow lose any nutrients?"

"I don't know the answer to those questions, and we need to get them. Here's another issue," Nick said, pointing further down the page. "Our assumptions regarding our 'replanting allowance.' We take a cutting from every plant and use it as the seedling that starts the next planting cycle, right?

"Can you find out more about this from one of your contacts? It has to do with the actual planting process. Are we better off taking a cutting from every plant, or are there some plants that are better breeding stock than others? See what I mean? For that matter, what is the best part of the plant to use for replanting—the top or the bottom?"

Keith nodded, his eyes glazing over slightly as he realized the amount of detail that they would have to master in order to succeed. "Right. Got it. I'll make some calls and see what I can get rolling in that area.

"OK," Keith continued. "Now, I've been focusing on the other end of the business chain—finding prospective customers."

"What have you found out?"

"Good news," said Keith, his enthusiasm rising perceptibly. "And it's not just the facts that I've learned, it's the attitudes that I've uncovered. Take the big processing companies, for example, the ones that have existing facilities in the Philippines. They have a relatively small list of customers, and I've been able to find out who many of them are."

"How?"

"I talked with one of their salespeople." Keith looked over at Nick with a sheepish expression. "He somehow thought I was a headhunter, and that I was calling him to recruit him into a better job somewhere else."

Nick smiled. "Geez, I wonder how he got that impression."

Keith went on. "He said that all of the people in his company's sales department are on salary, that they have no commission incentives, and that there is no focus whatsoever on new business development. They don't have anyone trying to find new customers. The company acts as if they're the only game in town, and if anyone wants to buy carrageenan, they'll have to buy from them.

"I found the same thing was true with the other big processing company. I talked with a salesman there," said Keith with an innocent shrug, "and from what I could find, both companies sell carrageenan at exactly the same price. It's as if they have an informal cartel.

"Then I called up one of their customers and talked to someone in their purchasing department."

Nick interjected, "Another recruiting call?"

"No. This guy must have gotten the impression that I was checking out some industry data for an MBA research project."

"He fell for that?" asked Nick.

"Yeah, and he told me that the reason they buy their carrageenan from HMC has nothing to do with price or product quality. It has to do with convenience. He cuts all of the purchase orders for his company, and he already buys other ingredients from HMC. If he can just add one more line item to an existing order, it's easier for him. It's just one less piece of paper for him to handle."

"Let's get back to the salesman for a minute," asked Nick. "Did he tell you the names of any prospects?"

"No, he wasn't *that* naive. I had to reverse engineer a list."

"How?" inquired Nick.

"Well, we know what types of businesses use carrageenan as an ingredient, right? So I came up with a list of the top ten food manufacturing companies in two different categories. I did some rough calculations and figured out about how much carrageenan each of the manufacturers would need per year, and added it all up. I already knew—and confirmed it in my conversation with both sales reps—about how much the big companies sell, so I just did some subtraction. If you assume that the largest food manufacturers in each category purchase their carrageenan supply from one of these big companies, you don't have to go very far down the customer list to know which companies have to buy their carrageenan from a different source."

"Good work," noted Nick.

Keith nodded at the compliment. "Hey, I learned from the master." He leaned forward. "Anyway, I called several of them, and actually was able to make appointments for us to meet with two that fit our profile perfectly. One of them, a mid-sized company in Minneapolis, is a pretty big manufacturer of chocolate milk. The Mother's Milk Company." Nick shook his head in wonder as Keith continued. "The other company, which packages gelatin, is based in Chicago, and is a bit smaller.

"I talked with the Presidents of both companies, and we've been invited to meet with them the week after next. They both seemed like great guys, and they were very interested in getting together with us."

"It was that easy to get an appointment?"

Keith nodded, smiling. "Hey, even a blind hog gets an acorn

every now and then. It's obvious that both of these guys are incredibly frustrated with the attitudes of the big carrageenan suppliers."

"Did you get into any specifics?"

"Nope. You're the question-meister, so I figured it would be better all the way around if you led that discussion. I did, however, arrange for a big block of their time so we'll be able to do it right."

"Good job," said Nick, reflecting on the possibilities. "You know, this whole situation is remarkable. We'll know in a few weeks how successful we'll be in setting up a farmers cooperative and purchasing the options on growing sites. If we can keep those efforts hidden from the big boys for just a little longer, we can't lose."

"It looks like we've got the capacity end nailed down, doesn't it?" added Keith.

"Yep. And with the market effectively cornered, we only need to nudge one customer off the mountain top to create an avalanche of business." Nick started to gather up the papers. "I'm not minimizing the amount of work ahead, but you have to admit all the pieces are coming together rather nicely."

Keith looked directly at him, their minds operating in unison. "I know. It's almost scary."

As he walked into the lobby of the Mother's Milk manufacturing company, the first thing that hit Nick was the smell—the sweet aroma of chocolate was overwhelming. Keith spoke to the receptionist, and she motioned for them to take one of the chairs in the small waiting area. They barely had time to seat themselves when a much older, gray-haired gentleman, wearing dark slacks and a short-sleeved dress shirt appeared.

"Welcome," he boomed. "I'm Carl Johanssen. Which one of you is Keith?"

Both Keith and Nick stood instantly, and Keith extended his hand. "Good Morning. I'm Keith Dickson, and this is Nick Gardner."

They shook hands briefly, and Carl turned to Nick. One of the techniques that Nick used to build rapport with a new prospect was to pretend that the person was someone he already knew very well. Looking at Carl's pale, weathered face and light blue eyes, he decided that Carl was like his favorite grandfather, who was gentle, about the same size, and very intelligent. The warmth that came through Nick's voice when he spoke was genuine. "Hello Carl. It's nice to meet you. I really appreciate your taking the time to fit us into your schedule."

Carl looked up at Nick, assessing him openly, and then responded in kind. "Nice to meet you too, son. I'm always willing to invest time with someone who can help me improve my business."

Nick nodded. "Well, let's see what we can do. I don't know if it's something you had planned to do first, but I know it would really help me if we could start with a tour of your facility."

Carl laughed, patting Nick on the shoulder. "That's good, son. My mama used to think the way to a man's heart is through his stomach, but I can see that you know differently. It's by getting him to talk about his business. Come on. I'll give you the fifty-cent tour."

For the next half hour, Carl walked them through the four buildings that comprised the Mother's Milk plant. He started the tour at the same place that his manufacturing process began—with the arrival of raw materials—and followed the process through to final packaging for the consumer. Because Carl knew of their interest in carrageenan, he highlighted its role whenever possible.

Carl showed them the enormous stack of burlap bags that contained the powdered carrageenan he purchased from his Japanese supplier. He showed them the machines—nothing more than industrial-sized mixing bowls—that blended the refined carrageenan with the powdered chocolate, sweeteners and other additives. As they walked through the buildings, Keith asked technical questions, the responses to which Nick tried to follow. He tuned out, however, when Carl said something about "the presence of lamellar layers of emulsifiers in the protein matrix," and Keith asked for a clarification of "the relationship between the hydrophilic and lipophilic parts." When the other men were through with the discussion, Nick asked Carl about the capital base of his business and some particulars about their management team, which Carl answered without hesitation.

The end of the tour was marked by the ceremonious opening of a chilled carton of Mother's Milk. In a small tasting room, Carl produced three polished glasses and emptied the contents of the carton into them. "Notice something?" he said, pointing to the milk. "See how the color is uniform throughout the glass? That's why we use carrageenan. It keeps the chocolate evenly distributed. Look inside—no lumps of chocolate or sludge, like you'd see in the bottom of our competitors' cartons."

Nick raised his glass to his lips, savored the aroma, and then, after an initial sip, nearly drained his glass in a couple of swallows. "Carl, that is delicious. It's a good thing my boys aren't here, or they'd empty your whole sampling case."

Carl laughed and thanked him, then led the way to his office, where they settled in for their meeting.

Nick wasted no time. "Carl, Keith has already told you why we wanted to meet with you, but let me summarize our situation briefly so we're all on the same page, OK?"

Nick waited for a response from Carl before proceeding, and Carl nodded. "You currently buy your carrageenan from a supplier with Philippine facilities, but not from one of the big boys. We're setting up a company that will dominate the supply end of the business throughout the Philippines, and are starting the process of finding our first partnering customers. We'd like to find out if it makes sense for you to do business with us." He made a small gesture with his eyebrows, as if to say "Everything OK, so far?"

This time Nick didn't have to search for a nonverbal response. Carl jumped right in. "Keith was a little more cagey about his comments on the telephone, but I sorta' read between the lines and thought that's what you boys had in mind. I'm interested in what you have to say, but first I've got a question. What do you mean by 'partnering'?"

Nick looked Carl right in the eye. "You probably already know this, but I want to make it crystal clear. We're in the early stages of launching this company. We're not here to strap some seaweed on your back and send you an invoice. We've got a much different view. We want long-term relationships, not just transactions, and the only way we can accomplish that is by creating a completely open line of communication—the kind of communication that partners use. We need people who will tell us when we're doing well, and tell us when we're screwing up. See what I mean?"

"You bet, son. That's what I thought you meant, but I wanted to hear you say it."

"Let me start with a couple of questions," Nick paused and looked over at Keith, "and I'm sure Keith will jump in with the things that are on his mind." He looked back at Carl, confirming that their thinking was in sync. "I'll assume that we wouldn't be sitting here if everything was going well with your current carrageenan vendor. What kinds of issues do you have with them?"

As he asked the question, Nick flipped open his notebook and produced his pen. He looked across the table in silence and prepared to jot down Carl's response. He didn't have long to wait, and he didn't need to prod the elder man along with clarification questions. Carl started talking in animated, sometimes even angry tones, and he didn't stop for a full ten minutes.

Nick looked down at his notebook, which now held half a dozen pages of comments. Carl was obviously—and justifiably—outraged by the treatment he had received from the hands of his supplier. In Carl's view, it was as if he was riding a go-cart on the freeway—and worse, going against the traffic. Everything, he said, went their way, and whenever he tried to negotiate something better—no matter how small or insignificant it might be—they steamrollered right over him.

Nick looked up at Carl. "Let me get this straight. They make you purchase a year's supply when you order?" Carl nodded.

"And you have to pay, in full, thirty days before it's shipped?" Nick asked, making sure that the incredulity in his voice was unmistakable.

Carl shot back, "And that's not the half of it. I also have to place a positional order for the following year, and they take a nonrefundable deposit for that as well."

Nick shook his head. "I guess they haven't heard about some of the more modern supply philosophies, have they? It looks like instead of practicing JIT they believe in JIID."

Carl looked back at him with a questioning look on his face. "Son, I've heard of 'Just In Time,' but I'm not familiar with the other one."

"Sorry, Carl," said Nick. "It stands for 'Jam It In Deeper,' and it looks like they've got it down to a science." Carl laughed.

"Moving right along, could you describe for us the process you use to qualify vendors?"

Carl answered, again at length, but this time with Keith and Nick periodically interrupting to clarify his statements. Keith asked why Carl didn't buy from one of the big companies, and was told that they thought Mother's Milk was too small a company for them to deal with. He added, "I wouldn't say they're arrogant, exactly. It's more like they simply don't care what people think about them. In a way, they're like some of the old timers in the manufacturing game."

Carl smiled at the expressions on their faces. "I mean the *real* old timers, not the young bucks like me. You know what I mean— the kind of guys who know how much they can build efficiently and then manufacture to that plan. They're satisfied to sell what they make, and not have to put up with the headaches of growing their business."

Nick nodded. "From what we've been able to learn, it appears that they pay their salespeople a straight salary, and the only time it makes any sense to do that is when you're not interested in growth."

Nick shifted his posture in the chair, subtly signaling a shift in the conversation. It was time for a trial close. "Carl," he began, "let me ask you this. I'm certain that our corporate philosophies are close enough to your own that we'll sail through your vendor qualification process, but I still want to do everything I can to let us start doing business as quickly as possible." He nodded his head almost imperceptibly, pausing only long enough for Carl to join him and nod his own.

He continued. "It's going to take us some time to make sure that we can deliver the right product. I'd like to begin preparing a sample for you to test and also start going through your vendor qualification process at the same time. Is there any way that you could let us have the exact product specifications that you require in the next day or so?"

Carl smiled. "No problem."

Nick, inwardly elated, remained outwardly calm. "What size sample do you think you will need to validate our product?"

"I'll need to check on that, but the amount we'll need for the laboratory testing will be minimal—probably five pounds. Once we get past that stage, of course, we'll need considerably more so that we can gradually incorporate it into our blending process. For the final production tests, we're probably talking about a sample of a metric ton."

"Right," agreed Nick. "That makes sense. OK. Well, assuming that our sample product meets with your approval, how much would you plan to purchase from us, on an annual basis?"

Carl looked him in the eye. "What price are we talking?"

"You're currently paying two dollars and twenty-five cents a pound?"

Carl seemed surprised. "For semi-refined, yes. I can see you've done your homework."

Nick shot back, "Of course. You'd be disappointed in me if I hadn't."

The smile broadened on Carl's face. He didn't speak.

"We're selling it at the same price."

Carl looked back at him, considering. After a moment, he said, "Are you sure you wouldn't like to give me a little discount, my being your first customer and all?"

Nick grinned. "When you hear the rest of my proposal, you'll consider yourself lucky that I'm not asking you for more. I'll charge you the same price that you're paying now, but I think you'll like my terms a whole lot better. We'll require a deposit of ten percent with your order, a letter of credit, and the balance due within fifteen days of delivery.

Nick studied the man's face before continuing. "Nothing will be nonrefundable, and we won't require you to order a year's supply.

You can, of course, order as much as you'd like, but we'll accept your orders, and schedule our shipments on a quarterly basis.

"If you think about it," said Nick, "we'll be freeing up a lot of your working capital and greatly reducing any interest or carrying costs you now have. With the benefits we can give you in cash flow and reductions in your cost of capital, why should we accept a lower price for our product? Why would you ask us to take a lower profit?"

Carl stared back at him, and then swallowed. "Son, you're absolutely right. I'm sure we can work something out."

Nick nodded. "Thank you. I appreciate your trust. And, in consideration of your becoming our first customer—our first partner—here's what I'll do. I'll give you the first metric ton for free, if you'll agree to pay the shipping costs."

"Done."

"So, back to my original question, once we successfully pass through the testing process, how much would you plan to purchase from us, on an annual basis?"

Carl looked over at both of them, and then spoke directly to Nick. "Normally, I'd start off by giving you a small percentage of my purchases—twenty percent or so—and see how well things went. But this is a different situation. I feel like those other guys are holding me hostage, and, frankly, I can't wait to tell them to take a hike. If you can deliver to my specifications, I'll give you all my business, right now."

Nick and Keith shared a quick glance of surprise. "Excellent," said Nick. "And just how much might that be?"

Carl didn't flinch. "Somewhere just under 600 metric tons."

Three hours later, Nick called Laurie from the Minneapolis airport as he waited for his flight to board. "You wouldn't believe it," he exclaimed. "When he told us how much he'd be willing to buy, you could have knocked us over with a feather. In a single year, this customer will be buying about one and half million dollars from us. We had no idea that he used so much carrageenan. It's unbelievable!"

"That's great, Nick," said Laurie, "It's all coming together, isn't it?"

Nick hesitated momentarily, "It sure looks that way."

Laurie lapsed into a brief silence herself. "So, are you coming home yet?"

"No, we're just getting ready to catch our flight to Chicago to meet with another prospect. They're in an entirely different kind of business, and I don't think they have the same kind of volume as the guy that we just met with. But after the way things went today, I can't wait to see what we discover. Our meeting is at nine tomorrow morning, and we ought to make our three-thirty flight without any problem. I should be home by dinner time. I love you, and I can't wait to see you. Kiss the boys for me."

It had taken Nick three faxes to the Philippines before he received a response from Romy. Given the inadequacy of the telephone systems in that part of the world, he didn't worry too much about not getting an earlier reply. Although he felt mildly frustrated, the lack of instant communication was something they'd have to learn to work around.

During their last meeting together, they had agreed to do most of their updates by fax. It was not only their most cost-effective method of keeping in touch, but it also solved many of the issues created by multiple time zones and unreliable postal service. At this point, however, they had made enough progress that a telephone conversation was appropriate, and scheduling that call had been the subject of their faxes.

At six o'clock in the morning, the telephone rang.

"This is Nick."

"Hello, Nick. How are you?" The connection was good. Even the slight static on the line couldn't mask the cheerfulness in Romy's voice.

"I'm fine, Romy. How about yourself?"

"Great, thank you. And how is the cowboy?"

Nick smiled. "She's well, and sends her love. It's a little too early for her to be up, or she'd say hello herself. It's good to hear your voice. We've got a lot to talk about."

"Good news, I hope?"

"That's what you pay me for, isn't it? But first, tell me what's been happening over there?"

"Certainly. I'll start with the work the attorney is doing. As you know, he has been leading our effort to secure options on all the properties we want, and of the two hundred and thirty two sites, he has already finalized a hundred and eighty-eight."

"That's great, Romy! I really didn't think he'd be able to move that quickly. How much money has he spent?"

Romy laughed. "Papa said that would be your reaction, and I will let him know that you did not disappoint him."

Nick chuckled in return. "What can I say?"

"You do not need to worry, the attorney is right on budget. Some of the options have been more expensive than others, but, on average, we are right where we thought we would be."

"Great. And how many of the people we've approached have declined our offer?"

"None of them."

"Excuse me? I thought you said that there were—," Nick hesitated for an instant, mentally doing the math, "forty-four sites we wanted that we hadn't been able to option."

"That is true, but that is not what you asked."

"Then you're saying that no one we've talked to has turned us down? Every piece of property we've tried to option we've been able to get?"

"Yes, Nick, that is correct."

Nick was silent for a moment. Remarkable, he thought, but strange, as well. He couldn't imagine that number of people being interested in accepting their offer—or, in fact, any kind of offer—in that short a time frame. "Romy," he asked, "this may sound like a stupid question, but I'm a little surprised. If everyone is agreeing to our offer this quickly, we must be overpaying, don't you think?"

"As I said before, Nick, you do not need to worry about the budget. The reason the attorney is succeeding is simply because he is very good at what he does."

"If you say so, Romy. How about the sites near Coron, have we finalized those yet?"

"Yes, and you can tell Laurie that her island is now the cornerstone of our company's production capacity."

"She'll be delighted. So, tell me, how are we doing on the tests?"

An almost tangible bubble of excitement burst through the telephone line as Romy spoke. "They are exactly where we thought they would be, Nick. Tying the plants closer together does not seem to make any difference in their rate of growth. Tripling the density of the tie lines actually does triple the growth capacity."

"Good work, Romy. Did all the sites get the same result?"

Romy paused. "Well, now that you mention it, two of the sites were virtually identical, and one of them was slightly less—about ten percent less, it seems."

Nick thought for a second. "Were all the cuttings you used from the same plant?"

"Yes."

"And everything else was the same?"

"Yes."

"Which test location had the slower growth rate?"

"The one just east of Camiguin."

"Hang on a second, Romy." It took Nick several seconds before he found the site on his map. "Right, here it is.

"You know, Romy, that's pretty far north, and it's also our only test site that's so exposed to the Pacific Ocean. Why don't you get a water sample and get it tested. Maybe there's a difference in the salinity or something. Come to think of it, when they get the sample, have them check the temperature of the water as well, and let's compare it to the temperature at the other sites. If it's only a ten percent differential, I'm not too concerned. But our supply position is the strategic advantage our company has. We might as well learn everything possible about how to make this stuff grow quickly."

"No problem, Nick."

"OK, let's see. Next on my list is Papa's progress in establishing the grower's cooperative. How's he doing so far?"

"I do not know, for sure. He left here last week, and telephoned me from Zamboanga, in southeast Mindanao, when he arrived there. He is scheduled for his first set of meetings the day after to-morrow, and then he goes out into the archipelago. They have no phones out there, Nick, so he will be out of touch for a couple of weeks."

"All right. Anything else on your end?"

"I met a few management candidates, but I have not found any-one I really like yet."

"Take your time on that one, Romy. I'm sure you're already doing this, but please make sure that you talk to as many people as you can. We're really not in any hurry, and we'll be living with your decision for a long time."

"That is exactly what I had in mind. So tell me, what is new over there? I received your specifications. You must be making some real progress."

"Yep. Did you have any questions about the spec?"

"No. I reviewed it with the chemist in Manila, and he thought that, because the microbial levels need to be less than fifteen parts per million, the request was for a dairy application. Is that true?"

"You'd have to talk to Keith to get the technical interpretation, but yes, the interest in the semi-refined kappa carrageenan is spe-cifically for chocolate milk. As I understand it, that's why the par-ticle size and solubility are so critical. One hundred percent of our test shipment must pass through a one hundred and twenty mesh screen, and dissolve fully in milk at thirty-five degrees Fahrenheit."

"Right, Nicholas. It sounds delicious, does it not?"

Nick laughed. "By the way, Keith wanted me to clarify that the viscosity needed to be measured on a Brookfield viscometer, spindle number two, and that the reading has to be less than fifty-five CPS. I don't know exactly what it means, but I think it has to do with tolerance for the high alkalinity of cocoa."

"I will check on it, Nick, and also make sure we have access to the Brookfield device."

"Great. We need to do absolutely everything we can to make sure that we meet this spec. This customer could be big—really big. I don't want to give you any specific forecasts at this point, but I'll tell you that we've gotten strong indications of pent-up demand."

"I understand."

"Good. Any idea when you think you'll have the sample ready?"

Romy thought for a moment. "Well, a lot will depend on drying time, Nick. But if the weather cooperates, we should be able to begin the refining process by the end of next month."

"The end of October? It'll take that long?" Nick did some quick calculations. A moment later he said, "OK. I guess that's right. I'd hoped it would be sooner. Once we've started our planting cycles, we'll have a steady source of product, and delays like this shouldn't be an issue. I guess it's just part of the startup process, but I have to tell you—I've never been in a business before where I had to rely on the weather. I'm going to have to get used to the idea that I can't make the rain stop or the plants grow faster.

"Anyway, if it won't be ready until then, we might just end up delivering the sample to the customer personally. We're scheduled to be in Mindanao for the ceremony the first week of November, so maybe Keith or I will carry it back home with us in our luggage."

"That is, I believe, what you would call excellent customer service."

"That's a fact. The only problem is that we'd be setting a pretty tough standard, Romy. I'd hate to have to make a delivery of two metric tons with my carry-on suitcase."

Romy laughed. "I will remember that, Nick. Anything else we need to discuss?"

"Nope, that's all from here."

"All right then. Take care of yourself, and please remember to give my regards to the Sultana."

September 26, 1991
San Francisco, California

Nick was sipping from his second cup of coffee when Keith walked into the lobby of the downtown Hyatt Hotel. Keith often ran a few minutes late. He was always trying to cram in one more telephone call from his car, or propose one more "final" thought to a client. Although Nick was normally irritated by Keith's tardiness, he didn't mind it so much today. He had put the finishing touches on their business plan the night before, something that signaled to him the end of the preparation stage of a new venture. The time to actually start doing things was approaching rapidly.

Nick didn't stand up to greet Keith. "Traffic a little heavy?"

Keith put his briefcase down and walked over to get a cup of coffee from the lobby bar. He returned a minute later with a full cup and saucer. "No, it really wasn't too bad. I had to finish up one more thought on a conference call. Sorry I'm late."

"Don't sweat it. So. Did you get a chance to go through the plan?"

"Yeah, and you were right. The numbers look *too* good."

Nick smiled. "I hate it when that happens, don't you? Anyway, I wanted to start by taking twenty minutes or so to walk through the nums, line by line. Not just as a sanity check, but also as a dry run for presenting this stuff. OK?"

Keith nodded. "Go for it."

"OK. Lets start with the first twelve-month operating plan and then look at figures for the second year. As you can see, the top line is as conservative as I could possibly make it. Just under three million dollars in sales for the first year," Nick flipped to the next page, "and five and a half million in the second year, are much less than we actually expect to do."

"You're right about that." Keith looked over at Nick. "This really is an unusual situation, isn't it? I mean, we already have orders for nearly six million dollars in our first year, and some of those customers will increase their orders the following year."

"I know, Keith, and it's only October. Our first year projections don't even start until January. It's inconceivable to me that we won't get any additional customers in the next fifteen months."

"So why did you cut back the projection for the first year? Why not go with six million?"

"You know the way I work, Keith—under-promise and over-deliver. No matter what goes wrong, what kind of surprises we get hit with, we'll be able to meet or beat three million in revenues. You and I might be disappointed not to hit seven or eight million, but I'd rather commit to doing less, and then look like heroes when we shoot out the lights and sell what we expect to sell.

"Besides, remember who is going to see this version—the venture capital guys down at Sand Hill Road. If we walk in there with a plan that showed what we thought we could really do, they'd think we'd been smokin' dope."

"OK. So what about the cost-of-sales figures?"

"I took exactly the opposite approach."

"They're fully-loaded."

"Right. And more than that, Keith. I stuck every single expense I could think of into them. What makes this business so amazing is that we really don't have any expenses for raw materials. Since we take a cutting for replanting at harvest, it's essentially free.

"In addition, you know how cheap our labor will be. Romy and I have gone around and around on this point, and the most we'll be paying each of the farmers in salary is about one thousand dollars a year. I wanted to pay more, but Romy convinced me that we'd create some real problems if we did that. Their average annual income per family is around eight hundred bucks, so you can see his point. We don't want people killing each other to come to work for us."

Keith nodded, so Nick continued. "Anyway, even if we sell eight million dollars in the first year, we're still talking about only eighteen hundred metric tons. All the cost-of-sales assumptions here are based on planting, growing, harvesting, drying, warehousing and shipping two thousand metric tons. And look. The most money I could credibly allocate to the cost-of-sales was only four hundred thousand dollars."

Keith looked over at him with a sly grin. "I don't think I've ever seen a plan before with gross profit margins of ninety percent."

"Tell me about it," laughed Nick. "It took balls to commit those figures to paper, knowing that I'm gonna be the one who has to explain them to a VC."

"See if you can keep a straight face."

"OK, now look at the next section. The operating expenses include every possible expense that the Philippine subsidiary unit might incur. We've got salaries for Romy and a ridiculously high number of the non-farming managers, as well as their overhead expenses. You know, the standard general and administration stuff—rent, office expenses, travel, depreciation, interest expense. I even plugged in a huge R&D budget, and look at the figure I used for outside services."

"What are you planning to do, Nick, have them hire every professional you know? How can a company in the Philippines with less than a hundred employees possibly spend half a million dollars on attorneys and accountants?"

Nick looked at Keith, serious for a moment. "Tell you the truth, Keith, I know we'll have to hire some 'consultants' over there to keep the skids greased. I'm not comfortable with it, but that's where I budgeted the spiffs we'll have to give to some of the local authorities."

"Outside services sounds a lot better than bribes, doesn't it? OK, so, even fully-loaded, you've still got an operating profit of nearly sixty-five percent. The last section—overhead—those are the numbers associated with the parent company?"

"Yep. As you look at those figures, do you see anything wrong?"

Keith didn't flinch. "No. I looked at them last night, and I don't see any way that we can spend more than six hundred thousand dollars on just the two of us." He grinned and shook his head. "Not if we take the market rate for compensation, and not if we don't need a fancy office. I can't see how we can spend that much on travel, unless you start to commute, first-class, to Minneapolis."

Nick nodded. "There are two reasons I made the travel number so high. The first one is that any venture capitalist who looks at it is going to know that it's too high, and I want them to see it as an indication of how conservative our numbers are."

"Besides, we might, in fact, end up sending some of our customers to the Philippines to see for themselves what we've created. But even that isn't the real reason."

Nick looked at Keith, squarely in the eyes. "It's funny. It's one thing to show a gross profit of ninety percent, but even I don't have the brass to show a pretax profit of more than fifty percent. Even though—if we only fill the orders we already have—our actual pretax profit should be significantly higher."

They were silent for a moment, digesting the exchange. Keith spoke first. "It's almost unbelievable. We're only talking about one percent of the existing market. If we earn a ten percent market share—"

Nick nodded. "I know. And if we wrap up the independent farmers and corner the market—"

"Jesus Christ—," breathed Keith softly.

"Pretty incredible, isn't it?"

"Sure is," replied Keith. "But I'm afraid that's not exactly what I was talking about." He indicated a couple of women who were walking through the lobby. "Look."

Nick glanced over his shoulder at the retreating, feminine forms. Both were tall and slender, wore fashionable business suits, and had great legs. Ah yes, he thought, the priorities of the single man.

He looked over at Keith, who was still watching the ladies walk away. "The brunette, right?"

Keith nodded, and finally looked back at Nick.

"Well, when you're done guessing what she looks like in a g-string, maybe you can guess how much capital we'll have to raise."

"Sorry, what was that?"

"The project. Our new company. Raising capital. So we can start making some money instead of spending our own," said Nick, regaining Keith's attention. "If you look at these figures, you'll see that the total of our expenses in the first year—even if we do six or seven million dollars in sales—is less than three million."

Nick looked at Keith with his hands spread open to emphasize his point. "When you consider the fact that we've already got orders and could actually ship product as early as the second quarter next year, we'll have positive cash flow way before the end of the year. You see what I mean? We don't need a large infusion of equity. We can damn near bootstrap this ourselves.

"Look at the cash flow projection, Keith. Even in a worst case scenario, the deficit never gets above two hundred thousand dollars. And that assumes *all* of these inflated expenses. If we defer some of them—if we simply don't take our own salaries, for example—then I could finance this myself. I take out a second on my house and put it into the business. Instead of getting a venture capital partner and giving away twenty-five percent of the company, you and I keep it. Instead of you getting only five percent of the company's stock, you could get twenty percent."

"And not take the company public?" asked Keith, carefully.

"It's an interesting position to be in, isn't it? I mean, here are our choices. Door number one, we do it ourselves and take a cash bonus every year. Each of us takes a million bucks or so, on top of salary. Door number two, we go to the venture capital guys and cut them in on it. We give up a certain amount of control, and don't run it like a small private company. They give us a couple of million dollars now, in exchange for probably twenty-five percent of our stock.

"You know the math as well as I do. Say that we discount the shit out of our projections, so that our pretax number is only thirty or forty percent. We're still talking about netting more than a million dollars, after taxes, and that's just in the first year."

Nick looked at Keith. "What valuation would you give this company? Given those numbers, what would you say the company is worth?"

Keith shook his head. "I see your point. It's hard to imagine a number of less than fifteen or twenty million."

Nick nodded, enthusiastically. "That's right. But say we knock that number down even further. Let's say we accept a valuation of twelve million. We sell a VC a quarter of the company for three million dollars—the complete amount of our first year operating expenses.

"Two years from now," Nick continued, "we go public. We're not showing after-tax profits of just one million dollars then—it's at least three or four million! What kind of multiple do you think the market would give us? Eight? Ten? Twenty-five times earnings?"

Keith leaned forward, hanging on Nick's every word.

"If it was only ten, which, given the margins and growth rate, seems ridiculously low, that means the market value of the company—in only two years—is forty million bucks."

Nick kept on rolling. "And look at the sex appeal of some of our markets. What do you think could happen if people start to recognize our company as the leading marketer of carrageenan—one of the best fat reduction products available. If the stock market heats up—"

Keith interrupted, finishing Nick's thought for him. "We could easily expect to get a price-earnings multiple of twenty-five, which would give the company a market value of at least a hundred million. The VC's stock would be worth twenty-five million, which would give them a return of almost ten times their initial investment."

"And?" Nick asked smugly, "How much is your own stock worth?"

The expression on Keith's face didn't change, but his eyes suddenly shone with a glitter that came from deep inside. Nick recognized it as the glimmer of greed. When Keith responded, it was in a husky voice that Nick had never heard from him before. "Five million. Jesus H. Christ. Five million bucks, probably more."

Nick sat back in the chair. "And we're still making a salary and a hefty bonus. So, like I said, some interesting choices. Have complete control over a smaller—but lucrative—pond, or go out and swim with the sharks in the ocean. What do you thing we should do?"

Keith raised his eyebrows. "Do you want me to make the appointment with the VC, or do you want to do it yourself? I mean, it's a no-brainer. It's the American way. More is better. If this is my shot at a quick five million, I'll do whatever it takes."

Nick looked over at his friend, slightly surprised. Not that he expected a different answer from Keith—it was the route he'd planned to take anyway. But the tone of Keith's voice had an insidious edge that made Nick uncomfortable. Maybe you never know what people will do for money, he thought to himself.

"OK, Keith, I'll make some calls. You know how busy those guys are. It might take some time to get in front of the right one. Whether we end up going with them or not, we might as well learn what they think of this."

Nick and Keith sat in a window booth at Buck's Restaurant having breakfast. The Old West decor and rustic charm of the place
belied the fact that many of the customers were talking about mul-
timillion-dollar deals over coffee and buckwheat pancakes. It was
easy to tell, Nick noted as he glanced at the other tables, which of
the players were from the nearby venture capital companies, and
which were the entrepreneurs seeking funding. It wasn't a simple
case of age versus youth. The ones in blue suit jackets, starched
shirts, and carefully-knotted neckties wanted the money; the more
casually—but expensively—clad diners were the venture capital-
ists.

Gesturing with his head towards one such table, Nick looked
over at Keith. "I'm glad we went California casual."

Keith nodded. "Look at these guys. They're so—earnest looking."

Nick grinned. "The last time I saw so many blue blazers was
when I was on a college campus, recruiting MBAs."

Keith took a bite of his toast. "Or at a convention of security
guards. So tell me, Nick, why Sand Hill Venture Partners? Those
guys have a great reputation, but they're supposed to be very
tough."

"It wasn't much of a decision, really. The truth is that, even with
our most aggressive terms, we're not asking for enough money to
interest the big name VC firms. The top tier guys want to invest a
minimum of ten or twenty million in a deal, and I just can't come
up with a reason for that much money. We're also a little small for
the next level of VCs, because even they don't get too excited un-

less a company needs five million or more."

He took a sip of his grapefruit juice. "I also think it's important that we work with someone who's been in the business for a while. So when you eliminate the big boys and the ones that are just getting started, you end up with a pretty short list.

"SHVP is the biggest of the boutique VCs—the ones that specialize in unusual situations. Besides, Bart Stevenson is their managing partner, and I knew he'd take my call. He was an investor in the first good-sized company that TGG turned around, and I know he thought I did a good job."

Keith was surprised. "Are you talking about TOT? Stevenson was one of their investors?"

Nick nodded. "Yep."

Keith's eyes lit up. "Geez, Nick, he must think you walk on water *and* change clothes in a telephone booth. TOT was so far dead that it would have been a waste of electricity just to hook them up to life support. When you got there, they weren't even warm to the touch."

"Well," Nick responded, with a shrug. "It's true that Bart not only escaped watching them go through a liquidation proceeding. We also found another investor to take him out of the deal. He probably made ten or eleven percent on his initial investment. Not his target rate of return, for sure, but, then again, not at all bad, under the circumstances."

Nick took another sip of his juice. "Anyway, Keith, PRMC isn't the typical technology or biotech venture that these guys are used to seeing. The most important thing they look for—aside from an obscenely high return—is the quality of the management team. I figured we'd start with someone who wouldn't question our management abilities."

"That makes sense. Did you try to get in to see anyone else?"

"Nope. I don't want to shop this around just yet. If Bart couldn't see us, or hadn't liked what he heard when we spoke on the phone, I would have gone to the next one down the list, but he was my first choice."

"Right. Sounds good, Nick." He slid across the red seat and stood up. "Excuse me for a minute. That coffee is going right through me."

Nick sat in silence, absorbed in his thoughts, until Keith returned to the booth with a mysterious look on his face. "What is it? You look like you just won the lottery."

Keith shook his head. "You wouldn't believe it. You know how the bathroom here is wall-papered with maps? Well, guess what map is in the stall. The Philippines! And, if I'm right, the holder for the toilet paper marks the location of our test site near Busuanga."

"You're kidding."

"Hey, it's a sign. It means that PRMC is destined to be a success. So where were we?"

Nick laughed. "The meeting."

"Oh, yeah." Keith took a sip of his water. "Now, I know we've both looked at this thing from a lot of different angles, but these VCs are famous for finding flaws in plans. Stevenson's supposed to be one of the best. What problems do you think he'll find with ours?"

Nick responded immediately. "There's only one I can think of—why we're bringing this opportunity to him so early. Given our cash flow projections, it's almost a bankable deal even without his funds, right?"

Keith looked at him, realizing that Nick was finished. "And? How are you going to answer that?"

"By telling him the truth." Nick pushed his plate to the side and brushed away some crumbs. "That we want an initial public offering within the next two years, and figure that if we align ourselves now with the right investment partner, getting through the IPO process successfully—and with the least amount of possible dilution—will be much easier for us. Remember, even though you and I have been with companies when they went public, neither of us were the company's CEO and we didn't work with the bankers. We were both farther down the food chain. So we could use someone with his reputation and experience.

"I think Bart's ego is big enough to bite on that one, but I'd still be surprised if he really swallowed such a superficial response. He'll question us a lot more. He'll keep drilling down deeper until he gets at the core. After all, Keith, the heart of the issue is basic: why does any company go public? I mean, look at PRMC. Aside from our own personal cash flow, what does the company need to raise money for?

"We don't need to hire a big sales force, because our market doesn't work that way. We'll have all the sales success we could ever hope for with just the two of us and a couple of major account reps.

"We also don't need money for a big Research and Development lab. The R&D in this industry is all done by the customers. We don't need any bricks and mortar, and asking for funding for a big marketing rollout budget is problematic, too. The investment community knows as well as we do that, in a market this size, the only cost-effective way to get customers is through direct selling.

"There is just no obvious necessity for PRMC to go public," concluded Nick, watching Keith carefully, "So I had to expand our vision a bit to come up with one."

Keith looked intently back at Nick, who remained silent, giving Keith time to digest this information. In a few seconds, Keith spoke. "We're going to integrate vertically, right? Not just supply the raw material, but get into the processing end of the business, as well."

Nick grinned. "I thought you might come to the same conclusion as I did." He continued. "It's the only logical scenario I could come up with in which PRMC required an initial public offering. It does, however, have some worms of its own."

"For example?"

"Well, if you follow the idea through, it goes something like this. For the first year or two, we concentrate on capturing—if not cornering—the supply end of the market, and pay the companies that already have large processing plants to do our refining work on a contract basis. Then, with our business concept proven, we go to the market and raise funds to build our own processing plant, right?"

Keith nodded, so Nick went on. "Where do we build the plant? As close as possible to the source of raw material, of course, and that means we ask U.S. investors to kick in fifteen or twenty million dollars to construct a facility in the Philippines."

Nick sat back in the seat for a moment. "There, my friend, is the first worm—the risks associated with owning property on foreign soil. We'll have to deal with a whole slew of issues that center on our ability to get our money out of there if something goes wrong. The Philippines don't have the best reputation in the business world, and their government has already nationalized at least one of their major agricultural industries, so the situation starts to look a little ugly."

Keith looked puzzled. "But I thought that was why we structured the two companies the way we did. PRMC owns the Philippine subsidiary, which means that the financial dealings of the sub are all controlled by us. None of the big money touches the sub; it all flows right to the parent company. PRMC sends out all the invoices, and the customers write the checks to us, don't they?"

Nick nodded. "That's right. The way we have these companies structured, PRMC is rock-solid, but the subsidiary unit is a different matter. It's a Philippine legal entity, a corporation operating in their country, so it has different elements of risk. You know how it works, Keith—potential for exposure increases in proportion to the value of assets.

"We might have to consider the processing plant as a cost of doing business, and be prepared—in a worst-case scenario—to simply abandon it. Then again, you would think our partners over there could pass legislation to eliminate the risk of nationalization."

"So, Nick, if Stevenson asks about this, how are you going to answer?"

Nick smiled. "Come on Keith, don't rush me. I still have at least half an hour." He signaled the waitress for the check. "Speaking of rushing, we'd better get out of here."

Two and a half hours later, Nick steered the car out of the Sand Hill Venture Partners parking lot on to Sand Hill Road, heading west towards Interstate 280. "Well," Nick began, glancing quickly over at Keith, "that was fun, wasn't it?"

Keith was still shaking his head. "You're not kidding. We couldn't have written a better script ourselves."

"Well, I wouldn't go quite that far, but it did illustrate the power of effective questioning, didn't it?"

"You did a super job, Nicholas."

Nick nodded, deflecting Keith's compliment, "I didn't actually sell him—I just asked him the right questions so that we could all reason things out together. And you know what? I enjoyed answering his questions. It made me feel like we *had* thought of everything."

Keith laughed. "It was hard to keep a straight face when he questioned you about the risks of fixed asset ownership in the Philippines. By the way, your response—did that just come to you on the fly?"

"Sort of. If you think about it, if we truly control the growing end of the business—which we'll be able to do through the growers' co-op and the prestige of the Sultancy—we're invincible when it comes to processing and selling. If we don't like the terms we get from the processing plants, we simply cut off their carrageenan supply."

"Right. That hadn't occurred to me. So it looks like it's a done deal."

"Well, don't forget, we still have work to do. It's not like he's wiring the money into our account today—although I sure wouldn't mind it. We still have to get the farmer's cooperative put together. But if we can get enough of the independent farmers on our side, nothing can stop us."

The family was seated at their long wooden trestle table for dinner. Almost on the eve of their journey, the boys were restless and trying to sit quietly, but were too excited to succeed.

"So," Nick began, "let me take a minute to walk you through the final schedule. OK?" Nick stopped and looked at each of them. "Keith and I leave tomorrow, arrive in Manila on Friday, and go to Quezon City to decompress for the weekend. You all leave here on Saturday, arrive there on Sunday, and I'll meet you at the airport. While you get some sleep and adjust to the changes in time zones, Keith and I will have meetings with our partners."

"Dad?" asked Sean, "Is the jet lag going to mess us up?"

Nick smiled. "It'll be easier for you guys to handle it than it will be for Laurie and me. It'll be a couple of days before you feel normal, but don't worry about it.

"Anyway, you won't do much of anything on Monday, and on Tuesday we'll all fly down to Mindanao for the ceremony, which happens the next day. From there, we'll visit a couple of the smaller, more remote islands, and then head back to Manila. Keith has some other meetings to go to, so he'll be off on his own after the ceremony. Our flight back here has a stopover in Hong Kong, so you'll get a chance to check that out, as well. Any questions?"

"Yeah. Are we gonna get to ride in a jeepney?" asked Max.

"You bet."

"Are we going to see Mom's Island?" asked Sean.

"I hope so," Laurie answered. "I keep telling your Dad to sell this house and move us all there." She looked over at Nick. "Each of the boys need to keep a journal of the trip for school, so I bought them bound books with blank pages to write in. They've also selected some things to take with them as gifts for people we meet."

"I'm taking a carton of my trading cards," Max announced. "I've got duplicate sets of the Forty Niners, so I'm gonna give them away, and I also have a lot of Chicago Bulls stuff. I talked to one of my teachers, and he said that basketball is their favorite sport."

"I'm bringing some maps," chimed in Sean. "Really big, colorful ones. They show not only the countries of the world, they also have a lot of scientific stuff on them. My homeroom teacher also gave me some posters that she doesn't use anymore. One of them shows the periodic table, another a timeline of world history, and another has diagrams showing the layers of human anatomy."

"Good job, you guys." Nick took a bite of steak, glancing down the table at Laurie. "And you, my dear, what are you bringing? A couple dozen cases of wine, perhaps? Some bowling balls?"

Laurie's responded tartly, "As a matter of fact, no." Then her voice eased as she spoke to the boys. "Your Dad is worried that our suitcases will be too heavy, even though that's only a temporary problem. The gifts we're bringing will be remembered by the people we give them to for a long time. If it's a little awkward for us to carry them, so what?"

"OK, OK," Nick backpedaled. "So, really, what are you bringing?"

Laurie put her fork down and launched into her explanation. "I went to the fabric store and loaded up on cloth. I got several bolts of the cotton prints that they liked so much in Coron, and then went into the city to get some things for Eleanor that are a little more special.

"Now that I've seen her and the way she lives, I was able to pick out some silks and embroidered fabrics that will look absolutely beautiful with her skin." She spoke to the boys. "Madame Dimakuta is a remarkable woman. Her father arranged her marriage to her husband when she was really just a girl—not much older than you, Sean."

Sean's eyes widened.

"Guys, we've already told you that Eleanor and Alec are Muslims," Nick said. "We've talked about their beliefs and they way they observe them. Does anyone want to give me a quick summary of what you remember?"

Sean spoke up first. "Instead of the Bible, they read the Koran, which is based on what God said to the prophet Mohammed. They get cleaned up and pray five times a day, bowing towards the east, towards Mecca."

"Perfect, Sean," said Nick, "except for one thing. Muslims pray facing the east, but in that part of the world, where is Mecca?" He paused for a moment. "See what I mean? In the Philippines, they pray facing the west. Anything else?"

"Yeah," said Max. "They don't smoke and they don't drink alcohol. And they never eat with their left hands. You're gonna be in trouble, Sean."

"It's true." Laurie addressed Sean, the only left-handed member of the family. "I'm afraid we'll have to tie your hand behind your back so you don't forget. What else?"

Sean chuckled. "Muslim men can have more than one wife."

"That's right," interjected Nick. "Men are allowed to have as many as four wives. When we're over there, you'll notice that women, even though they are equal to men in the eyes of the law, are treated differently. They're expected to cover their hair, and some Muslim sects require that women's faces be veiled, as well."

"Does Alec have more than one wife?"

"Actually, Max, he does."

Laurie exclaimed, "I didn't know that."

"Yep. Papa told me. He has two wives. Eleanor was his first, and then, a couple of years ago, he took another." He looked at Laurie. "She's much younger, I understand. Maybe we'll get the chance to meet her when we're in Mindanao."

Laurie shot back, a thin smile on her face, "Well don't start getting any ideas. Just because you're a Sultan doesn't mean you're going to have another wife."

"Don't worry, Sweets, you're more than enough for me."

Nick continued. "It's customary for the newly crowned Sultan to receive the gift of a ceremonial sword. So I thought it would be appropriate to give Alec a gift of thanks." He looked over at Laurie. "I've decided to give him my gold pocket watch."

She looked back at him, surprised. "The one you got from your grandfather?"

Nick nodded. "It's really the only small and transportable thing I have that means something special to me. If he is going to make me a brother, it seems like the right kind of gesture for me to make in return. Besides," he said, gesturing with his eyes at the boys, "it saves me the decision of which one of these guys to give it to."

"I also made a set of boxes for Eleanor, down in the shop. There's six of them, each one a little smaller than the next, so that they nest just inside each other. I used some contrasting hardwoods—some of that thin African Padauk and a spalted maple insert on the lid. It's nice."

"That's sweet," replied Laurie. "And giving Alec the watch is a great idea. I can just see him pulling it out of his vest pocket when he's on the floor of the Senate—telling everyone around that it was a gift from his American business partner."

Nick nodded.

"Can we please be excused?" chorused the pair of boys.

"Wait a second, guys. Listen up." Nick made eye contact with both of them. "This is important. I'm counting on you to make traveling easy for Laurie. Behave, stick together, and do whatever she says. The first time she asks. Without any questions. Understand?

"OK. And another thing. You're going to be guests, not just in someone else's house, but in someone else's country. Do not," Nick slowed his speech, "I repeat, do not do anything that will make me angry with you. And remember. The most important thing of all is to stay together. Got it?"

PART SIX

STONE MARKERS

Nick sat across the table from Keith in the restaurant of the Sulo Hotel. Sharing one of the larger booths along the wall, they sipped hot coffee, trying to force their bodies to shrug off the effects of jet lag.

"Your description of this place was perfect," Keith observed. "The room is clean and quiet, but it's also definitely rough. Since the only thing we're doing here is decompressing, though, it's fine. It's a great price-performer."

Nick laughed. Leave it to Keith to break everything down into marketing terms.

Keith gestured over to the buffet in the center of the restaurant. "Is this something special, or do they do this every day?"

"It must be Sunday brunch. They don't have anything this fancy on weekdays, that's for sure. Wait 'til you see this place tomorrow—every table will be taken by guys doing business over breakfast."

Keith grinned. "Just like Buck's, right?"

"Seriously, you may find it hard to believe, but some powerful people hang out here. I don't know if you remember, but when we took the taxi here from the airport, I pointed out a big building to you. The one that looks sort of like a hospital—not too far from here? That's the Philippine Mint, and the Director eats here every morning. I'll introduce you to him when I see him. He gave Laurie and I a great tour, and, if there's time, I'm going to ask him to show the boys. Maybe you'd be interested, too."

"In looking at a bunch of printing presses?" asked Keith skeptically. "Maybe. Given the number of publishing clients we've worked with though, I think I've been there and done that."

Nick took a sip of his coffee. "I don't think so, Keith. There's a lot more to the place than just printing presses. They also have facilities for minting coins and making bars of gold."

"Gold? I didn't think there was enough mining in the Philippines to warrant something like that."

Nick nodded. "That's what I thought as well, before we toured the place. But the gold doesn't come from mines, it comes from Yamashita's treasure."

Keith stared back at him blankly.

"Oh, I didn't tell you about that, did I? I forgot about it until just now. It's a great story." He took another sip.

"It seems that when the Japanese attacked Pearl Harbor, they conducted a simultaneous attack on Southeast Asia. A General named Yamashita led the secondary effort and blitzed through a bunch of countries in something like six months. He wasn't trying to take just the land, though, he was after the treasuries—the gold reserves—of each country. Yamashita amassed an unbelievable amount of wealth in just those few months. I can't recall the exact number, but it was at least several thousand tons of gold. Billions of dollars worth at the time, and, with inflation, worth more than a trillion dollars today."

"A *trillion* dollars?" asked Keith in disbelief.

"That's just part of the story. Yamashita tried to send the gold back to Japan to help finance the war effort, but some of the ships carrying his cargo were sunk. He spent the rest of the war holed up here in the Philippines, burying the treasure."

"You're kidding."

"Nope. According to the legend, he used POWs to dig tunnels throughout the Philippines to bury the treasure. He booby trapped the sites with bombs, and made maps of the hiding spots so that the only he—or someone with the maps—would be able to recover the fortune. He was captured and convicted of war crimes, and died without ever telling anyone how to get to his treasure."

"Has any of it ever been found?" asked Keith.

"That's what I've been told. The story takes an interesting twist here, because President Marcos gets involved. The stories about his greed and corruption are true. He had his hand in everything. But apparently a large part of his fortune came from the Yamashita treasure."

Keith, who was following his every word, simply nodded.

"And that's where the mint comes in. Marcos needed a way to melt down the gold statues and stuff that were recovered into bullion." Nick made a pointing gesture. "So, he builds the Mint."

"This is incredible," said Keith, leaning forward. "Why didn't you tell me this story earlier?"

"I've been so busy working on building our own fortune that I forgot about it. I guess I also forgot to tell you about the dinner Laurie and I had on our last visit with the head of The Committee.

"When Corazon Aquino was elected President, her first official act was to create the Philippine Commission for Good Government, or, as they call it here, The Committee. The charter of the PCGG is to locate all of the money hidden by Marcos and return it to its rightful owners, the people of the Philippines.

"The Committee has *carte blanche*. They can do, basically, anything they want. They talk to whomever they want, whenever they want. One of the first people they met with was Papa—he used to work with Marcos."

"Oh, shit," exclaimed Keith softly. "That's right."

"Relax. It's no big deal. The Committee has talked to Papa a lot of times, and they've never found anything wrong. As I see it, Papa is sort of the last honest man around here. He was in a position with Marcos where he would know a whole lot of valuable stuff, but he certainly doesn't have any money. I mean, not millions or billions of dollars.

"Papa told me that every time he gets involved in something new, the Committee chairman questions him again. The last time I was here, Papa, Laurie and I had dinner with a guy named

Ramierez, who heads up the Committee now. He spent an evening asking me questions—he'd checked us out pretty well. Anyway, Ramierez' job is to find assets hidden by Marcos so that he can return them to the government, but it's obvious to me that he plans to take a big cut for himself from everything that he finds. He's really a slimeball."

"Well, this is all news to me."

"Like I said, it's no big deal. But you see what I mean about this place? There's a lot more to it than meets the eye." Nick finished his coffee, and signaled to the waitress. "Could I please get a refill? It's Rita, isn't it?"

"Right away, Mr. Gardner," she exclaimed, looking up at him. "Welcome back. Will your wife be joining you?"

Nick smiled. " She arrives here later tonight. I'm sure you'll get to see her tomorrow. Our boys are coming with her as well, so you'll get to meet the whole family. This," he said, gesturing across the table, "is my partner, Keith Dickson. Keith, this is Rita."

"Welcome to the Philippines, Mr. Dickson, it's nice to meet you," she said warmly. "I'll be back in just a minute with fresh coffee."

"Thank you, nice to meet you as well," said Keith.

"Oh, Good!" said Nick suddenly. He slid across the bench to stand. "There's Romy."

"Romy, how are you?" called Nick, noting, as he approached, the gap in his exposed by a broad grin.

The two friends shook hands. "Nick, it is so good to see you again. Welcome back. Your flight was all right? You made it to the hotel without any problems, I hope?"

Nick laughed. "Aside from the usual case of buttlock, everything was fine. I'd like you to meet Keith Dickson."

"Hello, Romy, it's a pleasure to see you in person. I feel like I know you very well already."

Romy's grin grew even wider. "Thank you, Keith, but the honor is mine. Welcome to the Philippines." Romy grabbed the back of a chair and drew it up to their booth, so he could sit at the head of the table.

"So tell us what you've been doing," said Nick, as Rita returned with fresh coffee.

"I have good news to report," began Romy, enthusiastically. "I will start with the progress made by our attorney." Romy produced a three-ring binder, which contained a fat sheaf of loose leaf papers and slid it across the table to Nick. "Here is the documentation you requested, the list of all of our properties. The attorney has successfully secured options on all of the locations that we desired."

"All of them?" asked Nick incredulously, accepting the binder and giving it a cursory glance. "He was able to get an option to purchase every single one of them?" He ran his hands over his face and rubbed his eyes. "That's unbelievable."

Romy nodded, a big grin on his face. "Yes. I told you he was very good at what he did, Nick, and he completed his project right on budget as well."

"Good grief, Romy, I'm impressed," said Nick, reaching into the binder. After a moment of flipping through the thick stack of loose leaf pages, he pulled out a folded map. "This shows the locations of all of the properties we have optioned, right? It's the same one we discussed with Papa, isn't it, the last time I was here?"

As Romy nodded, Nick handed the map to Keith. "Take a good look at this. It will give you a idea of the sites that we now have under our control."

Keith accepted the map, folded it up, and put it in his briefcase without even looking at it.

"What this means, guys, is that we now have control over virtually every desirable location for growing carrageenan in the entire country. Maybe we'll use them, and maybe we won't, but the point is this—no one else will be able to get them and compete against us. I can't believe that the attorney got them all. It's amazing."

"Yes, and there is more good news," said Romy. "Using our new planting techniques, the growth rate for our crop during our most recent test actually exceeded the earlier results."

"In all of the sites?" asked Nick.

Romy looked at him, a serious expression dawning on his face. "Nearly all of them. Remember the one test location in the North? The one that had a slower growth rate?"

"In Camiguin?"

Romy nodded, appreciatively. "Yes. We did what you asked us to do. We took a sample of the water there for testing. The water temperature is significantly colder than the other sites, and that seems to be the reason for the slower growth. The longer the time of the test, the more pronounced the difference between the growth rate there and the growth rate in the test sites that have warmer water."

"Good," said Nick. "Since that location is the northernmost of our sites—and we don't have many sites that far north—we're in great shape. How are we doing on signing up farmers for the co-operative?"

Romy nodded his head, vigorously. "Papa is in Mindanao now. As you know, he was there for an extended visit about a month or so ago, but he met only with the tribal leaders in the small towns. Most of the men he met with hold the Muslim rank of *Hadj*. Once they understood who our partners are, they were very receptive. The *Hadjii* met with members of their own tribes during the last few weeks, and Papa went there to learn the results of those meetings.

"You know how poor the communication system is between here and the Mindanao Archipelago. But Papa sent me a fax last night, from Zamboanga. He had meetings with several *Hadjii* yesterday, and actually enrolled quite a number of farmers into the cooperative." Romy sat back in his chair, crossing his arms over his chest.

"And?" asked Nick, somewhat impatiently. "How many farmers did we sign up?"

Romy broke into a grin. "Nearly twenty thousand."

Nick's mouth fell open. He looked over at Keith, who appeared to be equally stunned. Nick spoke softly. "Did you say twenty thousand?"

Romy nodded. "Yes. And, Nick, that is only the first of several meetings that Papa will have down there. By the time he has traveled throughout the province, I would be surprised if that number does not grow considerably."

Nick looked over again at Keith. "Good Lord," he breathed, "this thing is gonna work. Everything is coming together perfectly." He asked Romy, "Have you heard anything about the sample we need for our chocolate milk customer? When will it be ready?"

"As I understand it, it will be ready later this week in Cebu. We made arrangements with one of the processing companies there to do the job specially for us."

"Great," enthused Keith. "If it's OK with the two of you, I'd like to volunteer to go there and pick it up. I want to go through one of the processing plants anyway. This way I'll be able to check them out and pick up the sample at the same time."

"Sounds good to me," said Nick.

"Certainly. I shall make the travel arrangements," added Romy.

"Thanks. I appreciate that," said Keith.

Nick took one last sip of his coffee. "Romy?" he started, "Did you get my latest fax? The one about my need to meet with Luis again?"

Romy nodded. "Yes, Nick, I did, and I was able to contact him and schedule a meeting for the two of you. He will stop by here tomorrow morning."

"Terrific," said Nick. "That's great. We never would have been able to get anywhere near this far along without you." He reached over and gave Romy's shoulder a hard squeeze. "Thank you. You've really done well.

Ignoring Romy's blush, Nick continued. "Things are going even better than we could have hoped for. There are only a couple of things left for us to button down, and then we're off to the races."

Nick got to the airport that night a half-hour early. Laurie and the kids' flight wasn't due in until after nine-thirty, and he waited outside the sliding glass doors of the customs area, enjoying the warmth of the evening. He was surprised to find so many people there, some busily milling about, others just standing idly. Nick paced the sidewalk along the length of the building, impatient for the safe arrival of his family, and aware that he stuck out in the crowd like the proverbial sore thumb.

It wasn't just the color of his skin, he thought, that drew people's eyes to him like iron filings to a magnet; it was his height. Even though there were no other Caucasians to be seen, he was aware that he towered over everyone else. Most of the older faces he saw glanced at him surreptitiously, not wishing to be rude, while the younger faces stared at him openly. Nick smiled back, not avoiding eye contact, but not speaking to anyone either.

Nearly at the end of the sidewalk that ran along the length of the building, Nick abruptly spun on his heel and reversed his direction, causing the man walking directly behind to bump into him. "Excuse me," said Nick, stepping aside.

The man looked up at Nick, a startled, almost alarmed expression on his face. As Nick started to repeat his apology, the man appeared to wink at him with his left eye, and then turned, melting back into the crowd without saying a word. Strange, thought Nick, as he resumed walking, it was almost as if the man had recognized him.

He walked nearly a hundred yards down to the other end of the building, arriving just as the sliding doors opened. He stepped inside, and found himself looking immediately into the faces of a dozen armed security guards who turned to look at him. Nick stopped, his eyes scanning the faces before him, and decided which of the men he should speak to. "Pardon me," he began, addressing the one with the most gold striping on his hat. "Is this where passengers come after they clear customs?"

"Yes, but you have to wait outside," the man replied.

"I'm here to meet my wife and children. Is it possible to wait for them at the gate?"

"Do you have your passport?"

"Yes," said Nick, reaching into his pocket and producing it.

The uniformed man examined his passport, and smiled. The other guards immediately seemed to lose interest in their conversations. "Yes," the guard said to Nick. "It is possible to wait for them inside. If you will pay their arrival tax now, I will see that you meet them at their gate."

"No problem," said Nick. "How much is it?"

The man hesitated for an instant. "Five hundred pesos."

Nick reached into his pocket and withdrew his money clip. He counted out the hundred-peso notes, and handed them to the man, who stuffed them into his pocket and turned, saying, "Follow me."

The guard escorted Nick to the gate, and they arrived just as the doors to the jetway opened. After perhaps twenty people had deplaned, Nick caught a glimpse of Laurie, bleary-eyed and tired. The boys followed, dragging, a few steps behind.

"Hey, Sweets!" he called, bringing a smile to her face. She scanned the crowd, looking for the source of the voice. Her eyes found him and she beamed.

"Dad!" came a chorus from the boys, who raced over for a hug.

Nick embraced them briefly and tousled their hair before stepping forward to hold Laurie in his arms for a long moment. She gave him a kiss, stopping only to ask, "How did you get out here? I thought you had to wait outside customs."

"Shhh." He said with a smile. "Don't tell anyone, but I bribed my way inside." He looked at them all, saw the exhaustion on their faces, and then said, "Welcome to the Philippines."

As Nick led the way to the baggage claim and customs area, the boys talked quietly but excitedly about their flight. Although they were exhausted, they were chatty and animated. Laurie, on the other hand, slumped against him slightly as they walked, relieved to have Nick's parenting support. "Relax, Laurie," he said softly. "We're almost there."

Twenty minutes later, they had collected their bags, whisked their way through customs, paid their arrival tax a second time, and jammed their luggage—and themselves—into one of the larger vehicles for hire waiting outside. As their driver pulled away from the curb, Nick saw something out of the corner of his eye that made him glance back at the crowd lining the sidewalk.

At first, all he saw was a sea of faces, looking back, slowly blurring together as their vehicle began to accelerate. None of the faces was familiar, thought Nick. None of the faces, that is, except one. The one that seemed to wink back at him.

November 4, 1991
Quezon City, The Philippines

Nick sat in the same booth of the hotel's restaurant that he had occupied the morning before, waiting for Keith. He was chatting with Rita when Keith walked up and joined him.

"Good Morning, Mr. Dickson," said Rita. "Would you like some coffee?"

"That would be great, Rita," Keith replied heartily. "Thanks. Morning, Nicholas, how'd things go at the airport last night?"

"Just fine. Laurie was really wiped out—I don't think she got any sleep at all on the plane. But the boys seem to be holding up pretty well. I checked in on them just before I came downstairs, and they were both snoring up a storm."

"You put the boys in an adjoining room?"

"Yep. They're in the room that's in between yours and mine. I expect they'll be in and out of bed all day today. How do you feel?"

"Good. I think I'm finally snapped in to the local time. My only problem is that I tried to call my answering machine last night and wasn't able to get through. I don't know if the circuits were unusually busy, or if that's just the way things work here, but no matter what I tried to do, I couldn't get the line to ring on the other end. I probably tried for two hours."

"The last time we were here," Nick responded, "the only time we were able to reach the boys by phone was when we called from downtown Manila. If you can't get through from here, you might try to call when we're at the airport. Once we get to Mindanao, trying to get an international connection will be even worse—and it'll be impossible if you travel to any of the outer islands."

Nick took a sip of his coffee. "Anyway, here's the schedule. Luis should be here any minute now, and then we need to get ready for our trip to Mindanao. I thought that after we meet with Luis, I'd go out and buy a bunch of bottled water. Laurie gave me a break by not packing a couple of cases of it in her luggage, and I promised her that I'd get some before we leave town."

"Sounds like a plan," said Keith. "When you decide to go to the store, let me know and I'll go with you. What's your agenda with Luis?"

"I want to get him to agree to create a mechanism that will eliminate any risk we face if the Philippine government decides to try and nationalize the carrageenan industry. Either they grandfather us into the legal code, or they give us a ninety-nine-year lease or something. I won't be able to get Sand Hill to fund us without something solid on that end."

Keith was on the same page. "Maybe he can simply create a loophole in any legislation that allows the government to specify a 'vendor of choice'."

Nick nodded. "Maybe. I just have to make sure we can protect our investors in the event something catastrophic happens. I'm sure he'll be able to figure this out—it can't be the first time he's seen this issue. With the amount of investment we're bringing to this country, and the number of his people that will be on our payroll, he has every incentive to have things work out our way."

There was a sudden commotion near the door of the restaurant. Nick smiled, sliding across the seat of the booth and rising to his feet. "We won't have long to wait before we find out what he has to say. Here he is."

Nick and Keith walked up the crowded sidewalk of the narrow street that led from the Sulo Hotel to the shopping district. The cement walkway was so cracked and broken, and the scraggly growth between the cracks so dense, that in many stretches, it looked more like a series of stepping stones than a paved pathway. Traffic on the street wasn't too heavy, and scores of people walked in all directions, some ignoring the sidewalk altogether, simply darting between the passing cars. The weather was perfect—not too warm, and not even a trace of humidity.

"He's an interesting man, isn't he?" said Nick, dodging a bicycle.

"Luis? Very. Intelligent, charismatic, and a consummate politician. Did you see the way he worked the room when he left? I'll bet he called every person there by their first name."

Nick nodded. "He didn't seem to have any problems with our request, did he?"

"It was pretty clear that he had anticipated it. It looks like the two of you are on exactly the same wavelength."

"Well," replied Nick, stopping for a moment to let an older lady cross in front of him, "it's nice to know that we've got friends in the right places." He looked over at Keith. "And you know what else it means?"

"Yeah. The only things that stand between us and success are wrapping up the farmer cooperative and getting a passing grade on our five pounds of seaweed."

Nick raised his eyebrows a couple of times. "Pretty cool, huh?" then pointed to a small storefront fifty yards ahead. "That's the place."

One of several retail businesses on the ground floor of a two-story building, the establishment was more like a convenience store than a supermarket. Walking into the store, they found stacks of packaged goods lining the industrial steel shelving and dingy linoleum aisles separating the display racks. They quickly found the bottled water in the back of the store, and, carrying as many of the plastic liter containers as possible, went to the checkout counter. The ancient cashier stared at them before she pushed the buttons of the manual cash register, and Nick paid the total as she slowly placed the heavy bottles into plastic bags.

"Thank you," he said, taking two of the bags and heading out the door. She smiled back in a toothless grin.

"Not exactly upscale, eh?" quipped Nick, as Keith fell into step beside him.

Keith shook his head. "At least the price was right."

Nick was about to comment when he noticed a man leaning against a parked car on the other side of the street, and his blood suddenly went cold. "Fuck!" he said softly.

Keith's head snapped over to look at him. "What's wrong?"

Nick kept walking, consciously exhaling once to compose himself. "Don't be obvious, but there's something I want you to look at." Nick stopped, bending down to place the bags on the ground for a moment, and pretending to look for something in the pockets of his pants. "Across the street—see the guy leaning against the red car?"

Keith looked casually up and down the street, as if looking for a street sign. "Yeah, I see him. Do you know him?"

Nick reached back down for the bags and then stood up, moving slightly so that he could position himself between Keith and the other man. "Can you still see him?"

Keith nodded.

"Look at his face. His left, eye, I think. Do you notice anything unusual about it?"

Keith looked past Nick and carefully studied the man, who was now looking off to his right. "Yeah," Keith said. "There's definitely something wrong with it. I mean, I can't really tell from here, but it almost looks like it's half-closed, or something." He looked back at Nick, and the two of them resumed walking. "Who is he? What the hell is going on?"

"He's following us," Nick said quietly. "Or more accurately, he's following me. I saw him at the airport last night—I'm sure it's the same guy. I never would have noticed him, but he almost ran into me."

"Are you sure? Why would he be following you?"

Nick shook his head, his mind racing, "The only thing I can

think of is that he's with The Committee. Remember when I told you about the Philippine Committee for Good Government? When I met with them on my last trip, they knew all about my travel schedule. I figured they were having me followed, but I thought they would stop once they realized I had no connection to the Marcos fortune."

Nick exhaled again. "It's probably no big deal."

They turned into the driveway of the Sulo Hotel. Keith looked once again, checking to see if the man was still watching them. "Well, whoever he is, he's still there."

Nick nodded. "Romy will be by later this afternoon with our tickets for Mindanao. I'll talk to him and see what he says. In the meantime, don't say anything to Laurie, OK?"

Standing at the helm of the *Makatà*, Buddy glanced at the luminous dial of his wrist watch. It was just after midnight. The faint light of the quarter moon shimmered off the calm surface of the sea and the only sound was the distant surge of waves breaking over the reef of the atoll. He studied the horizon to the south, his eyes straining to see the profile of the approaching ship.

As instructed, he had sent a signal out from his hand-held GPS at precisely 11:30 P.M. The device, which beamed an RF request to a series of orbiting satellites, accomplished more than just confirming his own location off the coast of Busuanga. Some eight hundred miles away, in Brunei, the Sultan's state-of-the-art communications toys intercepted the transmission and relayed the position coordinates to Hassonal, who was en route to the rendezvous point aboard one of the Sultan's vessels.

Buddy suddenly spotted the outline of the ship, the drone of it's powerful engines surprisingly gentle for the size of the craft. As the sleek two-hundred foot vessel coasted to a stop some fifty meters away, he could make out both the rakish tilt of it's funnel and a helicopter perched high atop the aft superstructure. On a lower deck, a few uniformed crewmen worked davits, lowering a launch. As soon as the smaller craft hit the water, its engine started, and it idled while awaiting a second load from the crew on deck. After a few minutes, the launch cast off from the mother ship and slowly approached the *Makatà*, towing behind it a large, black inflatable raft with a tarp covering its cargo.

Buddy called out to Hassonal, who stood on the deck of the launch, wearing clothing so white he appeared luminescent in the

310

darkness. "You're right on schedule."

The diminutive man squinted back at him and smiled. "Of course. Precision is important to the Sultan."

A faceless crewman untied the line to the inflatable boat and passed it over the side of the launch to Buddy, who attached it to a cleat on the stern of the *Makatà*.

"Your designs, Mr. Ripley, worked perfectly," called Hassonal as their boats drifted close together on the calm sea. "The long titanium tubes are only eight centimeters in diameter, but thick enough to carry a weight of several metric tons. The tripod's winch has a gearing ratio of more than a thousand to one—a mere ten kilos of pressure will easily lift the statue.

"Ironic, is it not? That one crane will be used to deliver another?" He chuckled softly—a high-pitched, irritating sound—before he continued. "When will you begin your excavations?"

"Not right away," answered Buddy. "I still have some logistical problems to solve. I'll signal you again when I'm ready."

"Good luck, Mr. Ripley," Hassonal said, looking back toward the raft. "Enjoy your mechanical Demoiselle."

The launch turned and sped away. Buddy stayed on deck and watched, waiting until the gleaming chrome on the stern of the huge vessel disappeared into the night.

Quezon City, The Philippines

Keith walked over to the newsstand, his eyes idly scanning the rack until a headline from that morning's *Philippine Reporter* jumped out at him. Stunned, he grabbed the paper and read, standing motionless.

Businessman and Son Kidnapped

Mindanao—A foreign businessman and his eleven-year-old son were kidnapped today, according to a report by local police. Eyewitnesses said that the pair, taken at gun-point while claiming their baggage at the airport, were forced into the back seat of what was described only as a large, dark sedan. As security guards, alerted by the pair's traveling companions, attempted to intervene, there was an exchange of gunfire. No one was reported injured. No ransom demands or further details were available at press time.

Keith was flipping through the pages of the newspaper, looking for more information about the incident, when his friend walked into the lobby and, seeing him, came over to the newsstand.

"Mornin', Keith. Let's get some coffee," said Nick, pausing as he noticed the expression on Keith's face. "What is it? Is everything OK?"

Keith handed him the paper. "Have you seen this yet?"

Nick shook his head as he accepted the paper and read the article almost instantly. "Jesus Christ." He looked over at Keith, pausing as he thought of his family upstairs and searched for the right words. "Well, it looks like it'll be an interesting trip today, doesn't it?"

Although they walked into the restaurant only moments after it had opened for business, a familiar figure was already seated at the large booth in the corner of the room. "Romy!" called Nick.

Romy, for once, wasn't smiling, but instead had a deeply worried look on his face. "Good Morning, Nick, Keith. I trust that each of you slept well last night. You have already seen this morning's newspaper, yes?"

Nick and Keith joined him in the booth, and Rita immediately appeared, carrying cups of coffee. Romy looked over at them. "I am sorry to say it, but, these things happen sometimes, particularly in Mindanao. There are two groups of people who kidnap visitors—usually businessmen—for modest ransoms. The victims are released as soon as the payment is made, and very rarely are they harmed in any way."

Romy looked directly at Nick. "The timing of this latest incident is unfortunate, however, because it creates additional difficulties for Alec."

"Oh?" asked Nick. "In what way?"

Traces of a smile appeared on Romy's face. "Alec is the Sultan of the Province. As your host, he must guarantee your safety. He will arrange additional security there as a result of what happened at the airport yesterday. I can assure you—there is positively no risk for you or your family—none at all. Things will be a little more complicated for Alec, and he may have to make some changes in the arrangements for tomorrow's ceremony, but please, believe me, you have absolutely nothing to fear."

Nick looked intently back at him, sensing an almost pleading quality coming from Romy's voice. "How can he guarantee our safety?"

Romy finally began to smile. "I said that there were two groups of people who do these things. Alec will contact each of them and let them know that you are his personal guests. He is a very powerful man there, and once he speaks with them, they will make sure that nothing happens."

"Who are these people?" asked Keith, seriously.

Romy looked slightly embarrassed, "One such group is small and unorganized. They are Communist rebels who hide out in the hills and use ransoms to finance their activities. The other group is much more organized. They have good information about who is traveling on which flights, and they use that information to perform the kidnappings. They take the ransom for themselves, but blame the Communist insurgents."

"And who are they?"

"The police," said Romy, looking away.

Nick and Keith exchanged surprised looks. Nick shook his head, muttering under his breath, "Good grief."

"Tell me, Romy," he said after a moment, "Am I being followed?"

Romy shot him a surprised look. "Why do you ask?"

Nick looked back at him carefully. "I—almost literally—ran into someone at the airport the other night when I met Laurie and the boys. I didn't think too much of it at the time, but then yesterday, I saw the same man again—here, outside the hotel." Nick shook his head. "It's possible, I suppose, that I could be wrong, but I'm almost positive it's the same guy."

Romy nodded. "What did he look like?"

"Male Filipino, maybe thirty years old, average height, but very muscular. The only really distinguishing thing about him is his eye. One of his eyes has a scar or something. It makes him look like he's winking."

Romy shook his head. "No, Nick. I am sorry, that is not what I meant. How was he dressed? What was he wearing?"

"I've seen him in a white T-shirt, I think. Oh, and dark, baggy pants. And sandals—no, not sandals, rubber thongs" He glanced over at Keith for confirmation.

Romy nodded, again looking away.

"What is it Romy?" Nick asked rapidly. "Who do you think it is? What's going on?"

Romy looked back at him, not quite meeting his eyes. "I am sorry, but I do not know, Nick." He continued, now looking Nick squarely in the face, "But I do not want you to worry. I will find out who it is. I will be traveling with you for the next several days. If you think you see him again, let me know at once."

Nick allowed some skepticism to creep into his voice. "Why did you ask me what he was wearing?"

Romy looked uncomfortable. He looked around the room, apparently checking to see if anyone had entered the restaurant that might overhear his comment. He lowered his voice, and said softly, "You have met some of the men on The Committee. It is unfortunate, but it is not unusual for them to have important people followed. If the person following you were wearing more formal clothing, then it would be probable that they were under orders from the PCGG. Many of those men are very dangerous, Nick. They can make people disappear."

Nick froze. "What about the guy I saw? Who's he working for?"

Romy, silent for a moment, finally looked directly at Nick. "I shall find out for sure, but I suspect Ramierez."

"Ramierez," exclaimed Nick in a harsh whisper. "But he's the head of the fucking Committee!"

Romy shook his head. "It is not that simple. True, he is the Chairman, and if the PCGG had an official interest in you, they might have had you followed by one of their own. But someone older, yes? Wearing business attire—a barong.

"What I suspect is that it is Ramierez *himself* who has an interest in your movements. Perhaps he hired someone to follow you so he could learn things for his own personal use. Perhaps he did so without informing the other members of The Committee of his actions. You have met him, Nick, and you understand the type of man he is. He may believe that he can learn something that will help him find some money, and if he discovers it in this manner, he would be able to keep it for himself."

Nick spoke softly, clarifying Romy's statement. "But if he used someone official—with The Committee's knowledge, that is—anything that he discovered he'd have to turn over to the government."

Romy smiled, sadly. "Yes. Or share it with other members of The Committee."

"Unbelievable," Nick said under his breath, digesting the information. "So what you're saying is that since the guy doesn't report to The Committee, we're not in any physical danger."

Romy nodded, an indecipherable expression on his face.

Nick tensed. He thought for a moment, then exhaled. "OK, here's what we'll do. I don't want to worry Laurie with this stuff, so let's keep it as quiet as possible." Seeing Romy's assent, he continued. "She'll be here in a few minutes. She's bringing the boys down for breakfast."

Nick sat back, took another deep breath. "They're looking forward to meeting you, Romy. When they get here, let's put this other stuff aside. Keith and I will keep an eye out for this guy, and you check around to see if Ramierez is responsible. Now, how soon can we get out of here?"

Manila, The Philippines

Ramierez toyed with his cigarette holder absentmindedly. He leaned back in the custom-made leather chair behind the massive antique desk in his office. Both furnishings were situated on a slightly elevated platform, high enough so that he looked down upon any person standing before him as if seated on a throne.

The powerfully built man with the disfigured left eye looked back up at him. He waited in silence until Ramierez finally spoke. "It's time for you to deal with another treasure hunter. An interesting man—an American, in fact. He pretends to pursue mundane interests here in the Philippines, but I am not fooled."

Ramierez flicked an imaginary piece of lint off his sleeve and straightened the razor-sharp crease of his trousers. After a moment, without looking at the other man, he continued. "I am told that he has a map. Several of them, actually. You must find out what he knows. Before you kill him. Take several of your men and make an example of him, and make it messy. Very messy this time. Oh, and use Intramuros again. I loved the way the media covered the last one."

His mouth twisted into what he intended as a smile as he dismissed his henchman with a backhand wave. "Let some more unfortunate tourists discover the results of your handiwork."

As their large, military-style van approached the airport, Nick saw through the darkly-tinted windows that the driver didn't follow the signs to the departing passenger area. Instead, he steered them rapidly through a maze of side roads, around and underneath the airport terminal buildings, a route which led directly onto the tarmac where the airplanes were parked.

They pulled to a stop in front of a small, two-engine aircraft. "Is this our plane?" asked Max, as Romy exited the vehicle, and opened the sliding door on the passenger side. "This is it, boys!" he said, enthusiastically, as everyone piled out.

The next several minutes were spent transferring their bags from the vehicle to the plane, a task that was supervised by a uniformed man wearing mirrored aviator glasses, who was so short that he stood eye-to-eye with the youngest boy. Helping the man load his backpack, Max asked, "Are you the pilot?"

The uniformed man returned a smile. "Yes, son, I am." He gave Romy a quick glance, nodded, and turned back to Max. "Would you like to be my co-pilot on this flight?"

Max's jaw dropped in surprise, and he looked over at Laurie quickly. "Can I Mom, please?"

"OK, Max, but do exactly what the Captain says. And don't touch anything." Her last words were spoken to the back of Max's head as he raced up the few steps of the gangway and into the plane.

Able to carry twelve passengers, the cabin had a central aisle that separated the seats on each side. It was not very tall, and everyone but Romy had to hunch down as they took their seats; Sean at the back, and the adults—at the pilot's request—toward the front. When everyone had climbed in, the pilot closed the door of the aircraft and walked to the cockpit. He took a moment to help Max adjust his seat belt harness, pointed out some of the controls to him, and then called back, "Seat belts, please!"

Nick looked back at Keith, who shook his head. Nick nodded—neither one of them had seen the man with the withered eye. A few minutes later, with a loud roar from the engines, the plane started to move forward, taxiing down the tarmac towards one of the runways. In no time at all, they were aloft, climbing slowly, the wings of the plane dipping to one side as the pilot banked into a southeasterly direction.

The plane leveled out at a comfortable cruising altitude, and the noise from the engines lessened. Romy unbuckled his seat belt and went back to sit with Sean, pointing out the window at various sights below, explaining what they were seeing. Glancing ahead at Max, Nick could see that their youngest son was having the time of his life. Every few minutes, the pilot would point to one of the dials on the console in front of them and ask Max to read it for him. The pilot would nod sagely at Max's response. Nick and Laurie relaxed, listening to Romy's narration and the drone of the aircraft's engines.

Mindanao, The Philippines

Two hours after takeoff, they landed in Cagayan de Oro, a small seaport on Mindanao's northern coast. As the pilot taxied the aircraft down the uncrowded airfield, Nick looked outside. Not far from the lone terminal building, waiting just outside the low hurricane fence, was a crowd of fifteen or twenty veiled women. Two of them carried tall poles that supported either end of a broad banner, the sign proclaiming in neat, large red letters, "Welcome to the Gardners!"

Nick looked inquisitively at Romy, who gave him an embarrassed shrug. The plane approached the fence, and the pilot shut down its engines. Unbuckling his own seat first, the pilot nodded to Max, who then did the same. "Good job, son," he said, reaching over to pat Max on the shoulder. "Nice landing."

The pilot walked down the aisle, opened the door, and everyone piled out. Nick thanked the pilot, while the boys helped Keith and Romy unload the baggage. Laurie, having seen a familiar face in the middle of the crowd, waved and called out, "Eleanor. Hi!" Nick watched as she trotted over to greet Eleanor. The small crowd parted as she approached, and the two women embraced.

"Welcome to Mindanao, Laurie!" Eleanor said.

"Thank you, Eleanor. And thank you so much for the sign—it was sweet of you to do that."

Eleanor indicated everyone standing around her, "These are some of my relatives. I've told them all about you, and they wanted to be the first to see the new Sultana."

Laurie blushed and looked around at the women. In response, they moved slightly forward, reaching out to gently touch her arm or hair, as Nick walked up with the boys.

Eleanor reached out to shake his hand. "Welcome, Nick, it is so good to see you. And these are your sons. My, my. They are so tall, and so handsome."

The boys looked uncomfortable, but endured the few minutes it took Nick to introduce them. Laurie, having disengaged herself from the group of women, joined Nick just as he was introducing Keith. Appraising Keith frankly, Eleanor said, "Welcome."

"Thank you. It is an honor to be here," replied Keith.

Eleanor smiled broadly in response, clearly approving of both Keith and his manners. "It is time for the drive to our home," she announced, indicating a row of half a dozen vehicles parked nearby. "Laurie, you will ride with my driver and me. Nick, if you would please take your sons, Alec's driver will take you. Keith and Romy, my sister, Michela, has offered to have you join her. Shall we go?"

Nick called to the boys, "Sean, Max, let's go." They each grabbed their backpacks and small suitcases and walked over the to the parked vehicles. While the make and model of each car was different, they all shared one feature—the glass of the windows was very darkly tinted.

As Keith and Romy approached Michela's sedan, the front doors of the silver car opened, and two well-dressed, sturdily built men wearing sunglasses got out. They opened the rear doors of the car, and the driver walked to the back and opened the trunk. Having loaded their bags inside, Keith and Romy got into the back seat, where Eleanor's sister waited. Nick couldn't get a good look at her as he walked by—it wasn't simply because he didn't wish to appear rude by staring into the car. He was distracted by the handguns holstered by the two escorts. Not very familiar with guns, Nick could tell that they weren't revolvers, but some kind of automatics instead. Whatever type they were, he thought, they were very, very large.

The process was repeated as Eleanor and Laurie entered the

next vehicle. Again, Nick noticed, the two men in the front seat were armed. He approached the lead vehicle, and another pair of men emerged from its front doors.

"This way, Sir," said the driver as he took their suitcases and backpacks and placed them in the trunk. As Nick and the boys got in the back seat, the two men closed their doors and then got in the front. "Seat belts, please. Tightly fastened," said the driver as he picked up a metallic radio and spoke softly into it in Tagalog.

A moment later, the driver, apparently satisfied with his radio exchange, started the car and began to drive. Both men in the front seat looked about constantly, Nick noted, in a measured, practiced, sweeping manner. At the exit to the small airport, the driver stopped, carefully examining the rearview mirror, and again used his hand-held radio. Finished with his communication, he reached down for his own seat belt and gave it another tug. Placing both of his hands on the steering wheel, he stepped on the accelerator and led the convoy onto the two-lane highway.

The next two hours were as exciting for the boys as an amusement park ride. They were driven swiftly along the curving roads that wound along the shore of northern Mindanao. They whizzed past other cars—sometimes spending several minutes at a stretch on the wrong side of the road—and zipped by tiny towns and villages, always easily under the control of the driver. Nick couldn't see the speedometer, but it felt to him as though they hit speeds on some straightaways of at least a hundred miles an hour.

Turning around to look behind, Nick saw that, whatever their driver did, the rest of the convoy did as well. Counterflow in the fast lane, he thought. After about thirty minutes, they turned inland, into the mountains. On the switchback curves of the steep grade, their speed decreased, but the convoy still jetted along, all the cars following closely behind. The terrain, Nick noted, was similar to what he had seen on Busuanga—huge expanses of green fields surrounded by a perimeter of dense, jungle-like vegetation. The major difference between the two islands was in size. And in the paved roads that they now raced along.

They passed only a few small buildings as they climbed, and saw virtually no people. At the top of the mountain, the view was inspiring. Nick could see the sparkling blue waters of the Sulu Sea, and a handful of islands in the distance. They sped along for another five minutes or so, heading due south, the late afternoon sun beginning to cast long shadows. Rounding a curve in the road, they got their first glimpse of Marawi City.

Spread out before them was a town of some twenty-thousand residents, a mass of small, low, white buildings nestled in the gently rolling hills that lay at the foot of a much taller peak. The city itself was probably at an altitude of several thousand feet, Nick thought. The mountain must reach a height of eight or even nine thousand feet. The driver slowed the vehicle to a reasonable speed as they entered the town, and applied the brakes even further when the streets became busy, slowing the convoy to a speed of around ten miles per hour.

People seemed to be everywhere. The streets were packed with men, women and children. Hearing the honking horns of the approaching vehicles, they scattered to one side of the street. The men and children turned to look directly at the opaque windows of the cars as the convoy passed by. The women, wearing veils over their faces, seemed disinterested. Looking over at his boys, Nick saw them peering out intently, fascinated by the sights of an unfamiliar world.

They drove past street vendors selling food from baskets under colorful cloth awnings edged with strings of beads and golden strands of rope. They passed slowly by building after building— all of them two-story affairs, all of them whitewashed, and all of them virtually indistinguishable, except for the flowers that grew from window boxes upstairs. The flowers, Nick thought, were remarkable. He didn't see a single variety that he recognized, and their colors spanned the entire spectrum of rainbow hues.

Turning a corner, the crowds suddenly thinned out, and the

vehicles approached a very tall stone wall that extended for several hundred yards along one side of the road. The driver picked up his radio and spoke into it as they neared a huge iron gate that occupied the only gap in the wall. The massive gate swung silently open for them, and the driver pulled into a cobblestone driveway that gracefully arced towards an enormous, three-story structure, flanked by several smaller, white stucco buildings.

The most prominent feature of each structure was its roof line. On a corner of each building stood a golden, onion-shaped dome, its shiny peak tapering to a dull point. The center of the largest building had a larger version of the dome at its summit, the sunlight providing highlights as its rays danced across the curved surface.

Nick looked around at the walled compound, which he judged to be the size of two or three city blocks. Their driver pulled to a stop at the end of the roadway, directly in front of the few stone steps that led to the entry of the largest structure. Nick turned to see the gates swing shut just behind the third vehicle. The other cars of the convoy had still been behind them when they arrived at the city. They must have gone to their own homes.

As the men in the front seats remained inside, everyone else piled out. Nick received a relieved glance from Laurie, and then, sensing movement behind him, turned in time to see the enormous, ornately carved, mahogany doors swing open, and Alec walk out. He wore baggy, white trousers, a loose-fitting shirt with broad, very colorful vertical stripes, and a simple, maroon felt garrison cap. He was barefoot. Looking out at his guests, he held his arms widely apart and called out, "Welcome!"

Nick walked over to him to shake hands. "Hello, Alec. Thank you for inviting us."

Alec smiled in satisfaction. "Nick, it is good to see you. I see that you arrived here safely. Good. Your journey was pleasant enough?"

Nick nodded. "Of course."

Laurie joined them, the boys in tow, and extended her hand to Alec, who took it in both of his. "Laurie," he said simply, but with genuine affection. "Welcome."

Alec looked over her shoulder at Sean and Max, as Eleanor walked up and stood by him. He turned to Nick. "I was expecting boys. Your sons are nearly men."

Nick smiled. "Alec, let me introduce you." The boys automatically came forward to meet their host. Each of them shook Alec's hand firmly, and looked him straight in the eye as they addressed him. "How do you do?"

Eleanor said softly to her husband, "Aren't they handsome?"

Alec nodded. "Very impressive, Nick."

"Thank you, Alec. We're very lucky. I also want to introduce you to our Associate, Keith Dickson."

Keith came up and, with just the slightest trace of a bow, shook hands. "It's a pleasure to meet you. Thank you for including me in your plans this week."

Alec shook his hand, studying him. "Nick has told me much about you. I understand that you have already made some important contributions to our success, and I thank you. Welcome to my home."

"And Romy," continued Alec, "*magadang tanghalli.*"

"*Asalaam-o-Aleikum,*" returned Romy.

"I am pleased that you all could join us," Alec announced. "Come. If you would please leave your shoes here," indicating an area to the side of the entry-way, "we shall show you inside."

Alec led the way as everyone kicked off their shoes and sandals and followed him. The interior was majestic. The ceilings were very high, probably fifteen feet, and they curved gently to meet the walls, which were covered with richly-colored tapestries. The designs woven into the hanging rugs depicted scenes of battles and celebrations.

The floors were of highly polished marble, mostly green, but with swirling streaks of white and gray intermixed. The entry area was quite large, stretching fifty feet in each direction, and it featured two sitting areas, at either side of the hall, with large Persian area rugs.

"How beautiful," exclaimed Laurie.

"Thank you," said Eleanor. "If you will please follow me, I will show you to your quarters. I know that you and your sons only recently arrived in this country, and I am sure you are tired from your travels. Perhaps you would care to rest for a while."

She turned to Michela. "I have made arrangements for an early dinner this evening, would you please check on the progress they are making in the kitchen?" Curious, thought Nick, exchanging a quick glance with Laurie. Although Keith and Romy had met Michela during their ride from the airport, Eleanor didn't bother to introduce her to the rest of them. Michela, though younger than Eleanor, had the same vibrant beauty as her sister. She silently complied with the request.

"This way, please," Eleanor said, and they all followed her down an expansive hallway to the stairs, which were made of marble, and bordered with intricately formed iron balusters and brass handrails.

The second story was as lavishly decorated as the first, although the ceilings were not quite as high. The hallway at the top of the stairs exposed a dozen or more mahogany doors fitted with brass hardware. Eleanor led them down the wide corridor, pointing out which rooms they would each be using. Looking for—and receiving—an approving nod from Laurie, Eleanor indicated that Sean and Max would share one room, and Laurie and Nick the room directly opposite theirs. Keith and Romy would each have their own rooms, near the end of the hall.

Eleanor turned to face her guests. "Although you will also find your suitcases in your rooms—if the drivers," she said with a smile, "were able to keep them all straight—you will also find some extra clothing. I'm sure that you will find something that fits you, and you are most welcome to change into our local dress. I shall excuse myself and give you time to rest. Please make yourselves comfortable, and join us downstairs whenever you are ready."

Keith and Romy each thanked her, and then headed down the hallway. The boys, with a quick glance of approval from Laurie, offered their thanks to their hostess, and excitedly ventured into their room. As Laurie opened the door to their room, Alec unobtrusively touched Nick's elbow.

"Nick," he said quietly, "if I may have a moment?"

"You bet," replied Nick. "Laurie, go ahead and get settled in. I'll be back in a bit." He turned and followed Alec, who was already walking back down the broad stairway.

Quickly catching up with him, Nick said, "I appreciate your hospitality, Alec. It really means a lot to all of us. Thank you."

Alec looked at him, shaking his head. "It is the least I can do. Come, in here please." He indicated an arched entry on the ground floor, and then led the way inside. It was, considered Nick, probably his private den. Compared to the other rooms he had seen, it was relatively small and square in shape—about fifteen feet across. It featured three oversized mahogany bookcases that contained hundreds of volumes, the faded leather bindings contrasting with the flecks of gold lettering down their spines. A magnificent desk dominated one side of the room, in front of which stood two large, overstuffed chairs.

Turning one of the chairs slightly so they could face each other, Alec gestured for Nick to sit, and then sat himself—somewhat stiffly, thought Nick—in the other. "I must apologize," he said, a trace of sadness creeping into his voice.

"Apologize? What for?"

Alec sat almost formally, his hands folded in his lap. "You have heard, I am sure, about the recent kidnapping."

Nick nodded. "I saw it in the paper at the hotel this morning."

"It is unfortunate. I can assure you that nothing like that will happen to you, but it has forced me to change my plans for our celebration."

"Oh?" said Nick.

"I had intended for you to join me tomorrow for the customary day of fasting and prayers, with the ceremony itself scheduled for Wednesday. Because of the kidnapping, we must now do everything in a single day."

Nick looked him in the eye. "Whatever you decide to do is fine with us."

Alec nodded, looking down at the floor between them. "I have been in contact with—" he hesitated momentarily, as if searching for the right word. Looking directly at Nick, he continued, "—people. I informed them of my plans, and they accepted my request that no disruptions occur anywhere within the province for the next twenty four hours."

Nick said, "Romy told me that you would have to make some special arrangements. I trust you to do whatever you think is best. My family and I are honored to be guests in your home, so please, don't feel that there is anything you need to apologize for."

Alec shook his head. "You do not understand. As your host, if anything were to happen, it is I who would be responsible for paying your ransom." He saw the surprised expression on Nick's face and continued. "It is the way things are done here. If you were here alone, it would be no problem. But, if anything happened to your entire family, I could not afford to pay the amount they would require." He looked beseechingly at Nick. "For that I am sorry. I can only guarantee your safety until sundown tomorrow."

Nick looked back at him. "Alec, please, there's no need to apologize. We will be happy to go along with whatever plans you've made."

Alec nodded, relief flooding his face.

Nick went on. "Anyway, Romy has probably told you that Keith and I have made a tremendous amount of progress back in the States. We're on the verge of achieving an enormous success, and all we need is to deliver a qualified sample and finalize things with the farmer's cooperative. Have you heard anything new from

Papa?"

Alec smiled, the animation now returning to his face. "Yes. He will be joining us early in the morning, but he radioed ahead to say he had good news. Excellent news, in fact."

"Terrific," exclaimed Nick.

"Just so, and his message also said that we would meet with some of the leaders of the cooperative immediately after the ceremony."

They were interrupted by the arrival of Keith and Romy, who appeared in the doorway wearing clothing similar to their host's. "Come in," said Alec cordially. "We were just talking about our schedule."

Nick stood, and, looking at Keith, said, "Pretty slick threads." Turning to Alec, he added, "Excuse me, but I think I'd better go and check on the boys."

Heading back upstairs, Nick opened the door to the boys' room. It was empty. He opened the door to the room he was sharing with Laurie, and was greeted by cries of, "Hey, Dad, what do you think?"

The boys both wore puffy white pants and large, blousy striped shirts. Max lifted up the hem of his shirt and said, "Look at what we have to use to hold up the pants," displaying a broad sash made of bright red cloth. They both wore solid-colored, velvet hats similar in style to the one worn by Alec.

He turned to face Laurie, who now wore a pale orange silk sari. One end of the fabric wrapped around her waist draped to the floor, the other covered her torso and flowed over her shoulder. It was held in place by a small, gem-studded gold pin—a carving of two long-necked nesting birds—and she wore a matching cloth to cover her hair. She smiled back at him, radiantly.

"Wow," he said.

"Can you believe all this? Look at this room. This place is a palace!"

Nick glanced quickly around at the appointments of their room—tapestries hanging from every wall, an ornately carved, polished mahogany armoire, a four-poster bed lined with fluffy maroon and green fabric draped over gold satin sheets. Before he could look around any further, however, Max yelled, "Come on, Dad. Check out our room."

Following Max across the hall, Nick saw two double beds, each four-posters as well, each billowing with richly-colored, lush fabric. Huge pillows lay in a pile in one corner of the spacious room, and a crystal chandelier hung from the center of the ceiling. Each of the off-white walls were nearly covered by a massive tapestry, whose muted colors added a feeling of warmth to the room.

"Pretty cool, huh?" Max asked.

"Very."

Max out the door, and Nick followed. Back in his own room, Laurie pointed to some clothes lying on the bed. "Why don't you change into those?" she asked, "and we'll meet you downstairs."

Nick laughed. "So much for taking a rest, eh?"

"We're all too excited to try to nap. See you in a minute." She gave him a quick kiss and then, with the boys close behind, left the room.

Nick took another minute to look around, then changed into the baggy white pants and striped shirt that had been set out for him on the bed. It was, he realized, very lightweight and comfortable, and he soon joined the group downstairs. No sooner had he found them than he heard first one, and then a series of melodic wails in the distance.

"You are just in time to join us for our evening prayer," said Alec. "I was just explaining to your sons this aspect of our faith. Come."

He and Eleanor led the way to the end of another corridor, which opened up onto a broad alcove. At one side of the hall was a large bowl of water, and, as everyone watched, Alec dipped his hands into it and spread water on his hands, face and feet. He reached over to one side of the bowl, took a small towel, and dried himself. He stepped to one side, while Eleanor performed the same brief ritual, and pointed to the broad wall at the end of the alcove.

"This," he said, "is our *mehrab*, it—"

"It shows which direction we need to face to bow towards Mecca," interrupted Sean excitedly.

"He is right," affirmed Alec with a broad smile of approval. "Very good, son. And do you know what these are?" he asked, holding out some tightly woven, towel-sized cloths.

"Prayer blankets?"

Alec nodded. "After you have cleansed yourself, please take the place next to me," and, turning to Nick, continued, "You, too, please."

Nick merely nodded, but Sean cried out, "All right!"

They each observed the cleansing ritual, and watched as Alec and Eleanor placed their mats on the floor, faced the wall, and knelt down—Alec front and center, Eleanor directly behind him. Alec took his hat off and placed it by his right side, and then, putting his hands out in front of him, leaned forward so that his forehead nearly touched the floor. Eleanor repeated the process.

Following the lead of their hosts, they each took a prayer rug and knelt down. As he stepped forward, Max whispered to Nick, "Dad, what are we supposed to pray about?"

Nick bent down and whispered in Max's ear, "Just think about all the things you have to be thankful for." Max nodded and, taking a mat, positioned himself next to Laurie.

Nick was next, and he joined Alec in the front row. As Nick bowed his head to the floor, he heard Keith, Romy and Michela fall in behind before he concentrated, reflecting on the moment. It was deeply moving to him that he and his family could be given this gift—welcomed not just into the home, but into the lives of such people. People who accepted them and honored them. People that had such different past experiences, and yet had such similar hopes for the future. People with whom he could share an opportunity for the enrichment of their lives, and the lives of others. Nick didn't consider himself to be religious, but, in that moment of reflection, he felt an awakening of understanding.

Nick sensed Alec push himself up from his deeply bowing position so that he knelt, sitting back on his ankles. Nick turned to watch Alec put his hat back on, place his hands on his thighs, and, in an effortless movement, rise to his feet. "*Allah o Akbar!*" he intoned, taking his prayer rug and returning it to its place outside the alcove.

Nick followed, gesturing to the boys that it was all right for them to rise as well. They stacked the prayer rugs in an orderly pile and followed their hosts down the corridor. Up ahead, Eleanor turned to them and excused herself as Alec led them into the dining room.

"Come," he exclaimed. "It is time to eat."

He motioned for everyone to enter the room, which had the same marble floors and tapestried walls of the rest of their home. The center of this room had a large Persian rug, upon which rested a wide circle of heavy, embroidered pillows.

Alec seated himself on the edge of one of the pillows, arranging his feet beneath his crossed legs. As he called their names, he pointed, indicating where each person should sit. Nick sat next to Alec, followed in order by Keith and Romy. Alec asked Laurie to sit on his other side, and, leaving a space for Eleanor, directed the boys to sit in line according to their age.

As soon as they were seated, Eleanor and Michela entered the room, delivering dinner plates and crystal drinking glasses to everyone. They left, returning a moment later with silver trays of food and plastic bottles of water. Everyone helped themselves to the water as more servings of food appeared. Where only a minute before the room had been vacant and lifeless, the aroma of exotic seasonings now filled the air.

Eleanor and Michela brought the final platters of food and seated themselves. Eleanor invited everyone to help themselves and she began to describe what they had served. Curried and steamed fish, broiled tiger shrimp, steamed white rice, coriander bread and a number of condiments. Sliced green onions, crushed pine nuts and a half dozen different types of raisins. For dessert, she said, there were dried, stuffed dates and *jelabi*, a deep-fried sweet that was twisted like a pretzel.

As they ate, Eleanor engaged Keith and the boys in conversation. She was apparently not only satisfying her curiosity, but also making sure that they felt welcome. The boys gave lengthy answers to her questions about growing up in the U.S. Keith enjoyed painting the picture for her of his life as a single man back home. The meal was, from both gastronomic and social perspectives, the best that Nick could remember.

As they sampled the dates and *jelabi*, Eleanor showed the boys how to use the finger bowls, and Alec talked about their schedule for the following day. It was apparent from the droopy-eyed expressions looking back at him that the excitement of the day was suddenly catching up with Laurie and the boys, so he ended the meal with the suggestion that everyone go upstairs and get some sleep.

Laurie nodded, gratefully, and glanced at Nick. They rose, thanked their hosts profusely, and with the boys following closely behind, walked up the stairs.

It was very dark and very early when the sound awakened Nick from a deep slumber. The rest of his body motionless, his eyes opened and his brain tried to register the source of the high-pitched tone. A faint shimmer from the satin sheets jolted his memory, and he instantly recognized the melodic timbres of the early morning call to prayer.

Rolling over quietly to look at Laurie, he saw that she was still asleep, so he gingerly lifted the bed covers and slipped out of bed. Reaching for the clothing he had deposited on the nearby chair the night before, he pulled on his loose-fitting pants and shirt, and made his way towards the bedroom door, navigating by the faint glow that shone beneath it. He turned the knob and entered the corridor, nearly colliding with someone coming out of the door across the hall.

"Dad?" came a hoarse whisper.

"Yeah, Sean, it's me," said Nick very softly. "Couldn't sleep?"

"I heard the prayer call. Are you going downstairs? Can I go with you?"

Nick reached over and put his arm on Sean's shoulder, leading him gently towards the stairs. "Sure, but keep it quiet. I don't want to wake everyone up."

They felt their way down the staircase, flickering lights from the floor below helping to guide them. Candles burned from a couple of sconces embedded in the wall, which threw a surprising amount of light into the hallway. They padded along toward the alcove, where Alec, Eleanor and Michela stood, just about to enter the area.

If their hosts were surprised to see Nick and Sean walking towards them, they didn't show it. Alec nodded once at them, his face a mix of curiosity and approval. Sean went ahead, dipping into the bowl, and rubbing his hands, face and feet. Drying himself off perfunctorily, he reached for a prayer rug and positioned himself next to Alec. Nick followed, taking the space on Alec's other side.

Nick knelt, and then bowed. He felt, to an even greater degree than during his prayer of the night before, the power of his connection with Alec. His mind raced through a series of things they would do to benefit Alec's people. It was all within their grasp. He was so close.

"*Allah o Akbar!*" said Alec, kneeling next to him.

"*Allah o Akbar!*" murmured Sean. He turned to Alec, whispering, "God is great?"

Alec nodded once solemnly.

When they had retreated from the alcove and replaced their prayer rugs, they all walked down the corridor to the kitchen. Eleanor smiled and spoke softly. "Would you like something to eat?"

Sean said, "Sure!" as Alec shook his head. "Not you, Nick. You and I must fast. Besides," he said, a smile flashing across his face, "we have some business to conduct. Come."

Nick followed Alec from the kitchen, looking back to see Sean climbing up onto one of the high stools that stood next to the large table in the center of the room. Up ahead, Alec walked into the bright light coming from the arched entryway of his den. He stepped around to the other side of his desk, and settled himself into the wooden, straight-backed chair that stood behind it. Nick was just about to take the same overstuffed chair he had used the previous afternoon, when he suddenly realized that it was occupied.

"Papa!" he cried out, startled.

Papa smiled, stood, and shook his hand. "Hello, Nick, it's good to see you. How are you?"

"Fine, Papa, just fine. It's good to see you, too. When did you get here?"

"Around midnight, actually." They both sat back into the large chairs that faced each other, in front of Alec's desk. Papa studied Nick for a moment, before saying, "I hear that you and your associate have been successful in getting our corporation set up."

"You bet," replied Nick happily. "Keith should be up soon, and you'll get a chance to spend some time with him. We've made a lot of progress. Pacific Resource Marketing Company is now a duly registered, official, U.S. corporation. I have some papers that both of you need to sign as Directors of the company.

"We prepared our business plan, using figures that were verified at our test sites here, and then completed our marketing plan. I brought a copy of those to share with you as well. They show that we've got the potential to make a profit of a couple million bucks in only our second year."

Nick looked over at both of his partners, who exchanged brief smiles. Pleased with their reactions, he continued. "If that happens, we're positioned for an IPO, which would net us a lot more—probably tens of millions of dollars."

Alec asked, haltingly, "Did you say IPO?"

Nick nodded. "Right, sorry. An Initial Public Offering. I was also able to find an investor who, provided that the right things fall into place, will give us a couple of million dollars for working capital up front, manage the public offering process down the road, and not need to take too much of our equity."

Papa asked, surprised, "You already found an investor?"

"Absolutely."

"And what things will they need to see before they will provide the necessary funds?"

"The investor said that he would fund us—for only a twenty-five percent stake in the company—if we met three conditions." Nick held up his hand and stuck out his thumb. "One. We find enough business to prove the fundamental math of our plan." He raised his forefinger. "Two. We block any competitors by locking up all the available growing areas. And three," he extended his middle finger. "We show that we have control over the independent farmers."

Alec leaned forward in his chair, idly picking up a pen from the desktop. "So how do we prove that our plan is achievable?"

Nick shot back, "Easy. We deliver some customers that buy enough from us to validate our cash flow projections."

"And you have made some headway in that area, right?" Papa inquired.

Nick laughed. "Papa, we not only found a perfect customer, we got our first order, as well. The way things look now, we'll get enough business from this single customer to make our entire year."

"That is where Romy's sample comes in?" asked Papa.

"Right," Nick nodded. "Romy harvested some of our crop from the pilot site and had it processed to the specifications provided to us by our initial customer. The sample we have to supply is only five pounds—that's all the customer needs to perform the chemical analyses that show that our product is viable. Before they'll give us a firm order, they'll require an additional metric ton of refined carrageenan to assimilate into their manufacturing process, but the fact is this—if the five-pound sample passes their tests, we're home free."

Nick looked at Alec. "You've heard, I assume, that our second requirement has already been accomplished. Our attorney here has wrapped up options on all the locations we discussed. No competitor will be able to access any of the prime growing sites anywhere in the Philippines—we've locked them all up." He looked over at Papa and grinned. "We even got the rights to those worthless plots scattered all over the interior."

Alec shot Papa a look and their eyes met for an instant. Nick went on. "Which leaves the third, and final, condition. We need to create an unbreakable link in the raw material supply chain. As long as our competitors can still get green carrageenan from the independent farmers, they're still in business—they're still a potential threat. If, however, the cooperative is large enough, we not only demonstrate that we have control over the independent farmers, but we've boxed in the competitive processing companies, as well. We corner the market."

Papa looked back at Nick, the traces of a smile forming on the corners of his mouth. He glanced over at Alec, and his grin broadened. He sighed deeply, and nodded, almost formally, and said, "Well, then, it looks like it truly is a day for celebration. Tell me, Nick, how large does the co-op need to be? How many members must we have?"

Nick raised his eyebrows, considering. "It depends, I suppose, on just how many independent farmers there are out there. But hey—," He looked back at Papa's suddenly impassive face, "forget that. Romy said that you already got something like twenty thousand people enrolled, and that's a big number, Papa. If you didn't get many more, don't worry about it. How many did you sign up?"

"About eighteen thousand."

"Oh," said Nick, hesitating briefly. "Well, that's fine. I thought Romy had told me that the total was a little more, but eighteen thousand is plenty."

Papa was grinning. "No, Nick, *another* eighteen thousand. Our cooperative now has a total of nearly forty thousand farmers."

"You're shitting me!"

Papa laughed, amused at Nick's reaction. "You're not the only one who's been working. I spent nearly five weeks traveling to every town and village in the Sulu Archipelago. Every island in the Samales, Pangutaran, and Tawitawi island groups, from Zamboanga to Bongao. Every one of them has hundreds of fishermen that farm seaweed, and I enrolled not only them, but their family members as well. We've got 'em all, Nick, and after today, none of them will ever want to sell to anyone but you."

"Me?"

Alec interjected, "Of course, Nick. They may be from many different tribes, but they are all Muslims. They feel it is a privilege for them to be able to do business with you."

Papa nodded. "I explained to them that Alec had finally found someone worthy of representing his people in the United States. That has never happened to them before. No one has ever offered them the opportunity to belong to a company that does business in America. This is a big step for them, and they are excited."

Nick swallowed, showing his embarrassment. "Well, that's good, I guess. They're an essential part of the equation."

Papa looked Nick directly in the eyes. "Your humility will serve you well, Nick. Particularly because I have described you to them in a way that they can truly appreciate. These are good, honest people, but they are also relatively simple and unsophisticated. That you are to be made a Sultan is, by itself, enough to motivate them to participate in the cooperative." He gestured in Alec's direction and continued. "If Alec thinks enough of you to give you that honor, that is all they need to know. Still, they are curious about you personally, and also about your family."

Alec spoke softly. "Our culture places a high value on families, and believes that sons are special. A man with two sons is doubly blessed."

Papa agreed. "When I told them that you were coming to Mindanao to be honored as a Sultan, many of the tribal leaders decided to attend the ceremony. They want to see the giant American who is President of their cooperative, his movie star wife, and his two handsome sons for themselves."

Nick laughed. "Well, if it means cornering the market in carrageenan, I guess you can handle a few curious folks."

It was Papa and Alec's turn to laugh. "Nick, it's going to be more than just a few folks." He turned to face Alec. "How many people do you expect to attend today?"

Alec answered in a matter-of-fact tone, "About ten thousand."

Nick looked back at them, stunned, when a knock came from the archway. It was Eleanor. "Alec," she said gently, "I'm sorry to interrupt your meeting, but you're ignoring your other guests. Michela is feeding them, but we have a lot to things we need to do this morning before the ceremony. Why don't you all join us in the great room for a few minutes so that we can get started?"

"Certainly," affirmed Alec, rising to his feet. "We were just finishing up here. Gentlemen? This way, please."

The mosque stood on the crest of a small hill that lay at the base of the mountain. Its stubby, golden spires and plain, whitewashed walls provided a contrasting backdrop for the three brightly-colored, fifty-foot-wide canvas pavilions that had been erected for the occasion. Yellow and silver banners streamed at the peak of each tent-like structure, and others, fixed to tall wooden poles spread across the open area, fluttered in the light breeze.

The doors to the mosque swung open, and the tribal Imam appeared. Wrapped in a flowing, floor-length ceremonial robe of black silk edged with gold, he walked slowly along the narrow rug that led down the stone steps, towards the first pavilion. Inside the mosque, Nick glanced back at his family, who stood in an orderly line, clad in the elaborate outfits provided by Michela. "Everyone OK?" he asked, softly. Their faces beamed back at him, without the slightest trace of nervousness, and he grinned. "You all look great. Remember what you're supposed to do? Good."

Nick turned to watch as Alec followed the Imam outside, walking in measured steps along the carpet, ten paces behind. The instant that Alec appeared, the music began. Ever so softly, a graceful melodic tone came from a single *shenai*, a sound, Nick thought, that was similar to a bassoon. He went next, keeping a distance of ten paces between himself and Alec. It was easy to walk slowly, he realized, because he and his boys each wore a ceremonial *lungi*—

a long, elaborately embroidered silk garment, broadly striped in white and red, that wrapped around the waist like a tight-fitting skirt.

As soon as he strode out into the sunlight, he was stunned to find himself surrounded by thousands upon thousands of people. Alec had told him that there would be a large number of people present to witness the event. What made this feel so overwhelming, though, was that every one of the faces in the mass of people was focused on him. The enormous throng began just beyond the edge of the three high canopies, continued up the slope of the opposing mountainside, and extended as far as he could see.

Row after row of native Filipino men and women stood shoulder to shoulder, staring intently back at him. Most of the men were shirtless, and wore plain velvet garrison-style caps. The women were dressed in saris, some with shawls covering their hair, others completely veiled with only their eyes exposed. A handful of men, the *Hadjii,* Nick thought, wore elaborate headdresses and coarsely woven barongs, finely and colorfully embroidered.

Although everyone was packed densely together, he noted that, other than the melodic, creeping cadence that came from the *shenai,* it was absolutely quiet. So quiet, in fact, that when Sean, following ten steps behind him, saw the crowd, Nick was able to hear his oldest son's awed reaction—a muted, "Whoa!"

Max followed Sean down the carpet, and Nick arrived at his place under the maroon pavilion just in time to look back at the entrance to the mosque and see Laurie make her appearance. A collective murmur came from the crowd that lasted for several seconds. It wasn't surprising, thought Nick. Wrapped in an emerald green sari made of shimmering silk, her hair covered by a golden *chadr,* she faced the crowd with a spontaneous, natural smile as she lifted an arm in salute.

The crowd roared in approval.

The cheers subsided as she took her place next to Nick under the canopy, their children standing slightly behind them. Alec and the Imam stood before them, while Eleanor, Michela and Nick's associates sat on enormous pillows under the adjoining blue canopy.

The music stopped, the Imam cried out a long string of unintelligible words in a high-pitched, sing-song chant, and the massive crowd of onlookers immediately fell silent. Finished, the Imam bowed slightly and retreated a few steps.

Producing a scrolled piece of parchment, Alec called out the written words in a slow proclamation loud enough for all to hear. "In the name of God, the beneficent, the merciful, know all men by these presents." He paused, and then spoke in Tagalog, repeating the words, presumed Nick. After another pause, he called out once again, this time in Arabic.

Alec continued this invocation for several minutes, before placing his hand upon Nick's shoulder and calling out the words, "Nicholas Gardner, *Sultanate a la Faez*." On this cue, Nick and Alec bowed deeply to each other, holding the position for fully ten seconds. They rose simultaneously, and Alec presented the scroll to Nick, extending it carefully from both hands.

"I am honored," Nick said.

Alec reached down to the knotted sash that supported his *lungi,* and removed the sheathed dagger that hung from it. Once again, with a slight bow, and using both hands, he presented the dagger to Nick. As he had been instructed, Nick placed the dagger on his own sash, and bowed as deeply as he could. Alec turned to face the crowd, and shouted out as Nick rose, "*Sultanate a la Faez*."

The crowd erupted into thunderous cheers. Nick, smiling now, extended both his arms up into the air, and the sound became even louder. He then stood next to Alec, and, as Laurie stepped forward to face them, the huge crowd quieted down quickly.

Eleanor and Michela took places on either side of Laurie. Once again Alec produced a parchment scroll, and called out the words written upon it in English, Tagalog, and Arabic. After several minutes of this, he reached out and touched her shoulder, this time with the solemn incantation, "Madame Gardner, *Sultana a bai a labi a Gaos al Emira.*"

She bowed at the waist towards them, receiving in return only a slight inclination of Alec's head. As she rose, he formally handed her the rolled proclamation and she looked back in appreciation. Following the choreographed plan, she then turned to face Michela, who placed an ancient necklace of delicately-worked silver and multicolored beads around her neck. Finally, she faced Eleanor, who gave her a small metallic box that was so heavy that Laurie needed both hands to carry it.

Alec then stood between Laurie and Nick, and called out in long, ponderous tones, "*Sultanate Faez y Sultana Emira!*" The crowd roared once again, and Alec led the group over to a group of satin cushions that were clustered underneath the third, bright yellow canopy. The deafening roar continued until they were all seated, cross-legged on the pillows, the men in front, the women and children slightly behind.

Once they were seated, the space under the maroon canopy was suddenly filled with a dozen musicians, who quickly set up a series of drums. Of various sizes, the lacquered instruments were made from hollowed logs, and each one was intricately carved with geometric patterns. As the drummers started to beat with powerful, pulsating precision, a group of brightly costumed young women appeared, gyrating rhythmically. The celebration had begun.

Three hours later, they were back in their rooms at Alec's compound, packing their bags. Nick took a moment to examine the dagger Alec had given him. He pulled the knife out of its sheath and admired its polished, wavy blade that bore dark stains in several places. Scraping it lightly against the hair on the back of his hand confirmed Nick's suspicion—it was razor sharp. Probably eighteen inches long, its handle was made of ivory and engraved with a tan pattern along either side. Etched silver capped the butt of the handle, the hilt, and the end of the sheath as well.

He was pleased that he had given Alec the pocket watch earlier that morning, before the ceremony. Although he knew that Alec had been surprised and delighted to receive it, he felt that the gold timepiece paled in comparison to the dagger. At their first chance, all the boys had rushed over to see it, sensing, as Nick had, that there was something almost magical about it.

During a break in the entertainment, Nick had taken an opportunity to study the box that had been presented to Laurie. Also an antique, it was designed to hold the meat of betel nuts, which natives chewed to keep their teeth clean. The inside of the box contained three partitions, each with its own hinged lid machined to a precise fit. The outside was a complicated design of silver and lead, and its smooth finish shone brilliantly.

Nick thought back to the final part of the celebration, and knew that he would recall its final moments as vividly as he would the gifts. He, Laurie and Alec had stood at the edge of the enormous maroon canopy and been introduced to the leaders of each tribe attending the event. It had taken more than an hour for the parade of men to pass by, each one stopping before the new Sultan and Sultana, and each one bowing in respect. Nick had followed Alec's lead and acknowledged their greeting with a slight nod of his head. At first, he had felt uncomfortable receiving their homage, but as the ritual progressed, the look in the eyes of the native men had begun to effect him deeply. In their faces, Nick found no suspicion, no skepticism, not even curiosity. What he saw was trust and hope.

Instead of feeling embarrassed by their obeisance, he instead drew motivation. He would justify their respect through the success of PRMC. As he packed the dagger carefully in the suitcase, Nick realized that, whenever he looked at it, he would see the faces of the Muslim seaweed growers.

Nick closed the large suitcase, and carried their bags downstairs.

Walking over to the den, he found Keith making a presentation to Alec, Papa and Romy. He stood in the archway and listened for a moment, careful to not interrupt, and realized that Keith was explaining why it might make sense for PRMC to eventually build its own processing plant.

As soon as he noticed that Nick was standing there, Alec spoke up. "Keith, I am sorry, but we will have to continue this conversation in the car." He made a show of reaching down and pulling out his gold pocket watch. He pressed the tip of the watch's stem, and its cover popped open with a satisfying click. "If we are to be at the airport by sundown, we will need to leave immediately."

They all followed Alec into the great room, where Laurie and the boys were listening attentively to Eleanor and Michela. "Come," said Alec. "I am afraid that it is time to go."

Alec announced that he would ride with the men, and Eleanor and Michela would ride with Laurie and the boys. Retrieving their shoes outside the front door, they stuffed their luggage in the trunk of each vehicle and piled inside. As before, there was an armed man riding shotgun, and the cars zipped along the winding roads at frightening speeds. Nick turned around every now and then to make sure the other car was still following closely behind them, but focused primarily on their conversation. Papa would remain behind with Alec until later in the week, when they would return to Manila. Romy would escort Nick and his family to the other islands, and Keith would head, alone, to Cebu.

Because Keith would return home as soon as his business was completed in Cebu, this would be their last chance to speak face-to-face for a while.

"Anything we need to cover?" Nick said.

Keith looked over at his friend. "I don't think so, Your Flatulence," he said with mock solemnity, adding quickly, "No offense, Alec."

Alec smiled and shook his head.

"Keith, give me a break," replied Nick. "When do you arrive

back in San Francisco?"

"I arrive in Cebu tonight and meet with the manager of the competitor's plant there tomorrow. On Friday, I go across town to pick up our sample. After that, I head back home. At this point I'm scheduled to fly out first thing on Saturday, with an overnight stopover in Hong Kong, but I'll just have to see how things go. In any case, I should be home by early next week."

"Right," said Nick, "that's what I thought." He glanced back to check on the other car, and continued. "It looks like we'll be out of touch, then. You'll have telephone service while you're on Cebu, but we'll be unreachable while we're on Busuanga and the other islands. By the time we get back to civilization, you'll be on an airplane.

"I'll call you at home, when we get to Manila. In the meantime, if anything comes up—if you have any problems at all—leave a message for me either at the Manila Hotel or on my answering machine back home. OK?"

"Certainly, partner."

They were back at the airport before sunset. The cars went directly out onto the tarmac, parking next to a twin-engine aircraft. As a short, uniformed pilot with mirrored glasses came down the steps, Nick realized it was the same plane they had arrived in a day earlier.

Exiting the car, he said, "Take care of yourself, Keith," adding with a wink, "but more importantly, take care of our sample. It's the only thing standing between us and a fortune."

"You bet, Nicholas. See ya' next week."

The other car came to a stop, and the boys bounded out. Keith went over to say his good-byes to everyone, and Nick turned to the older man. "Papa, thanks for all your help. I'll see you in a couple of days."

"You can count on it, Nick. Have a good flight."

Nick glanced over and saw that the boys were helping Romy load everything into the plane. Laurie smiled as she walked up to his side, and spoke softly. "Boy, do we have a lot to talk about."

Nick was about to ask what she meant, when the boys approached. "Thanks for everything," they said, each shaking hands quickly with Alec before, with a wave to Keith, they headed back onto the plane.

Eleanor spoke to Laurie. "Take care of yourself, *Emira*, and remember what I told you."

Nick watched as the two women embraced, and Michela stepped forward. Embracing Laurie briefly, she said, "Be well, and be safe."

"Thank you all," said Laurie, her eyes beginning to mist. She reached out her hand to Alec, who accepted it with both of his own. "And thank you," she said.

"You are welcome here anytime, *Sultana*," he said with a slight bow.

Nick said good-bye to Eleanor and Michela, then turned to face his host.

"Alec," he said as he shook his hand. "It's been an extraordinary visit. You've given all of us a day we will never forget. I appreciate it, and I want to thank you again for honoring me. The ceremony was magnificent, but, I have to tell you, second only to your trust, what I value most is the dagger. I'll always treasure it."

Alec, with an enigmatic smile, said, "You are welcome, *Sultan Faez*, and you are right about the dagger. It has an unusual history. Its previous owner was a natural leader, a powerful man who created a great fortune. You have the same opportunity, Nick, and your success will benefit all of us greatly."

Nick, his curiosity piqued, said, "It was owned by someone famous?"

"Not just famous," Alec answered, closely studying Nick's reaction. "Infamous. It was once was the personal property of General Tomoyuki Yamashita."

Nick woke up early, the familiar sound of dogs fighting on the street below ripping him out of his sleep. Taking the few steps to the door, he silently opened it and walked out onto the lanai of the second floor of the L&M Bakery. Wearing only his shorts, he sat in one of the bamboo chairs and looked out over the railing at the tin rooftops that defined the skyline of Coron. As the first rays of sunlight reflected off the maze of corrugated metal, Nick reflected on the previous twelve hours.

They had departed safely from Mindanao just before sundown. Their pilot had, once again, allowed Max to sit in the cockpit, while his brother rode in back with their parents and Romy. As soon as they were airborne, Laurie had begun to describe to Nick her conversation with Eleanor during their ride to the airport. Eleanor had told the story of Yamashita's gold to the boys, and they had been totally enthralled with the idea that the world's largest treasure was hidden close by.

Sean, who was seated directly behind them, had excitedly told Nick how Eleanor had described the system of markers that identified each of Yamashita's burial sites. The carving of a tiger, according to Eleanor, meant that the treasure was buried directly to the east. If a statue was in the likeness of a panther, the gold was buried to the north, and if it was the carving of an ox, it was buried to the south. There were also markers for decoy sites—a stone dragon, for example, indicated that the only things buried nearby were booby traps.

Laurie had also told him that her betel nut box was a wedding gift to Eleanor from Marcos himself. According to Eleanor, Marcos had discovered the ancient box buried along with a hoard of gold bullion and a statue of Buddha made of solid gold. Knowing the history associated with his dagger, Nick had been struck by the fact that he and Laurie now actually possessed some of Yamashita's treasure. Romy had stayed in the back of the plane, absenting himself from the discussion, seemingly content to look out the window.

It had been nearly eleven o'clock at night when they arrived in Coron in the back of the jeepney. Romy had checked them into the L&M Bakery and escorted them up the stairs on the side of the building. Nick and Laurie had taken the same room they stayed in on their earlier visit, the boys paired up in the next room, and Romy took the one next to them. They were so tired from the events of the day that they had all gone to sleep straightaway.

Nick heard a shuffling sound come from just behind him, and turned to see Sean walking towards him, rubbing the sleep from his eyes.

"Good morning," he said in a very soft voice. "How did you sleep?"

Sean nodded, stretching. "What's with those stupid dogs?" was all he said, looking out over the railing for the source of the disruption, and yawning hugely.

Nick held out his arms for Max, who climbed up onto his lap. They looked out from the balcony and watched the rest of the town slowly come to life.

The sun had long since settled over the hillside when Romy served them all dinner on the balcony. He had prepared a huge platter of grilled Lapu Lapu and another of steamed rice, and Max and Sean helped by bringing several large bottles of sparkling water up from the bakery. They jammed five chairs around the rectangular bamboo table, picked up their chopsticks and attacked their food.

Nick glanced over at his youngest son. "Max, what was your

favorite part of the day?"

Max, who was struggling slightly with his chopsticks, didn't hesitate. "The boat ride, for sure, and playing basketball with the kids at school."

"It looked like you were hitting every shot you took. Sean, how about you?"

"That's hard to say, Dad," he replied seriously. "Visiting the school was really pretty cool. It's so different from the one we go to that it was neat to check it out. And they really liked the stuff we brought for them. I can see why you wanted to do that, Mom."

Laurie smiled. "They'll use the things we brought for a long time."

"But I still like Calauit Island the best," finished Sean.

Nick momentarily tuned out the conversation and thought back about their day. As soon as they had finished their breakfast of fresh rolls and steamed rice that morning, Bongo's large diesel boat had picked them up at the pier by the fish market next door and taken them over to Calauit Island for a tour. Bongo had immediately taken to the boys, and shown them a couple of secret caves on their way to the animal preserve. The boys had loved riding in the caged vehicle around Calauit Island while Franco, their host, blathered on and on.

They had returned early in the afternoon, and spent the next several hours visiting the local school. Laurie had met first with the principal, a very short and slightly plump woman who immediately remembered Laurie as the donor of a large amount of school supplies several weeks earlier, and enthusiastically welcomed her. The principal had escorted them all into the classrooms, where the students had smiled and waved at Laurie and Nick, instantly recognizing them from their earlier visit. When the Gardner boys had entered the classrooms, however, the reaction was one of fascinated silence.

Nick was brought back from his brief reverie by the sound of laughter. "Did I miss something?" he said, looking up at them.

Sean explained. "I just said that I liked seeing the tiger eating the goat. But even that wasn't the best thing about the island."

"Oh? And what was?"

Sean, with a confirming look from his brother, said, "The statues of the panthers, of course."

"Why, Sean?" Nick said, obviously missing the point.

Sean was incredulous. "Duh!" he said, stretching it out to two syllables. "Because it means there's buried treasure there, that's why. Remember what Eleanor said—that a statue of a panther marked the location of a treasure that was buried to the north? The statues are at the southern tip of the island, which means that the stuff is buried somewhere up on the top of the hill, behind all the fences."

Max added, "Think about it, Dad, What better way to guard your treasure than with man-eating tigers?" He looked over at his brother. "Marcos was a pretty smart man, wasn't he?"

Nick thought for a moment. "Romy, didn't you tell us that the Marcos family owns the island?"

Romy swallowed once, looking suddenly uncomfortable. "Well, Nick, not exactly. What I said was that the old man bought the island with the intention of turning it into a game preserve, but I did not say that his family still owns it."

Nick listening to the reply, realized that Romy was picking his words very carefully. He probed further. "You're saying that the family doesn't own it anymore?"

Romy nodded.

Waiting a few beats, Laurie asked, "So, who does?"

Romy, with a barely noticeable hesitation, replied softly, "We do."

Four heads turned as one to face Romy. Nick put down his chopsticks and managed to say, "Excuse me?"

"Yes," replied Romy gingerly, an enigmatic expression crossing his face. "If you look at the documents in the binder I gave you earlier this week, you will see that it is one of the properties our

351

attorney acquired for us under option. We, or, should I say more precisely, PRMC, owns the rights to it."

"Jesus Christ," Nick mumbled almost to himself.

Max said, "That means the only thing we need to get to the treasure is the map."

"The map?" Nick asked.

"Eleanor's sister told us that the markers only show the general area of the treasure," Max answered. "There are secret maps that show exactly where you need to dig so the booby traps don't blow you up."

"No," said Sean smugly, "you're wrong."

"Am not!"

"Are too!"

"Stop!" said Laurie firmly. She put down her chopsticks and looked over at Sean. "It really doesn't matter, but I also thought it was Eleanor who told us about the treasure, and Michela who talked about the maps."

Sean nodded. "That's right, Mom, but that's not what I meant. Michela isn't Eleanor's sister, she's Alec's wife."

Nick turned to look at Sean, pausing as he thought about what he'd said. He looked over at Laurie, eyebrows raised, and she nodded back at him. "Now that you mention it, that makes sense." He turned to Romy. "Is it true?"

Romy appeared to relax, an amused and slightly surprised expression now on his face, "Yes. Westerners are often uncomfortable with a Muslim man having more than one wife. Alec did not want to make things awkward for your sons, so he chose to not introduce Michela." He looked at each of them. "He thought you both already knew."

Sean sat back in his chair with a satisfied expression on his face, and munched a mouthful of rice.

Nick shook his head, "I did hear something about another wife, but—I'm sorry to say—I just didn't make the connection." He said to Laurie, "Did you?"

She nodded back at him. "Sure," she said with a smile. "I thought you figured that out, too."

Nick shook his head, wondering how he could have been so blind to something so obvious to everyone else around him. "I completely missed it," he said. "I guess I had other stuff on my mind. Anyway," he continued after a pause, wanting to change the subject, "we still haven't heard from you, Laurie. What was the highlight of your day?"

She leaned forward, immediately warming to the subject, and launched into her response. "Well, the morning was great—Bongo was so nice, and Franco was—well, Franco. But, for me, the best part of the day was at the school.

"I loved the way the kids in the classes looked at all of you when you walked into their rooms," she announced. "None of them had ever seen a white person before—at least, not one that was their own age. And I know that they appreciated the things that we brought them."

She added with a curious smile, "I also think several of the girls there fell in love. When we wrote our address on the blackboard, some of them copied it down. I'd be surprised if you didn't hear from them."

Relieved to have the conversation back on a lighter note, Nick looked over at the boys. "And I think I enjoyed most watching you play basketball after school."

"A lot of their guys were good," Max observed. "I mean, they aren't very tall, but they sure know how to play."

Romy smiled, very broadly. "Yes. That is true. Basketball is a very big sport over here. It is almost as popular as cockfighting."

The boys tried, unsuccessfully, to suppress their laughter. Romy continued, either oblivious to the cause of their reaction or choosing to ignore it, explaining that Filipino men keep roosters for weekend fights.

The laughter from the boys subsided as they politely listened to Romy, but Nick couldn't resist the temptation to indulge them further. "He's right. In fact, the last time we were here, Max, I saw a man walking down the street in Manila holding his cock in his hands."

That brought laughter from the boys, and Laurie shot him a stern look, "Nick!" But even Romy smiled.

"Sorry, guys," Nick said, obviously lying. "Hey, we've got another big day tomorrow. You need to take care of the dishes, and get to bed."

With mild groans, the boys stood up from their chairs, grabbed a couple of plates, and carried them downstairs to the bakery's kitchen. Nick announced that he was tired, and needed to hit the sack. He went back into their room and turned on the bare light bulb that dangled in the middle of the room from a thin black cord. He was shuffling through his canvas briefcase when Laurie entered the room.

"Are you OK?"

He found the thick binder he was looking for. "Everything's fine. It's just that—well, you know I don't like surprises." He looked up at her, not wanting to alarm her. "It was news to me that PRMC has the rights to Calauit Island, that's all. When I talked to Romy earlier about the work the attorney was doing, he didn't mention it. It's probably no big deal, but I think I should take another look at these papers."

He reached out to take her hand. "Don't worry, I'm sure everything's fine. Why don't you check on the boys and get them tucked in. This won't take very long."

As Laurie left to go and see to the boys, Nick opened the three-ring binder and flipped through it, looking for the map. When he didn't find it, he carefully read the first few pages and realized that each of the properties the document referred to was described only by it's legal plot number and street address. He shook his head. Something wasn't right. How could there be a street address for beach-front property in the Philippines? And where was the map?

He sat back for a moment, thinking, and finally remembered

N

LUZON

MANILA·

·LEGAZPI

CALAUIT
ISLAND

BUSUANGA
·CORON

·TACLOBAN

·CEBU

·CAGAYAN DE ORO
·MARAWI

MINDANAO

CARAGEENAN
SITES

that he had given it to Keith. Resuming his search, he rifled through the rest of the pages and came across something inserted inside the back cover of the binder.

Taking it out and unfolding it, he saw that it was a large, black and white map of the Philippines. He laid it out on the bed, and noticed immediately that, unlike the map that Keith now had, this one had hundreds of tiny holes spread all over it. He flipped over a corner of the paper and ran his hand over the back side. The holes were pin pricks. Someone had put this map up on a wall and marked each of the sites with a pin.

He looked at one of the pages in the binder and then back at the map, matching up the descriptions with the pinpointed sites on the map. He flipped through the pages in the binder until he found their test site at the Old Man's Island and then inspected the map again. Hearing Laurie's footsteps approach their door, he quickly refolded the map and put it back in its slot at the back of the binder. He went back to the descriptive pages and began to study them carefully.

November 8, 1991
Busuanga, The Philippines

It was late afternoon as they rode in the back of the jeepney up the curving road leading to the inland airstrip. Laurie chatted with Romy and the boys watched the landscape pass by, while Nick thought back on the events of the day. It had been eye-opening.

After they had eaten their minimal breakfast, they had again been met by Bongo and his diesel water craft at the fish market pier. They had motored out to the east, through the gently rolling swells and the sapphire blue water towards The Old Man's Island, where the boys had experienced for themselves what Nick and Laurie had enjoyed only two months before.

The long boat, its engine idling, had drifted slowly towards the sandy shore of the island, and gracefully kissed the sand as it had come to a stop. The boys had bounded out, racing down the beach and marveling at the number and size of the seashells they had found. Pedro, Tony and Maria, had greeted them warmly, Pedro still wearing the T-shirt they had given him on their last trip.

Tony had bonded immediately with the boys, and had spent the morning teaching them the skills necessary for living on a tropical island. He'd shown them how to climb the trees for coconuts, and the art of throwing a net into the shallow water to catch fish. The boys had fared well. Sean had been unable to climb a coconut tree, but was the only one who had caught any fish. Max had not only been adept at climbing trees, but had also shown an enormous appetite for coconut milk.

Tony had led them on a brief hike over the spine of the island so they could view the seaweed plantation, which had grown dramatically. Where before the lines of plants had only occupied a

357

fraction of the lagoon, they now covered about eighty percent of the area. One of the workers had then met them in a small inflatable boat and ferried them out to Laurie's Island.

Nick recalled the beautiful expression on Laurie's face as their family had posed for a picture on the island named for her. She had been happy to see that, even though changes had been made around the lagoon, her namesake would be left alone. Despite the presence of several floating workstations that had been installed at the far end of the reef and the rows of carrageenan plants that were much more densely packed together, the turquoise water was still crystal clear, and the sand on the bottom still bleached perfectly white.

They had gone back to the encampment on the larger island for lunch—a meal of coconut, rice and freshly-netted grilled fish, accompanied by coconut milk. While everyone feasted, Nick had, as unobtrusively as possible, reexamined the stone base of the cooking stove, confirming what he had seen on his earlier visit. He again found himself looking at the carved face of a snarling tiger.

Fortunately, no one else had noticed it. He had remembered Sean saying that an image of a tiger meant that treasure was buried to the east. Looking around as casually as possible, he had considered the place in a completely different light. What might it have looked like, he had wondered, fifty years before? As fast as the jungle-like vegetation grew, it was impossible to know, and senseless to even guess.

He had tried a different tack. If he were going to bury anything, he had thought, it would be incredibly difficult to do it on the hard lava rock that made up the island's hillside. The only logical hiding place east of the stone marker would be under water in the middle of the shallow atoll on the other side of the island. He had wondered, considering the possibility—had the reef been the same for the past fifty years, or had some enormous storm wiped out a section of it? Did the lagoon look today like it did in the early 1940s? Was the water then the same depth that it was now, or had the passing decades filled the underwater expanse with more sand? How deep might it have been during the war?

Nick shook his head, remembering the conflicting feelings that had overcome him during his lunch. When he had stood on Laurie's Island and looked out at the beautiful atoll, the water glittering in the late morning sun and the red strands of idly floating carrageenan, he had seen the fortune they could make by selling it. But was it possible, he had asked himself, that a fortune in gold lay buried beneath it as well?

They had returned to Coron just after lunch, as the more successful of the town's fishing fleet was beginning to head home. Sitting in the cockpit of the boat, Laurie had pointed out the rugged, vertical cliffs that they passed and told the boys how native boys their same age climbed them in search of nests. They had passed by the fishing boats and watched the men gripping their drop lines, occasionally seeing the flashing form of a helplessly struggling fish being hauled, hand over hand, up to the surface and into the boat.

Lurching along the dusty road, Nick next recalled the twisting sensation he had felt in his stomach the night before as he reviewed more carefully the binder of papers their attorney had prepared for him. Checking the descriptive pages contained in it against his own map of the Philippines, he had confirmed what Romy had said—PRMC did, in fact, hold an option to purchase Calauit Island. Nick had also verified that they had actually purchased The Old Man's Island, its surrounding atoll, and Laurie's Island. But as he continued his investigation, he had learned that those were not the only parcels of land in the immediate area to which they now held ownership rights.

There was another location on Busuanga, an inland area. Because the scale of his map lacked the necessary detail, he couldn't be certain, but he could tell from the topographical descriptions contained in the binder that the site was either the pasture that defined the airstrip they now approached, or somewhere directly adjacent to it.

The jeepney's driver turned off the roadway, stopping a few yards before the crude, makeshift bridge leading to the airstrip. They all piled out of the back, and the boys raced over the heavy timbers that bridged the gap. The adults followed behind at a leisurely pace, and then gave hand signals to the driver so he could bring the vehicle across. Everyone climbed back aboard for the short ride to the end of the grass runway—everyone except for Nick.

"You guys go on ahead. I'll just walk the rest of the way."

As the jeepney pulled away, he examined the area around him. Except for the southern end of the large field, where the ravine prevented grazing animals from escaping, a barbed wire fence stood around its perimeter, and the grass within was kept short by the now-absent water buffaloes. He could make out dozens of piles of their droppings. The area just beyond the fence was dense with vegetation, which appeared to be so thick that the fence was almost unnecessary. At the other end of the airstrip, however, was a gap. As Nick walked towards it, he could see that the trees behind the fence had been cleared, presumably so that planes had a little more room for maneuvering on their takeoffs and landings.

He stopped at the fence at the clearing, and realized that more than a few trees had been cut away. The entire area appeared to be perfectly level, and unnaturally smooth. At some point, he guessed, it been graded with heavy machinery. Other than that, there was nothing noteworthy about the property except for the profile of a lone water buffalo resting in the deep grass, perhaps thirty yards way.

Nick turned around and started to walk away when it hit him—the grass on the other side of the barbed wire fence was much higher than it was where he stood, and, even though there wasn't an animal to be seen grazing now on his side of the fence, there was on the other. He spun around and looked again. Hesitating to believe what he saw, he climbed through the strands of wire and waded through the tall grass towards the bovine figure. It was made of stone.

Another marker.

Fuck me, he thought. Three PRMC properties, three stone markers.

"Nick? Are you OK?" It was Laurie, calling to him from just the other side of the fence.

He looked back at her and answered. "Yeah, I guess so. My stomach is a little off. Maybe it's something I ate. I thought a few minutes walk would do me good before I got on the plane."

"What are you doing over there?"

He spread two of the wires apart and carefully crawled back through the fence. "Oh," he replied, with a sheepish expression, "I thought I'd try to get some distance between me and the smell of the yak shit. When is the plane due in?" he said, trying to change the subject.

"That's why I came to get you," she replied. "Romy said it would be here any minute, and they can't land if you're standing on the runway."

"Oh. Right," he said, as they walked back towards everyone else.

"Are you sure it's your stomach that's bothering you?" she asked.

He wasn't yet sure what he should say, but nodded. "I'm also a little frustrated by not being able to get in touch with Keith. Today is the day that he's supposed to pick up our test sample from the processing plant in Cebu. I'm sure that he had a chance to look at a report of some kind that detailed the chemical composition of the stuff when he picked it up. I'd like to know what he found out."

He looked over at Laurie, his eyebrows raised. "Know what I mean?"

Laurie didn't answer, instead putting her arm around his waist.

"You've done everything right so far, Nick. Try to relax a little, OK?"

The last part of her sentence was drowned out by the roar of an airplane. Flying only a hundred feet or so over their heads, it headed away from them, going north, before turning back. Coming in low over the fence at the other end of the field, its wheels touched down and it taxied noisily towards them and came to a halt twenty yards away. A minute or so after the engines died, the propellers stopped turning, the door opened, and the stairway unfolded. A uniformed man got out and waved to them, so they picked up their suitcases and helped load everything into the plane.

There were no other passengers, Nick noted with some surprise, but—unfortunately for Max—there was a uniformed copilot. As they each took a seat and buckled up, the copilot folded the stairway and shut the door while the pilot started the engines. In no time, they were airborne, heading in a northwesterly direction towards the southern tip of Luzon.

As everyone else looked out their windows at the view below, Nick stared ahead at the bulkhead wall in front of him and mentally ticked off the questions that scrolled through his brain.

What the hell, he wondered, was really going on?

Who was the puppetmaster pulling the strings?

It had to be one of his partners, but why?

Why go to the trouble of setting up an exporting business?

Why involve outsiders?

Why not just keep the money for themselves?

They landed in Legazpi City and boarded a small bus that Romy had arranged for them. They would be spending the night on the campus of the local university where Romy occasionally taught. Nick would use one of the classrooms the next morning for a meeting with some of the cooperative members, while Laurie and the boys would take a tour of Mount Mayon, an active volcano nearby.

Although it had only a fraction of the major city's population, Legazpi shared more than a trace of the claustrophobic intensity that characterized Manila. They rode in the bus, slowly weaving through the uncrowded, narrow streets, the multiple story buildings packed densely together on either side of them. Nick, his mind racing through the possibilities he faced as darkness began to fall, felt like a rat in a maze.

The bus turned into a driveway with a guarded gate house standing on one side. Stretching along the street in either direction of the driveway were tall cement walls, which completely blocked the view of whatever stood inside. Not bothering to stop, the driver honked the horn of the bus and the iron gates swung open.

Once inside, Romy turned and announced, "The big buildings over there are the academic halls, and the smaller ones over this way are the dormitories. I have reserved one of them for us for the night," indicating a very plain, single story, cinder block structure. The bus came to a halt, and the driver pushed the lever to open its door.

They grabbed their belongings and followed Romy inside the building. It was, Nick saw at a glance, a very simple affair—a narrow central hallway with eight doors on each side. The rooms were evidently unlocked, and Romy turned the knob to the first door and opened it for Laurie. Clean and spartanly-furnished, it held a single large futon and a couple of wicker chairs. The boys would take the room directly across the hall from theirs, and Romy the one next door.

"Please take a few minutes to rest and get cleaned up, if you wish," Romy said. "When you are ready for dinner, just knock on my door."

Forty-five minutes later, they were all set to go. Romy had arranged for them to eat in the student cafeteria, and, although school was in session, the place was not crowded. Either they were eating at an unusual hour, or the place wasn't very popular. Following Romy's lead, they each took a tray and walked down the line, helping themselves to the food.

Seated on benches at a single large table, they had a very quiet dinner. Laurie and the boys were clearly tired from their travels, and they all seemed to concentrate on their food. When they had finished their meal, Nick and Laurie walked the boys to their room and, making sure that Sean would lock the door behind them when they left, kissed them goodnight. They returned to their own room, took off their clothes, and got into bed.

As they settled into the sheets of the futon, Laurie snuggled up close. Putting her arm over Nick, she pulled him towards her and gently kissed him. When he didn't respond, she said, very softly, "It's been an incredible day. We've had an experience we'll never forget. You're on the verge of an enormous success, and yet, ever since last night, you've been a million miles away. What's going on?"

He hugged her tightly for a long moment before replying. "We need to talk."

November 9, 1991
Legazpi City, The Philippines

A gentle knocking on their door awakened Nick. "Mom? Dad? Are you in there?"

Nick got up and unlocked the door, finding Max wide awake and fully dressed . "Mornin', sport," said Nick. "How'd you sleep?"

"Great. Hey, Dad, some guys are out there playing basketball, can I go out and play with them?"

Nick checked his watch and was surprised to see that it was just after seven thirty. Well, he thought, it wasn't really too surprising. He and Laurie had stayed up talking until nearly three in the morning. "I don't know. Where are they?"

Max pulled his Dad down the short hallway and opened the door. "See? Just over there."

Standing in the doorway, Nick looked outside. Out in the courtyard, just behind one of the other dormitory buildings, stood some basketball goals, where several boys were practicing shots.

"Sure. Why don't you see if your brother wants to play, too? And Max, make sure you stay inside the courtyard where we can see you, OK?"

Max's only response was to race back to his room to wake up Sean.

Returning to their room, Nick sat on the futon next to Laurie. "Laurie," he said softly, brushing a few strands of hair away from her face with his fingers. "You need to get up. It's showtime."

Nick waved good-bye as the twelve-seat school bus pulled away, noting that the smiles on the faces of the boys were bigger and more sincere than Laurie's. As they had agreed during their late-night conversation, they would go along with the plan for the day, and both of them would try to act as if it was business as usual. Laurie and the boys would go with Romy to tour the city's volcano, and Nick would stay behind to meet with members of the seaweed cooperative.

Nestled in each other's arms, Nick had told Laurie his suspicions, his voice never once rising above a whisper. When he had started to outline his ideas, her response had been to gradually increase the pressure of her fingers that rested on his biceps. By the time he had finished with his story, her fingernails had dug into his arm so deeply that they almost drew blood.

Nick had told Laurie about the properties the attorney had secured for their company, explaining that most of them were, in fact, seaside expanses that were perfect for growing carrageenan. Many of the locations, however, he had explained, were not. Too many. And, although he had only seen two of those unsuitable sites—Calauit Island and the Busuanga airstrip—both of them had stone markers. While it was impossible for him to visit all of the other inland sites, there was one other location that had a similar profile that they could easily check out. That location, according to Nick's interpretation of the documents in the binder and his map, was at the base of the Mayon volcano.

Laurie would go on the tour of the volcano caves with Romy and look for another stone marker. If he had pieced the puzzle together correctly, she ought to find the carved image of a Tiger. Whatever was going on, he'd told her, they would be all right as long as they stayed with Romy and did what was expected of them. Don't do anything that suggests that we know anything, he had told her. Stay in the spotlight and everything will be OK. As long as they were conspicuously visible, nothing would happen to them. Whoever was orchestrating this, Nick had explained, needed them, so they were too important to be in any real danger.

Laurie had rolled over onto her elbows, her face only inches away from his. "Who is doing this?" she had finally asked.

Laying on his back, Nick had just stared at the ceiling in the darkness, silently shaking his head.

Now, as their pudgy bus turned out of sight, Nick took a deep breath, held it for a moment, and then exhaled. It was time for him to meet with the farmers from the co-op and he could only pray that he was right about his family being safe.

Nick walked towards the school's central administration building in search of a telephone. His meeting had been interesting, but less important than it might have seemed a few days earlier. Papa had evidently told the independent seaweed growers that they would have a chance to meet with the company's President, a giant American, and nearly thirty people had decided to take advantage of the invitation.

While most of the co-op's farmers were from the Philippine's southern region and had been able to see Nick at the ceremony, there were also a large number of families that fished and farmed the fertile shallows of eastern Luzon, Samar, and the islands surrounding the Visayan Sea, which were quite a distance from Mindanao. Romy had chosen Legazpi City for their meeting because it was a central site for assembling the northern contingent of the group.

In passably good English, the men and women had asked him questions that ranged from the predictable to the curious. What price they would get for their crops? How tall was he? When would they get paid? Was it true that his wife was a movie star? Nick had patiently answered them all. When the questioning had come to an end, he stood by the door and shook hands with each of the farmers as they left the meeting.

Now, waiting for Laurie and the boys to return, he had an urgent task to complete—checking his telephone messages back home to see if there was any word from Keith. As directed, he found the telephone just inside the entry of the administration building. It was large, red, and looked as much like a slot machine as it did a telephone. He lifted the receiver, dropped the coin into the slot, and listened for the dial tone before it dawned on him that the telephone had a rotary dial.

"Christ," he said, realizing that he couldn't retrieve his messages without a telephone with a push button keypad. He hung up the receiver, shook his head, and sighed in frustration.

His coin fell into the return drop. He retrieved it, put it back in the slot and dialed the international operator. When she came on the line, Nick gave her Keith's office number, his own credit card number, and waited for Keith's voice to come on the line. Because Keith was scheduled to be in an airplane all day, Nick knew it would be some time before he was able to speak to him personally. When the machine answered on the other end of the line, he did the next best thing—he left a lengthy message that detailed all of his findings and concerns.

Soon enough, he figured, he'd be able to discuss the situation in person with Keith. Until then, he'd just have to wait until they arrived in Manila where the phone system was better. At least now, he knew, Keith would have the same information that he did and could help him figure out what to do next.

Cebu, The Philippines

Keith had spent the last two days making sure he did everything possible to ensure proper delivery of their carrageenan sample back to the States. Not wanting to create any unnecessary delays in getting it cleared through customs, he had decided against carrying it himself and sent it via an overnight courier service instead.

He had planned to head back home today, and, knowing that he'd be inaccessible for the next couple of days, he used the phone in his room at the Holiday Inn to check his office answering machine before he packed. Stunned by Nick's message, he decided to delay his flight and consider his next move over lunch in the restaurant downstairs.

Buddy Ripley walked into the Holiday Inn just before noon. He had arranged to pick up his new resistivity detector at a time that coincided with Jenessa's next Cebu layover. He checked his watch. She wouldn't arrive here for another two hours, so he went into the restaurant to wait.

The hostess seated him right away, handed him a menu, and walked back to her station. It always happens, he thought, looking around. Only one other diner in the entire restaurant, and she seats the two of us practically on top of each other. Buddy glanced at the man seated at the next table, who intently studied a map spread out before him. He was, Buddy could tell instantly, an American. Buddy picked up his menu and was about to scan it when the impact of what he'd seen hit him like an electric shock.

Buddy had spent so long studying his own maps that he instantly recognized the one spread out on the other table. What jolted his sensibilities, however, was not the map itself, but the markings on it. Even from a distance of six feet, he could tell that the places that were highlighted were locations that held Yamashita's gold.

Buddy closed his eyes, and, for almost a minute, breathed slowly, contemplating the turn of events. Then, opening his eyes, he stood up, took a step toward the other diner, and said, "Pardon me, but I have to ask—you're from the States, aren't you?"

"Is it that obvious?"

"Takes one to know one, I guess. I'm an American myself, and I don't see that many folks around here from back home. Mind if I join you?"

"Not at all," the man said, folding the map and putting it away. "Pull up a chair."

"I'm Buddy Ripley."

"Keith Dickson," came the reply as the men shook hands. "Nice to meet you."

Buddy signaled the waitress and ordered some tea, and the two men chatted casually about the Philippine weather and the food. After several minutes, Buddy asked, "So, what brings you to this part of the world?"

"A business venture. We're setting up an export company," Keith said vaguely.

"Oh, really? For a minute, I thought you were another treasure hunter."

Keith's was unable to conceal his shock. "Why do you say that?" he asked.

"First," Buddy said, "Americans that come to the Philippines mainly visit Manila. The ones that visit the other islands usually come to look for treasure. And then, when I walked by your table, you were studying a map. From what I could tell by the way it's marked, it looks like it belongs to someone who has a good idea of where to look for Yamashita's gold."

"No shit. What do you know about that?"

"I've studied the General's activities myself and I know enough about them to distinguish fact from fiction."

"So you're a treasure hunter?"

Buddy launched into his stock answer—the story he always gave when he first met someone. There was probably no one else in the world that knew as much about Yamashita's treasure as he did, but he needed to find out more about what this Yank was up to.

"You could say that. I was born and raised here, and I've been fascinated with Yamashita ever since I was a kid. I had a dream that I could find his treasure. Read everything about him that I could get my hands on."

He was interrupted by the waitress who brought his tea, and they both ordered sandwiches. Buddy continued. "Anyway, then my life changed. I moved to the States to finish high school and eventually went to college. Couldn't wait to get back here, though, get back home. I guess I never grew up, because I just took up where I'd left off—I started looking for the treasure."

Keith asked, "Have you ever found anything?"

Buddy looked away. "Well, I do know where some of it is buried, which is why I was curious about your map."

"But you haven't dug anything up yet," said Keith.

"Not yet," replied Buddy casually. "There are a couple of problems I've been waiting to solve."

"Like the markers?"

Well, Buddy thought, this guy knows the locations *and* about the markers. Though surprised, he didn't show it, asking instead, "What do you know about them?"

"I've been told that Yamashita used stone carvings of animals to mark the entrance to each burial site."

"What kinds of animals?"

Keith laughed. "What is this, a test?" Seeing the blank expression on Buddy's face, he leaned forward and continued. "It is, isn't it? You're trying to decide how much I know."

Buddy nodded. "It's an interesting dance, isn't it? You try to figure out what I know while I try to figure out what you know." Their eyes met and they both laughed.

The waitress brought their sandwiches and drinks and, as they ate their lunch, their conversation shifted. They talked about their impressions of the Philippines and the States, and about their families and education. More than an hour passed before Buddy asked, "So, have you thought about what you'd do if you got your hands on Yamashita's gold?"

"You know, it's funny." Keith sidestepped the question. "I first heard about this treasure only a couple of days ago, but now it seems as though it's being handed to me on a silver platter. As far as I can tell, all I have to do is figure out the answer to one problem, and then I'm going after it."

"What's your problem?" asked Buddy. "How to launder the gold once you find it?"

Keith smiled. "Actually, no. I already have that figured out. What bothers me are the booby-traps." He took a bite of his sandwich and asked, "So, what's standing in your way?"

Buddy hesitated for only a second. "From my standpoint, there are two things. The first one is logistical, the second one legal. The logistical one is troublesome, but not impossible. Most of the treasure is buried pretty deep. It would take me a long time to dig it up by hand."

"So you bring in some heavy equipment."

"Maybe, but that leads to the legal issue—getting permission from the property owners to excavate on their land. How can you convince someone to let you dig up their land without first telling them what you're looking for?"

Keith smiled and pressed on. "What about the booby-traps? Aren't you worried about them?"

"Nope. After high school I went into the Marines. Learned everything I need to know about using—and disarming—bombs."

Keith sat back in his chair and looked at Buddy in a new light.

"Is that so?"

Buddy took the last bite of his sandwich, watching Keith consider the information. Watching Keith watch him. Buddy's instincts told him that Keith was debating whether or not to suggest that they should team up together. If that was the case, there was only one thing left for Keith to know—how they'd split what they found, and Buddy had an answer to that question that would reel him in.

It was less than a minute before Keith spoke again, "What do you plan to do with this fortune once you find it?"

Buddy smiled. "That one's easy. I don't do anything. I just walk away."

"What?"

"I just want to be known as the guy that found it."

Keith looked at him carefully. "That's all?"

Buddy grinned. "Look, my needs are simple. I've got everything I need to be happy. But this is the Mount Everest of treasures. I want to be known as the guy who found Yamashita's gold—you know, just because it's there—and walked away from a trillion dollar fortune."

Keith stared back at Buddy, openly assessing him. After a few moments, he said, "You speak Tagalog, right?"

Buddy nodded.

"Well, I've decided to stick around here for a little while. A couple of weeks, anyway." Keith paused momentarily before committing himself. "Suppose I can solve your problem about getting access to the sites, and I give you all the credit for finding it. Will you show me how to get past the booby-traps?"

That's the way it always works, Buddy thought. The only reason to share a piece of the pie is if you're convinced that the other guy's contribution is essential to your own success. In this case, the fact that Buddy didn't believe the booby-traps existed didn't matter. The only thing that mattered was that Keith believed in them. And the more Keith worried about them, the more he'd value Buddy.

He still needed to know how Keith could solve the property access problem. If it was a solid approach, Buddy would play along with the arrangement. For now.

"OK, Keith, I'm in. But only if I get to pick which site we dig first."

Unsure of what to say, Keith simply nodded.

Buddy pressed. "So, tell me. What's your angle? How do you get us on the property?"

"We can go to every one of the sites and, as long as you're with me, no one will bother us."

Buddy raised his eyebrows. "Oh? And how do you figure that?"

Keith smiled smugly. "My company owns the rights to every one of these locations."

"Your company? How the hell did you accomplish that?"

"It's a long story."

"So what?" countered Buddy, for the first time truly stunned by someone else's information. "I've got time."

Nick was in his room at the university, thinking about the situation and poring over the documents in the binder. He asked himself for the thousandth time, who was behind this? Getting the inland properties had been Papa's idea, he thought, or had it? Nick knew that the attorney had managed the process of getting the options to the properties and that Romy had managed the attorney, but—it just couldn't be him, he felt. Romy was their companion and protector.

Nick was wondering if Papa could have possibly eluded The Committee for so long when the sound of footsteps approaching made him look up. "Hey, Dad," said Max, passing through the open door and plopping down on the futon. "You should have been there. It was really cool."

Sean followed him inside and joined them on the bed.

"There were these really neat caves," Max continued. "They were huge. One of them was so big that, during the second World War, the people in the town used to have dances in it, with bands and lights and everything."

"Yeah," corrected Sean. "But not during the whole war, only at the beginning. The guide said that when the Japanese got here and gained control, they made the caves off-limits to the local people." He looked up at Nick. "I'll bet they used the caves as bomb shelters, Dad. They go really deep underground."

Just as Nick was about to respond, Laurie entered the room, with Romy a step behind. One look at her face was all it took Nick to know that she'd found another marker.

"Hey, Laurie," he said rising and giving her a quick kiss. "How did your tour go?"

Laurie smiled thinly and nodded knowingly at him. "It was informative, just like you thought it would be."

Romy, who had been listening politely, asked, "And how was your meeting with the cooperative members, Nick?"

"It was fine. About thirty people showed up. I think they were mostly just curious. It was amazing, though. Some of them came from quite a distance."

"Yes, Nick," he said enigmatically. "Quite a number of people here have heard about you and are interested in following your progress." He made a show of checking his wristwatch. "I am sorry, but the tour took a great deal longer than I had anticipated. Your sons insisted on seeing the entire network of caverns. Now, if you could all please hurry, the bus driver is waiting for us, it is time to go to the airport."

The boys disappeared with Romy to grab their bags, and Laurie said, "Did you hear anything from Keith?"

Nick shook his head. "No. I had to leave a message. I'll try again when we get to Manila." He raised his eyebrows, asking the question silently.

She glanced over her shoulder, aware that the door was open and that Romy could reappear any instant. She came into his arms for a hug, and whispered up to him, "It was so dark that I almost missed it." Stepping back a bit so she could look him in the face, she said softly, "Another tiger."

Instead of methodically plodding along as he had earlier, the bus driver raced through the streets of Legazpi City like a maniac. Shifting gears furiously, he constantly wove in and out of the traffic, honking his horn and tailgating dangerously.

Nick, seated in the twin front seat with Laurie, turned around and asked, "What's going on, Romy?"

Romy, leaned forward in his seat, "Our scheduled flight to Manila has been canceled. We are trying to get to the airport in time to catch another plane."

Fifteen minutes later they approached the airport, screeching to a halt in front of the terminal. Romy bounded out of the bus and raced inside, moving with remarkable speed for a man of his size and age. A moment later he returned, walking now, and breathing heavily. He shook his head. They were too late.

Romy walked back up the steps of the bus and spoke in Tagalog to the driver. Their conversation started slowly but built quickly in intensity, culminating in an incredibly rapid staccato exchange. Suddenly, Romy stopped talking and nodded, satisfied. He turned to Nick and said, "He will drive us."

"Excuse me?" he asked in near disbelief.

With a dismissive wave of Romy's hand, the driver pulled the lever that shut the door to the bus, and engaged the gear. As the bus lurched away from the curb, Romy continued. "There are no other flights until Monday. He will drive us to Manila."

"Wait a minute, isn't it over two hundred miles?"

Romy hesitated for only an instant, his face breaking into an approving grin. "Very good, Nick, you are right. It is almost three hundred kilometers exactly."

"How long will it take?"

Romy shook his head, "The roads are not very good. If we drive straight through, it will probably take us around ten hours. We should get there early tomorrow morning."

Nick instantly did the math; twenty miles an hour for ten hours. "Christ," he breathed, softly. They'd be spending the night on the open road. If anyone wanted to get at them, now was their chance; they'd be completely exposed.

Laurie gently nudged him in the ribs, aware that the boys were listening to their conversation anxiously. "Hey!" she said cheerfully, mustering some credible enthusiasm, "we'll just camp out on the bus. There's plenty of room to stretch out—it'll be another adventure."

Romy grinned broadly enough to expose the gap in his upper molars, "There you go, Laurie. Still a cowboy."

She smiled, relaxing. "Romy, let's stop somewhere in town and get something to eat, and some food and drinks we can take with us. Oh, and some blankets, too. OK?"

"Certainly." Romy turned and spoke to the driver, at some length.

Sometime after midnight, Nick woke up as the bus lurched through another hairpin turn, causing his head to bump against the window. His brain instantly kicked into gear, but he didn't open his eyes. He didn't want any sights to distract him from this thoughts, which shot back and forth like a tennis ball at Wimbledon.

His first thought was that it would be nice to be back in his office so that he could work out his problems on his white board. Yeah, right—as if there were a magic wand he could wave that would make this mess go away. Or transport him and his family back to the safety of the States. No. His best option was getting them to the security of the Manila Hotel. He glanced at his watch. They would be there in just a few more hours.

He reflected on the facts. What did he know? And what did he only suspect?

He knew they'd been followed, but by whom? Was it The Committee, or was it that asshole Ramierez? He was powerful enough, and motivated. Or was it someone else?

What did they want? What might they do?

And what about his partners? Who was in on it, and who wasn't?

There were too many unknowns. With so many uncertainties, he had no specific target. There was no one to confront. Nothing to fix. A bad combination for a consultant.

One thing was for sure—he was in way over his head. And there was no one he could turn to for help. He'd have to get them out of this one by himself.

More than ever, he realized, it was essential that his family stick together. Without Romy's protection, he couldn't risk letting Laurie or the boys out of his sight. A kidnapping would be easy to arrange. If something happened to any of them, he knew, he'd have to go along with whatever it was that they wanted. He had to get his family on the airplane and out of the country. Only then would they truly be safe.

He sat up straight, looking around and orienting himself. The roads, he saw through the glow of the headlights, were even worse than he had pictured. Paved only with packed gravel, they weren't much wider than a single lane. Looking out at the darkness of the night, the isolation of the area gave him an overwhelming sense of exposure. Headlights of another car speeding towards them lit up the inside of the bus.

Still bouncing the possibilities back and forth in his mind, he looked around. He saw Max curled up asleep in one of the seats across from him, while Sean slept on the floor, in the aisle. Romy had taken the bench seat in the back, and Laurie was in the seat just behind him, wide awake.

"Hi, there," she said, softly, moving up and joining him in his seat.

He put his arm around her and she leaned against him. "Did you get any sleep?" he asked.

"Not much."

Just as he began to respond, the sound of an explosion echoed through the interior of the bus, which suddenly veered to the right as the driver struggled for control. They bolted upright, each looking quickly around.

"What was that?" Laurie cried, as the driver, wrestling with the steering wheel, brought the bus to a skidding stop on the shoulder of the road. "It sounded like gunshot."

Nick, looking at the boys, called out, "Is everyone OK?"

Max, who had been thrown to the floor by the sudden stop, rubbed the side of his head with his hand and got back up on the seat. "What's going on? Where are we?" he asked.

Laurie, seeing that Sean was all right, went over to Max and put her arm around him. The driver opened the door and stepped out cautiously into the darkness, with Nick following just behind. Romy, who had also been bounced onto the floor, climbed over Sean and was sitting down next to Laurie when Nick stuck his head back inside the bus. "It's only a flat tire," he said with relief. "I'll give the driver a hand. I don't want this to take any longer than necessary."

By the time Nick had gone back down the steps, the driver had retrieved an oil lantern and a few pieces of equipment from a compartment in the back of the bus. The jack he produced was small, almost like a toy, but it managed to lift the bus high enough to do the job. With both of them working together, it took a half hour to remove the right front tire and replace it with the spare.

Dusty and dirty, they were again underway, reaching the outskirts of Manila just as dawn began to break. Laurie, the boys and Romy all slept, but Nick, though bone-tired himself, sat in the front seat and talked, making sure that the driver stayed awake. The man spoke virtually no English, so Nick simply asked questions about the places they passed, which the appreciative driver responded to in Tagalog.

Nick recognized their route as they approached Rizal Park. "Wake up, Laurie," he said gently. "We're almost there."

A few minutes later, they turned into the driveway leading to the Manila Hotel. "Why don't you take the guys inside and get us checked in?" Nick said, as she stretched and rubbed the sleep from her eyes. "I'll take care of the baggage and meet you at the front desk."

The driver stopped the bus at the entrance, which was directly across the driveway from a long row of parked taxis. Laurie gathered the boys and led them into the hotel, while Nick and Romy walked towards the back of the bus. They were just starting to reach for their bags when a uniformed bellman appeared with a brass luggage cart.

Happy to have the assistance, and comforted by the more civilized—and secure—surroundings, Nick glanced idly around. Off in the distance, he could see the twinkling lights of boats moored out in the bay, and, just in front of him, an eclectic collection of taxis, waiting for passengers to come out of the hotel. Some of the drivers were slumped in their seats, napping, and others stood outside, leaning against their vehicles and smoking cigarettes. The sight of a muddy school bus disgorging a family of American passengers was enough to draw more than a few curious stares from them.

As Nick turned back to watch the bellman finish taking their suitcases off the bus, he realized with an almost physical shock that one of the taxi drivers had seemed to wink at him. He spun around, and looked again. There, only twenty yards away, was the man with the withered eye. His mind raced and he turned back, gesturing to Romy.

"Romy," he said, softly but urgently. "Come here. Quickly. It's the man who has been following me. Look over my shoulder. Do you see the guy leaning against the red car across the street?"

Romy stepped forward and looked past Nick.

"Where?" asked Romy. "Who?"

Nick turned around. The man was gone.

N

PASIG RIVER

RUINS OF
INTRAMUROS

MANILA HOTEL•

RIZAL PARK

Manila
BAY

ROXAS BOULEVARD

MANILA
DETAIL

Nick stretched out, luxuriating in the clean, crisp sheets of the king-size bed. Sunlight poked through the sides of the heavy curtains, and he rolled over to look at the clock. It was almost noon.

He got out of bed and walked over to the open door which led to the adjoining room where the boys had slept. He found them lying on one of the big beds, quietly watching television.

"Hey, Dad," said Max. "You should see this. It's really funny."

"Yeah," explained Sean. "It's an old American cartoon that they've dubbed in Chinese."

Nick entered the room and sat on the edge of the bed, watching for a moment. The high-pitched dubbing contrasted starkly with the normal voices of the characters, and the speech was completely out of sync with the movement of their mouths. "Guys, I know it's been over a week since you've had the chance to watch any TV, but I didn't think you'd be this desperate. Anyone hungry?"

The serenity of the moment was instantly broken as both boys leapt to their feet, shouting at the same time, "Yeah. Let's go!"

Their voices had awakened Laurie, who appeared in the doorway in her nightgown.

"Mornin', Laurie," Nick said, giving her a hug. "I told the boys we'd go get something to eat. Care to join us?"

She nodded, snuggling her face into his chest. "Of course," she said with a yawn. "Give me a couple of minutes, and I'll be all set to go."

With everyone dressed, they went down the hall to the elevator for the short ride to the ground floor. The lobby was bustling with activity, and they wove their way through the crowds to the Champagne Room for Sunday brunch. Although the restaurant was packed with people, they were able to get a large corner table immediately.

As soon as they were seated, a tuxedoed waiter appeared, carrying a tray of crystal flutes filled with champagne. "Compliments of the house, Mr. Gardner," he said with a slight bow, placing one glass in front of Laurie and another in front of Nick.

The boys eyes grew wide as the waiter served champagne to each of them as well. Nick looked over at Laurie, who winked back at him. "One sip, boys—that's it," she said. Both of the boys immediately reached for their glass and took a taste, which was followed by similar facial expressions of disgust.

"Yuck!" said Max, his shoulders shuddering slightly. "How can you drink that stuff?

Nick and Laurie clinked their glasses together, "To Laurie's Island," he said.

"Cheers," she responded.

He raised his eyebrows and sipped the sparkling wine, his thoughts uncomfortably at odds with the spirit of the toast.

The waiter returned, took orders for drinks and directed them to the buffet, which was so large that it was set up in a separate, adjoining room. Leaving their table, they discovered that the selection and presentation of the buffet was overwhelming. No less than half a dozen long tables were covered with food, spread out in sweeping twin arcs, each artfully packed with covered chafing dishes. A diner could choose from breakfast, lunch, dinner or dessert, and eat either western or eastern food. Four chefs stood at the end of the room, manning portable ranges for making omelets and hot sandwiches.

"OK, boys," said Laurie. "Help yourselves to whatever you want, and meet us back at the table. Don't waste anything. And remember—walk, don't run."

Nick and Laurie went to the end of one of the long tables and collected a plate from the rack. She turned to him and said, "How did your telephone call go with Keith last night—or should I say this morning?"

Nick shook his head. "It didn't. I was finally able to retrieve the messages from my answering machine, but none of them were from Keith. It's frustrating"

"Isn't he supposed to be home by now?" she asked, a note of concern in her voice.

"I don't know," he lied, looking down at his plate so that he would avoid meeting her eyes. "Maybe I misunderstood his schedule. I'll try him again after we eat."

"Don't worry, Nick. I'm sure he's OK."

They walked the length of each side of the buffet, occasionally serving themselves. By the time they returned to their table, the boys were already seated. Nick checked out their plates, curious to see what they had selected. Max had managed to fill a plate entirely with food that was white. He had two kinds of fish. He had rice. He had bread. And everything was white. Sean had amassed an impressive array of shellfish—his plate a heaping pile of lobster, tiger shrimp, clams and mussels.

Laurie returned to the buffet for seconds and the boys went back for thirds, but Nick ate sparingly, distracted throughout the meal by a gauntlet of his own thoughts. When they were finished, they left the restaurant to return to their rooms, and were nearly to the elevators when Laurie turned to Nick. "You know, between the long bus ride and all that food, I really need to take a walk. Is it OK if we take the boys to see Intramuros?"

Nick thought for a moment. Like Laurie, his body craved exercise, and he felt dull and sluggish, as well as the effects of the champagne. He knew that it was a beautiful day outside but he had planned for them all to spend the day safely within the confines of the hotel.

"I really don't think that's a very good idea. Why don't we just go for a swim in the hotel pool?"

"Come on, Nick," she pushed. "The boys can always go swimming, but they'll never get another chance to see the ruins here. We'll be fine."

He sighed, reconsidering. The ruins really were something the boys should see and they were just across the street. There would be lots of other people around, so they ought to be safe enough. He looked back at her, the tone of his voice indicating that it was clearly against his better judgment, and said, "All right. But just for a little while, OK?"

Laurie went over to the concierge and returned a moment later with a brochure that described the historical site, which had been built by the Spaniards some four hundred years earlier. Having gathered the boys, she read from the pamphlet, sharing some of the key points of the site's history with them as they walked past the hotel security guards and out the door.

"Listen to this. 'The stone walls surrounding the ancient city of Intramuros are over fifteen feet high and, in many places, are as thick as forty feet.' She read further and summarized, "The area inside the walls covers about two square miles, and the meadow outside the walls, which is now used as a golf course, used to be a protective moat that was filled with water, like a medieval castle."

They walked down the driveway to the intersection. Waiting for the light to turn green, they could see other people milling about at the entrance to the site, which lay directly across the busy boulevard. She continued to look at the brochure. "During the second World War, this was the site of the final battle where the Allied forces—that's the Americans, boys—recaptured the Philippines from the Japanese. The fighting during that battle was so intense that the entire place was reduced to what it is today.

"My God, Nick," she continued. "Over sixteen thousand Japanese soldiers died here."

Looking over at the historic site, they could see into the maze of ten-foot-high brick walls arranged in concentric geometric patterns, and a few groups of people walking within the walls along pathways of unmowed grass and gravel. As the light changed and they entered the crosswalk, the boys surged ahead. Laurie called after them, "Remember, boys—stick together!"

Without taking her eyes off them, Laurie reached over and took Nick's hand. Their fingers interlaced automatically, and they strolled for a minute in silence, following several yards behind their children.

"So, Nick, would you like to tell me what in the world you think is going on?"

He nodded. "I can tell you what I know, and I can tell you what I think, but the simple fact is that I really don't know very much." He looked over at her as they walked toward one of the entrances to the ancient city. "What I do know is this—the only thing that stands between us and a ton of money is a five-pound bag of processed carrageenan. That test sample may already be back in California with Keith, but since I haven't been able to contact him yet, I don't know that.

"I also know that PRMC, of which I am President, indirectly owns the rights to a lot of land over here—land that *might* hold buried treasure." He stopped for a moment.

"Wait a minute, are you saying you still doubt that there's a treasure? Are you out of your mind?" she cried.

He shook his head. "No, I didn't say that. I just said I can't prove it's on land that's controlled by our company."

"Right," said Laurie, "because we don't have those Japanese maps that Eleanor told us about."

"I suppose," he said, starting to walk again. "But I mean—really—a trillion dollar buried treasure? Doesn't it still seem just a little bit unbelievable to you?"

"Don't give me that, Nick. Where there's this much smoke, there's gotta be fire. The treasure is real, and we both know it.

"Don't get too far ahead!" Laurie called out to the boys, who were now twenty yards ahead of them, dodging in and out of the openings in the brick walls of the ruins. Max, who was closest to them, turned around and waved back in acknowledgment.

Nick nodded. "OK, you're right. I do believe that the treasure exists. Someone is using us to get at it, but I don't know who that someone is." He looked at her, adding, "And I sure as shit don't know why."

"Why what?"

"Well, if you had the key to the treasure, why on earth would you wait to uncover it? Why would you want to share it with anyone? Why would you bother to include us?" He lowered his voice as they passed a large group of Asian tourists.

She considered for a moment. "So, who do you think it is? Papa?"

Nick shook his head. "Even though he's the most logical possibility, I really doubt it. For starters, he's been investigated up the wazoo by The Committee for the past ten years, and, with all of their resources, they haven't found anything. Second, if he had access to any serious money, he wouldn't have asked me to go and find an investor for the company. That's the last thing he'd do—he'd have just given me the money himself.

"I mean, it's one thing if you and I know what's going on, but there's just no way that he'd risk having very many people know about it. He's bound to realize that any U.S. investor is going to ask questions.

"The same is true for Alec," he said as the boys ducked around the corner in front of them, momentarily out of sight. "Besides, Alec is so devout that his faith dictates his actions and his priorities. He's got so much visibility that I can't see him risking the heritage of his Sultancy by being publicly associated with something as shady as a treasure conspiracy. It just doesn't make sense."

She looked up at him. "So who does that leave? You don't think it's Luis, do you?"

"Not a chance. He's a senior member of the government and he lived through the ugliness of the final years of the Marcos regime. He wouldn't dare put himself in a situation where his reputation, his lifelong contributions to the Philippine people, could be painted with the same brush that tarnished Marcos.

"No, none of them fit. Unless they suddenly come up with a couple of million bucks to capitalize the company, it can't be any of them. It has to be someone else. That's why I keep getting back to the question of why." He turned to her. "Why orchestrate all of this? Why us?"

They reached the brick wall at the end of the broad grassy walkway and stopped. Looking to the left, they saw a number of other people who were touring the site, but neither of them could see the boys. They looked to their right just in time to see Max and Sean duck out of a gap in the wall.

"Guys!" called out Nick. "Wait up!"

As they continued walking, Laurie asked, "Have you ever thought about what you would do if you found the treasure?"

"Truthfully, no. It may be hard for some people to accept, but, I really don't care about it." He chuckled. "I may be the only one around here who doesn't. I want the business to succeed."

She squeezed his hand.

"Look, if PRMC goes public, we can make twenty-five or thirty million dollars. We'd be set for life, the boys would be taken care of. We're just not the kind of people who would ever be able to spend it all. What would we do with any more?"

She looked up at him. Their eyes met and they both smiled and shook their heads. Then Laurie answered, seriously, "You could give it back to the people here."

"I'm afraid there are too many greedy fingers in the hands of the government. Pricks like Ramierez. It'd never reach the people who really need it."

"So you set up a foundation." She stopped. "No, you've already got your own company. You just use PRMC to do what needs to be done. You take the treasure and build hospitals and sewers. Power plants. More schools. Set up companies here to supply businesses back home, and to hire and train people.

Although he faced her, Nick's eyes looked past her, searching for the boys.

"That's what I'd do," she said, looking up at him. "What do you think?"

"It's wrong, and I just can't do it," adding almost under his breath, "God only knows how many laws I'd be breaking." His eyes surveyed the sparse crowd, scanning for any sign of the boys. They were nowhere to be seen.

"Boys?" he shouted out. "Boys!"

He waited a few seconds for a response, then dropped Laurie's hand and bolted down the wide grassy pathway. "Come on!" he yelled back to her. She was already racing after him. He reached top speed in a couple of strides, sprinting in the direction of his last glimpse of them, looking into the openings and gaps in the walls that he whizzed past. "Boys!" he hollered.

Laurie, suddenly on the verge of panic, screamed as well, "Boys!"

As Nick reached the end the path, he heard a voice call out and he stopped, turning around. "Dad! Over here!" It was Max, sticking his head out from one of the unframed doorways he had just run past. "What is it Dad?" he asked, as Laurie caught up with them. "What's going on?"

Laurie rushed over and put her arms around him. "Thank heaven! There you are. Where's Sean?"

Max shrugged, shaking his head.

Nick, slightly winded, demanded, "Where did you see him last?"

Max pointed to spot a dozen yards away, where the corners of ruins formed an intersection of pathways. "He was standing right over there and he ditched me, so I decided to hide over here."

"How long ago?" he barked.

"Just a minute or so, Dad. He can't be far away."

"Wait here," he said to Laurie as he started to run towards the intersection. "If you see him, yell."

Heading in the direction that Max had indicated, he took off, running as fast as he could. He picked the path in the middle, his eyes darting left and right as he looked around the corners of every ruin he passed, desperate for a sign of him. In the labyrinth of ancient rubble, however, there were simply too many places to look, too many places to hide. "Sean!" he yelled.

He sped down another grassy gap between ruins—long, windowless brick walls on either side of him—and slowed down when he reached the next intersection.

He looked both ways and ran to the right. He kept calling out for Sean, but heard nothing but the sound of his feet hitting the ground. Two minutes passed. No sign of Sean. He kept running, his lungs starting to ache. He backtracked, racing down new paths.

Turning yet another corner, he immediately saw a pool of blood.

He skidded to a stop, his heart pounding wildly. A second puddle of blood lay a few feet away, and another beyond that one. Walking numbly, he followed the crimson trail through a doorway when he first saw the body. Or what was left of one.

It wasn't Sean, he realized instantly, but a white male with light-colored hair. The partially-clad body lay face-down and was almost entirely bathed with blood. A few insects swarmed around the head. Nick was about to turn around to look for Sean when he noticed the whiteness of the dead man's tennis shoes. His stomach nearly heaved—it might be Keith. He walked around to the other side of the body and bent down to look at the face.

Good God, he thought in shock and revulsion as he examined the bloody mass of hair and flesh. The man's features had been horribly slashed and battered. They'd cut him in other places as well. His penis was sticking out of his mouth. Poor bastard, thought Nick. At least he could discern from what remained of the corpses's features that it wasn't Keith.

He didn't know how much time had passed when he heard someone call his name in the distance. Stepping outside, he cried out, "Sean?"

Laurie's voice called back faintly, "He's here!"

"Stay where you are," he shouted back, heading in the direction of her voice. Breaking into a long, loping gait, Nick quickly found his way back to them. Laurie stood huddled with an arm around each boy, her face a mixture of anger and relief.

Nick walked the last few steps towards them, the sweat pouring down his shaking body. His heart began to regain its normal rhythm. "Dammit, boys, you scared the shit out of me. Come on, let's get back to the hotel."

Nick escorted them upstairs to their room. The boys, chastised during the long walk back, went to watch television, and Laurie escaped to the bathroom to soak in the tub. Nick announced that he needed to take care of something with the concierge downstairs and that he'd be back as soon as possible. There was no way he was going to tell Laurie about the body, but he had to tell the authorities.

It was nearly two hours before he was able to return to his room, and the first thing he did was to reach for the telephone. He got through to the answering machine in his office and punched in the numbers of his access code. No messages. He dialed Keith's office number, which was answered by a machine as well.

Nick hung up the phone and looked out the window at the boats in the harbor. What the hell could have happened, he wondered? Where could Keith be? Was he safe? He flipped open his calendar and confirmed that he was, in fact, supposed to have already landed in San Francisco. Frustrated and worried, he realized that he'd just have to try again later.

They were nearly finished with their meals at the hotel's Roma Ristorante Italiano when the three partners unexpectedly entered the dining room. Seeing them first, Nick rose and walked towards them, outwardly calm, but inwardly apprehensive.

"Papa—Alec—Romy," he said, shaking hands with each of them. "I wasn't expecting to see you tonight. I thought we were supposed to get together first thing in the morning."

"Something's come up, Nick, and we won't be able to make it then, so we thought we'd try to catch you now," said Papa smoothly.

"Sure," replied Nick tersely. "We're just finishing our dinner. Why don't you come over and join us for dessert?"

"Great," said Romy, grinning broadly.

The uniformed *maître d'*, who had been hovering nearby, stepped forward and ushered the newcomers to the table next to theirs. Laurie smiled up at them, saying, "What a nice surprise."

As Nick reached for the back of his chair, he turned to the *maître d'*. "Do you have zabaglione?"

With a crisp, shallow bow, the uniformed man said tartly, "But of course, sir."

"Good. Servings for everyone, please."

"Right away, sir."

He seated himself as their guests settled into their chairs. "Hello, boys," said Romy, and they greeted him excitedly. Alec acknowledged the boys with a wave.

Papa turned to Nick. "So, you leave tomorrow morning."

"Yep," replied Nick. "We're on the first flight out. We have a stopover in Hong Kong, and return to San Francisco the next day."

"Ah, that is good," smiled Romy, approvingly. "Your family will get to see what it looks like before it reverts to the Chinese. Where will you be staying in Hong Kong?"

"At the Marriott. Laurie would love to go back to the Peninsula Hotel, but, as you can imagine, it's just too expensive for all of us. Besides, the subway has a station right underneath the Marriott, so it's really convenient for getting around the city."

The *maître d'* returned, leading a parade of uniformed men.

First to follow was a very short chef pushing a cart, whose classic, starched white hat was so tall he seemed to be the same size as the others around him. Five musicians brought up the rear, four with violins held almost carelessly at their sides, and one with a mandolin that he carried like a baby. The cart was wheeled into position behind Nick, so that most of the people in his party could observe the preparation.

Papa leaned forward. "What have you heard from Keith?"

The *maître d'* departed, and the chef, using a single hand, broke two eggs into a large aluminum mixing bowl.

Nick shook his head. "Nothing. I've tried to reach him several times, but I haven't been able to get through to him yet. I assume that he got the sample and made it back all right." Nick noticed the surprised looks on the men's faces and continued. "If he had a problem, I'm sure he would have left a message for me on my answering machine. Something probably came up at the last minute."

Papa considered, and spoke again. "I see. And once the sample is approved, what is your next step?"

The chef added some Marsala to the eggs and lit the small, portable gas burner on top of the cart.

"We meet with Bart Stevenson, the investor. As soon as our sample passes the customer's tests, we'll have an order for a whole lot of seaweed. We'll need to get our money lined up so that we can finance our processing, shipping and marketing."

Placing the bowl over the portable range, the chef began to stir the eggs with a wire whisk, and the musicians began to play softly behind him. Although Nick didn't recognize the tune, it had a distinctive, Italian style.

"That's what we thought," replied Papa neutrally, "And that's what we need to talk about."

"Oh?"

As the sounds of the violins subsided slightly, the chef began to whip the zabaglione in time with the beat of the strumming of the mandolin. The musician picked up the pace of his strumming, and the chef matched his rhythmic whisking of the mixture in the bowl as it heated, the hard, flexible wires of the utensil clinking against the metallic rim of the bowl.

Papa looked over at his associates and then back at Nick. "Yes. Since it seems that things are going so well, maybe we don't need an outside investor."

Nick's eyes widened. "Excuse me?"

Papa looked down at the table. "How much money do you need?"

"For now, three million—minimum—and when we decide to build the processing plant, another twelve."

The strumming of the mandolin built to a loud crescendo, and the chef completed his whisking with a simultaneous flourish. A handful of diners at other tables briefly applauded.

Papa smiled. "No problem. Let us know when you need it, and we'll arrange a wire transfer into the corporate account."

Nick looked back at him in disbelief.

The chef ladled the thick custard into small, delicate glass bowls and served them.

Papa sat back, gesturing modestly with one of his hands. "Why dilute our holdings at this stage? Besides," he said, glancing over at Alec and Romy, "they would just ask a lot of unnecessary questions. It is better if we keep things amongst ourselves.

"You have done very well, Nick," continued Papa. "Very well indeed. You've accomplished everything we expected you to, and then some. Go home now and take care of business. Take care of your family. We'll be in touch. Soon."

Nick looked down at the golden-brown dessert in front of him. Absentmindedly reaching for his spoon, he dipped it into the bowl. Papa's lips continued to move, but Nick didn't hear any of the words. His mind a million miles away, he brought the spoon to his lips. The warm, sweet custard had a cold and bitter taste in his mouth. His mind was consumed by a single thought—getting his family out of there.

Sitting in the jam-packed passenger lounge at their departure gate, he glanced at his watch for the thousandth time that morning. A little after seven. They didn't have long to wait.

After they had put the boys to bed the night before, he and Laurie had returned to their room and simply looked at one another, then melted into each other's arms for a long, tight, silent embrace. Although there was no sense of friction between them, neither of them had said so much as a single word to the other as they prepared for bed. While Laurie slept, Nick had tossed and turned, his brain racing through an endless sequence of questions and options.

They had arisen very early and then packed, checked out of the hotel, and taxied to the airport. Nick had, as unobtrusively as possible, looked constantly around them to see if they were being followed. Although he couldn't be absolutely sure, he hadn't seen any familiar faces observing them.

They had passed through the emigration process, checked in for their flight, and proceeded uneventfully down the terminal concourse to the gate. Despite the lulling effect of following a routine he had performed countless times before, Nick was intensely focused on getting his family on the airplane. He wouldn't be able to relax until they were out of the Philippines.

Waiting to board the airplane, Nick watched the door that led to the waiting area, certain that men from The Committee would barge through it at the last minute and detain him for questioning. What would he tell them, he wondered? What could he tell them? That he was just an American businessman traveling with his family? That although he'd heard rumors about the treasure, he didn't know anything? No, he realized, they'd see through that. And what protection would he have? How could he protect his family?

Lost in his own thoughts, he almost jumped out of his skin when Laurie nudged him with her elbow. "My God, Nick! Did you see this?" she nearly shouted as she pointed to her morning newspaper. They found a dead body yesterday at Intramuros." As she continued to read, the blood drained from her face. Then she turned to look at him directly. "The body was discovered by an American tourist." She looked into his eyes deeply, and Nick made no effort to manufacture an expression of innocence—that wasn't an option. "It was you, wasn't it?"

He nodded. "Shhh. Keep your voice down. God, it was awful. I've never seen violence like that before. I didn't want to freak you out, so I didn't say anything."

"No wonder you've been acting so strangely. How horrible! That's why you took so long getting back to the room."

Still staring straight ahead, he nodded again. Numb and momentarily distracted by the image of the battered body, he didn't notice the man with the withered eye enter the boarding area.

He sat forward in the chair, resting his elbows on his knees, and glanced down at his watch again. He heard the sound of a heavy metallic door swinging open and looked up quickly. His heart stopped. It was only the ticket agent opening the door to the jetway for their flight. The next few minutes melded into a series of announcements and moving in crowded lines as they were allowed to board the plane and take their seats.

Nick buckled in, outwardly calm but inwardly reeling, waiting for the sound of the plane's door closing. At last, it came. The engines started, the plane pushed back from the gate, taxied out to the runway, and took off.

Nick took a very deep breath and audibly exhaled.

They landed in Hong Kong an hour and a half later and breezed through customs. Everyone carried their suitcases outside, where the sun was shining and the temperature a perfectly comfortable seventy degrees.

"Whoa!" exclaimed Max, pointing to a very long Mercedes limousine approaching the curb. "Look at that."

The black stretch vehicle rolled to a stop in front of them, its front door opened, and a uniformed Chinese chauffeur emerged. He looked directly at Nick, and said, with a touch of a British accent, "Mr. and Mrs. Gardner, welcome to Hong Kong."

"Thank you," said Nick, as the chauffeur stepped over and opened the passenger door for them. Nick gestured to Laurie to get in, while the boys stood numbly still, their mouths open. The driver began loading the suitcases into the trunk.

"Come on, boys, don't just stand there. Hop in."

They arrived at the Marriott within twenty minutes, and checked in with the concierge.

Their room was a small suite on the twenty-seventh floor. The large front room was appointed with a couple of designer sofas that converted into beds, and several comfortable chairs arrayed in front of an impressive entertainment center. The second room had a king-size bed and a writing desk. Each room had its own private bath. It was not, however, the floor plan or the furniture that made the setting so spectacular, it was the view.

The entire outside wall was glass, floor to ceiling, so that beyond and beneath them lay the magnificent panorama of Hong Kong Harbor and Tsim Sha Tsui, the Kowloon Peninsula.

"Can we go down there?" said Max, pointing to the mass of small boats down in the harbor.

"OK. As soon as I make a couple of quick phone calls and we change into some walking-around clothes, we're outta here."

He walked briskly to the desk and dialed Keith's number. Goddammit, he thought, still no answer. He left another message on the machine and called his own office to check his messages. Nothing from Keith. Fuck!

Laurie walked over and gave Nick a big hug. "Are you going to be able to relax now?" she said.

Sean looked up. "Yeah, Dad, did something go wrong during your meeting last night? You didn't even finish your dessert."

Nick nodded. "I didn't realize you were watching my food so closely. Haven't we been feeding you enough?" He gave Laurie a quick kiss. "I've had a lot on my mind, that's all. Come on, let's go."

The rest of their stay in Hong Kong flew by. They spent the first part of the afternoon checking out the Stanley Market, then took the subway into Kowloon where they roamed the bustling, densely-pack streets until early evening. They rode the Star Ferry back across the harbor to the island, and had an inexpensive dinner in one of the hotel restaurants.

Returning to their room, Nick was elated to see the blinking red light on the telephone. Finally, a message from Keith. Punching in his access code, he retrieved the single awaiting message. He felt his skin crawl and a tightness in his throat as he listened to a voice he'd never heard before.

"Mr. Gardner. You have a collection of documents in your possession. If you give them to me, I will not harm your children." A pause. "Or even your beautiful wife. You will meet me tonight—"

Nick listened to the rest of the instructions numbly, his stomach churning at the speaker's final words. "Come alone, and re-member Intramuros." He hung up the phone.

"What is it, Nick? Did you finally hear from Keith?"

"No. Something else has come up." He glanced at his watch. "I have to go."

He looked her in the eyes. "Lock the door behind me."

As instructed, he took the elevator to the subway station beneath the hotel lobby. The place was almost empty, and he exchanged his money for a token at a machine. Following the color-coded line on the wall, he boarded the first train that was headed north, under the harbor waters, to the Kowloon Peninsula. Clutching his canvas satchel in his lap, he sat gazing out at the black-stained walls of the tunnel.

He was the only rider who got off the train at the third exit, the Yaumati Station. Nick stood on the platform next to the tracks, in between two large, tiled, supporting pillars, exactly as he had been instructed. Just standing there, waiting in the empty station, he felt so exposed. He tried to visualize what was about to happen.

The train departed, leaving him completely alone. A few min-utes passed and he glanced at his watch. It was time. The metallic voice announcing the arrival of the next train covered the sound of the approaching footsteps. Nick sensed the presence of a figure and turned. It was the man with the withered eye. The man paused a few yards away, studying Nick. Then he began to step forward, slowly, as if stalking his prey. Although Nick watched his every move, it was only when the man stopped a few feet away, just be-yond arms reach, that Nick saw the gun. It was big. And pointed right at him.

The man finally spoke. "Did you bring it?"

Nick nodded. Bending down, he put the satchel on the ground, opened the flap, and reached inside with both hands. With his left hand, he withdrew the binder and its precious map. Underneath it, his right hand grabbed the razor sharp dagger. When he stood, his hands held the binder as if it were a serving tray.

"Here. This is what you want. Now leave us alone."

The man reached out with his free hand and sneered. "Fuck you. Your wife will be my bonus." Nick could only hear the first few words he spoke before the rushing air of the approaching train drowned out everything else.

Just before he could touch the binder, Nick dropped it. The man looked down, momentarily surprised, and Nick slashed upwards at his neck with the naked blade. As if in slow motion, Nick felt only a slight tug as the knife connected. Desperate to evade the assault, the man leapt backwards, stumbling once on the platform before falling backwards onto the tracks. If he screamed, Nick didn't hear. The train roared over him in a flash.

Tossing the dagger back into his satchel, Nick grabbed the binder and ran up the stairs, where the bright neon lights of Nathan Street welcomed him. He flagged the first taxi he saw and was back at the hotel in fifteen minutes.

He entered the suite as quietly as possible and bolted the door, thanking God that his boys were softly snoring and that Laurie was asleep. Closing the door to the bathroom behind him, he was just starting to clean the blood off the dagger when Laurie knocked softly.

"Nick? Are you OK?"

He quickly wiped off the blade and returned it to the sheath in his briefcase. He opened the door and took her in his arms. "Yeah, everything's gonna be all right, but I'm afraid there's been another accident."

Nick didn't sleep at all, convinced that the police would arrive at any moment. Finally, he stepped over to the desk by the window, turned on the table lamp, and picked up the phone, punching in Keith's number. It was 5:30 A.M., still dark outside, and he took a moment to look out at the city, the lights reflecting off the water in the harbor reminding him of the view back home. Christ, he thought, as he listened to the machine answer again and heard Keith's taped greeting, he's still not there.

Nick spoke softly into the phone. "Keith, this is Nick again. It's Tuesday morning, the twelfth—I think it's Monday night there. I've been going nuts trying to reach you.

"We're going to be leaving on an eight-thirty flight this morning so I don't see any way that I'll be able to connect with you today in person. If you haven't already done it, please leave me a message on my machine. I've been really worried about you and need to find out how the rest of your trip went. I'll give you a call as soon as I get back home. Be careful, partner."

He hung up the phone and dialed his office number. On signal, he entered his access codes and soon heard a welcome voice coming from the tape on his machine. "Nick, it's Keith. Sorry that this is the first time I've been able to get through to your machine, but you know what the phone lines are like over here.

"Anyway, here's a quick update. I learned a lot more about the problems associated with building and running a food processing plant while I was in Cebu, and, of course, I got our sample. It didn't make sense for me to try and carry it with me—I would have had all sorts of problems trying to carry a five-pound bag of dirty white powder through customs—so I sent it by next day air freight instead.

"Something else came up, though, so you'll need to follow up with Johanssen yourself to make sure it got there and passed all his tests. I'm not sure when you're getting back, but I'll track you down in a couple of days. Take care."

Nick hung up the phone and sat back in the chair, digesting the information. Keith was safe. But where had he called from? What was that comment about the quality of the phone lines "over here" all about? Was he still in the Philippines?

Nick still had a problem—he'd have to figure out a way to tell Keith that he was going to pull the plug on PRMC and destroy it before it even got started. That conversation, as difficult as it might be, would have to wait until he could track Keith down and speak to him in person.

They didn't bother with breakfast, knowing that they'd be sitting in an airplane for the next fifteen hours, where there would be more than enough to eat. The bellman came and loaded all of their suitcases onto a cart, and they left their room and rode the elevator down to the lobby.

While Laurie and the boys went outside to begin loading into the vehicle that would transport them to the airport, Nick went to the front desk to check them out of the hotel. He briefly scanned the items on the bill, and was signing the credit card voucher when the concierge handed him an overnight express mail envelope.

No return address, he noted. "Do you know when this arrived?" Nick asked, pulling the tab and tearing it open.

"No, Mr. Gardner. I'm sorry."

Inside the large cardboard mailing packet was a small, sealed envelope with his name handwritten on it. Nick broke the seal, pulled out the single piece of paper within, and read it quickly.

"Did you enjoy your stay, Mr. Gardner?" asked the concierge.

Nick looked at her, nodding. "Yes. It was quite exciting, in fact. This city seems to be full of surprises." He put the note back in its envelope and placed it in his briefcase.

Nick had used his frequent flier account for their tickets, so he and Laurie enjoyed the luxury of First Class while the boys sat together in the compartment behind them, in the oversized seats of Connoisseur Class. Halfway through their flight, most of the passengers had turned off their reading lights and were trying to get some sleep. Nick sipped from a glass of sparkling water and reconsidered his options.

Reaching under the seat in front of him for his briefcase, he retrieved the letter he had received at the hotel, opened it, and re-read it. In crisp, bold handwriting, he was instructed to receive a telephone call from a Mr. Sakura, a resident of San Francisco. Mr. Sakura, it seemed, was a Japanese theologian, and he would present Nick with some important papers for safekeeping. Nick glanced at the final lines of the letter again. Important, my ass, he thought, as the final piece fell into place, those papers were priceless.

He could see it now. Unless he intervened, it was only a matter of time before they'd start shipping Yamashita's gold into the United States. The first few shipments of carrageenan would proceed without a hitch. Then, when PRMC had established a routine of shipping cargo containers into the U.S., they'd start putting gold bars inside. After all, who would ever know? When you're shipping that much physical volume—something that weighs metric tons—there's got to be room for a few gold bars. It would be easy for them to have someone retrieve the bullion for them once it was stateside.

They'd keep the initial shipments small, until they figured out how to launder larger amounts. How do you sell a metric ton of gold bullion, anyway, he wondered? He thought about it for a while, and realized that, while it wouldn't be easy, it sure wasn't impossible. He shook his head. Within a year—two at the out-side—they'd be selling as much gold as the world markets could absorb. Until, that is, someone fucked up.

Somewhere along the way, of course, there would be a prob-lem, and they'd get caught. He shook his head regretfully, and took another sip of water. Even if he could stay out of jail, he'd certainly lose his business, and his reputation would be shattered.

But the company hadn't shipped anything—yet—so they hadn't broken any laws. The key now was to not let anything get started, and the easiest way to do that was to shut down PRMC. Terminating the official corporate entity was simple—all he had to do was go into the city and file the necessary paperwork. The tougher part was figuring out how to put some distance between PRMC and his partners back home.

What would he tell Bart Stevenson? What would he say to Keith? He had to come up with a plausible reason for backing away, and the reason he stated had to be something that couldn't be solved. It couldn't be a technical problem, because VCs like Bart ate those challenges for breakfast. If they couldn't out-think an obstacle, they just threw money at it until it went away.

Nick decided to tell him that he was withdrawing from the op-portunity, hinting at personal reasons. With him out of the deal, that would be more than enough to kill Bart's interest, and the idea that Nick had doubts about the ethics of his Philippine con-tacts would be assumed, but unspoken.

Keith, on the other hand, was too smart to allow any single prob-lem to stand between him and this fortune. Whatever Nick said, he'd come up with a workable solution for it. Nick smiled at the irony of the situation. They had, in fact, solved every problem they'd encountered, and now he had to manufacture one that they couldn't.

Finally it came to him. Nick would express his fear that their sample might not have actually been produced from their own crops—the thought had passed through his mind, in fact, more than once already. Without personally supervising the harvesting and processing, they had no way of knowing whether their associates hadn't simply bought a five-pound bag from a competitor, or stolen it, for that matter. If Keith came up with a solution to that problem, he'd tell him the truth.

Nick felt the letter in his fingers. There was still the question of his Philippine associates. He knew what he knew, and they knew that he knew. They'd come after him—of that he was certain. He reached down for his briefcase so that he could put the letter away, looking down one more time at the final line of the note and its signature. "By the way, I hope you enjoyed your tour of Intramuros. —Romy."

Nick sat back in his seat and closed his eyes. The next several months would be interesting. Romy and his partners weren't about to let the venture die easily. Even after he pulled the plug on PRMC, they'd arrange for him to meet with Sakura, the man with the maps. And even if Nick didn't take possession of them, the next thing they'd do is have him contacted by someone who just happened to have experience in trading gold on the world markets.

How would they approach him? Would it be direct, or subtle? Would they simply call him one day and schedule a meeting, or would one of them just show up at his doorstep, unannounced. Maybe he would get a letter from his bank, confirming the arrival an enormous wire transfer or an abnormally large deposit. No, he concluded. They'd be more devious.

Nick imagined his firm being approached by a hot, new off-shore client who would insist on paying him an exorbitant amount of money for a relatively trivial service. Or contract with his firm to acquire a shell company on behalf of another, apparently legitimate company. Christ, he realized, the contact could come from anywhere. One day, the phone would ring, and that would be it.

One thing was for sure, he thought, as he closed his eyes and drifted off to sleep, he wouldn't have long to wait.

PART SEVEN

THE BIRDS OF CIREBON

The telephone rang in his office. On any other day, he would have picked it up at once, but this morning he let it ring. He'd spent a lot of time on the phone since his return—too much time. He'd made some progress, but not enough.

As soon as he had arrived home the first thing he did was call Keith's office. He hadn't gotten an answer, of course. Keith was still out of touch. He was apparently still in the Philippines. Why? What had happened to make him stay? All Nick had to go on was the strange message that he'd gotten a few days before. Since then—nothing.

Nick had waited almost a full day before calling Bart. He'd wanted to shake the jet lag cobwebs from his mind before speaking with their potential lead investor. He knew that Bart would ask tough questions, and he wanted to be at his sharpest for their conversation. The call had been difficult enough, but had gone according to plan. There was no way that Sand Hill Investment Partners was going to participate in the deal if he wasn't going to be part of it.

Then he'd called Carl Johanssen at Mother's Milk Company. That had sure been a surprise. The sample Keith had delivered to them had arrived and been immediately tested. It was perfect, Carl had said. But there was more. Because of the improvement in the payment terms that PRMC offered, Carl, thinking that he was doing them all a favor, had made some telephone calls of his own. He'd called the heads of the other companies that made chocolate milk and told them what PRMC was doing. If Nick could make them the same deal that he had offered to him, Nick could sell nearly seven thousand metric tons per year. It was Carl's way of making sure that Nick's new company had enough critical mass to stay in business.

Instead of PRMC selling three to five million dollars worth of product in the first year, with the additional contacts that Carl had made, now they'd sell nearly forty million. The market value of the company skyrocketed proportionately, and Nick's personal equity stake now looked like it would have been worth over a hundred million dollars. Twist the knife, thought Nick. It had nearly broken his heart to tell Carl that he'd discovered some potential problems with the Philippine partnership and was not going to pursue the business.

He had driven over to Keith's house in the Oakland hills—not that he really expected to find him there, but out of sheer desperation. Perhaps, he had thought, he'd find someone who had received a message from Keith about the timing of his return, maybe a neighbor who was collecting his mail. It didn't matter who, but perhaps there was someone.

He looked down at the ringing phone. Maybe it was Keith. He picked it up. "This is Nick."

"Hello, Nick," came the familiar voice on the line. "I was afraid that I wouldn't be able to get a hold of you. How was your flight home?"

"Fine, Papa. Just fine."

"Good. And what is the news from your end?"

"It's too early to tell," Nick said, stalling for time to think. "I haven't been able to talk with Keith, so a lot of things are still up in the air."

"Yes, Nick, that is what I wanted to talk to you about."

"Excuse me?"

"We need to talk about Keith."

Nick lurched in his seat and felt a bead of sweat roll down his spine. "Is he all right?"

Papa seemed almost to laugh on the other end of the line. "Yes, of course we know where he is. He's fine."

"Why hasn't he called me then?"

There was an instant of hesitation before Papa spoke. "He has been—occupied."

"But you're sure he's OK?"

"Yes, yes. Now what is this I have heard about closing down the business?"

Nick froze. How did Papa know that?

"We need to meet," continued Papa casually, "before you take any action. We need to discuss what steps to take next. We need to talk about the future."

"Fine, Papa. I'll be happy to do that, but let me talk to Keith first."

"I am afraid that will not be possible. Don't worry, though. You have my word that he will be safe until you get here."

"What?" Nick exclaimed, not quite sure that he'd heard Papa correctly.

"You need to come back, right away."

"What? You mean to Manila?"

"It's the only way, Nick."

Nick's mind raced. He'd just escaped from there and felt lucky to be alive. Now he had to return? It wasn't possible. There must be another way. "Look, Papa," he said, desperation creeping into his voice. "Why don't we meet in Hawaii? I just got back and I've barely even unpacked from the last trip. Keith will need to come back home with me anyway, so why don't the two of you go to Honolulu? I'll meet you there. It'll be easier for all of us." At least that way, he reasoned, he'd still be on American soil, and it would get Keith out of the Philippines.

"No. It has to be here. I've already prepaid a ticket for you on United and made a reservation for you at the Manila Hotel—I know how much you appreciate it. You leave tomorrow morning. Give my best to Laurie and the boys. Good-bye."

The line went dead in Nick's hand.

November 19, 1991
Coron, The Philippines

Keith awoke from the sleep of the dead. It was still dark, and the damn dogs were barking outside his room. The manual labor of the past several days had been exhausting, and, even though he was in excellent physical shape, ten hours of shoveling the day before had been more than he could take.

After his meeting with Buddy in Cebu, he'd traveled to Manila to meet with Romy and Papa. It had been easy enough to convince them that Nick could handle the business issues back in the States, and that the best use of his own time was to learn as much as possible about the operational details of growing and harvesting carrageenan. That, of course, meant that he'd need to extend his stay in the Philippines for another few weeks. High on his list of priorities was a visit to many of their sites. They'd been only too happy—and curiously unsurprised—at his decision.

He had to wait until Saturday to catch a flight to Busuanga, and, like Nick and Laurie before him, he'd taken the jeepney from the pastoral airport to the L&M Bakery. Buddy had met him there, and they'd hired a truck for the week as well as this room. What a dump, he thought, pulling a pillow over his head in an attempt to drown out the sound of the dogs below. Oh well, he thought, in a day or two they'd be done. Never again would he have to stay in a shitty, stinking little village like this. He closed his eyes and tried to go back to sleep.

Buddy awoke to the sound of dogs fighting somewhere on the shore. Comfortably nestled in his berth on the *Makatà*, he relaxed and enjoyed the gentle rocking of the boat and reviewed the progress they'd made.

After meeting Keith ten days before, he had cut short his visit with Jenessa. He'd sailed west, and met Keith in Coron on Sunday morning, right on schedule. It had been easy enough for them to hire a vehicle to take them and their equipment to the airport, and they had spent the entire first day surveying the site.

It had been, he thought with a smile, incredible. The statue of the ox was right where it was supposed to be. And they had been lucky. They'd dragged the GPR system over the ground in a grid-like pattern to isolate the gold, and had quickly found what they were looking for. They had repeated the process four times to make sure that they got the same readings, because they both agreed that they should limit their excavation to the smallest area necessary.

While the entire area gave positive indications of buried metal, there was one particular spot that had such a concentration of gold that it pegged the needle on the monitor of the resistivity detector. That much gold, he knew, could only be one thing—the Birds of Cirebon. The best news, from his perspective, was that the cache looked like it was only buried thirteen or fourteen feet down. If it had been forty or fifty feet underground, they would have delayed digging until they could get some heavy equipment in to help them, but, again, fortune had been on their side.

By yesterday, they had been able to dig just over eleven feet down into the ground, and so, with something less than four feet to go, they'd certainly hit pay dirt today. The journey started thirty years ago, he thought, and now it was down to a mere thirty inches. Buddy knew how much his father had dreamt about this day, and wished he could be here now. Perhaps he was. Almost there, Dad. Today is the day.

Manila, The Philippines

They met in the Manila Hotel dining room over breakfast. Just as the travel had drained the energy from Nick's body, so, too, had the pretenses been stripped from the past. The three men studied each other as they waited for the waiter to deliver their coffee.

"OK," started Nick. "I'm here."

"And how is Laurie?" asked Romy politely.

"Cut the crap, Romy. How do you think she is? She's so pissed at me for coming back here that she can't see straight."

"Doesn't she want PRMC to succeed?" probed Papa.

"Give me a break. The company is finished. I've already prepared the documents necessary to shut down the corporation and I've got them in a place where you can't find them. If anything happens to me, they'll be received immediately and processed by the Secretary of State."

"Nick, please. Do not worry about your personal safety," said Romy. "You may not like our agenda, but we're not violent men. We are not the ones with blood on our hands."

Nick looked over at Romy's forced smile, ignoring the last statement. "You'd use me and lie to me, but you wouldn't resort to violence? We're talking about enough money to control the economic future of the entire Pacific Rim. It's your government, your Committee, and you against me. Too bad if I find your words a little hard to believe. The only reason I came back is to make sure that Keith's all right, and get him safely out of the mess I got him into."

Papa and Romy exchanged a glance and remained silent.

The waiter returned with their coffee. None of the men touched their cups.

"So where is he? Where's Keith?" asked Nick.

Papa cleared his throat. "He is fine, Nick, just fine. He has decided to stay here for a while to pursue some—local interests."

"What's that supposed to mean?"

"He's reviewing some of our operations."

Nick looked at Papa, then at Romy, and then back to Papa. "This is bullshit. Let me talk to him. If he can convince me that it's in his interest to stay here, then fine—I'll walk away. But not until I talk to him."

The two men across the table exchanged looks again. This time it was Romy who spoke. "That is impossible, Nick. Keith is out on one of the other islands now, and—well—you know how difficult inter-island communications are."

Romy continued, "Besides, his standards are a little different from yours. He asked us to give you this note."

Nick accepted an envelope from Romy. It was sealed, he saw, but that didn't mean anything. He examined the writing on the front, and recognized it as Keith's distinctive hand. Tearing it open, he flicked out the folded piece of paper it contained and read its brief message.

He closed his eyes and took a deep breath. Exhaling, he knew—it was definitely from Keith. He looked over at Papa and Romy. "Keith's going after the treasure. He's out chasing Yamashita's gold."

"With our blessing, Nick. You don't need to worry about him. He'll be fine."

Nick's mind was still fuzzy from the jet lag and he felt the conversation was going nowhere. Even though he thought it was like trying to push a rope uphill, he decided to try one last tack. "Guys, do you know what will happen when I file the corporate dissolution papers? Every U.S. agency, from the IRS down, is gonna know about it, and soon. If you go ahead and try to ship a PRMC container into the U.S., there's no way that our customs department will let it through. It's over."

Papa shook his head, sadly. "It doesn't have to be that way, Nick. As you've so aptly pointed out, we all have a tremendous amount at stake—you as much as any of us. Think about it."

"No way. I'm finished."

"I like you, Nick," said Romy. "We all like you. We know you, and we trust you. So let me make you one final offer." He glanced over at Papa, who nodded. "If PRMC goes public, how much would your share be worth? Thirty million? Forty million dollars? You're a young man, and managing the wealth we are about to harness is a role you could enjoy for the rest of your life."

Romy leaned forward. The subtlety was gone from his voice. "What would you say to thirty *billion* dollars?"

Nick leaned back in his chair and looked across at the table at them. His body went limp, and it wasn't the jet lag. His mouth was dry. "You guys know what I'm good at. If you need some business advice, give me a call. But if you want me to get involved in laundering a trillion dollars in gold, my answer is simple. It hasn't changed. I'm sorry guys, but I'm out." He pushed back his chair, stood up, and walked away.

Busuanga, The Philippines

Their progress had been slowed by the density of the clay soil they'd encountered in the last hour, and the last two feet in particular seemed to be taking forever. According to all of Buddy's equipment, they were only inches away from their prize. How many more times would he have to repeat the digging motion that burned the muscles in his body like fire, Keith wondered? Five, ten? Certainly not more than a hundred. He had to be close.

He put his foot on top of the blade of the shovel and leaned into it. The sweat poured down his forehead and into his eyes as the business end of the shovel suddenly hit something solid with an audible *clink*. He stopped instantly, looking above him to the berm of the hole. From the look on his partner's face, he could see that Buddy had heard the same thing. Metal against metal.

Keith pulled the spade out of the earth and aimed for a spot a few inches away. Gingerly this time, he pushed the blade back into the soil. Another *clink*. Just as he was about to push the handle down and pull the dirt free, he realized that Buddy had joined him in the bottom of the pit, shovel in hand. Keith withdrew the spade from the ground and extended his hand out, palm up. Buddy excitedly gave him "five" and then moved into position to unearth their prize. Grinning fiercely at each other, they simultaneously drove their implements into the ground.

Coron, The Philippines

Rose Marie Escador stood at the front of her third-grade class-room, pointing to a place on one of the new maps that hung on the wall. About to recite the answer to the teacher's question, she was interrupted by a sudden jolt that rocked the floor beneath her feet. It lasted only for a second or two and then stopped.

Everyone in the class froze, anticipating the instructions from their teacher that usually accompanied an earthquake. The earth, however, didn't move again. In the silence of the moment, they all heard it—a deep, booming, thundering echo that resonated through the town for several seconds. The sound of an enormous explosion that appeared to come from the center of the island, somewhere by the airport.

PART EIGHT

YAMASHITA'S GOLD

Manila—The Mayon Volcano exploded this morning in a spectacular thirty-minute eruption that killed 68 people and required the evacuation of 60,000 others. Eyewitnesses were astounded by a series of explosions that rocked the countryside as the molten lava snaked its way down the volcano's slope.

The pyroclastic flows forever buried the town's famous caves and tunnels under several hundred feet of lahar, rocks and poisonous gas. The most active volcano in the Philippines, the mountain, which previously rose to a height of over 1,700 meters, stood guard over the city of Legazpi, 300 kilometers southeast of Manila.

Manila—In an isolated area a few kilometers outside Quezon City, a car ran off the road and crashed into a tree, apparently exploding upon impact. Although the local coroner's office stated that the lone occupant was burned beyond recognition, the body is presumed to be that of the vehicle's registered owner, Mr. Alfredo "Papa" Villangca.

Nick Gardner, President of TGG, announced today the sale of one of his corporate clients to an undisclosed Pacific Rim company for $42 million in cash. The acquired company, which advised foreign corporations on strategies for penetrating the U.S. market, was named Pro-5. Headquartered in Tiburon, California, Pro-5 was founded only four years ago.

Honolulu—A jury today awarded $22 billion from the estate of Ferdinand Marcos to the family of a Filipino locksmith and amateur treasure hunter. Roxas, the plaintiff, had discovered a golden Buddha in 1971 in Northern Luzon, which was later, the jury found, stolen by Marcos. Roxas died under mysterious circumstances while he was preparing to leave Manila to attend the trial.

Manila—Reports came today from the Philippines that two more treasure hunters died while digging for the infamous "Yamashita's Gold."

Although details were still sketchy at press time, the two men were apparently buried alive when a small explosion rocked their excavation, causing a wall of debris to fall on them.

May 9, 1997
The Philippine Reporter

Only Fraction of Marcos Fortune Recovered

THE END

About the Author

TATE HOLT is an entrepreneur and founder of a management consulting firm. He has been honored as a Sultan as a result of his business involvements in the Philippines. He lives in Marin County, California with his wife, Laurie, and four boys.